Or, the Secret of a Royal Mirror

MONA
Or the Secret of a Royal Mirror

By MRS. GEORGIE SHELDON

AUTHOR OF

"Virgie's Inheritance," "A True Aristocrat,"
"Trixy," "Lost A Pearle," "Helen's
Victory," etc.

A. L. BURT COMPANY

PUBLISHERS   NEW YORK

MONA

MONA

CHAPTER I.

A FASCINATING YOUNG WIDOW OPENS THE STORY.

"Appleton, don't look quite yet, but there's a woman just behind you whom I want you to see. I never before saw such a face and figure! They are simply perfection!"

The above remarks were made by a young man, perhaps thirty years of age, to his companion, who, evidently, was somewhat his senior.

The two gentlemen were seated at a private table in the dining-room of a large hotel in Chicago, Illinois, and were themselves both handsome and distinguished in appearance.

"There!" the speaker continued, as a slight commotion near them indicated that some one was rising from a table; "she is about to leave the room, and now is your chance."

The gentleman addressed turned to look as the lady passed; but the moment she was beyond the possibility of hearing he broke into a laugh of amusement.

"Oh, Cutler!" he exclaimed; "I never would have

3

believed that you could rave so over a red-head—
you who all your life have held such hair in detes-
tation!"

"Well," returned Mr. Cutler, flushing guiltily, "I
acknowledge that I have always had a peculiar aversion to red hair; but, truly, hers is an unusual shade
—not a flaming, staring red, but deep and rich.   I
never saw anything just like it before.   Anyhow, she
is a magnificent specimen of womanhood.   See! what
a queenly carriage! what a figure!" and his glance
followed the lady referred to, lingeringly, admiringly.

"Yes, she certainly is a fine-looking woman," his
companion admitted; "and, if I am any judge, the
diamonds she wears are worth a small fortune.   Did
you notice them?"

"No; I saw only herself," was the preoccupied response.

"Aha! I see you are clean gone," was the laughing
rejoinder of Mr. Appleton.

The lady referred to was indeed a strangely attractive person.   She was rather above the medium height,
straight as an arrow, with a perfectly molded figure,
although it was somewhat inclined to *embonpoint,*
while her bearing was wonderfully easy and graceful.
Her complexion was exquisitely fair, her features
round, yet clearly cut and regular.   She had lovely
eyes of blue, with a fringe of decided, yet not unbe-
coming red upon their white lids, while her hair was
also a rich but striking red, and was worn short, and
curled about her fair forehead and down around her
alabaster neck in bewitching natural rings.

She was apparently about twenty-five or twenty-
eight years of age, with all the strength and *verve* of
perfect health in her movements.   She was dressed

wholly in black, which served but to enhance her fairness, while in her ears and at her throat she wore peculiar ornaments shaped like small crescents, studded with diamonds, remarkable for their purity and brilliancy.

For several days Mr. Cutler and Mr. Appleton sat at the same table, and were quietly observant of this lovely woman.

She came and went, apparently unconscious of their notice or admiration, was gently dignified in her bearing and modest in her deportment, and the two gentlemen became more and more interested in her.

Upon inquiring, they learned that she was a young widow—a Mrs. Bently, whose husband had recently died very suddenly. He was supposed to have been very wealthy, but, there being no children, there was some trouble about the settlement of the property, and she was boarding in the city until matters should be adjusted, when she contemplated going abroad.

She seemed to be an entire stranger to every one, and very much alone, save for the companionship of a maid, by whom she was always attended, except at meal-time. Mr. Appleton was called from the city about ten days after his attention was first called to her, but his friend, Mr. Cutler, was still a guest at the hotel, and before the expiration of another week he had managed to make the acquaintance of the fascinating widow.

The more he saw of her the more deeply interested he became, until he began to realize that his interest was fast merging into a sentiment of a more tender nature.

Mr. Cutler was an energetic young broker, and report said that he was rapidly amassing a fortune, and ere long would be rated rich among rich men. He was fine-looking, very genial and social in his nature, and so, of course, was a general favorite wherever he went.

His admiration for Mrs. Bently soon became the subject of remark among his acquaintances at the hotel, and they predicted that the fair and wealthy widow would soon capture the gallant and successful broker.

Six weeks spent in the attractive widow's society convinced Justin Cutler that she was as lovely in character as in person. She was remarkably sweet-tempered, very devout, and charitable beyond degree. She would never listen to or indulge in gossip of any kind; on the contrary, she always had something kind and pleasant to say to every one.

Upon several occasions, Mr. Cutler invited her to attend the theatre, lectures and concerts, and she honored him by graciously accepting his attentions; while, occasionally, he was permitted to accompany her to church.

That faultless face, her unvarying amiability, her culture and wit, were fast weaving a spell about him, and he had decided to ask her to share his fate and fortune, when he suddenly missed her from her accustomed seat at the table, and failed to meet her about the house as usual.

For three days he did not see anything of her, and he began to be deeply troubled and anxious about her. He could not endure the suspense, and made inquiries for her. He was told that she was ill, and this, of course, did not relieve his anxiety.

On the fourth day, however, she made her appearance again at dinner, but looking so pale and sad, that his heart went out to her with deeper tenderness than ever.

He waited in one of the parlors until she came out from the dining-room. She made her appearance just as a lady, one of the hotel guests, was leaving the room. With eagerness he stepped forward to greet her, and then, with kind solicitude, inquired regarding her recent illness.

"Thank you, Mr. Cutler; I have not been really ill," she said, with a pathetic little quiver of her red lips, "but—I am in deep trouble; I have had bad news."

"I am very sorry," returned the young broker, in a tone of earnest sympathy. "Shall I be presuming if I inquire the nature of your ill-tidings?"

She smiled up at him gratefully.

"Oh, no, and you are very kind. It—it is only a business trouble," she said, a vivid flush dyeing her fair cheek; "but being a woman, perhaps I cannot meet it with quite the fortitude of a man."

"Can I help you in any way?" the gentleman asked, eagerly. "Come into the little reception-parlor yonder—there is no one there—and confide in me, if you will honor me so far."

The fair widow took the arm he offered her, and he led her within the room, and shut the door.

"Sit here," he said, placing a comfortable rocker for her, then he sat opposite her, and waited for her to open her heart to him.

"You know," she began, falteringly, "that I have lost my husband; he died several months ago, and there has been some trouble about the settlement of his estate.

"His relatives contested the will, but my lawyer has always assured me that he could at least secure a handsome amount for me, even if he could not win the whole. But the first of this week, I learned that I am to have almost nothing—that there was not nearly as much as at first supposed, and Mr. Bently's relatives will get that; and so—I am penniless."

"Oh, not so badly off as that, I hope!" exclaimed Mr. Cutler, looking grave.

"It is true. My lawyer's charges will take every dollar that is coming to me, and—oh! it is humiliating to tell you of it—I owe a great deal of money here at this hotel, besides. I never dreamed," she went on, hurriedly, and flushing hotly again, "but that I could pay my bills. I thought that I should have a large fortune, and I—I am afraid that I have been very extravagant; but now—I do not know *what* I shall do."

Mr. Cutler saw that she was in a very perplexing situation, and she seemed so crushed by it that all his tenderest sympathies were enlisted.

"If you would allow me to lend you any amount," he began, when the widow showed him the first burst of temper that he had ever seen her exhibit.

"Sir, do you suppose I would *borrow* what I could never expect to pay?" she cried, with almost passionate scorn, and flushing to her temples.

"I beg your pardon," Justin Cutler returned, feeling almost as if he had been guilty of an inexcusable insult; "believe me, I would not wish to put you under any obligation that would be burdensome."

Then he asked himself if it would be safe for him to tell her of his love then and there, lay his fortune at her feet, and thus relieve her from her present trouble and all anxiety for the future.

But he feared she might resent the offer, coming at

such a time—think it was prompted more by pity than affection, and reject it as scornfully as she had refused his offer of a loan.

She was very attractive as she sat there before him, her white hands folded on her lap, her eyes cast down in troubled thought, and a grieved expression about her beautiful mouth, and he longed, with all the earnestness of his generous nature, to help her in this emergency.

Suddenly his face lighted.

"Are you willing to confide in me the amount of your indebtedness, Mrs. Bently?" he gently asked.

She falteringly named a sum that staggered him, and told him that she had indeed been very extravagant.

"I—I have always had what I wanted. I have never had to count the cost of anything, for my husband was very generous and indulgent," she apologized, with evident embarrassment, as she met his grave look.

"May I make a practical suggestion without the fear of offending you?" the young man questioned, with some confusion.

"Oh, if you would!" cried his companion, eagerly, her face brightening, while she uttered a sigh of relief, as if she expected that his suggestion, whatever it might be, would lift the burden from her heart.

"You have some very costly jewels," Mr. Cutler remarked, the color deepening in his cheek as he glanced at the flashing stones in her ears; "perhaps you would be willing to dispose of them and thus relieve yourself from your present embarrassment."

"Oh, you mean sell my—my diamonds?" cried the lovely widow, with a little nervous sob, and instantly

her two white hands went up to her ears, covering the
blazing gems from his sight, while a painful flush
leaped to her brow and lost itself beneath the soft
rings of her burnished hair.

"Yes," pursued Mr. Cutler, wondering at her confusion. "If I am any judge, they are very valuable
stones, and I suppose you might realize a handsome
sum upon them."

He was secretly planning to redeem them and re-
store them to her later, if she should favorably regard
his suit.

"But—but," and her confusion became intensified
a hundred-fold, "they aren't *real*. I'd be glad enough
if they were, and would willingly sell them to cancel
my indebtedness, but they are only *paste,* although an
excellent imitation."

Her companion regarded her with astonishment.

"You surely do not mean that?" he exclaimed, "for
if I ever saw pure white diamonds, those which you
wear are certainly genuine."

"No, they are not," she returned, shaking her head
with a positive air. "I am very fond of diamonds
and I had some very nice ones once, but they were
stolen from me just after my husband died. I could
not afford to replace them, just then, and I had these
made to wear until I could do so. They were made
in Paris, where they are very clever at such work.
I hoped when my husband's estate was settled, I could
have some real stones again; but, of course, I cannot
now," she regretfully concluded.

"Will you allow me to examine them, please?" Mr.
Cutler asked, still sure that the stones were genuine.

Mrs. Bently unhesitatingly removed one of the

crescent ornaments from her ear and laid it in his hand.

He examined it critically and was still confident that it was really composed of precious gems. He believed that if she had had them made to order to replace the stolen ones, either the jeweler had been guilty of a wretched blunder, or else some friend had interposed to replace the jewels which she so regretted.

"I am sure there is some mistake. I am confident that these are real diamonds and very valuable," he asserted, positively.

"Oh, no, they are *not*," she repeated, with grave assurance.

Then she naïvely added, and with a little ripple of laughter:

"I am glad to know that they are so good an imitation as to deceive you. There is some comfort in that, although it is not pleasant to have to acknowledge the sham."

Still her companion was not convinced. Surely no paste jewels ever emitted such a brilliant white light as those which lay upon his palm, catching and reflecting the various colors about them in such dazzling gleams.

"Would you be willing to go with me to some reliable jeweler and have them tested?" he asked.

The lovely woman flushed crimson.

"No, I couldn't do that; I should not like to—to have it known that I had been wearing such things," she said. "To be sure," she added, with a quick upward glance that made her companion thrill with secret joy, "I have confessed it to you, but you were so kind and sympathetic I—I trusted you involuntarily."

"Thank you," Justin Cutler returned, a brilliant smile lighting his face, and he longed to open his heart to her, but deemed it better to wait a while. "Then, if you would not like to go with me, will you trust the stones with me, and allow me to have them tested for you?"

"Of course I will, if you want to take that trouble; though," she added, with a little skeptical laugh, as she removed the crescent from her other ear and gave it to him, "I assure you the trust isn't such a responsible one as you imagine."

"We shall see," he smilingly responded, as he put the ornaments carefully in his purse and arose. "I shall submit them to some reliable dealer in diamonds, get him to set a value upon them, and will inform you of the verdict this evening."

"Thank you, Mr. Cutler—you are very kind to be so interested for me," the beautiful woman gratefully murmured.

"I would I might," the young man began, eagerly, then suddenly checked himself and added, "might assist you in some way regarding your other troubles."

Again he had been on the point of declaring himself, but told himself that the moment was not a propitious one.

"I am afraid it is too late for that," she responded, with a sigh; "the case is settled, and Mr. Bently's relatives have won. But, good-by—do not let me detain you longer."

"I will see you again this evening," he returned, adding, as he passed out of the room: "I will be very careful of your property, and hope to bring you a good report."

Mrs. Bently shrugged her graceful shoulders in-differently, as if she had no faith in his belief, and felt that it would be but a small loss if the jewels were never returned. Then, with a smile and a bow, she went up stairs to her own rooms.

CHAPTER II.

THE VICTIM OF A WOMAN'S WILES.

Justin Cutler, after leaving the hotel, went directly to one of the first jewelers of the city, a well-known diamond expert, and submitted Mrs. Bently's orna-ments to his judgment.

"They are remarkably fine stones," Mr. Arnold remarked, after having carefully examined them through a microscope; "very pure and clear, most of them without a flaw. So far as I can see, there is not one of them that is in the least off-color."

"I thought so," was Mr. Cutler's inward and exul-tant comment; but he simply asked, as if he accepted the man's verdict as a matter of course: "What is your estimate of their value?"

"Well," said the jeweler, smiling, "if you wish to know their real value just for your own satisfaction, I can give it; but that might considerably exceed the amount I should be willing to name in case you might wish to dispose of them to me."

"I understand," Mr. Cutler returned; "but what would they be worth to you—what would you be will-ing to give for the stones?"

Mr. Arnold considered the matter a few moments, and then named a sum which Mr. Cutler deemed a fair price under the circumstances, and one which he felt sure Mrs. Bently would be only too glad to secure in her emergency.

"You make that offer for them, then—you will purchase them if the lady agrees to take the sum you have named?" he asked.

"Yes, and the offer shall be open for her acceptance or refusal for three days."

"Thank you; I will see you again before the time expires," Mr. Cutler replied; and, taking up the diamonds, which Mr. Arnold had placed in a small box, he put them carefully away in an inside pocket and left the store.

When he returned to his hotel he sent his card up to Mrs. Bently, with a request that she would see him for a few moments in the reception-room. But he was greatly disappointed when the waiter returned and said that the lady was out.

He had an engagement for the evening, and thus he would not be able to see her until the next morning. He was somewhat troubled, for he did not like to retain her diamonds over night; but since he could not return them to her, he judged they would be safer about his person than anywhere else, and so did not remove them from his pocket.

The next morning he was early in his place at breakfast-time and anxiously awaiting the appearance of Mrs. Bently.

She soon came in, looking much brighter and fresher than she had been the day before, and he noticed that she was in her traveling-dress.

Could she be contemplating leaving the hotel? he asked himself, with a sudden sense of depression.

She smiled and bowed as she passed him, and he remarked, in a low tone, as he returned her salutation:

"I will wait for you in the reception-room."

She nodded assent, but a gleam of amusement shot into her expressive eyes, which he interpreted to mean that she believed he had failed in his errand and would be obliged to acknowledge the truth of what she had told him about her ornaments.

This thought greatly elated him, and he chuckled to himself as he imagined her astonishment when he should inform her of the offer of the diamond merchant.

He soon finished his breakfast and repaired to the reception-room, where he drew forth his morning paper to while away the time until Mrs. Bently should appear.

But she did not hurry, and he began to grow impatient. Evidently she had no faith in the genuineness of the stones, and had no intention of spoiling her breakfast just to be told what she already knew.

It was nearly half an hour before she came to him, but he could forgive her for making him wait, for her greeting was unusually cordial, and she seemed lovelier than ever in her pretty dress of dark gray trimmed with black. It was made very high at the throat, and fitted her perfect form like a glove. Her face was like a flawless pearl, and he had begun to think the soft ruddy rings that crowned her milk-white brow and made her look so youthful, the most beautiful hair in the world.

He sprang to his feet, his face all aglow, and went forward to take the hand she extended to him.

"I have such good news for you, Mrs. Bently," he said, as he drew the little box from his pocket. "Your gems are real after all," and he slipped them into her hand as he spoke.

She lifted a startled, incredulous look to his face.

"You cannot mean it—you are only jesting!" she cried.

"Indeed no; I would not jest, and I do mean just what I have said," he persisted.

"Impossible! Why, Mr. Cutler, I gave less than ten dollars for the crescents."

The young man looked blank.

"Then some one has made an expensive blunder, and set real diamonds for you instead of paste. Where did you purchase them—or order them made?"

"Of Hardowin & Leroux, under the Palais Royal, Paris, less than a year ago," Mrs. Bently promptly responded.

"It does not seem possible that any one could have made such a costly mistake," Justin Cutler said, looking perplexed. "It is almost incredible."

"Yes, and I am just as astonished by your report," his companion said, lifting the cover of the box and gazing upon the blazing stones. "They do look wonderfully real," she added, "and yet I can hardly believe, Mr. Cutler, that any one would be willing to purchase them and give me the value of diamonds."

"But the gentleman to whom I submitted them—a jeweler and an expert—made me an offer for them," and he named the sum.

"So much?" murmured the fair woman, flushing. "Ah, it would be such a help."

"This offer," Mr. Cutler resumed, "is to remain open to you for three days, and you can take them to him within that time if you see fit, and Mr. Arnold will give you the money."

Mrs. Bently made a sudden gesture of repulsion, her head drooped, a flush swept up to her brow, and tears rushed to her eyes.

"Poor little woman!" said Justin Cutler to himself, "it humiliates her to think of selling her jewels—of course it must."

Then he asked, after a moment of thought:

"Would you accept the amount that Mr. Arnold offered?"

"Why, yes, if—if you are sure that they are real, and think it would be right for me to do so," she answered, with a somewhat troubled expression on her fair face.

"Of course it will be perfectly right; the man knew what he was talking about, for, as I told you, he is a diamond expert, and he examined them with the utmost care."

"The amount would be very acceptable," said the fair widow, musingly, "and I shall be glad to sell them; but——"

"The thought of going personally to sell your jewels humiliates you," the generous-hearted young man added; "then let me do it for you, and relieve you of the disagreeable task."

"How kind you are; how you read my very thoughts; but I do not like to trouble you," murmured the beautiful woman, with a quiver of her red lips and a thrilling glance. "And yet," she continued, "I must have money at once. I was going to my lawyer this morning to beg him to try and raise something for me in some way, for I must settle my bill here to-day. I have dismissed my maid and engaged a room at No. 10 ———— street, and am going there this afternoon. Oh! Mr. Cutler, it is very hard to be obliged to confess my poverty," and she had to abruptly cease her remarks, in order to preserve her self-control, for she seemed upon the point of breaking down utterly.

"Mrs. Bently," said the young man, with sudden impulse, "let me relieve you from all unpleasantness; let me advance you the sum which Mr. Arnold named; then I can take the crescents to him and he will make it right with me."

A peculiar smile lingered about his lips as he concluded.

"That is exceedingly kind of you," Mrs. Bently said, gratefully, "but, truly, Mr. Cutler, I am almost afraid to take you at your word."

"Why?"

"Because I have always regarded the crescents as paste, and—and I cannot quite divest myself of the idea even now, in spite of your assurance," she answered, with a clouded brow.

Her companion laughed aloud.

"I will be responsible for their genuineness," he returned. "See!" he added, drawing a card from his pocket and writing rapidly upon it. "I will give you this to ease your conscience."

She took it and read:

"I, the undersigned, purchase of Mrs. Bently a pair of crescent ornaments which she affirms are paste, but which I am content to accept as genuine, for the sum agreed upon."

The price was carried out in figures, and his full name signed underneath.

She looked up at him with tears in her eyes.

"You are determined to befriend me, in spite of my scruples," she murmured, brokenly.

"I would gladly do a hundred-fold more for you," he replied, with tender earnestness. "Will you let me have the crescents now?"

"Yes, and thank you more than I can express," she answered, with drooping lids.

He drew forth a wallet filled with bills, and began to count out the sum he had named.

"Wait a moment," said Mrs. Bently, the color mounting to her temples; "I have a handsome case for the ornaments. I will go and get it for you."

She turned suddenly and vanished from his presence, before he could tell her he would rather take them in the little box.

"How sensitive the poor child is!" he murmured, with a tender smile; "she could not even bear to see me count out the money."

Mrs. Bently soon returned with a handsome morocco case in her hands.

"They look better in this," she remarked, as she lifted the lid, and revealed the crescents lying upon a rich black velvet bed; "and," with a nervous little laugh, "now that I know they are genuine, I really am very loath to part with them, in spite of my necessity."

She closed the case with a snap, and passed it to him, and he slipped a roll of crisp bank-bills into her hand.

"This arrangement will smooth all difficulties, I trust," he said, "and now," with a slight tremor in his voice, "I have a special favor to ask. May I come to see you at No. 10 ——— street?"

"Certainly, you may, Mr. Cutler," she replied, lifting a bright, eager face to him, "and I assure you I shall have a warmer welcome for no one else. I cannot tell you how grateful I am——"

"Do not speak of that," he interposed. "I am amply repaid for anything I have done by seeing the look of trouble gone from your face. I must bid you good morning now, but I shall give myself the pleasure of calling upon you very soon."

He held out his hand to her, and she laid hers within it. He was surprised to find it icy cold and trembling, but he attributed it to emotion caused by the parting with him.

"Then I shall only say *au revoir,*" she responded, smiling.

She looked so lovely that he longed to draw her within his arms and take a more tender leave of her, but again putting a curb upon himself, he simply bowed, and left her, when with a quick, elastic step, she swept up stairs to her own apartments.

Justin Cutler was very busy all the morning, and did not find time to go to the jeweler's until the afternoon.

He had no intention of disposing of the crescents— he simply wished to tell him that he had himself concluded to purchase them, and then ask the privilege of depositing them in Mr. Arnold's safe for a few days; for they were to be his gift to the woman he loved, if she received his suit with favor.

The gentleman was in, and his eyes lighted as his glance fell upon the case which Mr. Cutler laid upon the show-case, for he believed that, in purchasing the crescents, he was going to get an unusually good bargain.

"Ah," he remarked, "the lady has decided to dispose of the stones?"

"Yes; but——" Mr. Cutler began, when he suddenly stopped, and gazed, astonished, at the man.

He had taken the case, opened it, and started in dismay as he saw what were within, while a look of blank consternation overspread his face.

Then he turned sternly, almost fiercely, upon the young man.

"What is the meaning of this?" he demanded, in a threatening tone. "Did you imagine you could cheat me in this miserable way? You have got hold of the wrong customer if you did."

"What do you mean, sir?" inquired Mr. Cutler, amazed, but flushing angrily at being addressed so uncivilly.

"These are not the stones you brought to me yesterday,'" said Mr. Arnold, who was also very angry.

"Sir!" exclaimed Justin Cutler, aghast, but with haughty mien.

"They are nothing but paste," continued the jeweler, eyeing the beautiful crescents with disdain; "and," he added, menacingly, "I've a mind to have you arrested on the spot for attempting to obtain money under false pretenses.

Mr. Cutler grew pale at this with mingled anger and a sudden fear.

He reached across the counter and took the case from Mr. Arnold's hand.

He turned the stones to the light.

At the first glance they seemed to be all right—he could detect nothing wrong; for aught that he could

see the crescents were the same which he had submitted to the merchant the day before. But as he
studied them more closely the gleam of the gems
was entirely different—the fire of the genuine diamond was lacking.

"Can it be possible that I have been duped, swindled?" he exclaimed, with white lips and a sinking
heart.

"I should say, rather, that you were attempting to
dupe and swindle some one else," sarcastically retorted the diamond dealer. "The stones are a remarkably fine imitation, I am free to confess, and
would easily deceive a casual observer; but if you
have ever tried and succeeded in this clever game
before, you are certainly caught this time."

"Mr. Arnold, I assure you that I am blameless in
this matter—that I honestly believed these jewels to
be the same that I brought to you yesterday," the
young man said, with an earnest directness which convinced the gentleman that he spoke the truth. "I see
now," he continued, "that they are not; and"—a feeling of faintness almost overpowering him as he realized all that this experience would cost him, aside
from his pecuniary loss—"I have been outrageously
deceived and hoodwinked, for I have already advanced
the sum you named to the woman who wished to dispose of the diamonds."

Mr. Arnold searched the manly face before him,
and was forced to believe in the truth of his statements.

"If that is so, then you have indeed been wretchedly swindled," he said; "for these crescents are but
duplicates in paste of those I examined yesterday.
How did you happen to be so taken in?"

Mr. Cutler briefly related the circumstances, and when he concluded, Mr. Arnold remarked:

"The woman was an accomplished cheat, and led you on very adroitly. Your mistake was in advancing the money for the stones; if you had brought these things to me first, you would have saved yourself this loss. But of course she never would have allowed that; her game was to get the money from you, and she worked you finely for it."

Mr. Cutler groaned in spirit as he realized it all, and how he had tied his own hands by what he had written on the card that he had given to the wily woman.

He kept this portion of the transaction to himself, however; he could not confess how foolishly weak he had been. Surely his infatuation for the beautiful widow had led him beyond all bounds of common sense and good judgment; but he had no one but himself to blame, and he must bear his loss as best he could. His lost faith in womanhood was the heaviest part of it.

"I sincerely regret having put you to so much trouble, Mr. Arnold," he courteously remarked, as he closed the jewel-case and put it out of sight, "and as a favor, I would ask that you regard this matter as strictly confidential. I have been miserably fooled, and met with a heavy loss, but I do not wish all Chicago to ring with the story."

"You may trust me, and accept my assurance that I am sincerely sorry for you," the jeweler returned, in a tone of sympathy, and now entirely convinced of the honesty of the young man. "And let me tell you," he added, "for your personal benefit, while examining those crescents yesterday, I put a private mark on the back of the settings with a steel-pointed instrument; it was like this"—making a cipher on a card and passing it to him. "If you should ever be fortunate enough to come across them again, you could identify them by it."

"Thank you," Mr. Cutler returned, as he put it carefully away.

Then he wished the gentleman a polite good-day, and went out of the store, a wiser, but a somewhat poorer, man than he had been the previous day.

He was almost crushed by the wrong which had been perpetrated against him. He had been thoroughly and artfully deceived. Mrs. Bently—if indeed that was her real name, which he doubted—had seemed such a modest and unassuming woman, so frank, and sweet, and ingenuous, that he would have indignantly resented it had any one hinted to him that she was not all that she appeared to be.

He had never met any woman who possessed such power to charm him, and yet she had never seemed to seek his notice—had never appeared to thrust herself upon him in any way. He had instead sought *her* and been especially attracted to her by the very simplicity and naturalness of her deportment; and this rude awakening to the fact of her duplicity was therefore far more bitter than the loss of his money, although that was considerable.

He was greatly depressed, but, on leaving Mr. Arnold's store, he proceeded directly to the street and number which she had given as her future place of residence. It proved to be an empty house with the sign "To Rent" staring at him from several windows.

He next sought for the lawyer who, Mrs. Bently

had told him, had conducted her business affairs.
There was no such person to be found.

Then, his indignation getting the better of his grief
and disappointment, he sought a detective, told his
story, and gave the case into his hands.

"Keep the matter quiet, Rider," he said, "but spare
no expense to find the woman. If she is a professional thief, she will try the same trick on some one
else; and though we may not be able to bring her to
justice in this case, since I so rashly tied my hands
by giving her that writing, yet I should like to give
my evidence against her for the benefit of some other
unfortunate victim."

Thus the matter rested for the time, and Justin
Cutler once more threw himself heart and soul into
business, vowing that he would never trust a woman
again.

"But I'll keep the bogus crescents, to remind me of
my folly, for of course I shall never see the real ones
again."

Did he?

CHAPTER III.

MONA.

"Mona, come here, dear, please."

A gentleman, of perhaps forty-five, looked up from
the desk where he had been writing, as he uttered this
request; but his voice trembled slightly, and was replete with tenderness, as he spoke the name which
heads this chapter.

The girl whom he addressed was sitting by a win-

dow on the opposite side of the room, and she lifted
her bright brown head and turned a pair of dark,
liquid eyes upon the speaker.

"Yes, Uncle Walter," she cheerfully responded, as,
laying down her book, she arose and moved gracefully across the room toward the handsome, aristo-
cratic-looking man at the desk, who watched her every
motion with a fond intentness that betrayed a deep
and absorbing affection for her.

He frowned slightly, however, as she spoke, and a
half-bitter, half-scornful smile curled his finely chiseled lips for an instant.

The young girl was tall and exquisitely formed, but
her face was one not easily described. Her features
were delicate and clearly defined, yet with a certain
roundness about them such as one sees in a faultlessly
sculptured statue, while unusual strength of character
was written indelibly upon them. Her hair was slightly curly, and arranged with a careful carelessness that
was very becoming, while here and there a stray
ringlet, that had escaped the silver pin that confined it,
seemed to coquet with the delicate fairness of her neck
and brow.

Reaching her uncle's side, she laid one white hand
upon his shoulder, then slid it softly about his neck.

"What is it, Uncle Walter? What makes you look
so sober? Have I done something naughty that you
are going to scold me for?" she concluded, playfully,
as she bent forward and looked archly into his eyes.

His face grew luminous instantly as he met her gaze,
while he captured her small hand and toyed with the
rosy, taper fingers.

"Do I look sober?" and a brilliant smile chased the
gloom from lip and brow. "I did not mean to, while

you know I could not scold you if you were ever so naughty, and you are never that."

"Perhaps every one does not look upon me with your partial eyes," the lovely girl returned, with a musical little laugh.

The man carried the hand he held to his lips and kissed it lingeringly.

"Let me see," he remarked, after thinking a moment, "isn't it somebody's birthday to-day?"

"So it is! but I had not thought of it before," exclaimed the maiden, with a lovely flush sweeping into her cheeks. "And," with a far-away look in her eyes, "I am eighteen years old."

"Eighteen!" and Walter Dinsmore started slightly, while a vivid red suddenly dyed his brow, and a look of pain settled about his mouth.

But he soon conquered his emotion, whatever it might have been, and strove to say, lightly:

"Well, then, somebody must have a gift. What would you like, Mona?"

She laughed out sweetly again at the question.

"You know I have very strange notions about gifts, Uncle Walter," she said. "I do not care much about having people buy me pretty or costly things as most girls do; I like something that has been made or worn or prized by the giver—something that thought and care have been exercised upon. The little bouquet of blue-fringed gentians which you walked five miles to gather for me last year was the most precious gift I had; I have it now, Uncle Walter."

"You quaint child!" said the man, with a quiver of strong feeling in his tone. "You would like something prized by the giver, would you?" he added, musingly. "Well, you shall be gratified."

He turned again to his desk as he spoke, unlocked
and pulled out a drawer.

"Would you like this?" he asked, as he uncovered
a box about eight inches square.

"Why, it is a mirror! and what a queer one!" exclaimed the maiden, as she bent forward to look, and
found her lovely, earnest face reflected from a square,
slightly defaced mirror that was set in an ebony frame
richly inlaid with gold and pearl.

"Yes, dear, and it once belonged to Marie Antoinette. Doubtless it reflected her face many times during the latter half of the last century, as it now re-
flects yours, my Mona," said Mr. Dinsmore.

"To Marie Antoinette?" repeated Mona, breathlessly, "to the Queen of France? and would you give it to
me—*me*, Uncle Walter?"

"Yes, I have kept it for you many years, dear," the
man answered, but turning away from her eager, delighted eyes and glowing face, as if something in them
smote him with sudden pain.

"Oh! thank you, *thank* you! It is a priceless gift.
What can I say? How can I show you how delighted
I am?" Mona cried, eagerly.

"By simply accepting it and taking good care of it,
and also by giving me your promise that you will never
part with it while you live," Mr. Dinsmore gravely
replied.

"Of *course* I would never part with it," the young
girl returned, flushing. "The mere fact of your giving
it to me would make it precious, not to mention that
it is a royal mirror and once belonged to that beautiful
but ill-fated queen. How did it happen to come into
your possession, Uncle Walter?"

The man grew pale at this question, but after a moment he replied, though with visible effort:

"It was given to your great grandmother by a Madame Roquemaure, an intimate friend, who was at one time a lady in waiting at the court of Louis the Sixteenth."

"What was her name?" eagerly asked Mona—"my grandmother's, I mean."

"She was a French lady and her maiden name was Ternaux, and when her friend, Madame Roquemaure, died, she bequeathed to her this mirror, which once graced the dressing-room of Marie Antoinette in the Tuileries."

"What a prize!" breathed Mona, as she gazed reverently upon the royal relic. "May I take it, Uncle Walter?"

"Certainly," and the man lifted it from the box and laid it in her hands.

"How heavy it is!" she exclaimed, flushing and trembling with excitement, as she clasped the precious treasure.

"Yes, the frame is of ebony and quite a massive one," said Mr. Dinsmore.

"It looks like a shallow box with the mirror for a cover; but of course it isn't, as there is no way to get into it," observed the young girl, examining it closely.

Her companion made no reply, but regarded her earnestly, while his face was pale and his lips compressed with an expression of pain.

"And this has been handed down from generation to generation!" Mona went on, musingly. "Have you had it all these years, Uncle Walter—ever since you first took me?"

"Yes, and I have been keeping it for you until you

should reach your eighteenth birthday. It is yours now, my Mona, but you must never part with it—it is to be an heir-loom. And if you should ever be married, if you should have children, you are to give it to your eldest daughter. And, oh! my child," the agitated man continued, as he arose and laid his hands upon her shoulders and looked wistfully into her beautiful face, "I hope, I *pray,* that *your* life may be a happy one."

"Why, Uncle Walter, how solemn you have grown all at once!" cried the young girl, looking up at him with a smile half startled, half gay. "One would think you were giving me some sacred charge that is to affect all my future life, instead of this lovely mirror that has such a charming and romantic history. I wish," she went on, thoughtfully, "you would tell me just how you came to have it. Did it descend to you from your father's or your mother's ancestors?"

The man sat down again before he replied, and turned his face slightly away from her gaze as he said:

"It really belonged to your mother, dear, instead of to me, for it has always been given to the eldest daughter on the mother's side; so, after your mother died, I treasured it to give to you when you should be old enough to appreciate it."

"I wish you would tell me more about my mother, Uncle Walter," the young girl said, wistfully, after a moment of silence. "You have never seemed willing to talk about her—you have always evaded and put me off when I asked you anything, until I have grown to feel as if there were some mystery connected with her. But surely I am old enough now, and have a right to know her history. Was she your only sister, and how did it happen that she died all alone in London? Where was my father? and why was she left so poor when you had so much? Really, Uncle Walter, I think I ought to insist upon being told all there is to know about my parents and myself. You have often said you would tell me some time; why not now?"

"Yes, yes, child, you are old enough, if that were all," the man returned, with livid lips, a shudder shaking his strong frame from head to foot.

Mona also grew very pale as she observed him, and a look of apprehension swept over her face at his ominous words.

"Was there anything wrong about mamma?" she began, tremulously.

"No, no!" Mr. Dinsmore interposed, almost passionately; "she was the purest and loveliest woman in the world, and her fate was the saddest in the world."

"And my father?" breathed the girl, trembling visibly.

"Was a wretch! a faithless brute!" was the low, stern reply.

"What became of him?"

"Do not ask me, child," the excited man returned, almost fiercely, but white to his lips, "he deserves only your hatred and contempt, as he has mine. Your mother, as you have been told, died in London, a much wronged and broken-hearted woman, where she had lived for nearly three months in almost destitute circumstances. The moment I learned of her sad condition I hastened to London to give her my care and protection; but she was gone—she had died three days before my arrival, and I found only a wee little baby awaiting my care and love."

A bitter sob burst from the man's lips at this point, but after struggling for a moment for self-control, he resumed:

"That baby was, of course, yourself, and I named you Mona for your mother, and Ruth for mine. The names do not go together very well, but I loved them both so well I wanted you to bear them. I gave you in charge of a competent nurse, with instructions that everything should be done for your comfort and welfare; then I sought to drown my grief in travel and constant change of scene. When I returned to London you were nearly two years old and a lovely, winning child. I brought you, with your nurse, to America, resolving that you should always have the tenderest love and care; and Mona, my darling, I have tried to make your life a happy one."

"And you have succeeded, Uncle Walter, I have never known a sorrow, you have been my best and dearest friend, and I love you—I love you with all my heart," the fair girl cried, as she threw her arm about his neck and pressed her quivering lips to his corrugated brow.

Mr. Dinsmore folded her close to his breast, and held her there in a silent embrace for a moment.

But Mona's mind was intent upon hearing the remainder of his story; and, gently disengaging herself, she continued:

"But tell me—there is much more that I want to know. What was the reason—why did my father——"

She was suddenly cut short in her inquiries by the opening of a door and the entrance of a servant.

"There is a caller for you in the drawing-room, Miss Mona," the girl remarked, as she extended to her the silver salver, on which there lay a dainty bit of pasteboard.

Mona took it and read the name engraved upon it.

"It is Susie Leades," she said, a slight look of annoyance sweeping over her face, "and I suppose I must go; but you will tell me the rest some other time, Uncle Walter? I shall never be content until I know all there is to know about my father and mother."

"Yes—yes; some other time I will tell you more," Mr. Dinsmore said, but with a sigh of relief, as if he were glad of this interruption in the midst of a disagreeable subject.

"I will leave the mirror here until I come back," Mona said, as she laid it again in its box in the drawer; then, softly kissing her companion on the lips, she went slowly and reluctantly from the room.

The moment the door had closed after her, Walter Dinsmore, the proud millionaire and one of New York's most respected and prominent citizens, dropped his head upon the desk before him and groaned aloud:

"How can I ever tell her?" he cried. "Oh, Mona, Mona! I have tried to do right by your little girl—I have tried to make her life bright and happy; must I cloud it now by revealing the wrong and sorrow of yours? *Must* I tell her?"

A sob burst from him, and then for some time he lay perfectly still, as if absorbed in deep thought.

At length he lifted his head, and, with a resolute look on his fine face, drew some paper before him and began to write rapidly.

At the expiration of half an hour he folded what he had written, put it in an envelope, and carefully sealed it, then turning it over, wrote "For Mona" on the back.

This done he took up the mirror which he had but just given the young girl, pressed hard upon one of the pearl and gold points with which the frame was thickly studded, and the bottom dropped down like a tiny drawer, revealing within it a package composed of half a dozen letters and a small pasteboard box.

The man was deadly pale, and his hands trembled as he took these out and began to look over the letters.

But, as if the task were too great for him, he almost immediately replaced them in their envelopes, and restored them to the drawer in the mirror. Then he uncovered the little box, and two small rings were exposed to view—one a heavy gold band, the other set with a whole pearl of unusual size and purity.

"Poor Mona!" he almost sobbed, as he touched them with reverent fingers. "I shall never be reconciled to your sad fate, and I cannot bring myself to tell your child the whole truth, at least not now. I will tell her something—just enough to satisfy her, if she questions me again—the rest I have written, and I will hide the story with these things in the mirror; then in my will I will reveal its secret, so that Mona can find them. She will be older, and perhaps happily settled in life by the time I get through, and so better able to bear the truth."

He replaced the box and letters in the secret drawer of the mirror, also the envelope which contained what he had written, after which he carefully closed it, and returned the royal relic to the box in his desk.

"There! everything is as safe as if it were buried in Mona's grave—no one would ever think of looking for that history in such a place, and the secret will never be disclosed until I see fit to reveal it."

He had scarcely completed these arrangements when Mona re-entered the room, her face bright and smiling, a lovely flush on her cheeks, a brilliant light in her liquid brown eyes.

"Well, my pet, you look pretty enough to kiss," exclaimed Mr. Dinsmore, assuming a lightness of manner which he was far from feeling. "Have you had a pleasant call?"

"Indeed I have, Uncle Walter, and I have also had an invitation to attend the opera to-night," Mona replied, with increasing color.

"Ah! then I imagine that Miss Susie did not come alone, eh?" and Mr. Dinsmore smiled roguishly.

"No; Mr. Palmer was with her; and just as they were at the door, he discovered that he had forgotten his cards, so he just penciled his name on the back of Susie's; but I did not see it, and of course did not know he was here until I went into the drawing-room," the young girl explained.

"Palmer! Ray Palmer, the son of Amos Palmer, the diamond merchant?" questioned Mr. Dinsmore.

"Yes, I have met him a number of times during the past year, and at Susie's birthday party last week he asked permission to call. May I go to-night, Uncle Walter?" Mona asked, with downcast eyes.

"Who else is to be in the party?" gravely inquired her uncle.

"Susie, and Louis, her brother."

"Then I have no objection to your going also," said Mr. Dinsmore; then he added, as he searched the beautiful face beside him: "I know that Ray Palmer is an exceptionally fine young man, and any girl might feel honored in receiving his attentions. Is he agreeable to you, Mona?"

A vivid scarlet suffused the maiden's face at this pointed question, and the gentleman laughed out softly as he beheld it.

"Never mind, dear," he continued, lightly. "I am already answered, and Mr. Ray Palmer has my best wishes for his future success and happiness. There, run back now, and tell your callers that you will join their party."

A shy, sweet smile wreathed Mona's lips as she again left the room.

But she was not gone long—scarcely five minutes had elapsed before she returned, and gliding to Mr. Dinsmore's side, she said, with quiet resolution:

"Now, Uncle Walter, I want to hear the remainder of what you have to tell me about my father and mother."

CHAPTER IV.

MONA ASKS SOME PERTINENT QUESTIONS.

Mr. Dinsmore's face clouded instantly at Mona's request, but after thinking a moment, he threw back his head with a resolute air, and said:

"There is not so very much more to tell, Mona—it is the oft repeated story of too much love and trust on the part of a pure and lovely woman, and of selfish pleasure and lack of principle on the part of the man who won her. When your mother was eighteen—just your age to-day, dear—she fell in love with Richmond Montague, and secretly married him."

"Then she was *legally* his wife!" burst forth Mona, with pale and trembling lips. "Oh, I have so feared, from your reluctance to tell me my mother's history, that—that there was some shame connected with it."

"No—no, dear child; set your heart at rest upon that score. She was legally married to Richard Montague; but his first sin against her was in not making the fact public. He was just starting on a tour abroad and persuaded her to go with him. He claimed that he could not openly marry her without forfeiting a large fortune from an aunt, whose only heir he was, and who was determined that he should marry the daughter of a life-long friend. She was in feeble health and wanted him to be married before he went abroad, as she feared she might not live until he should come back. This he refused to do, although he allowed her to believe that he intended to marry Miss Barton upon his return. But he did marry your mother, and they sailed for Europe.

"They spent a few months traveling together, but while they were in Paris, your father suddenly disappeared, and it became evident to your mother that she had been deserted. To make matters worse, the people of the house where they had been living became suspicious of her, accused her of having been living unlawfully, and drove her away. She was desperate, and went directly to London, intending to return to America, but was taken ill there, and was unable to go on.

"Three months later I learned, indirectly, of her wretched condition, and I hastened to her, as I have already told you, only to find that I was too late—she had died just three days before my arrival, and only a few hours after your birth. Oh, Mona! I was heartbroken, for she was all I had, and the knowledge of her wrongs and sufferings drove me nearly wild; but —I cannot live over those wretched days—I simply

endured them then because I could not help myself.
But, as time passed, I gradually learned to love *you*—
you became my one object in life, and I vowed that
I would do everything in my power to make your life
happy, for your mother's sake, as well as for your
own," he concluded in tremulous, husky tones, while
tears stood in his eyes.

"Dear Uncle Walter, no one could have been more
kind than you have been," the young girl said, nestling
closer to him; "you have been both father and mother
to me, and I am very grateful——"

"Hush, Mona! Never speak of gratitude to me,"
he said, interrupting her, "for you have been a great
comfort to me; you have, indeed, taken the place of
the little girl who never lived to call me father—and
—have helped me to bear other troubles also," he concluded, flushing hotly, while a heavy frown contracted
his brow.

Mona glanced at him curiously, and wondered what
other troubles she had helped him to bear; but her mind
was so full of her own family history she did not pay
much attention to it then. The remark recurred to
her later, however.

"There is one thing more, Uncle Walter," she said.
after a thoughtful pause. "What became of my
father?"

Her companion seemed to freeze and become rigid
as marble at this question.

"I wish you would not question me any further,
Mona," he said, in a constrained tone. "Your father
forfeited all right to that title from you before your
birth. Cannot you be satisfied with what I have already told you?"

"No, I cannot," she resolutely replied. "Where did

he go? What happened to him after my mother died? Has he ever been heard of since?" were the quick, imperative queries which dropped from her lips.

"Oh, yes," said Mr. Dinsmore, replying to the last query; "he married Miss Barton—the girl his aunt had chosen for him—shortly after his return to this country. The woman had set her heart upon the match, and died a month after the marriage, leaving her nephew the whole of her fortune."

"Did he—my father—know that he had a child living?" demanded Mona, in a constrained tone.

"Certainly."

"And—and——" she began, with crimson cheeks and blazing eyes, then choked and stopped.

"I know what you would ask—'did he ever wish to claim you?'" supplemented her companion, a bitter smile curling his white lips. "I have never been asked to give you up, Mona," he continued, apparently putting it thus so as to wound her as little as possible; "but I should not have done so under any circumstances."

"Did he never offer to settle anything upon me out of his abundance?" the young girl asked, bitterly.

"No; no settlement, no allowance was ever made. I alone have cared for you. But do not grieve—it has been a very delightful care to me, dear," Mr. Dinsmore said, tenderly, while he stroked her soft hair fondly with a hand that was far from steady.

"Is the—man living now?" Mona demanded, a cold glitter in her usually gentle eyes.

Mr. Dinsmore threw out his hand with a gesture of agony at this question.

Then suddenly pulling himself together, he hoarsely responded:

"No."

But he turned his face away from her gaze as he said it.

"When and where did he die?"

"Do not ask me. Oh, Mona, for pity's sake, ask me nothing more. I cannot, I will not bear this inquisition any longer," the man cried, in a despairing tone.

The young girl's face blanched suddenly at this, and she turned a wild, startled look upon her companion, as a terrible suspicion flashed into her mind.

Had her uncle avenged her mother's wrongs?—was his hand stained with her father's blood, and was this the reason why he was so fearfully agitated in speaking of these things?

It was an awful thought, and for a moment, every nerve in her body tingled with pain. All her strength fled, and she dared not question him further on that point, for her own sake, as well as his.

There was a dead silence for several moments, while both struggled for the mastery of their emotions; then Mona said, in a low, awed tone:

"Just one thing more, Uncle Walter—is—his other wife living?"

"I believe so."

"Where is she?"

"I do not know."

"Did she care nothing for me?"

"No, she hated your mother, and you a hundred-fold on her account."

"That is enough—I have heard all that I wish," Mona said, coldly, as she started to her feet and stood erect and rigid before him. "You said truly when you told me that the man deserved hatred and contempt.

I do hate and scorn him with all the hate and strength of my nature. I am glad he is dead. Were he living, and should he ever seek me, I would spurn him as I would spurn a viper. But oh, Uncle Walter, you must let me lean upon you more than ever before, for my heart is very, very sore over the wrong that has been done my poor mother and me. How good you have been to me—and I love you—I will always love and trust you, and I will never ask you any more questions."

She flung her arms around his neck, buried her face in his bosom, and burst into a passion of tears. The sorrowful story to which she had listened, and the fearful suspicion which, at the last, had so appalled her, had completely unnerved her.

The man clasped her to him almost convulsively, though a strong shudder shook his frame, laid his own face caressingly against her soft brown hair, and let her weep until the fountain of her tears was exhausted, and he himself had become entirely composed once more.

"My dear child," he said, at last, "let these be the last tears you ever shed for the wrong done you. I beg you will not allow the memory of it to make you unhappy, my Mona; for as I have assumed a father's care for you in the past, so I shall continue to do in the future; you shall never want for anything that I can give you while I live, and all that I have will be yours when I am gone. I have made an appointment with my lawyer for the day after to-morrow," he went on, in a more business-like tone, "when I purpose making my will, giving you the bulk of my property. I ought to have done this before; but—such matters are not pleasant to think about, and I have kept putting it off. Now dry your tears, my dear; it pains me to see you weep. And here," he added, smiling, and forcing himself to speak more lightly, "I almost forgot that I had something else for your birthday. Come, try on these trinkets, for you must wear them to the opera to-night."

He took a case from his pocket as he spoke, and slipped it into her hands.

Mona looked up surprised.

"But you have already given me the mirror, Uncle Walter," she said. "I could not have anything that I should prize more."

"Ah, well, but I could not let a birthday go by without spending a little money on you," he returned, fondly; "so look at your gifts, and let me see how they will fit."

Mona obediently opened the case, and found within a pair of narrow gold bands, studded with diamonds, for her wrists.

"They are lovely," she cried, a smile of pleasure breaking over her face, "and—I really believe it is the very pair that I was admiring in Tiffany's window only a few days ago!"

"I shouldn't wonder—sometimes the fairies whisper maidens' wishes in older ears, eh?" Mr. Dinsmore archly returned, and glad to see the gloom fading from her face.

"The fairies are great tell-tales then, for you are continually anticipating my wishes," Mona replied. "But," she added, glancing at the clock, "I have some little things to attend to before going out this evening, and I must be about them. A thousand thanks for my diamonds," and she kissed him softly as she said it, "and I shall surely wear them to-night."

"And here is your mirror," he said, taking the box containing it from the drawer of his desk. "Remember your promise, dear, never to part with it."

"It shall never go out of my possession," she gravely replied, as she took it, and then quietly left the room.

She was very grave as she went slowly up stairs, and once or twice a long, sobbing sigh escaped her.

"Oh, why did such a thought ever come to me?" she murmured. "It is too dreadful, and I will not harbor it for a moment. He is good and noble—his whole life has been grand and above reproach, and I love him with all my heart."

That evening, about seven o'clock, Mona Montague went down to the elegant drawing-room of her uncle's residence, exquisitely clad for the opera.

Her dress was a fine black lace, of a delicate and beautiful pattern, made over old gold silk, with the corsage cut low and sleeveless, thus leaving her neck and arms to gleam like alabaster through the meshes of delicate lace. The heavy edging at the throat was just caught together with a shell of Etruscan gold, studded with diamonds. Costly solitaires gleamed in her ears, while her dainty wrists were encircled with Mr. Dinsmore's gift of the morning. Upon her head she wore a jaunty hat of black lace, surrounded by a wreath of old gold crushed roses, that contrasted beautifully with her clear, fair skin and dark eyes. Her face was bright with anticipation, her cheeks were slightly flushed, and she was a vision of loveliness to gladden the heart of any beauty-loving man.

"I have come down to receive your verdict, Uncle Walter," she remarked, smiling, and sweeping him a

graceful courtesy, as he threw down his paper and
arose to meet her, "Will I do?"

His face lighted with love and pride as he ran his
eye over her.

"Really, Mona," he said, "you make me almost wish
that I were going to see 'Il Trovatore' with you in Ray
Palmer's place. You are a very queen of beauty to-
night."

Mona flushed as he uttered Ray Palmer's name, but
she put up her lips to kiss him for his compliment, and
at that moment the young man himself was announced.

His eyes lighted with admiration, as he approached
to salute the beautiful girl, and a thrill of delight ran
through him as he clasped the hand she so cordially
extended.

He was several inches taller than Mona, and a
young man of singularly noble bearing, and perhaps
twenty-three years of age.

Dignity of character and sincerity of purpose were
stamped upon every feature of his intelligent face,
and gleamed from his frank, genial eyes, which met
yours with a directness that won the heart and confidence at once, while his manner and bearing as well
as every detail of his dress, betrayed the thorough gentleman.

Mr. Dinsmore smiled complacently as he marked
the exchange of greetings between the two young
people. He saw that Mona was deeply interested in
her handsome escort, as her deepening color and drooping eyes plainly betrayed.

He followed them to the door, and wished them a
genial good-night, after which he went back to his
library, saying to himself:

"I could wish nothing better for her. If I can but see her safely settled in life, I should have little to fear for the future, in spite of the miserable past. Young Palmer is a fine fellow, and I will favor his suit with all my heart. Then, with my will signed and sealed, my mind will be at rest."

Alas! alas! "Man proposes and God disposes."

CHAPTER V.

MONA'S APPALLING DISCOVERY.

Mona Montague was very happy throughout that memorable evening as she sat beside Ray Palmer, and listened to the opera of "Il Trovatore."

The four young people occupied a proscenium box, and made a very interesting group. Many a glass was turned upon them, many an eye studied their bright, animated faces, and found the sight almost as entertaining as the scene being enacted upon the stage.

To Ray Palmer's partial eye the fair girl beside him was the most beautiful object in the world, for he loved her with all his heart, and he made up his mind to win her if it were possible.

When the opera was over, the quartet repaired to a fashionable *café*, where they had a delicious little supper, and spent another happy half-hour discussing the merits of "Il Trovatore"; then they separated to go to their homes.

"You have given me great pleasure this evening, Miss Montague," Ray Palmer remarked, as he lingered for a moment beside her at the door of Mr. Dinsmore's residence, and loath to bid her good-night.

"Then I am sure the pleasure has been mutual, Mr. Palmer, for I have enjoyed myself exceedingly," Mona replied, as she lifted her flushed and smiling face to him.

"You are very kind to give me that assurance," he returned, "and you embolden me to crave another favor. May I have your permission to call upon you occasionally?"

"I am only very happy to grant it; pray consider yourself welcome at any time," Mona answered, cordially, but dropping her eyes beneath his earnest look.

"Thank you; I shall gladly avail myself of your kindness," the young man gratefully responded; and then, with a lingering clasp of the hand, he bade her good-night and ran lightly down the steps.

With a rapidly beating heart and throbbing pulses, Mona softly let herself in with a latch-key, turned out the hall gas, which had been left burning dimly for her, and started to mount the stairs, when she espied a gleam of light shining beneath the library door.

"Why! Uncle Walter has not gone to bed yet! Can it be that he is sitting up for me?" she murmured. "I will go and tell him that I have come in, and get my good-night kiss."

She turned back and went quietly down the hall, and tapped lightly at the door. Receiving no response, she opened it, and passed into the room.

The gas was burning brightly, and Mr. Dinsmore was sitting before his desk, but reclining in his chair, his head thrown back against the soft, bright headrest, the work of Mona's skillful fingers.

"He has fallen asleep," said the fair girl, as she

went to his side and laid her hand gently upon his shoulder.

"Uncle Walter," she called, "why did you sit up for me? Wake up now and go to bed, or you will be having one of your dreadful headaches to-morrow."

But the man did not make or show any signs of having heard her.

He was breathing heavily, and Mona now noticed that his face was unnaturally flushed, and that the veins upon his temples were knotted and swollen.

A startled look swept over her face, and she grew white with a sudden fear.

"Uncle Walter!" she cried out, sharply, and trying to arouse him; "speak to me! Oh! there is something dreadful the matter with him; he is ill—he is unconscious!"

With a wild cry and sob of fear and anguish, she turned and sped with flying feet from the room.

A moment later she was knocking vigorously at the door of the serving-man's room, begging him to "get up at once and go for Doctor Hammond, for Mr. Dinsmore was very ill."

Having aroused James, she called the other servants, and then flew back to her idolized uncle.

There was no change in him; he sat and breathed just the same. Instinctively feeling that something ought to be done immediately for his relief, with trembling fingers she loosened his neck-tie, unbuttoned his collar, then drenching her handkerchief with water from an ice pitcher, she began to bathe his flushed and knotted forehead.

She imagined that this afforded him some relief, and that his breathing was not quite so labored, but his condition drove her nearly frantic with fear and anxiety.

James was very expeditious in his movements, and in less than half an hour returned with the family physician.

"Oh, Doctor Hammond, what is the matter with him?" Mona cried, with a sinking heart, as she saw the grave expression that settled over the doctor's face the moment he reached his patient's side.

"An apoplectic attack," he replied, thinking it best that she should know the truth, and so be somewhat prepared for what he feared must soon come.

The unconscious man was borne to his chamber, and everything which human skill could devise was done for him. He rallied somewhat toward morning, but Doctor Hammond gave them no hope that he would ever be any better, or even retain his consciousness for any length of time.

The whole of his right side was helpless, and his tongue was also paralyzed, so that he was entirely speechless.

His efforts to talk were agonizing to witness, for he appeared to realize that his hours were numbered, and seemed to have something special on his mind that he wished to make those around him understand.

Mona alone, who never left his side, seemed able to interpret something of his meaning, and she asked him question after question trying to learn his desire; but he could only slowly move his head to signify that she did not yet understand.

"Oh, what shall I do?" she moaned, in despair; then a bright thought flashed upon her. "Is there some one whom you wish to see, Uncle Walter?" she asked.

His eyes lighted, and a faint nod of the head told her that she had got hold of the right thread at last.

"Who is it?" she said, eagerly; then remembering his helplessness, she added: "I will say over the letters of the alphabet, and when I reach the right one you must press my hand."

This method proved more successful, and Mona finally spelled out the name of Graves.

"Graves—Graves," she repeated, with a puzzled look; then she cried, her face lighting: "Oh, it is Mr. Graves, your lawyer, whom you want."

Again the sufferer nodded, and weakly pushed her from him with his left hand to show that he wanted her to be quick about summoning the man.

In less than an hour Mr. Graves was in the sickroom, and by signs and questions and Mona's use of the alphabet, he finally comprehended that Mr. Dinsmore wished him to draw up a will for him, leaving everything he had to Mona.

While the lawyer was thus engaged in the library, the invalid tried to make Mona understand that there was something else he wished to tell her, and she spelled out the word "mirror."

"Oh, you want me to remember my promise never to part with it—is that it, Uncle?" she asked.

"No," he signaled, and looked so distressed that the much-tried girl sobbed outright. But she quickly controlled her grief, and finally spelled the word "bring," though her heart almost failed her as she realized that his left hand was fast becoming helpless like the other so that she could scarcely distinguish any pressure when she named a letter.

But she flew to her room and brought the royal mirror to him, and he tried to make her understand that there was something he wished to explain in connection with it.

We who have learned the secret of it, know what he wanted, but he could not even lift his nerveless hand to show her the gilded point beneath which lay the spring that controlled the hidden drawer and its contents.

Mona asked him question after question, but all that she could elicit were sighs, while great tears welled up into the man's eyes and rolled over his cheeks; and when at last a groan of agony burst from him, she could bear it no longer, and went weeping from the room, bearing the ancient relic from his sight.

She remained in her own room a few moments to compose herself before going back to him, and during her absence, Mr. Graves went up to him with the will which he had hastily drafted.

Mr. Dinsmore had had some conversation with him, in a general way, about the matter previous to this, and so he had drawn up the instrument to cover every point that he could think of. He read it aloud, and Mr. Dinsmore signified his satisfaction with it, and yet he looked troubled, as if it did not quite cover all that he desired.

Doctor Hammond and the housekeeper were summoned to act as witnesses; then Mr. Graves placed the pen, filled with ink, within the sick man's fingers, for him to sign the will. But he could not hold it—there was no strength, no power in them.

In vain they clasped them around it, and urged him to "try;" but they instantly fell away, the pen dropped upon the snowy counterpane making a great, unsightly blotch of ink, and they knew that he was past putting his signature, or even his mark, to the will.

As he himself realized this, a shrill cry of despair burst from him, and the next instant he lapsed into unconsciousness from a second stroke.

"The end has come—he will not live an hour," gravely remarked Doctor Hammond, as his skilled fingers sought the dying man's feeble pulse.

In half that time Walter Dinsmore was dead, and Mona Montague was alone in the world.

We will pass over the next few days, with their mournful incidents and the despairing grief of the beautiful girl, who had been so sadly bereft, to the morning after the funeral ceremonies, when Mr. Graves, with Mr. Dinsmore's unsigned will in his pocket, called to consult with Mona regarding her uncle's affairs and her own plans for the future.

He found her in the library, looking sad and heavy-eyed from almost incessant weeping, her manner languid and drooping.

She was engaged in trying to make up some accounts which the housekeeper had requested her to attend to, hoping thus to distract her mind somewhat from her grief.

She burst into tears as the lawyer kindly took her hand, for the sight of him brought back to her so vividly the harrowing scenes of that last day of her idolized uncle's life.

But she strove to control herself after a moment, and invited the gentleman to be seated, when he immediately broached the subject of his call.

"Perhaps you are aware, Miss Montague," he began, "that Mr. Dinsmore, on the morning of his death, tried to make his will, in which he stated his wish to leave you all his property; but he was unable to sign it; consequently the document cannot stand, according to law. I was somewhat surprised," Mr. Graves continued, looking thoughtful, "at his excessive anxiety and distress regarding the matter, as he had previously given me to understand that you were his only living relative. Still he might only have wished to make assurance doubly sure. Do you know of any heirs beside yourself?"

"No," Mona answered, "he had no relatives as near to him as I. There are, I believe, one or two distant cousins residing somewhere in the South."

"Then you are of course the sole heir, and will have the whole of his handsome fortune—the will would only have been a matter of form. Mr. Dinsmore was a very rich man, Miss Montague, and I congratulate you upon being the heiress to a large fortune," the lawyer continued, with hearty sincerity in his tone.

But Mona looked up at him with streaming eyes.

"Oh! but I would rather have my uncle back than all the wealth of the world!" she cried, with quivering lips.

"True. I know that your loss is irreparable—one that no amount of money can make up to you," was the kind and sympathetic response. Then the man returned to business again. "But—do you mind telling me your age, Miss Montague?"

"I was eighteen the day before my uncle died," the stricken girl replied, with a keen heart-pang, as she recalled that eventful day.

"You are very young to have care of so much property," said the lawyer, gravely. "What would be your wish as to the management of it? You ought really to have a guardian for the next few years. If you will designate some one whom you would wish, and could trust to act as such, I will gladly assist in putting Mr. Dinsmore's affair in convenient shape for him."

"You are very good, Mr. Graves," Mona thoughtfully returned. Then she added, wistfully: "Why cannot *you* act as my guardian? I know of no one in whom I have so much confidence. Uncle Walter trusted you, and surely there can be no one who understands his affairs as well as you do."

The man's face lighted at this evidence of her trust in him.

"Thank you, Miss Mona," he said. "It is of course gratifying to me to know that you desire this, and I really think that Mr. Dinsmore would have suggested such an arrangement had he been able to do so; but of course I felt delicate about proposing it. Walter Dinsmore was a dear and valued friend, as well as my client, and, believe me, I feel a deep interest in you, for his sake, as well as your own. I will accept the trust, and do the best I can for you, my child, thanking you again heartily for your confidence in me."

He spent a long time, after that, talking over business matters and looking over some of Mr. Dinsmore's papers, and when at length he took his leave, Mona was really greatly comforted, and felt that she had found a true friend to rely upon in her loneliness.

CHAPTER VI.

A BOLD AND CUNNING SCHEME.

On the afternoon previous to Mr. Dinsmore's death a woman of perhaps sixty years alighted from an ele-

gant private carriage before the door of a fine residence on West ——— street, in New York city.

She was simply but richly clad in heavy, lustrous
black silk, and was a woman of fine appearance, although her face wore a look of deep sadness which
seemed to indicate some hidden trouble or sorrow.

Her hair was almost white, but carefully arranged,
and lay low upon her placid, but slightly wrinkled,
brow in soft, silken waves that were very becoming to
her. Her complexion was unusually clear and fair
for one of her years, although it might have been en-
hanced somewhat by the fine vail of white tulle which
she wore over it. She was tall and commanding in
figure, a little inclined toward portliness, but every motion was replete with graceful dignity and high-bred
repose.

After giving directions to her coachman to wait for
her, she mounted the steps leading to the door, pausing for an instant to read the name, "R. Wesselhoff,
M.D." engraved upon a silver plate, before ringing
the bell.

A colored servant soon answered her call, and responded affirmatively to her inquiry if the noted physician was in, then ushered her into a small but elegantly appointed reception-room upon the right of the
lofty hall.

Five minutes later an elderly and singularly prepossessing man entered and saluted his visitor in a
gracious and respectful manner.

"Mrs. Walton, I suppose?" he remarked, just glancing at the card which she had given the servant.

The woman bowed, then observed, with a patient but
pathetic sigh:

"I have called, Doctor Wesselhoff, upon a very sad

errand, and one which I trust you will regard as strictly confidential."

"Certainly, madame; I so regard all communications made by my patients," the gentleman courteously responded.

"I have a son," madame resumed, "who has of late betrayed symptoms of the strangest mania, although he appears to be in perfect health in all other respects. He imagines that some gigantic robbery has been committed; sometimes he declares that bonds to a large amount have been stolen, at other times it is money, then again that costly jewels have disappeared; but the strangest phase of his malady consists in the fact that he accuses me, and sometimes other members of the family, of being the thief, and insists that he must have me arrested. This has gone on for some time, and I have been obliged to adopt every kind of device in order to keep him from carrying out his threats and thus creating a very uncomfortable scandal. This morning he became more violent than usual, and I felt obliged to take some decided step in regard to proper treatment for him; therefore my visit to you."

"It is a singular mania, truly," said the physician, who had been listening with the deepest interest to his companion's recital. "I think I never have met with anything exactly like it before in all my experience. How old is your son, Mrs. Walton?"

"Twenty-four years," the woman replied, with a heavy sigh; "and," she added, tremulously, "I cannot bear the thought of sending him to any common lunatic asylum. I learned recently that you sometimes receive private patients to test their cases before sending them to a public institution, and that you have frequently effected a cure in critical cases. Will you take my son and see what you think of his case—what you can do for him? I shall not mind the cost—I wish to spare nothing, and I do not wish any one, at least of our friends and acquaintances, to know that he is under treatment for insanity until you pronounce your verdict. He seems sane enough upon all other topics, except now and then he persists in calling himself by some other name, and I know he would be very sensitive, should he recover, to have his condition known. He does not even suspect that I am contemplating any such thing, and I shall be obliged to use strategy in bringing him to you."

Doctor Wesselhoff was evidently very deeply interested in the case; he had never heard of anything like it before, and all his professional enthusiasm was aroused.

He spent some time questioning his visitor, and finally decided that he would receive the young man immediately—to-morrow afternoon Mrs. Walton might bring him, he said, if she could conveniently arrange to do so.

"I think, perhaps, it will not be best for me to come with him myself," the lady said, after considering the matter for some time. "Truly," she added, with a sad smile, "I almost fear to go out with him, lest he put his threats into execution and have me arrested. But I think I can arrange with my sister, Mrs. Vanderbeck, to persuade him to come with her as if to call upon a friend."

The matter was arranged thus, and madame arose to take her leave, the physician accompanying her to the door and feeling deep sympathy for the cultured and attractive woman in her strange affliction.

The next day, about one o'clock—the day following Mona Montague's attendance at the opera with Ray Palmer, and only a few hours after Mr. Dinsmore's death, a brilliantly beautiful woman, who might have been forty-five years of age, entered the handsome store of Amos Palmer & Co., diamond merchants and jewelers.

She was exquisitely dressed in an expensive, tailormade costume of gray ladies' cloth, with a gray felt bonnet trimmed with the same shade of velvet as her dress. Her hands were faultlessly gloved, her feet incased in costly imported boots, and everything about her apparel bespoke her a favorite of wealth and luxury.

Her appearance was the more marked from the fact that her hair was a deep, rich red, and curled about her fair forehead in lovely natural curls, while she wore over her face a spotted black lace veil, which, however, did not quite conceal some suspicious wrinkles and "crow's-feet," if that had been her object in wearing it.

She had driven to the store in a plain but elegant *coupé,* drawn by a pair of black horses in goldmounted harness. Her driver was apparently a man of about thirty years, and of eminently respectable appearance in his dark-green livery.

She approached a counter on entering the store, and, in a charmingly affable manner, asked to look at some diamonds.

As it happened, at that hour, one of the clerks was absent, and Mr. Amos Palmer was himself in attendance in his place, and politely served the lady, laying out before her a glittering array of the costly stones she desired to examine.

He saw at once that she was a judge of the gems, for she selected not the largest and most showy, but the purest and the best, and he could but admire her discernment and taste.

When she had made her selections, and she took plenty of time about it, chatting all the while with the gentleman in the most intelligent and fascinating manner, she remarked that she wished her husband to see them before she concluded her purchase.

"But," she added, thoughtfully, "he is something of an invalid, and not able to come to the store to examine them; have you not some one whom you could trust, Mr. Palmer, to take the stones to my home for his inspection? If he sanctions my choice he will at once write a check for their price, or the attendant could return them if they were not satisfactory."

"Certainly," Mr. Palmer graciously responded; "we frequently have such requests, and are only too willing to accommodate our customers. Will madame kindly give me her address?"

Madame smiled as she drew a costly card-case from her no less costly shopping-bag, and taking a heavy card with beveled edges from it, laid it upon the counter before the jeweler, remarking that she should like to have the clerk accompany her directly back in her own carriage, as she wanted the matter decided at once, for the diamonds were to be worn that evening if they suited.

"Mrs. William Vanderbeck, No. 98 —— street," Mr. Palmer read, and then slipped the card into his vest pocket, after which he beckoned a clerk to him.

"Ask my son to step this way a moment," he said.

The man bowed respectfully, bestowing an admir-

ing glance upon the attractive woman on the other
side of the counter, and then withdrew to a private
office at the other end of the room.

A moment later Ray Palmer made his appearance
and approached his father.

Mr. Palmer introduced his son to Mrs. Vanderbeck,
mentioned her desire that some one be sent to her
residence with the diamonds she had selected for her
husband's approval, and asked if he would assume
the responsibility.

The young man readily consented, for the duty was
not an unusual one, and immediately returned to the
office for his coat and hat, while his father carefully
put up the costly stones in a convenient form for him
to take, and chatted socially with the beautiful Mrs.
Vanderbeck meantime.

When they were ready Ray slipped the package
into one of the outside pockets of his overcoat, but
retained his hold upon it, and then followed the lady
from the store to her carriage, and the next moment
they drove away.

The young man found his companion a most charming woman. She was bright, witty, cultured and
highly educated. She had evidently seen a great deal
of the world, and was full of anecdotes, which she
knew how to relate with such effect that he forgot
for the time everything but the charm of her presence
and conversation.

The drive was rather a long one, but Ray did not
mind that, and was, on the whole, rather sorry when
the carriage stopped, and Mrs. Vanderbeck remarked,
in the midst of a witty anecdote:

"Here we are at last—ah——"

This last ejaculation was caused by discovering

that she could not rise from her seat, her dress having been shut into the door of the *coupé.*

Ray bent forward with a polite "allow me," to assist her, but found that he could not disengage the dress.

Just then the coachman opened the door, but in spite of the young man's utmost care, the beautiful cloth was badly torn in the operation.

"What a pity!" he exclaimed, in a rueful tone.

But madame looked up with a silvery laugh.

"Never mind," she said lightly, "accidents will happen, and I ought to have been more careful when I entered the carriage."

Ray stepped out upon the sidewalk, where he stood waiting to assist his companion, who, however, was trying to pin the rent in her skirt together. Then gathering up some packages that were lying on the seat opposite, she laughingly inquired:

"Please may I trouble you with these for a moment?"

"Indeed you may. Pray excuse my negligence," Ray gallantly exclaimed, as he extended his hands for them.

She filled them both, and then gracefully descended to the ground.

"You can wait, James, to take Mr. Palmer back," she quietly remarked, as they turned to mount the steps of the residence before which they had stopped.

"Pray do not ask your man to do that, Mrs. Vanderbeck; "I can take a car just as well," the young man exclaimed.

"No, indeed," she returned, with a brilliant smile, "I am sure it would be very uncourteous in me to allow you to do so after your kindness in coming with me."

She rang the bell, and the door was almost immediately opened by a colored servant, when the beautiful woman led the way to a small reception room on the right of the hall, where she invited her companion to be seated, while she went to arrange for the interview with her husband.

She glided gracefully from the room, and Ray, depositing upon the table the packages he held, began to remove his gloves, while he glanced about the elegant apartment, noticing its hangings and decorations and many beautiful pictures.

Presently a gentleman of very prepossessing appearance entered, and Ray, arising, was astonished to behold, instead of the invalid he had pictured to himself, a man in the prime of life and apparently in perfect health.

He bowed politely.

"Mr. Vanderbeck, I presume?" he remarked, inquiringly.

The gentleman smilingly returned his salute, without responding to the name, then courteously asked him to take a seat.

Ray took the proffered chair, and then observed, although he wondered why Mrs. Vanderbeck did not return:

"As I suppose you know, I have called, at the request of Mrs. Vanderbeck, to have you examine some—— Good heavens!"

And he suddenly leaped from his chair as if shot from it by some powerful but concealed spring, his face as pale as his shirt bosom, great drops of cold perspiration breaking out upon his forehead

He had put his hand in his pocket as he spoke, to take from it the package of diamonds, but—*it was gone!*

"Pray do not be so excited, my young friend," calmly observed his companion, "but sit down again and tell me your errand."

But Ray Palmer did not hear or heed him. He had rushed to the window, where, with a trembling hand, he swept aside the heavy draperies and looked out upon the street for the *coupé* in which he had been brought to that house.

It was not in sight, and the fearful truth burst upon him—he had been the victim of an accomplished sharper.

He had been robbed, and the clever thief had suddenly vanished, leaving no trace behind her.

CHAPTER VII.

A DESPERATE SITUATION.

For a moment all Raymond Palmer's strength fled, leaving him almost as helpless as a child, while he gazed wildly up and down the street, vainly searching for the woman who had so cunningly duped him, for he knew, if his suspicions were correct, the firm of Amos Palmer & Co. would lose thousands of dollars by that day's operations.

But the young man was no irresolute character. He knew that he must act, and promptly, if he would regain the treasure he had lost, and this thought soon restored strength and energy to both heart and limb.

"I have been robbed!" he cried hoarsely, as he rushed back to the table and seized his hat and gloves, intent only upon getting out upon the street to trace the clever woman who had so outwitted him.

Doctor Wesselhoff was also a victim of the sharpers; for, of course, it will be readily understood that the whole matter was only a deeply laid and cunningly executed scheme to rob the wealthy jewelers of diamonds to a large amount. He was watching Ray's every movement with keenest interest, and with a resolute purpose written upon his intelligent face. He quietly approached him, laid his hand gently upon his arm, and his magnetic power was so strong that Ray was instantly calmed, to a certain extent, in spite of his exceeding dismay at the terrible and unexpected calamity that had overtaken him.

"My young friend," he said soothingly, "you say you have been robbed. Please explain yourself. There is no one in this house who would rob you."

Ray searched the man's face with eager, curious eyes. Then he shook off his hand with an impatient movement.

"Explain myself!" he repeated hotly. "I have had a small fortune stolen from me, and I believe that *you* are an accomplice in the transaction."

"No, no; I assure you I am not," returned the gentleman gravely, and exactly as he would have addressed a person whom he believed to be perfectly sane. "I was told that a caller wished to see me, and I find a man claiming that he has been robbed in my house. What do you mean? Tell me, and perhaps I can help you in your emergency."

The young man was impressed by his courteous manner, in spite of his suspicions, and striving to

curb his excitement, he gave him a brief explanation
of what had occurred.

His account tallied so exactly with the statements
of his visitor of the previous day that Doctor Wesselhoff became more and more interested in the singular
case, and was convinced that his patient was indeed
afflicted with a peculiar monomania.

"Who was this woman?" he inquired, to gain time,
while he should consider what course to pursue with
his patient.

"I do not know—she was an utter stranger to me—
I never saw her before. She called herself Mrs.
Vanderbeck."

That was the name of the "sister" whom Mrs.
Walton had told him she would send with her son,
so the celebrated physician had no suspicion of foul
play.

"And who are you?" he asked, searching the fine
face before him with increasing interest.

"My name is Palmer," Ray answered. "I am the
son of Amos Palmer, a jeweler of this city."

Doctor Wesselhoff glanced keenly at him, while he
thought that, if he was mad, there was certainly
method in his madness to make him deny his own
name, and claim to be some one else.

The physician had always been a profound student,
he was thoroughly in love with his profession, devot-
ing all his time and energies to it, consequently
he was not posted regarding the jewelers of New
York, or, indeed, business firms of any kind; therefore he did not know Amos Palmer—if indeed there
was such a man—from any other dealer in the vani-
ties of the world.

He firmly believed the young man before him to be

a monomaniac of an unusual type, although he could plainly see that, naturally, he was a person of no ordinary character and intelligence.

"I regret very much that you should find yourself in such deep trouble," he remarked in his calm, dignified manner, "and if you have been decoyed here in the way you claim, you are certainly the victim of a very clever plot. Perhaps I can help you, however; just come this way with me. I will order my carriage, for of course you must act quickly, and we will try our best to relieve you in this unpleasant predicament."

"Thank you sir; you are very kind to be so interested," returned Ray, beginning to think the man had also been made a tool to further the schemes of the thieves, and wholly unsuspicious that he was being led still farther into the trap laid for his unwary feet. "My first act," he continued, "will be to go to the superintendent of police, and put the matter in his hands."

"Yes, yes—that would be the wisest course to pursue, no doubt. This way, Mr.—Palmer. It will save time if we go directly to the stable," and Doctor Wesselhoff opened a door opposite the one by which Ray had entered, and politely held it for him to pass through.

Ray, wholly unsuspicious, stepped eagerly forward and entered the room beyond, when the door was quickly closed after him, and the sound of a bolt shooting into its socket startled him to a knowledge of the fact that he was a prisoner.

A cry of indignation and dismay burst from him, as it again flashed upon him that his companion of a moment before must be in league with the woman who had decoyed him to that place.

He sprang back to the door, and sternly demanded to be instantly released.

There was no reply—there was not even a movement in the other apartment, and he was suddenly oppressed with the fear that he was in the power of an organized gang of robbers who might be meditating putting him out of the way, and no one would ever be the wiser regarding his fate.

He felt that he had been very heedless, for he did not even know the name of the street he was on. His fascinating companion had so concentrated his attention upon herself that he had paid no heed to locality.

He repeated his demand to be released, beating loudly upon the door to enforce it.

But no notice was taken of him, and a feeling almost of despair began to settle over him.

He glanced about the room he was in, to see if there was any other way of escape, when, to his dismay, he found that the apartment was padded from floor to ceiling, and thus no sound within it could be heard outside.

It was lighted only from above, where strong bars over the glass plainly indicated to him that the place was intended as a prison, although there were ventilators at the top and bottom, which served to keep the air pure.

The place was comfortably, even elegantly, furnished with a bed, a lounge, a table and several chairs. There were a number of fine pictures on the walls, handsome ornaments on the mantel, besides books, papers and magazines on the table.

But Ray could not stop to give more than a passing glance to all this. He was terribly wrought up at finding himself in such a strait, and paced the room from end to end, like a veritable maniac, while he tried to think of some way to escape.

But he began to realize, after a time, that giving way to such excitement would do no good—that it would be far wiser to sit quietly down and try to exercise his wits; but his mind was a perfect chaos, his head ached, his temples throbbed, his nerves tingled in every portion of his body, and to think calmly in such a state was beyond his power.

Suddenly, however, he became conscious of a strange sensation—he felt a peculiar influence creeping over him; it almost seemed as if there was another presence in the room—a power stronger than himself controlling him.

This impression grew upon him so rapidly that he began to look searchingly about the apartment, while his pulses throbbed less heavily, his mind grew more composed, his blood began to cool, and he ceased his excited passings up and down the floor.

All at once, in the wall opposite to him, he espied a hole about the size of a teacup, and through this aperture he caught the gleam of a pair of human eyes, which seemed to be looking him through and through.

Once meeting that gaze, he could not seem to turn away from it, and he began to feel very strangely—to experience a sense of weariness, amounting almost to exhaustion, then a feeling of drowsiness began to steal over him—all antagonism, indignation, and rebellion against the cruel fate that had so suddenly overtaken him appeared to be gradually fading from his mind, and he could only think of how tired he was.

"What can it mean?" he asked himself, and made a violent effort to break away from the unnatural influence.

He believed that those eyes belonged to the man whom he had met in the other room—that having hopelessly ensnared his victim he was now availing himself of a panel in the wall to watch and see how he would bear his imprisonment.

"Who and what are you, sir, and what is the meaning of this barbarous treatment?" he demanded; but somehow the tones of his own voice did not sound quite natural to him. "You are aiding and abetting a foul wrong," he went on, "even if you are not directly concerned in it, and I command you to release me at once."

There came no word of reply, however, to this demand; but those strange, magnetic eyes remained fixed upon him with the same intense, masterful expression.

He tried to meet them defiantly, to resist their influence with all the strength of his own will; but that feeling of excessive weariness only seemed to increase, and, heaving a long sigh, he involuntarily began to retreat step by step before those eyes until he reached the lounge, when he sank upon it, and his head dropped heavily upon the pillow.

The next moment his eyelids began to close, as if pressed down by invisible weights, though he was still vaguely conscious of the gaze of those wonderful orbs gleaming at him through the hole in the wall.

But even this faded out of his consciousness after another moment, and a profound slumber locked all

his senses. Ray Palmer was hypnotized and a helpless prisoner in the hands of one of the most powerful
mesmerists of the world.

CHAPTER VIII.

THE HEIRESS BECOMES A SEAMSTRESS.

Poor Mona Montague was almost heartbroken
over the sudden death of her uncle. She could not be
reconciled to her great loss, and grieved so bitterly and continuously that her health began to be
affected, and she lost all her lovely color and became thin and weak.

With the exception of the housekeeper and servants, Mr. Dinsmore had been her sole companion for
many years, and they had been all in all to each
other, so that this loss was a terrible blow to her.

Mona had always been an especially bright child,
unusually mature for her years, and probably her
natural precociousness had been increased by having
had so much of the companionship of her uncle. He
had always interested himself in all her pleasures and
made a confidante of her in all things which he
thought she could comprehend; so in this way she had
become very thoughtful for others, while it had also
served to establish a very tender comradeship between them.

He had gratified her every wish whenever he could
consistently do so, and had taken care that she should
have the best of advantages and the most competent
teachers. His home, also, had been filled with every-

thing entertaining and instructive, and thus to her
it had been rendered the dearest and happiest place
in the world.

But the charm and center of attraction were gone,
now that he had been laid away, and, though she
believed that his death had left her independently rich,
the knowledge gave her no pleasure—in fact, she
scarcely gave the subject a thought, except when it
was forced upon her.

A fortnight had elapsed since Mr. Dinsmore died,
and everything had moved on as usual in his elegant
home, while Mrs. Marston, the housekeeper, strove
in every way to comfort Mona and to keep her mind
occupied so that her thoughts would not long dwell
upon her bereavement.

But the young girl's condition troubled her greatly.
She was listless and languid; she lost her appetite,
and had seasons of depression and outbursts of sorrow that were really alarming.

Susie Leades came to her almost every day and
tried to cheer her. Mona appreciated her kind efforts,
and was somewhat comforted by them, while she
also had many letters of sympathy and condolence
from her numerous friends.

But to her great surprise Ray Palmer had never
once come to inquire for her; neither had he written
her one word to tell her that he felt for her in this
bitter trial.

She was both grieved and hurt over his apparent
indifference, especially after the request he had made
on the evening of their attendance at the opera, and
the many unmistakable signs of regard which he had
betrayed for her at that time.

She was brooding over this one afternoon when

Mr. Graves, the lawyer and her future guardian, was announced.

He looked serious and troubled; indeed, he was so unlike himself that Mona observed it, and asked him if he was ill.

"No, Miss Mona, I am not really ill, but I am laboring under trouble and anxiety enough to almost make me so," he responded, as he took her extended hand and gazed down upon her own colorless face with a sorrowful, wistful look.

"Trouble?" she repeated, with a quivering lip. "Oh, trouble is so much harder to bear than illness."

"My poor child, your remark only makes my burden all the heavier," the gentleman returned, in an unsteady voice. "Alas, my trouble is all on your account, for I am the bearer of ill news for you."

"Ill news—to me?" exclaimed the young girl, in a wondering tone. "After losing Uncle Walter, it does not seem as if *any* trouble could move me; *nothing* can compare with that," she concluded, passionately.

"Very true; but there are other troubles in life besides death," said Mr. Graves, gently; "such as—the loss of fortune, poverty——"

"Do you mean that I am to have no fortune—that I am to be poor?" exclaimed Mona, astonished.

"Ah, I fear that it is so."

"How can that be possible? Uncle Walter was very rich, wasn't he? I certainly understood you to say so."

"Yes, I did; and I find, on looking into his affairs, that he was worth even more than I had previously supposed."

"Well, then, what can you mean? I am his only

near relative, and you said that I should inherit everything," Mona said with a perplexed look.

"I know I did, and I thought so at that time; but,
Mona, I was waited upon by a noted lawyer only a
few days ago, and he claims the whole of your uncle's
great wealth for another."

"Why, who can it possibly be?" cried the girl in
amazement.

"Your uncle's wife, or, I should say, his widow."

"My uncle's wife?" repeated Mona, with a dazed
look. "Uncle Walter had no wife!"

"Are you sure?"

"Why, yes, of course. I have always lived with
him, ever since I can remember, and there has been
no one else in the family except the servants and the
housekeeper. I am sure—I think—and yet——"

Mona abruptly paused as she remembered a remark
which her uncle had made to her on her eighteenth
birthday. He had said: "You have taken the place
of the little girl who never lived to call me father,
and—you have helped me to bear other troubles also."

Could it be possible, she now asked herself, that her
uncle had had domestic troubles, that there had been
a separation from his wife, and that this had been a
lifelong sorrow to him?

She had always supposed that his wife was dead,
for he would never speak of her, nor allow Mona to
ask him any questions. From her earliest childhood
she had somehow seemed to know that she must not
refer in any way to such a subject.

"Ah, I see that you are in some doubt about it,"
Mr. Graves observed. "The matter stands thus, however: A woman, claiming to be Mrs. Walter Dinsmore, has presented her claim to her husband's prop-

erty. She proves herself, beyond the possibility of doubt, to be what she pretends, bringing her marriage certificate and other papers to substantiate her title. She asserts that about a year after her marriage with Mr. Dinsmore they had trouble—of what nature I do not know—and the feeling between them was so irreconcilable they agreed to part, Mr. Dinsmore allowing her a separate maintenance. They were living in San Francisco at the time. There was no divorce, but they never met afterward, Mr. Dinsmore coming East, while she remained in California. She says there was a child——"

"Yes," Mona interposed. "Uncle Walter told me of the birth of a little girl, but that she never lived to call him father."

"I wonder what he meant by that?" said Mr. Graves with a start; "that the child came into the world lifeless? If such was the case, then your claim to the estate is still good."

"I supposed from what he said that it was born lifeless; still his words were somewhat ambiguous—even if she had lived several months, she might not have lived long enough to call him father!"

"Well, the woman asserts that the infant lived for a few hours, and brings the records to prove it, and claims that *she* is Mr. Dinsmore's only legitimate heir, through her child," Mr. Graves explained.

"And is she?—is that true?" Mona asked.

"Yes, the court will recognize her claim—to all appearance, it is indisputable; and now I can understand what puzzled and troubled me when Mr. Dinsmore was so helplessly ill," Mr. Graves said, reflectively. "You doubtless remember how distressed he was when he tried to make me understand something in connection with his will."

"Yes," said Mona with streaming eyes. "Oh, poor Uncle Walter!"

"Doubtless he knew that his wife was still living," Mr. Graves resumed, "and that she would be likely to claim his property. He wanted *you* to have it—that I know—and he must have suffered untold anguish because he could not make me understand that he wanted to have me insert something in his will, which would provide against this woman's demands. Even if he had been able to sign the document which I drew up, she could have broken it, because she was not mentioned and remembered in it, and he knew this, of course."

"Then she will have all—I am not to have anything?" said Mona inquiringly, but without being able to realize, in the least, what such utter destitution meant.

"My poor child, she utterly refuses to release a dollar of your uncle's money to you. I have fought hard for you, Mona, for I could not bear to come to you with this wretched story; but she is inexorable. She seems, for some reason, to entertain a special spite— even hatred—against you, and asserts, through her counsel—*I* have not had the honor of meeting this peculiar specimen of womanhood—that you shall either work or beg for your bread; you shall have *nothing* of what legally belongs to her.

"Then I am absolutely penniless!" said Mona, musingly. "I wonder if I can make myself understand what that means! I have always had everything that I wanted. I never asked for anything that Uncle Walter did not give me if he could obtain it. I have had more money than I wanted to spend, and so I have given a great deal away. It will seem *very* strange to have an empty purse. I wonder where I shall get my clothes, when what I have are worn out. I wonder how I am to get what I shall need to *eat*— does it cost very much to feed one person? Why, Mr. Graves!" putting her hand to her head in a half-dazed way. "I *cannot* make it seem *real*—it is like some dreadful dream!"

"Mona, my dear child, do not talk like that," said the man, looking deeply distressed, "for, somehow, I feel guilty, as if I were, in a measure, responsible for this fresh calamity that has befallen you; and yet I could not help it. If I had only *known* that Mr. Dinsmore's wife was living, I could have made the will all right. Ah! no, no! what am I saying? Even if I *had*, he could not have signed it, for his strength failed. Still, I know that he wanted you to have all, and it is not right that this woman should get it from you."

"Must I go away from my home and from all these lovely things of which Uncle Walter was so fond?" Mona asked, looking about the beautiful room with inexpressible longing written on her young face. "Will she claim his books and pictures, and even this dear chair, in which I loved to see him sit, and which seems almost like a part of himself, now that he is gone?" and unable to bear the thought of parting from these familiar objects, around which clustered such precious associations, the stricken girl bowed her face upon the arm of Mr. Dinsmore's chair, and burst into a passion of tears.

"My dear girl, don't!" pleaded the tender-hearted lawyer, as he gently stroked her rich, brown hair with one hand, and wiped the tears from his own eyes with the other, "it almost breaks my heart to think of it, and I promise that you shall at least have some of the treasures which you prize so much. You shall not want for a home, either—you shall come to me. Mr. Dinsmore was my dear and valued friend, and for his sake, as well as your own, you shall never want for enough to supply your needs. I have not great wealth, but what I have I will share with you."

Mona now lifted her head, and wiped her tears, while she struggled bravely to regain her self-possession.

"You are very kind, Mr. Graves," she said, when she could speak, and with a newly acquired dignity, at which her companion marveled, "and I am very grateful to you for your sympathy and generosity; but I could never become an object of charity to any one. If it is so ordered, that I am to be bereft of the home and fortune which Uncle Walter wished me to have, I must submit to it, and there will doubtless be some way provided to enable me to live independently. It is all so new and so—so almost incomprehensible, that, for the moment, I was overcome. I will try not to be so weak and childish again; and now," pausing for a deep breath, "will you please explain to me just my position? When must I go, and—and can I take away the things that Uncle Walter has given to me from time to time? The pictures in my own rooms were given to me on certain birthdays and holidays; the piano he gave me new last Christmas, and I have a watch and some valuable jewelry."

"Of course, you may keep all such things," Mr. Graves answered with emotion, for it was inexpressively sad to have this girl so shorn of all that had made life beautiful to her so many years, "unless," he added, "it be the piano, and that you may have if there is any way to prove that it was given to you. You are to have a week in which to make your arrangements, and at the end of that time everything will pass into the possession of madame."

"Only a week longer in my dear home!" broke from the quivering lips of the stricken girl; "how can I bear it? Oh, Uncle Walter! how can I bear to have strangers handle with careless touch the things that you and I have loved so much? these dear books that we have read together—the pictures that we selected and never tired of studying to find new points for each other! Oh, every one is sacred to me!"

The strong man at her side was so moved by her grief that he was obliged to rise and walk to a window to conceal his own emotion.

But after a little she controlled herself again, and discussed everything with him in a grave, quiet, yet comprehensive way that made him sure she would in time rise above her troubles and perhaps become all the stronger in character for having been thus tried in the furnace of affliction.

He went every day after that to assist her in her arrangements for leaving; helped her to pack the treasures she was to take away with her, and to put in the nicest order everything she was to leave; for on this point she was very particular. She had secretly resolved that her uncle's discarded wife should have no fault to find with his home.

When the end of the week arrived Mr. Graves tried to persuade Mona to go home with him and remain until she could decide what she wished to do in the future, or, he told her, she was welcome to remain and make it her home indefinitely.

But she quietly thanked and informed him that she had already arranged to go as seamstress to a lady on West Forty-ninth street.

"You go as a seamstress?" exclaimed the lawyer, aghast. "What do you know about sewing—you who have always had everything of the kind done for you?"

"Oh, no; not everything," said Mona, smiling slightly. "I have always loved to sew since I was a little child, and my nurse made me do patchwork; and I assure you that I am quite an expert with my needle in many ways."

"But to go out and make it a business! I cannot bear the thought! What would your uncle say?" objected good Mr. Graves.

"I do not believe that Uncle Walter would wish me to be dependent upon any one, if it was possible for me to take care of myself," Mona gravely replied. "At all events," she continued, with a proud uplifting of her pretty brown head, "I could never allow another to provide for my needs without first trying my best to earn my own living—though, believe me, I am very grateful for your kindness."

"You are a brave and noble girl, Mona, and I admire your spirit; but—I have no daughter of my own, and, truly, both my wife and I would be glad to have you come to us," Mr. Graves urged, regarding her anxiously.

"Thank you; it is very comforting to know that you are so kindly disposed toward me, but I know that I shall respect myself more if I try to do something for my own support," was the firm yet gentle response.

Mr. Graves sighed, for he well knew that this delicately reared girl had a hard lot before her if she expected to earn her living as a sewing girl.

"At least you will regard me as your stanch friend," he said, "and promise me, Mona, that if you ever get into any difficulty you will appeal to me; that if you should find that you have undertaken more than your strength will allow you to carry out you will make my home your refuge."

"Yes, I will," she said, tears of gratitude starting to her lovely eyes, "and I am greatly comforted to know that I have one such true friend in my trouble."

"What is the name of the family into which you are going?" her companion inquired.

"I do not know, and it is a little singular that I do not," Mona replied, smiling. "I applied at an employment bureau for a situation a few days ago; yesterday I went to ascertain if there was a place for me and was told that a lady living on West Forty-ninth street wanted a seamstress, and I am to meet her at the office this afternoon. I, of course, asked the name, but the clerk could not tell me—she had lost the lady's card, and could only remember the street and number."

"Rather a careless way of doing business," the lawyer remarked, as he arose to go. "However," he added, "let me know how you succeed after you get settled, and if anything should occur to throw you out of your place, come straight to us, and make our home headquarters while you are looking out for another."

Mona's self-possession almost forsook her as she took leave of him. It seemed almost like losing her only friend, to let him go; but she bade him good-by with as brave a front as possible, though she broke down utterly the moment the door closed after him.

The remainder of the day was spent in packing her trunk and looking her last upon the familiar objects of the home that had always been so dear to her.

But her severest trial came when she had to bid the housekeeper and the servants farewell, for the loved and loving girl had been a great favorite with them all, and their grief was as deep and sincere at parting with her.

This over, she stepped across the threshold of Walter Dinsmore's elegant home for the last time, and entered the carriage that was to bear her away, her heart nearly bursting with grief, and tears streaming in torrents over her cheeks.

CHAPTER IX.

MONA RECEIVES A SHOCK.

When Mona arrived at the office of the employment bureau, at the hour appointed, she found awaiting her the carriage belonging to the woman who had engaged her services.

A pretty serving girl admitted her when she arrived at the elegant brown stone mansion, and remarked, as she showed her up to the room she was to occupy, that "the mistress had been called out of town for the day, and would not be at home until dinner time."

The girl seemed kindly disposed, and chatted socially about the family, which consisted only of "the mistress and her nephew, Master Louis." The mistress was a widow, but very gay—very much of a society lady, and "handsome as a picture." She was upward of forty, but didn't look a day over thirty. She was very proud and high spirited, but treated her help kindly if they didn't cross her.

Somehow Mona did not get a very favorable impression of her employer from this gossipy information; but her fate was fixed for the present, and she resolved to do the best that she could, and not worry regarding the result.

As the girl was about to leave the room to go about her duties, she remarked that dinner would be served at six o'clock, and that Mona was to come down to the basement to eat with the other servants.

Mona flushed hotly at this information. Must she, who all her life had been the petted child of fortune, go among menials to eat with she knew not whom?

But she soon conquered her momentary indignation, for she realized that she was nothing more than a servant herself now, and could not expect to be treated as an equal by her fashionable employer.

"Will you tell me your name, please?" she asked of the girl, and trying not to betray any of her sensitiveness.

"Mary, miss," was the respectful reply, for the girl recognized that the new seamstress was a lady, in spite of the fact that she was obliged to work for her living.

"Thank you; and—will you please tell me the name of your mistress, also; the card which she left at the office was lost, and I have not learned it," Mona said as she arose to hang her wraps in the closet.

"Lor', miss! that is queer," said the girl in a tone of

surprise, "that you should engage yourself and not know who to."

"It didn't really make much difference what the name was—it was the situation that I wanted," Mona remarked, smiling.

"True enough, but my lady's name's a high-sounding one, and she's not at all backward about airing it; it rolls off her sweet tongue as easy as water off a duck's back—Mrs. Richmond Montague," and the girl tossed her head and drew herself up in imitation of her mistress's haughty air in a way that would have done credit to a professional actress. "But there," she cried, with a start, as a shrill voice sounded from below, "cook is calling me, and I must run."

She tripped away, humming a gay tune, while Mona sank, white and trembling, upon the nearest chair.

"Mrs. Richmond Montague!" she repeated, in a scarcely audible voice. "Can it be possible that she— this woman, to whom I have come as a seamstress— is my father's second wife—or was, since she is a widow! How strange! how very strange that I, of all persons, should have been fated to come here! It is very unfortunate that I could not have known her name, for, of course, I should never have come if I had. It may be," she went on, musingly, "that she is some other Mrs. Montague; but no—it could hardly be possible that there are two persons with that peculiar combination of names. This, then, is the woman for whom my father deserted my mother in order to secure the fortune left by his aunt! How unworthy! —how contemptible! I am glad that I fell to Uncle Walter's care; I am glad that I never knew him— this unnatural father who never betrayed the slightest interest in his own child. But—can I stay here with her?" she asked, with burning cheeks and flashing eyes. "Can I—his daughter—remain to serve the woman who usurped my mother's place, who is living in affluence upon money which rightly belongs to me?"

The young girl was trembling with nervous excitement, and a feeling of hot anger, a sense of deep injustice burned within her.

This startling discovery—for she was convinced that there could be but one Mrs. Richmond Montague—stirred her soul to its lowest depths. She felt a strange dread of this woman; a feeling almost of horror and aversion made her sink from contact with her; and yet, at the same time, she experienced an unaccountable curiosity to see and know something of her. There was a spice of romance about the situation which prompted her, in spite of her first impulse to flee from the house—to stay and study this gay woman of the world, who was so strangely connected with her own life.

She could leave at any time, she told herself, should the position prove to be an uncongenial one; but since she had chosen the vocation of a seamstress, she might as well sew for Mrs. Richmond Montague as any one else; while possibly she might be able to learn something more regarding her mother's history than she already knew. She felt sure that her uncle had kept something back from her, and she so longed to have the mystery fully explained.

But, of course, if she remained, it would never do for her to give her own name, for this woman would suspect her identity at once, and probably drive her out into the world again. It was not probable that she would knowingly tolerate the child of a rival in her home.

Mona was glad now that she had not told Mary her name, as she had once been on the point of doing.

"What shall I call myself?" she mused. "I do not dare to use Uncle Walter's name, for that would betray me as readily as my own; even Mona, being such an uncommon name, would also make her suspect me. There is my middle name, Ruth, and my father was called Richmond—suppose I call myself Ruth Richards?"

This rather pleased her, and she decided to use it. But she was strangely nervous about meeting Mrs. Montague, and several times she was tempted to send Mary for a carriage and flee to Mr. Graves's hospitable home, and start out from there to seek some other position.

Once she did rise to call her. "I cannot stay," she said. "I must go." But just then she heard voices in the hall below, and, believing that Mrs. Montague had returned, she turned back and sat down again with a sinking heart, assured that her resolve had come too late.

At six o'clock she went down to the basement, where she had been told dinner would be served, and where she found no one save Mary and Sarah, the cook, who proved to be a good-natured woman of about thirty-five years, and who at once manifested a motherly interest in the pretty and youthful seamstress.

Mary informed her, during the meal, that Mrs. Montague was going out that evening to a grand reception, and had sent word that she could not see her until the next morning; but that she would find some sheets and pillow slips in the sewing room, which she could begin to work upon after breakfast, and she would lay out other work for her later.

Mona uttered a sigh of relief over the knowledge that the meeting, which she so much dreaded, was to be postponed a little, and after dinner she returned to her room, and sat down quite composedly to read the morning paper, which she had purchased on her way to Mrs. Montague's.

While thus engaged, her eye fell upon the following paragraph:

"No clew has as yet been obtained to the mysterious Palmer affair, although both the police and detectives are doing their utmost to trace the clever thief. It is most earnestly hoped that they will succeed in their efforts, as such successful knavery is an incentive to even greater crimes."

"What can it mean?" Mona said to herself; "and what a blind paragraph! Of course, it refers to something that has been previously published, and which might explain it. Can it be that Mr. Palmer's jewelry store has been robbed?"

This, of course, led her thoughts to Ray Palmer, and she fell into troubled musings regarding his apparent neglect of her, and in the midst of this there came a rap upon her door.

She arose to open it, and found Mary standing outside.

"Please, Miss Richards, will you come down to Mrs. Montague's room?" she asked. "She has ripped the lace flounce from her reception dress while putting it on, and wants you to repair it for her."

Mona was somewhat excited by this summons; but, unlocking her trunk, she found her thimble, needles, and scissors, and followed Mary down stairs to the second floor and into a large room over the drawing-room.

It was a beautiful room, most luxuriously and taste-fully fitted up as a lady's boudoir, and was all ablaze with light from a dozen gas jets.

In the center of the floor there stood a magnificently beautiful woman.

She was a blonde of the purest type, and Mona thought that Mary had made a true statement when she had said that, though she was upward of forty, she did not look a day over thirty, for she certainly was a very youthful person in appearance.

Her skin was almost as fair as marble, with a flush on her round, velvet-like cheeks that came and went as in the face of a young girl. Her features were of Grecian type, her hair was a pale gold and arranged in a way to give her a regal air; her eyes were a beautiful blue, her lips a vivid scarlet, while her form was tall and slender, with perfect ease and grace in every movement.

"How lovely she is!" thought Mona. "It does not seem possible that she could have even an unkind thought in her heart. I can hardly believe that she ever knew anything of my poor mother's wrongs."

Mrs. Montague was exquisitely dressed in a heavy silk of a delicate peach ground, brocaded richly with flowers of a deeper shade. This was draped over a plain peach-colored satin petticoat, and trimmed with a deep flounce of finest point lace. The corsage was cut low, thus revealing her beautiful neck, around which there was clasped a necklace of blazing dia-monds.

Her arms were bare to the shoulder, the dress hav-ing no sleeves save a strap about two inches wide, into which a frill of costly point was gathered. Long gloves of a delicate peach tint came above her elbow, and between the top of each of these and the frill of lace there was a diamond armlet to match the necklace.

Magnificent solitaires gleamed in her ears, and there was a star composed of the same precious stones among the massive braids of her golden hair.

She was certainly a radiant vision, and Mona's quick glance took in every detail of her dress while she was crossing the room to her side.

Mrs. Montague bent a keen look upon her as she approached, and she gave a slight start as her eyes swept the delicately chiseled face of the girl.

"You are the new seamstress, Mary tells me. What is your name—what shall I call you?" she questioned, abruptly.

"M——" Mona had almost betrayed herself before she remembered the need of concealing her identity.

But quickly checking herself, she cried:

"Ruth Richards, madame; call me Ruth, if you please."

"Hum! Ruth Richards—that's rather pretty," remarked the lady, but still searching the fair face before her with a look of curious interest. "But," she added, "you look very young; I am afraid you are hardly experienced enough to be a very efficient seamstress," and the lady told herself that those delicate, rose-tipped fingers did not look as if they had been long accustomed to the use of a needle.

"I do not understand very much about dressmaking," Mona frankly replied, although she ignored the reference to her youthfulness; "but I can do plain sewing very nicely, and, indeed, almost anything that

is planned for me. I distinctly stated at the office that
I could neither cut nor fit."

"Well, I can but give you a trial," with a little sigh
of disappointment, as if she regretted having engaged
one so young; "and if you cannot fill the place, I
shall have to try again, I suppose. But, see here! I
caught the thread that fastened this lace to my skirt,
and have ripped off nearly half a yard. I want you to
replace it for me, and you must do it quickly, for I am
a little late, as it is."

Mona dropped upon her knees beside the beautiful
woman, threaded her needle with the silk which Mary
brought her, and, though her fingers trembled and her
heart beat with rapid, nervous throbs, she quickly
repaired the damage, and in a manner to win commendation from Mrs. Montague.

"You are very quick with your needle, and you
have done it very nicely," she said, with a smile that
revealed two rows of the most perfect teeth that Mona
had ever seen. "And now tell me," she added, as she
turned slowly around, "if everything about my costume is all right, then you may go."

"Yes," Mona returned; "it is perfect; it fits and
hangs beautifully."

"That is the highest praise any one could give,"
Mrs. Montague responded, with another brilliant
smile; "and I believe you are really a competent judge,
since your own dress hasn't a wrinkle in it. Did you
make it yourself?"

"I—I helped to make it. I told you I do not know
how to fit," Mona answered, with a quick flush, and
almost a feeling of guilt, for she had really done but
very little work upon the simple black robe which had
been made since her uncle's death.

"Well, I shall soon find out how much you do know," said the lady in a business-like tone. "You can begin upon those sheets and pillow slips to-morrow morning—Mary has told you, I suppose. That will be plain sewing, and you can manage it well enough by yourself. Now you may go," and the elegant woman turned to her dressing-case, gathered up an exquisite point-lace fan and handkerchief, while Mona stole softly out of the room and up to her own, where, no longer able to control the nervous excitement under which she was laboring, she wept herself to sleep.

The poor grief-stricken girl felt very desolate on his, her first night beneath a strange roof, and real-ized, as she had not before, that she was utterly alone in the world, and dependent upon the labor of her own hands for her future support.

Aside from the grief which she experienced in losing her uncle and the lovely home which for so many years had been hers, she was both wounded and mortified because of Ray Palmer's apparent indiffer-ence.

She could not understand it, for he had always seemed so innately good and noble that it was but natural she should expect some evidence of sympathy from him.

He had been so marked in his attentions to her during that evening at the opera, he had appeared so eager for her permission to call, and had implied, by both words and manner, that he found his greatest pleasure in her society, she felt she had a right to expect some condolence from him.

She had begun to believe—to hope that he enter-tained a more tender sentiment than that of mere friendship for her, and she had become conscious that

love for him—and the strongest passion of her nature
—had taken deep root in her own heart.

How kind he had been to her that night—how
thoughtful! anticipating her every wish! How his
glance and even the tones of his voice had softened
and grown tender whenever their eyes had met, or
he had spoken to her!

What, then, could be the meaning of his recent
neglect? Could it be possible that it had been occasioned by the loss of her wealth?—that it had been
simply the heiress of the wealthy Mr. Dinsmore in
whom he had been interested, and now, having lost
all, his regard for her had ceased?

It was a bitter thought, but she could assign no
other reason for his strange silence and absence during her sorrow.

Must she resign all the sweet hopes that had begun
to take form in her heart?—all the bright anticipations
in which he had borne so conspicuous a part?

Must she lose faith in one who had appeared to be
so manly, so noble, and so high-minded?

It certainly seemed so, and thus the future looked
all the darker before her, for, humiliating as it was
to confess it, she knew that Ray Palmer was all the
world to her; that life without him would be almost
like a body without a soul, a world without a sun.

Her uncle's death had come upon her so like a
thunderbolt out of a clear sky, almost benumbing all
her faculties with the grief it had hurled upon her so
remorselessly, that she could think of nothing else until
Mr. Graves had come to her with that other fatal
piece of news—the loss of her fortune.

She had scarcely looked into a daily paper until
that evening, for she felt no interest in the outside

world; she could apply her mind to nothing but her own afflictions; consequently, she had not known anything of the mysterious and exciting circumstances connected with Ray Palmer's sudden disappearance and the stolen diamonds. That little blind paragraph, which she had seen just before she was called down to Mrs. Montague's room, was the only hint that she had had of any trouble or loss in the Palmer family.

So, of course, it is not strange that she so misjudged Ray; she could not know that only a great wrong kept him from speeding to her side to express the deeepst interest and sympathy for her in her sorrow.

And it was well, perhaps, that she did not know, for it would only have added to her troubles and caused her greater suffering.

CHAPTER X.

MONA MEETS MRS. MONTAGUE'S NEPHEW.

The next morning, as soon as she had finished her breakfast, Mona asked Mary to conduct her to the sewing-room, and there she found a pile of work, which would have been exceedingly disheartening to a less resolute spirit.

But the young girl had bravely determined to do the best she could and not worry about the result.

Fate had willed that she must work for her living, and she had resolved not to murmur at her lot, but, putting forth all her energies, hope to please her employer and meet with success in her undertaking.

So she arranged her chair and table by a pleasant window overlooking the street, and then boldly attacked the mountain before her.

"I wonder if Mrs. Montague intends to have these done by hand or machine?" she mused, as she shook out the folds of snowy cloth and began to turn a hem on one of the sheets. "And then"—with a puzzled expression—"how am I to know how broad to make the hems?"

She feared to go on with the work without special directions, for she might make some mistake. But after considering the matter, she determined to leave the sheets altogether and do the over-and-over sewing on the pillow-slips, until she could ascertain Mrs. Montague's wishes.

Mona was naturally quick in all her movements, and, being also very persevering, she had accomplished considerable by ten o'clock, when Mrs. Montague, in an elegant morning *negligée* of light-blue cashmere, and looking as lovely as an houri, strolled languidly into the sewing-room to see what her new seamstress was about.

"Oh, you are sewing up the slips," she remarked, as she nodded in reply to Mona's polite good morning and observed her employment. "I forgot to tell you about the hems last night, and I have been afraid ever since I awoke this morning that you would not make them broad enough."

"Yes, I feared I might make some mistake, so left them," Mona answered, but without stopping her work.

"How beautiful your seams look!" the lady said, as she examined some of the slips. "Your stitches are very fine and even; but over-and-over sewing must be very monotonous work. You might vary it by hemming a sheet now and then. I want the hems three inches wide on both ends."

"Do you have them stitched or done by hand?" Mona inquired.

"Oh, stitched; I have a beautifully running machine, and I want to get them out of the way as soon as possible, for there is dressmaking to be done. Can you run a White machine?"

Mona was conscious that her companion was regarding her very earnestly during this conversation, but she appeared not to notice it, and replied:

"I never have, but if I could be shown how to thread it, I think I should have no difficulty."

She was very thankful to know that all that mountain before her was not to be done by hand.

"Do you like to sew?" Mrs. Montague inquired, as she watched the girl's pretty hand in its deft manipulation of the needle.

Mona smiled sadly.

"I used to think I did," she said, after a moment's hesitation, "but when one is obliged to do one thing continually it becomes monotonous and irksome."

"How long have you been obliged to support yourself by sewing?" the woman asked, curiously, for to her there seemed to be something very incongruous in this beautiful high-bred girl drudging all day long as a seamstress.

Mona flushed at the question.

There was nothing she dreaded so much as being questioned regarding her past life.

"Not very long; death robbed me of friends and home, and so I was obliged to earn my living," she returned, after considering a moment how she should answer.

"Then you are an orphan?"

"Yes."

"Have you no relatives?" and the lovely but keen blue eyes of the lady were fixed very searchingly upon the fair young face.

"None that I know of."

"You do not look as if you had ever done much work of any kind," Mrs. Montague observed. "You seem more like a person who has been reared in luxury; your hands are very fair and delicate; your dress is of very fine and expensive material, and—why, there is real Valenciennes lace on your pocket-handkerchief!"

Mona was becoming very nervous under this close inspection. She saw that Mrs. Montague was curious about her, though she did not for a moment imagine that she could have the slightest suspicion regarding her identity; yet she feared that she might be trapped into betraying something in an unguarded moment, if she continued this kind of examination.

"I always buy good material," she quietly remarked. "I think it is economy to do so, and—my handkerchief was given to me. How wide did you tell me to make the hems on these pillow-slips?" she asked, in conclusion, to change the subject, but mentally resolving that Mrs. Montague should never see any but plain handkerchiefs about her again.

"I did not tell you any width for the slips," was the dry, yet haughty rejoinder, for madame could not fail to understand that she had been politely admonished that her curiosity was becoming annoying to her fair seamstress, "but you may make them to match those upon the sheets—three inches."

She arose, immediately after giving this order, and swept proudly from the room, and Mona did not see her again that day. It seemed to the poor girl, with her unaccustomed work, the longest one she had ever known, and she grew heavy-hearted, and very weary before it was over.

She had all her life been in the habit of taking plenty of exercise in the open air. While she was studying, Mr. Dinsmore had made her walk to and from school, then after lunch they would either go for a drive or for a canter in the park or the suburbs of the city.

She had never been subjected to any irksome restraint, and so it seemed very hard to be obliged to sit still for so many hours at a time and do nothing but "stitch! stitch! stitch!" like the woman in the "Song of the Shirt."

But six o'clock came at last, to release her from those endless seams and hems, and after she had eaten her dinner she was so completely wearied out that she crept up to her bed and almost immediately fell asleep.

But the next morning she was pale and heavy-eyed, and Mrs. Montague evidently realized that it was unwise to make her apply herself so steadily, for she made out a memorandum of several little things which she wanted and sent Mona down town to purchase them.

The girl came back looking so bright and fresh, and went at her work with so much vigor, the woman smiled wisely to herself.

"She hasn't been used to such close application, it is plain to be seen," she mused, "and I must take care

or she will give out. She sews beautifully, though,
and rapidly, and I want to keep her, for I believe she
can be made very useful."

So every day after that she sent her out for a while
on some pretext or other, and Mona felt grateful for
these moments of respite.

One day she was sent to Macy's with a longer list
than usual, and while there she came face to face with
a couple of acquaintances—young ladies who, like
herself, had only that winter been introduced to society.

They had been only too eager, whenever they had
met her in company, to claim the wealthy Mr. Dinsmore's niece as their friend.

Mona bowed and smiled to-day, as she met them,
but was astonished and dismayed beyond measure
when they both gave her a rude stare of surprise, and
then passed on without betraying the slightest sign
of recognition.

For a moment Mona's face was like a scarlet flame,
then all her color as quickly fled, leaving her ghastly
white as she realized that she had received the cut
direct.

Her heart beat so heavily that she was oppressed
by a feeling almost of suffocation, and was obliged to
stop and lean against a pillar for a moment for support.

She did not see that a young man was standing
near, watching her with a peculiar smile on his bold
face. He had observed the whole proceeding, and
well understood its meaning, while, during all the
time that Mona remained in the store, he followed her
at a distance. Her emotion passed after a moment,
and then all her pride arose in arms. Her eyes

flashed, her lips curled, and she straightened herself haughtily.

"They are beneath me," she murmured. "Home-less, friendless as I am to-day, I would not exchange places with them. I am superior to them even in my poverty, for I would not wound the humblest person in the world with such rudeness and ill-breeding."

Yet, in spite of this womanly spirit, in spite of the contempt which she felt for such miserable pride of purse and position, she was deeply wounded and made to realize, as she never yet had done, that Mrs. Rich-mond Montague's seamstress would henceforth be regarded as a very different person from Miss Mona Montague, the heiress and a petted beauty in society.

She did not care to go out shopping so much after that; but when obliged to do so she avoided as much as possible those places where she would be liable to meet old acquaintances.

She would take her airing after lunch in the quiet streets of the neighborhood, and then return to her tasks in the sewing-room.

She was not quite so lonely after a dressmaker came to do some fitting for Mrs. Montague, for the woman was kind and sociable, and, becoming inter-ested in the beautiful sewing-girl, seemed to try to make the time pass pleasantly to her, and was a great help to her about her work.

Mona often wondered how Mrs. Montague would feel if she should know who she was. Sometimes she was almost inclined to think that she did suspect the truth, for she often found her regarding her with a curious and intent look. It occurred to her that the woman might possibly have known her mother, and noticed her resemblance to her, for Mr. Dinsmore had told her that she looked very much like her.

One day Mona was standing close beside her, while she tried on a fichu which she had been fixing for her to wear that evening, when the woman broke out abruptly, while she scanned her face intently:

"For whom are you in mourning, Ruth?"

Mona did not know just how to reply to this direct question; but after an instant's reflection she said:

"The dearest friend I had in the world. Do you not remember, Mrs. Montague, that I told you I was an orphan? I am utterly friendless."

Mrs. Montague regarded her with a peculiar look for a moment, but she did not pursue the subject, and Mona was greatly relieved.

"If she knew my mother," she told herself, "and has discovered my resemblance to her—if she knew Uncle Walter, and I had told her I was in mourning for him—she would have known at once who I am."

It was very evident that her employer was pleased with her work, for she frequently complimented her upon her neatly finished seams, while the dressmaker asserted that she had seldom had one so young to work with her who was so efficient.

On the whole she was kindly treated; she was in a pleasant and luxurious home, although in the capacity of a servant; her wages were fair, and for the present she felt that she could not do better than to remain where she was, while she experienced a very gratifying feeling of independence in being able to provide for herself.

She had seen Mr. Graves only once since leaving her own home, and then she had met him on the street during one of her daily walks.

He had told her that Mr. Dinsmore's property had all passed into the hands of his wife, although the house had not as yet been disposed of; it had been rented, furnished, to a family for a year. He said he had never met Mrs. Dinsmore; all her business had been transacted through her lawyer, and the woman evidently did not like, for some reason, to appear personally in the settlement of the property.

He kindly inquired how she endured the confinement of her new life, and urged her cordially to come to him whenever she was tired and needed a rest, telling her that she should always be sure of a warm welcome.

A day or two after this meeting with her old friend, and just as she was returning from her usual walk, Mona encountered a young man as she was about to mount the steps leading into Mrs. Montague's residence.

He was dressed in the height of fashion, and might have been regarded as fairly good-looking if he had not been so conceited and self-conscious.

The young girl did not bestow more than a passing glance upon him, supposing him to be some stranger whom she might never meet again.

She ran lightly up the steps, when, what was her surprise to find him following her, and, just as she was on the point of ringing for admittance, he stayed her hand, by remarking, with excessive politeness:

"I have a latch-key, miss—pray allow me to admit you."

Of course, Mona knew then that this young exquisite must be the nephew of Mrs. Montague, of whom Mary had told her—Mr. Louis Hamblin.

She observed him more closely as she thanked him,

and saw that he was apparently about twenty-five years of age, with light-brown hair, blue eyes, and somewhat irregular, yet not unpleasant, features. He was well formed, rather tall, and carried himself with ease, though somewhat proudly.

He was evidently impressed with Mona's appearance, as his look of admiration plainly indicated.

He appeared to regard her as some visitor to see his aunt, for his manner was both respectful and gentlemanly as he opened the door, and then stood aside to allow her to pass in.

Mona bowed in acknowledgment of this courtesy, and, entering, passed directly through the hall and up stairs, greatly to the young man's astonishment.

He gave vent to a low whistle, and exclaimed, under his breath, as he deposited his cane in the stand and drew off his gloves:

"Jove! I imagined her to be some high-toned caller, and she is only some working girl. Really, though, she is as fine a specimen of young womanhood as I have encountered in many a day, and I should like to see more of her. Ah, Aunt Marg," he went on, as Mrs. Montague came sweeping down the stairs, just then, in an elaborate dinner costume, "how fine you look, and I'm on time, you perceive! How about the McKenzie reception to-night?"

"We must go, of course," responded the lady, in a somewhat weary tone, "for Mrs. McKenzie would be offended if we should remain away, though I am really too tired after the Ashton ball last evening to go out again; besides, I do not like to wear a dress that isn't properly finished; but I shall have to, for the girls cannot possibly do all that needs to be done."

"You are too particular, Aunt Marg. What if

every seam isn't bound just as you like it? Your
general make-up is always superb. By the way, who
was that girl in black who just came in and went up
stairs?" the young man concluded, as if it had only
just occurred to him to inquire regarding her.

"Oh, that was Ruth Richards, my seamstress; she
had just been out on an errand," Mrs. Montague in-
differently returned as they passed into the drawing-
room.

"Ruth Richards? Pretty name, isn't it?" her companion remarked, "and the girl herself is a stunner—
one does not often meet so lovely a seamstress."

Mrs. Montague turned upon him sharply.

"Nonsense, Louis," she said, impatiently; "don't
allow your head to be turned by every pretty face that
you see. There are plenty of fine-looking girls in our
own set, without wasting your admiration upon a poor
sewing-girl."

"I never should have imagined that she was a
sewing-girl," Mr. Hamblin returned. "I supposed
her to be some aristocratic young lady of your acquaintance, who had come for a social call. She carries herself like a young queen; her form is simply
perfect, and her face!—well, were I an artist I should
love to paint it," he concluded, with unusual enthusiasm.

Mrs. Montague shrugged her graceful shoulders,
and curled her red lips scornfully.

"What would Kitty McKenzie say if she could hear
you run on like this about a girl who has to work for
her living?" she sneered.

"Kitty McKenzie cannot hold a candle to Ruth
Richards. Dress her as Kitty rigs herself out and

all New York would be raving about her," the young man replied.

"Louis Hamblin, I am all out of patience with you! Kitty would feel highly complimented with your opinion of her charms," cried his aunt, angrily. "But let me tell you," she added, resolutely, "I shall not countenance any fooling with that young lady; you have shown her very marked attention, and she has a right to expect that you have serious intentions. You know that I should be only too glad to have you marry Kitty; she is a sweet girl, to say nothing about her beauty, while the McKenzies are all that could be desired, both as to wealth and position; and the day that Kitty becomes your wife I will match her dowry as a wedding-gift to you."

"Thank you; I know that you are all that is kind and good in your plans for me, Aunt Margie," Louis responded, in a conciliatory tone, "and you need not fear that I am rashly going to throw Kitty over; we are the best of friends, although not acknowledged lovers. I cannot quite make up my mind to propose, for, really, I do not feel like tying myself down just yet."

"It would be a good thing for you—you have sown wild oats enough, Louis, and it is time that you began to think of settling down in life. If you please me you know that a brilliant future awaits you, for you are my only heir," Mrs. Montague concluded, as she searched his face earnestly.

"My dear Aunt Margie, you well know there is nothing I like to do better than to please you," was the gallant response, and Mrs. Montague believed him, and smoothed her ruffled plumage.

"Nevertheless," Mr. Louis Hamblin remarked later,

while smoking his cigar by himself, "I shall try to see more of that pretty seamstress, without regard to the McKenzie expectations. Jove! what eyes she has! and her low 'thank you,' as I let her in, had the most musical sound I've heard in many a day. Stay," he added, with a start, "now I think of it, she must be the same girl to whom those proud upstarts gave the cut direct in Macy's the other day. I thought her face was familiar, and didn't she pull herself together gloriously after it. There's a romance connected with her, I'll bet. She must have been in society, or she could not have known them well enough to salute them as she did. Really, Miss Ruth Richards grows more and more interesting to me."

CHAPTER XI.

RAY'S EXPERIENCE.

While Mona was plodding her monotonous way among sheets and pillow-slips, table linen and dressmaking, in Mrs. Montague's elegant home, Raymond Palmer was also being subjected to severe discipline, although of a different character.

We left him locked within a padded chamber in the house of Doctor Wesselhoff, who was a noted specialist in the treatment of diseases of the brain and nerves.

It will be remembered that Ray had been hypnotized into a profound slumber, from which he did not awake for many hours.

When at last he did arouse, he was both calmed and refreshed, while he was surprised to find that a small table, on which a tempting lunch was arranged, had been drawn close beside the lounge where he lay.

He was really hungry, and arose and began to partake with relish of the various viands before him, while, at the same time, he looked about the artfully constructed chamber he was in with no small degree of curiosity.

He remembered perfectly all that had occurred from the time he left his father's store in company with the charming Mrs. Vanderbeck until he had been so strangely overpowered with sleep by the influence of those masterful eyes, which had peered at him through an aperture in the wall.

As his mind went back over the strange incidents of the day he began to experience anew great anxiety over the loss of the rare stones which had been so cleverly stolen from him, and also regarding the fate in store for him.

He knew that the diamonds were in his pocket when the carriage stopped before the house, for he had not removed his hand from the package until Mrs. Vanderbeck discovered that her dress had been caught in the door of the carriage.

That very circumstance, he felt sure, was a part of the skillfully executed plot, and he was convinced that the woman must have robbed him during the moment when he had bent forward and tried to extricate it for her; while she must have concealed the package somewhere in the *coupé* while she was apparently trying to pin together the rent in her dress.

Then, as soon as he alighted, how adroitly she had filled his arms with her bundles and kept his attention so engaged that he did not think of the diamonds again, until the gentleman of the house appeared in the room where Mrs. Vanderbeck had left him.

Oh, how negligent he had been! He should not have released his hold upon that package under any circumstances, he told himself; and yet, he argued, if he had been ever so careful he might have been overpowered and the stones taken by violence, if the woman's cunning had failed to accomplish the desired object.

He firmly believed that he was in a den of thieves, and that the man who had come to him in the reception-room and conducted him into that chamber was in league with the beautiful Mrs. Vanderbeck, who had so fascinated him and hoodwinked his father into sending out such costly jewels for examination.

Then his mind reverted to the strange sensations which he had experienced beneath those human eyes after being trapped into the padded chamber, and a shiver of repulsion ran over him. Was he a captive in the hands of, and at the mercy of, a gang of conjurers and mesmerists? The thought was horrible to him. He had courage enough to defend himself in a hand-to-hand encounter, but he felt powerless to contend against such diabolical influences as he had already been subjected to.

While he was pondering these things, he heard the bolt to the door shoot back, and in another moment a strange man entered the room.

Ray started to his feet, and boldly confronted him.

"Who are you?" he haughtily demanded.

"My name is Huff, sir," the man returned, in a calm, respectful tone, "and I have come to see what I can do for you."

"There is but one thing I desire you to do—release

me instantly from this wretched place!" Ray responded authoritatively.

"Yes, yes; all in good time. Doctor Wesselhoff will attend to that," Mr. Huff mildly replied.

"Doctor Wesselhoff?" exclaimed Ray, astonished. "I have heard of him. He is the noted brain and nerve specialist, isn't he?"

"Yes, sir."

"And—am I in *his house?*" the young man demanded, his amazement in nowise abated.

"Yes, this is Doctor Wesselhoff's residence."

"That is very strange! I cannot understand!" Ray remarked, deeply perplexed. "Why am I here?"

"You—have not been quite well of late, and you are here for treatment."

"For *treatment?* Do you mean that I am here as a patient of Doctor Wesselhoff?" cried Ray, aghast.

"Yes, sir, for a little while, until you are better."

"Who brought me here? Who made arrangements for my coming here?"

"Your own friends; and really, sir, it would be better if you would accept the situation quietly," said the man, in a conciliatory tone.

Ray began to get excited again at this information, and the more so, that he did not believe it, while the mystery of his situation seemed to deepen.

He had heard of Doctor Wesselhoff, as he had said; he knew that he was regarded as one of the finest brain specialists in the metropolis, if not in the country, and that, as a man, he stood high in the estimation of the public.

This being the case, he certainly would not lend himself to such an outrageous trick as had been practiced upon him that day.

He did not believe what the old man told him—he did not believe that he was in Doctor Wesselhoff's house at all. It was only a lie on the part of the diamond thieves to further their own schemes, he thought, and yet the man's manner was so respectful, and even kind, that he was deeply perplexed.

"There is nothing the matter with me—I am as sane as you are," he said, flushing angrily at the idea of being regarded as a lunatic.

"Yes—yes; we will hope so," was the gentle response, as the attendant began to gather the dishes and remnants of Ray's lunch.

"You say that my friends brought me here," persisted the young man; "that is false; I was brought here by a woman whom I never saw before, and who robbed me of valuable diamonds. If she arranged for my coming, it is all a trick. But what did she claim was my special malady?" he concluded, with considerable curiosity.

"We will not talk any more about it now, sir, if you please," said his companion, in a soothing tone. "Doctor Wesselhoff will explain it all to you when he returns."

"When he returns? Where has he gone—how long will he be absent?" Ray demanded, with a sinking heart, for time was precious, and he was almost wild to get away to hunt for the thieves who had robbed him; while, too, he knew that his father must already have become alarmed at his long absence.

"The doctor was called away by a telegram only an hour ago," the attendant replied, hoping by this explanation to divert the mind of his charge from his mania of robbery. "His wife, who went South a week ago to visit friends, has been taken suddenly ill, and he was obliged to hasten to her; but he will return at the earliest possible moment."

"Gone *South!* and I must remain here until his return?" Ray cried, in a voice of agony. "I *will* not," he went on fiercely, his face growing crimson with angry excitement. "I tell you I am perfectly well, and I have been only tricked into this place by some cunning thief who has robbed me. Whether Doctor Wesselhoff is concerned in it or not, I cannot tell. I confess it seems very like it to me, although I have always heard him well spoken of. Stay!" he cried, with a start, "you tell me the doctor has already left the city! oh! then he must be a party to the foul wrong of which I am the victim. Let me out—I tell you I *will* not submit to such inhuman treatment," and he turned fiercely upon the attendant, as if he meditated attacking and overpowering him, with the hope of forcing his way from the place.

But the attendant quietly retreated before him, looking him calmly in the eye, and, as Ray pressed closely upon him, he made a few passes before his face with his hands.

Instantly the young man began to experience that same sense of weariness and drowsiness that had overpowered him when those masterful eyes had fastened themselves upon him through the hole in the wall.

"Don't! don't!" he cried, throwing out his arms as if to ward off the influence, while he tried to resist it with all his will-power.

But his arm fell powerless by his side and he sank into a chair near which he was standing, and the attendant turned and left the room, a smile of peculiar satisfaction on his face.

"That was very well done, I think, for a pupil of

the great Doctor Wesselhoff," he muttered, as he shot the bolt into the socket and turned to go about other duties. "It will not be long before I shall be able to exert the power as skillfully as he does."

Ray sat as one half dazed for a few moments after the departure of Mr. Huff, and tried to combat with all the strength of his will the strange desire to sleep.

Then suddenly his glance became riveted upon something that was clinging to the leg of his trousers.

He stooped to pick it off, examining it closely, and uttered an exclamation of surprise upon finding that it was a small piece of ladies' cloth of a delicate mauve color.

"Ha!" he cried, excitedly; "it is as precious as gold dust, and may prove to be very useful to me. How fortunate I am to have found it!"

It was a small piece of woolen goods that had been torn from Mrs. Vanderbeck's dress, and Ray, after a moment, put it carefully away in his pocket-book, in the hope of some time finding the rent that it would fit.

It was true that Doctor Wesselhoff had been suddenly called away to his sick wife.

No other summons would have had the power to draw him away from New York at that time, for he experienced great anxiety and interest regarding the new and peculiar case that had just been confided to his care.

He really believed that Ray—or young Walton, as he believed his patient's name to be, in spite of the fact that he had given it as Palmer—was a monomaniac; for his words and manner fully corroborated the statement which his visitor of the previous day had made to him. He had not the slightest suspicion

that he also was the dupe of a cunning plot to secure
diamonds that were worth a large sum of money.

But before leaving the city he gave the most careful
directions to his pupil, Doctor Huff, who had been
studying with him for more than a year, regarding
the treatment of his patient, and then he was obliged
to hurry away, promising, however, that he would
return just as soon as it would do to leave his wife.

It took him two days of continuous travel to reach
his destination, and then he found Mrs. Wesselhoff so
very ill that all his thought and care were concentrated upon her.

The place to which he went was a remote Southern
town, where Northern newspapers seldom found their
way; consequently he could not know anything of the
intense excitement that was prevailing in New York
over the mysterious disappearance of Raymond
Palmer and the costly stones he had taken with him.

To his pupil he had hastily explained all that he
could regarding the young man's case, and had told
him that his name was Walton; so, of course, Doctor
Huff, on reading an account of the diamond robbery
and the strange disappearance of the merchant's son,
never dreamed that the patient left in his charge was
the missing young man.

Mr. Palmer did not seem to be at all troubled over
the non-appearance of his son until the time arrived
to close the store for the night; then he began to feel
some anxiety.

Still, he told himself, Ray might possibly have been
detained longer than he had anticipated, and finding
it rather late to return to the store, had gone immediately home, where there was also a safe in which
the diamonds could be deposited for the night.

With this hope to rest upon, he hastened to his residence, but was made even more anxious upon being told by the housekeeper "that Mr. Raymond had not come in yet."

He kept hoping he might come, so he ate his supper and then tried to compose himself to read his papers; but his uneasiness only continued to increase.

He endured the suspense until nine o'clock, and then went down town to consult with the superintendent of police.

He confided to him what had occurred, and his fears regarding the safety of his son, and he was by no means reassured when that official at once exclaimed that "the whole thing was a put-up job."

"Keep quiet," he advised, "for a day or two, and we will see what we can do."

He set his detectives at work upon the case immediately, while the anxious father endeavored to endure his suffering in silence. But the "day or two" brought no revelations, and his agony could no longer be controlled; he believed that his son had been murdered for the sake of the diamonds, and thus the matter became public.

The newspapers were full of the affair, and caused great excitement. The city offered a large reward for any intelligence regarding the missing young man or the diamonds, and this was doubled by Mr. Palmer himself.

But days and weeks passed, and no clew was obtained regarding either the stolen jewels or Ray's mysterious fate; therefore the belief that he had been foully dealt with prevailed very generally.

Mr. Palmer had placed in the hands of a private detective a detailed account in writing of the woman's visit to the store, and also a minute description of herself, and the moment he had finished reading it the man's face lighted up with eager interest, even enthusiasm.

"Great Scott!" exclaimed the detective, with a resounding slap upon his knee, "I'll wager my badge that it's a sequel to that Bently affair, when a young broker of Chicago was wretchedly fooled with some diamonds about three years ago!—that woman also had short, curly red hair."

He related the story to Mr. Palmer, and informed him that he had been engaged upon the case, off and on, for a long time; but since he had come to New York to reside he had about given it up as hopeless.

"This may put me on the trail again, however," finally remarked Mr. Rider, who was the detective that Justin Cutler had employed.

Of course, the house which Mrs. Vanderbeck had given as her place of residence was visited, but as in the Bently affair, it proved to be empty, and Mrs. Vanderbeck seemed to have vanished as completely as if she had been a visitant from some other sphere.

All this had occurred while Mona was so absorbed in her grief for her uncle; when she had had no interest in anything outside her home, and so not having read any of the newspapers, she was entirely ignorant of the excitement that had prevailed over the robbery, and Ray's disappearance. Thus she believed that he had deserted her, like most of her other fair-weather friends, and was trying to make herself believe that he was unworthy of her regard.

Poor Ray! it had fared hard with him during all this time, although not in the way that his father and the detectives feared.

We last saw him just after he had discovered the shred that had been torn from Mrs. Vanderbeck's dress; but when Doctor Huff again went to him he found him prostrate upon the floor in a high fever and delirious.

For four weeks he lay thus. He had taken a severe cold, and that, with the excitement and anxiety caused by the loss of the diamonds, had brought on the illness.

When Doctor Wesselhoff returned after a hard fight with disease in his wife's case, he found him very low, and just at the turning point in his fever.

He bestowed great commendation upon his pupil, however, for his management of the case, which, he said, he could not have treated better himself.

He expressed himself as very much surprised, because none of the young man's friends had called to make any inquiries about him; it certainly showed a lack of interest, if not a positive neglect, he thought.

He believed that the fever would turn favorably, for the young man had a naturally vigorous constitution, and he had known of persons recovering who had possessed far less vitality.

Ray did pass the crisis successfully, but he was very weak for many days longer; too weak even to notice where he was, or who was caring for him.

But, as he gained a little strength, he looked curiously about him, then memory began to assert itself —he recalled the events which had occurred on that fateful day, when he had been made a captive, and he realized that he had been moved from that dismal padded chamber to a large and airy room in another portion of the house.

The next time Doctor Wesselhoff came to his bedside, after he had come thoroughly to himself, he said, in a grave but authoritative voice:

"Doctor Wesselhoff, sit down if you please; I want to talk with you for a few moments."

The physician obeyed, but with some surprise, for both the look and manner of his patient convinced him that he was perfectly rational.

"I have been very ill, have I not?" Ray inquired.

"Yes, but you are much better and steadily improving."

"How long have I been sick?"

"It is more than five weeks now since you were attacked."

Ray frowned at this information.

How must his father feel regarding his strange absence? What had become of that cunning thief and the diamonds? were questions which suggested themselves to him.

But he simply asked:

"When did you return to New York?"

"About a week ago," the physician replied. "I was very sorry to have to leave you as I did, but the summons to my wife was imperative, and of course my duty was by her side."

A sarcastic smile curled Ray's lips at this last remark.

"I am only surprised that you returned at all," he quietly responded.

"Why?" inquired the physician, with some astonishment.

"It is not always safe, you know," Ray answered, looking him straight in the eye, "for one who has aided and abetted a stupendous robbery to appear so soon upon the scene of his depredations."

Doctor Wesselhoff's face fell.

He had hoped that, when the young man should recover, all signs of his peculiar mania would disappear;
but this did not seem much like it, and he began to
fear the case might prove a very obstinate one.

"I think you must rest now," he remarked, evading
the subject; "you have talked long enough this time."

"Perhaps I have, but I do not intend to rest until
I have come to some definite understanding regarding
my relations with you," Ray responded, resolutely.

"Well, then, what do you mean by a definite understanding?" the physician asked, thinking it might be
as well to humor him a little.

"I want to know how far you are concerned in this
plot to keep me a prisoner here? I want to know in
what way you are connected with that woman who
called herself Mrs. Vanderbeck, and who enticed me
here with valuable diamonds, only to steal them from
me? I believe I am in the power of a gang of thieves,
and though I cannot reconcile it with what I had
heard of you previously, that you must be associated
in some way with them."

Ray had spoken rapidly, and with an air and tone
of stern command, which puzzled while it impressed
the doctor.

"You bring a very serious charge against me, my
young friend," he gravely remarked, but without betraying the slightest resentment; "but perhaps if you
will tell me your side of the story I shall understand
you better, and then I will explain my authority for
detaining you here."

Doctor Wesselhoff was strangely attracted toward
his patient. He did not seem at all like an insane person, except upon that one subject, and he would not

have regarded that as a mania if he had not been assured of it by Mrs. Walton. He began to think there might at least be some misunderstanding, and that it would be as well to let the young man exhaust the subject once for all; then he could judge the better regarding the treatment he needed.

"Well, then, to begin at the beginning," Ray resumed. "A woman, giving her name as Mrs. William Vanderbeck, called at my father's store on the day I came here, and asked to look at diamonds. You will remember, I told you my father is a diamond dealer. They were shown to her, and she selected several very expensive ornaments, which she said she wished to wear at a reception that evening. But she represented that she could not purchase them unless they were first submitted to her husband for examination and his sanction. He was an invalid; he could not come to the store, consequently the stones must be taken to him; was there not some reliable person who could be sent to her residence with them, when, if Mr. Vanderbeck was satisfied with the ornaments, a check for their price would be filled out and returned to my father. This seemed fair and reasonable, and I was commissioned to attend the lady and take charge of the diamonds. I put the package in my pocket, and my hand never left it until the *coupé* stopped before this house, when Mrs. Vanderbeck suddenly discovered that her dress had caught in the carriage door, and she could not rise. Of course I offered assistance in disengaging it; but in spite of our united efforts, the garment was torn during the operation. I suppose she robbed me at that moment, but am not quite sure, as I did not discover my loss until you—whom I supposed to be the lady's husband—entered the room, and I slipped my hand into my pocket for the diamonds, only to find that they were gone. You know the rest, and the treatment I received from yourself. Is it any wonder that I believed you an accomplice when I found myself in that padded chamber and losing all sense and reason beneath the influence of a powerful mesmerist?"

Doctor Wesselhoff had listened gravely throughout the young man's recital, and, though astonished and puzzled by what he heard, felt that he was relating a very connected story.

He was upon the point of replying to his questions, when he chanced to glance at his assistant, Doctor Huff, who had been in the room all the time, and saw that he was startlingly pale, and laboring under extreme agitation.

"Sir," cried the man, hoarsely, "can it be possible that he is the victim of the recent diamond robbery, which has created so much excitement? The newspapers have been full of the story that he has just related."

CHAPTER XII.

AMOS PALMER FINDS HIS SON.

"What do you mean?" Doctor Wesselhoff sharply demanded, and losing color himself at the sudden suspicion that he also might have been the dupe of a set of rogues.

"Haven't you seen an account of the affair in the papers?" Doctor Huff asked. "They were full of it for two weeks after you left home."

"No, I did not see a New York paper from the time I started until I returned. I could not get one, even if I had not had too many cares and been too much absorbed in my wife's critical condition to think of or read news of any kind," Doctor Wesselhoff replied. Then, with a sudden thought, as he turned again to Ray: "Young man, is not your name Walton?"

"You know it is not," said Ray, with a flash of indignation. "I told you, the day I came, that my name is Palmer—Raymond Palmer."

"He is the man!" cried the assistant, starting up and regarding the invalid with a look of fear, "and it was Amos Palmer, the diamond merchant, who was robbed!"

"Can it be possible!" exclaimed the physician, amazed at this intelligence. "That woman—Mrs. Walton—told me that he was her son, only at times he denied his own name, so when he told me his name was 'Palmer' that day I imagined it only a freak produced by his mania."

Ray had been regarding the man curiously during this speech. He surely did not appear like a person who would have anything to do with so daring a crime as that of which he had accused him. He was strikingly noble in appearance; his manner was quietly dignified and self-possessed—he had a finely shaped head, a kind eye, a genial smile, while his astonishment and dismay over what he had just been told seemed too genuine to be feigned.

"Did you not expect to find me in your reception-room? Did no lady inform you of my arrival on the day I came here?" Ray inquired, searching his face earnestly.

"No, I saw no lady—a servant came to tell me that a gentleman was waiting to see me," responded the doctor.

"Then she must have gone immediately out and made off with all possible speed," said Ray, musingly.

"But," Doctor Wesselhoff continued, as if he had not heard his remark, "the woman I spoke of—a Mrs. Walton—called upon me the previous day and arranged with me to take you as a patient. She was upward of fifty years of age, her hair was white, and she had the look of one who had known much care and sorrow."

He then proceeded to relate all that had occurred during the interview, and Ray was astonished at the daring scheme which had been so successfully planned and carried out.

When the physician concluded his account, Ray gravely and positively declared:

"I do not know any person by the name of Walton. If this woman told you that she was my mother, she uttered a falsehood, for I have no mother—she died more than ten years ago, and her place has been filled, as well as another could fill it, by a housekeeper. My home is No. 119 ——— street; but, Doctor Wesselhoff, if you still doubt my statements, and imagine that I am laboring under a peculiar mania, you can easily ascertain the truth by bringing my father here to prove my assertions. I beg that you will do so without delay, for he must be suffering the most harrowing suspense on my account."

Doctor Wesselhoff looked very much disturbed, for the more he talked with Ray, the more fully convinced he was that he had been unconsciously lending his aid to further an atrocious crime.

But as he saw how pale and weary his patient was, he was recalled to a sense of his duty as a physician.

He arose and kindly took the young man's hand.

"I am very much afraid," he said, "that we are both the victims of a complicated plot; but let me assure you that so far as I am concerned, the wrong to you shall be made right without a moment's delay. Now I want you to go to sleep, and while you are resting I will seek an interview with the man whom you claim as your father."

Ray's weak fingers closed over the hand he held in a friendly clasp at this assurance, and he was at once inspired with implicit confidence in the physician.

"Thank you," he said, a trustful smile wreathing his thin lips, "I will be obedient and go to sleep, but I shall expect to find my father here when I awake."

"If Amos Palmer is your father, you will surely find him by your bedside after you have had your nap," Doctor Wesselhoff responded, and with another hand-clasp he withdrew from the room.

In less than five minutes Ray was sleeping quietly and restfully.

Half an hour later the great brain specialist rang the bell of Amos Palmer's handsome residence. The servant who answered it replied in the affirmative when asked if the gentleman of the house was in, and ushered the visitor into a richly furnished reception-room leading from the hall.

A few minutes later a sorrowful, despondent-looking gentleman entered, and politely, although somewhat absently, saluted his caller.

He did not look much like the upright, energetic and affable gentleman who had so courteously served the elegant Mrs. Vanderbeck a few weeks previous.

His face was wan and drawn with anguish, his cheeks were hollow, his eyes sunken, heavy and luster-less; his form was bowed, his steps feeble and faltering.

After saluting Doctor Wesselhoff, he threw himself, with a heavy sigh, into a chair, where he immediately became absorbed in his own painful thoughts, appearing to forget that there was any one present, or that there were duties devolving upon him as host.

"Mr. Palmer," said the physician, breaking in upon his sorrowful reverie, "my name is Wesselhoff, and I have called to consult with you regarding the very peculiar circumstances connected with your son's disappearance."

Amos Palmer was like one electrified upon hearing this. He sat erect, and stared with wondering eyes at his companion, and began to tremble violently.

"My son! my son!" he cried, in quavering tones. "Oh, if you can tell me *anything*—if you can tell me that he—lives," the word was scarcely audible, "you will put new life into me."

"Tell me his full name, if you please," said Doctor Wesselhoff, who was scarcely less excited than the trembling man before him.

"Raymond Palmer."

"Describe him to me."

Amos Palmer gave him a minute description of the young man as he appeared on the day that he had been trapped into the physician's house, even to the clothing which he had worn, and the doctor was at last convinced that, all unwittingly, he had assisted in the perpetration of a double crime.

"Yes," he said, when the eager father had concluded, and feeling that he must at once relieve the terrible suspense under which his companion was laboring; "your son lives, and is longing to see his father."

"Oh, then, I have nothing more to wish for—the world will be bright to me once more, for he was my all, Doctor Wesselhoff—my last, and best beloved. I have laid six children in the grave, and all my hopes were centered in Ray. My boy! my boy! I am content to know that you live—that you are not lost to me!"

The overwrought man broke down utterly at this point, bowed his face upon his hands, and sobbed almost convulsively.

Doctor Wesselhoff was also greatly moved at the sight of his emotion, but as soon as he could control himself sufficiently, he remarked:

"I have a very strange story to tell you, Mr. Palmer, and you may be inclined, as your son was at first, to suspect me of complicity in the affair. I am, however, willing to be subjected to a rigorous investigation, if you demand it; but let me assure you that the moment I discovered the truth, I saw that I, as well as you, had been wretchedly imposed upon, and I was anxious to do all in my power to right the wrong."

He then related all that he had told Ray, and all that we already know, while Amos Palmer listened with wonder to the unfolding of the bold and cunning scheme which had so baffled the police and the best detectives in New York.

"It is the most devilish plot I ever heard of if you will excuse the expression," Mr. Palmer excitedly exclaimed, when his visitor had concluded his narrative.

"It certainly was a very brazen one, yet very cleverly arranged, and just as artfully carried out," Doctor Wesselhoff remarked; and then he inquired, while he regarded his companion with earnest interest: "But have you no doubts as to the truth of my statements? Have you no suspicions that I might also be concerned in the plot?"

"No, sir; I am impressed that you are a man of truth and honor. I have heard of you, and know something of your reputation; and I can but feel thankful that my son fell into your hands, rather than into the clutches of some unprincipled villain," Mr. Palmer replied, with a hearty confidence in his tones that could not be doubted. Then he added: "Excuse me for a few moments while I order my carriage, then you shall take me at once to my son."

Amos Palmer seemed a changed man now that hope throbbed once more in his heart, and he started up with all his old-time vigor and energy to leave the room.

But Doctor Wesselhoff stopped him.

"My own carriage is at your door—do not wait for yours; come at once with me and I will have you sent home when you are ready to return; but Mr. Palmer, you must be prepared to find your son greatly changed, for he has been very ill; the worst is over, however, and he will gain rapidly now, if we take proper care of him."

In a few moments the two men were driving rapidly toward the physician's residence, while they more fully discussed the affair of the robbery, and the skillful way in which it had been managed.

"I would never have believed that a woman could have nerve enough to attempt anything so daring," Mr. Palmer remarked. "I should have been willing to take my oath that she—this Mrs. Vanderbeck, so called—was just what she pretended to be—a refined

and cultured lady accustomed to the most polished society. She did not overdo her part in the least, and
had one of the most frank and beautiful faces that I
have ever seen. Her figure and carriage were superb,
her manner charming. The only peculiar thing about
her was her hair, which was a decided red, as were
also her eyebrows, and lashes. She had fine teeth,
and she was very richly, though modestly, dressed.
She came to the store apparently in her own carriage,
with a colored driver, and everything seemed to indicate that she belonged in the ranks of high life."

"The woman who came to me, to make arrangements for the treatment of her pretended son, was a
much older woman than you describe," Doctor Wesselhoff said, in reply, "her hair was almost white, her
face was somewhat wrinkled, and she appeared sad
and depressed. It must be that there were two women
concerned in the affair, for my visitor remarked that
since her son, when under the influence of his mania,
was so determined to have her arrested, she would
send her sister, whom she called Mrs. Vanderbeck,
with him."

"Hum—maybe my adventuress was the same person in disguise," Mr. Palmer thoughtfully observed.

"But you said she had red hair, brows, and lashes,
and was quite young in appearance; while Mrs. Walton was old and wrinkled, with white hair; the brows
and lashes I did not notice particularly, but they certainly were not red," Doctor Wesselhoff responded,
doubtfully.

"Well, whether they were one and the same or not,
the whole thing is a perplexing puzzle, and I would
sacrifice a good deal to have it solved," said Mr.
Palmer. "But," he added, with a sigh, "I am afraid

that it never will be, for the thieves, in all probability, left New York immediately, and were sharp enough to remove the diamonds from their settings before attempting to dispose of them."

"They may overreach themselves yet and be brought to justice," Doctor Wesselhoff remarked. "But is there no way of identifying the diamonds unset?"

"Some of them—two in particular—could be identified; they were a pair of magnificent solitaires, and I am sure my expert could tell them anywhere," Mr. Palmer replied.

"It is strange that you were not suspicious of a person who wished to purchase so many diamonds at one time," said the physician, thoughtfully.

"She did not pretend that she wished to buy all that she laid out, only that her selections from the lot were to be made with the advice and sanction of her husband; and in this way—don't you see?—the clever sharper got possession of a great deal more than she would otherwise have done."

"True, she showed herself very shrewd. But your son has in his possession a clew, though a very slender one, which may possibly lead to a solution of the mystery. It is a small piece of cloth that was torn from the woman's dress," Doctor Wesselhoff returned.

"I am afraid that won't amount to much, for, probably, if the woman is still in New York, which I doubt, she will never wear that dress again," Mr. Palmer responded. "But," he continued, cheerfully, "I shall not complain as long as I am to have Ray back again. I fully believed that he had been murdered. My loss I can never tell you what anguish I have endured, for will of course eat deeply into the profits of my business for this year, but that is of comparatively little consequence. I am more troubled to have such wickedness prosper than I am about any pecuniary loss."

The carriage stopped just then, and the conversation ended. Both gentlemen alighted, and Doctor Wesselhoff led the way into his house, and straight up to the chamber which Ray occupied.

He had not aroused once during the doctor's absence, but awoke almost immediately after their entrance, and the meeting between the father and son was both joyful and tender.

Neither had ever before realized how much they were to each other, or believed that life could be so dark if they were separated.

Doctor Wesselhoff would not allow them to talk very much that night, for he said that his patient was liable to have a relapse if he became too weary or was subjected to too much excitement; so Mr. Palmer was permitted to remain only a short time with him, but promised to return again at as early an hour in the morning as the physician would allow.

He visited Ray twice every day after that, and both father and son were fully convinced of the truth and honesty of purpose of the noted specialist, who had given Ray such excellent care, and whose interest in him continued to increase throughout his recovery.

The Palmers found him very genial and entertaining, and an enduring friendship grew up between the three.

Ray improved very rapidly, and was able by the end of two weeks to return to his own home; but, though he was very thankful to be restored to health and to his father once more he was saddened and dismayed upon learning of Mr. Dinsmore's sudden death, and that Mona had been deprived of her inheritance.

He was still more appalled when, upon making inquiries, he could learn nothing of her movements since
leaving her home. No one seemed to know anything
about her—even her friend Susie Leades was in ignorance of her whereabouts, for Mona had shrunk, with
extreme sensitiveness, from telling any one, save Mr.
Graves, of her plans for the future.

Ray did not know who had been Mr. Dinsmore's
man of business, so, of course, he could not appeal to
the lawyer, and he was finally forced to believe that
Mona had left New York.

He could not be reconciled to have her vanish so
completely out of his life, just when he had begun to
entertain such strong hopes of winning her for his
wife.

For more than two years he had loved Mona Montague in secret, but only during the last few months
had he allowed himself to show her marked attention.

She had been in school until the previous June, and
he had felt sure that Mr. Dinsmore would not countenance anything that would distract her mind from
her studies, therefore he had waited, with commend-
able patience, until she graduated before making it
manifest that he experienced any especial pleasure in
her society.

Mr. Dinsmore and Mona had spent the months of
July and August at Lenox, Massachusetts, and Ray,
having learned their plans, arranged to be there at the
same time. Therefore the young people had seen considerable of each other during the summer, and before their return to New York, Ray Palmer had begun to have strong hopes that he should eventually
win the beautiful girl for his wife.

They met several times in society during the early winter, and Mona always appeared so happy with him that he gradually grew bolder in his attentions, and finally formally requested the pleasure of acting as her escort in public. This request was granted, as we know, and cordial permission to call was also given him, and when Ray left Mona that night, after their attendance at the opera, he resolved to seek Mr. Dinsmore at an early day and ask the privilege of paying his addresses to his niece with the view of winning her.

But he was very unhappy over his fruitless efforts to find her, and he grew strangely silent and depressed, greatly to his father's surprise, even while he was every day gaining in health and strength.

Finally Mr. Palmer questioned him outright as to the cause; and Ray, longing for both sympathy and advice, frankly told him the truth.

"That is too bad, Ray, and I am extremely sorry," the royal-hearted man remarked. "I should be very sorry to have you disappointed in such a matter, but do not be discouraged; we will do our best to find the young lady, and then you shall bring her home as soon as you please."

"Then you approve of my choice!" Ray remarked, with some surprise at his father's interest and even anxiety to have him succeed in his suit.

"Why not? I do not know Miss Montague, but I am sure that a niece of Mr. Dinsmore, and reared with the care which he would be likely to bestow upon her, could be objectionable to no one. Mr. Dinsmore was one of the noblest of men," said Mr. Palmer, with hearty commendation.

"But Mona is only a penniless girl now," Ray responded, determined that his father should fully comprehend the situation. "Mr. Dinsmore's wife has claimed all his property, I have been told, and even if I could find and win her, my bride would have to come to me without any dowry."

"That wouldn't trouble me in the least, my boy, provided the girl herself was all right," his father gravely returned. "We have enough," he continued, smiling, "without desiring to enrich ourselves by marrying money. You shall choose your own wife, Ray, be she rich or poor, plain or beautiful; only find a sensible little woman who will be a true wife and make you happy, and I shall be more than satisfied."

"Thank you, father," Ray gratefully returned. "I wish there were more men like yourself in the world —there would surely be fewer ill-assorted marriages if there were. Only let me find Mona, and I will soon convince you that she will be a girl after your own heart, as well as mine."

CHAPTER XIII.

AT THE RECEPTION.

One evening, after Ray's entire restoration to health, he and his father attended a reception given by an old friend of Mr. Palmer's.

It was an unusually brilliant affair, for the Merrills were wealthy people, and very socially inclined, and many of the best people of New York were present.

Mr. Palmer was conversing with his host in a quiet way during a few moments while he was at liberty, when his attention was attracted by the entrance of a new arrival, whose advent seemed to create an unusual flutter of interest.

"Who is she?" he inquired, as the lady slowly approached them, smiling, bowing, and responding to the eager greetings on every hand. "She is a magnificent-looking woman."

"She is Mrs. Montague—a wealthy widow, and a great favorite in society," his friend replied, while his own eyes rested admiringly upon the lady.

"Montague! Montague!" Mr. Palmer repeated reflectively, while he said to himself: "That is the name of Ray's little lady-love; perhaps this woman is a relative, and the girl has gone to live with her. I must find out about that." Then, with this thought in view, he added, aloud: "Introduce me, will you, Merrill?"

His host glanced roguishly at him, and a smile of amusement hovered about his lips as he replied:

"Certainly, if you wish, but I give you fair warning that she is a dangerous party, and especially so to widowers—there are a dozen, more or less, who have already had their wings thoroughly singed."

Mr. Palmer smiled with an air of calm superiority.

"Well, Merrill, I admit that she is as fine-looking a woman as I have ever seen," he said, "but I believe that I am proof against the blandishments of the fair sex upon principle; for," more gravely, "I have never had any desire to change my condition since I lost my wife. My reason for requesting the introduction was, I thought Mrs. Montague might be able to give me some information regarding another lady of the same name."

"All right; an introduction you shall have; but pray take heed to my warning, all the same, and look out

for yourself," was the laughing rejoinder. "Ah," as
he bowed graciously to the lady approaching them,
"we are very glad to be favored with your presence
this evening, and now allow me to present a friend;
Mrs. Montague, Mr. Palmer."

The brilliant woman shot one sweeping glance out
of her expressive eyes at the gentleman and then extended her faultlessly gloved hand to him in cordial
greeting.

"I am very glad to make Mr. Palmer's acquaintance," she said, graciously, "although," she added,
with a charming smile, "I cannot look upon him quite
as a stranger, for I have friends who frequently speak
of him, and in a way that has made one wish to know
him personally."

Mr. Palmer flushed slightly as he bowed in acknowledgment of such high praise, and remarked that he felt
himself greatly honored.

Mrs. Montague then adroitly changed the tenor of
the conversation, and kept him chatting some time,
before he thought of Mona again, and when he did,
he hardly knew how to broach the subject to his companion.

"Have you resided long in New York, Mrs. Montague?" he inquired, after a slight pause in their conversation.

"Only about six months, but, Mr. Palmer, during
that time, I have found your city a most delightful
one, socially," the lady returned.

"I understand that Mrs. Montague is quite a favorite in society, which accounts, in a measure, perhaps,
for her own enjoyment of its people," the gentleman
gallantly responded.

Mrs. Montague flushed slightly and lowered her

white lids, modestly, for an instant, and Mr. Palmer
continued:

"Allow me to ask, Mrs. Montague, if you ever met
Mr. Walter Dinsmore?"

"Dinsmore—Dinsmore," repeated his fair companion, with a puzzled expression; "it seems as if I have
heard the name, and yet—I am quite sure that I have
met no such person since my residence in New York.
Let me see," she added, as if suddenly remembering
something—"did I not read in the papers, a short
time ago, of the death of the gentleman—he was quite
a prominent citizen, was he not?"

"Yes, and much respected; he died suddenly, leaving a large fortune. The reason I inquired if you
knew him," Mr. Palmer explained, "was because he
left a niece whose name is the same as yours, and I
thought possibly you might be a relative of the family. Miss Mona Montague is the young lady's name."

"Mona Montague?" repeated Mrs. Montague, bury-
ing her face for an instant in the bouquet she carried as if to inhale its perfume. "No, I think not—I
have no relatives in New York except a nephew, who
is the same as a son to me. We came to your city
entire strangers to every one. But how old is this
Miss Montague?"

"About eighteen years of age, I believe. She was
said to be a very beautiful girl, and every one supposed her to be Mr. Dinsmore's heiress; but it seems
that he had a wife living, although he was supposed
to be a widower—who claimed everything, and thus
Miss Montague was rendered homeless and penniless.
She has certainly disappeared from the circle in which
she hitherto mingled."

"How exceedingly unfortunate!" murmured Mr. Palmer's fair listener, with apparent sympathy.

"Very," said the gentleman; "and as we—I feel deeply interested in her, I hoped, when I heard your name, that you might prove to be a relative, and could give me some information regarding her."

"I should be most happy to oblige you, Mr. Palmer," Mrs. Montague sweetly returned, "but I have never met the young lady, and I know nothing about her present circumstances. Is she a connection of yours?"

"No, madame—that is, not as yet," Mr. Palmer answered, with a slight twinge of embarrassment. "I knew Mr. Dinsmore, however, and it seems a very sad thing that his niece should be deprived of both home and fortune, as well as her only friend, especially when he was so fond of her and intended that she would inherit his property. I would give a great deal to know where she is; she would not long be without a home if I could find her."

"Does the man want to marry the girl?" was Mrs. Montague's mental query, as she glanced keenly at her companion. "I begin to believe I should like to see this wonderful creature."

"You say she is very beautiful?" she remarked, aloud.

"So I have been told, and very lovely in character, also."

"Then you have never seen her? Surely you are very philanthropic to be so deeply interested in an entire stranger," Mrs. Montague observed. Then, without giving him an opportunity to reply, she asked, abruptly: "Mr. Palmer, who is that lady just entering the room? She is very striking in appearance, and what a profusion of magnificent diamonds she has on her person!"

Mr. Palmer started at this last observation, and turned to look at the new arrival.

He saw a woman of about thirty-five, rather stout in figure, very showily dressed, and wearing a great many exquisite diamonds of great value.

The man's keen eyes went flashing over her with eager scrutiny, his heart beating rapidly, as he asked himself if it might not be possible that some of his own precious gems were among the jewels that she wore.

The suspicion flashed upon him, in spite of the fact that the woman was a guest in the house of his friend, for he knew that thieves had been found mingling with the brilliant throngs attending regular receptions in New York, and might be again.

But of course he could recognize none of them under such circumstances, and his face fell after one sweeping glance.

"It would be impossible to identify any of the stones without a glass, even if they were there," he said to himself; "for, of course, the thief, whoever she was, would have had the stones reset before wearing them anywhere."

"Yes," he said, aloud, "the lady has a fortune upon her person; but I do not know her. Speaking of diamonds," he continued, glancing at the ornaments which Mrs. Montague wore, "you will pardon me, I am sure, if I tell you that you, also, have some very fine stones. I consider myself a connoisseur regarding diamonds and capable of judging."

"Yes," Mrs. Montague quietly responded, "I have some choice ones, and I am very fond of diamonds;

but I have never seen any one, unless it was an actress, with such a profusion of them as that lady. I do not think I should care to wear so many at one time, even if I possessed them."

"No, it hardly seems in good taste," Mr. Palmer replied, then added: "My son is beckoning me; will you excuse me for a moment?"

"Your *son*!" exclaimed the lady, with a light laugh and an arch look. "Surely, Mr. Palmer, *you* cannot have a son old enough to mingle in society like this?"

"Indeed I have, and you can see for yourself—he is standing yonder by that large easel," the gentleman returned, laughing also, and evidently well pleased to be regarded younger than he really was.

"I must confess my surprise," said the charming widow, as she darted a curious glance at the young man, "but since you assert it I must not doubt your word, and I will say, also, that you have every reason to be proud of your son. But—I will not detain you," she added, bowing gracefully; "only I trust that I may have the pleasure of meeting you again."

"Thank you, madame; you honor me," the diamond merchant replied, as he, too, bowed, and then passed on.

"Merrill said truly," he muttered, as he made his way through the crowd toward Ray; "she is certainly a very charming woman; I don't wonder that she is a favorite in society. Well, what is it, Ray, my boy?" he asked, as he reached his son's side.

"Did you notice that woman who entered the room a moment or two ago?" the young man asked, in a low tone.

"The one wearing so many diamonds?"

"Yes; and, father, I believe there is some of our property about her."

"I thought of it, too, Ray, but only because she wore so many stones, I suppose. We surely have no right to suspect her of being the thief," said Mr. Palmer, gravely.

"Perhaps not; but I did, all the same."

"She does not look at all like that Mrs. Vanderbeck," Mr. Palmer remarked, as he again singled out the woman, and observed her closely.

"I don't know; her form is not unlike; and put a red wig on her, she might pass——"

"Pshaw, Ray," interrupted his father, "you are letting your imagination run away with you; she cannot be the same person; her features are entirely different, and she is too stout."

"Well, that may be; but I am impressed that some of those stones belong to us," Ray said, following the woman with a critical glance.

"If any of them are ours, we have no means of identifying them," Mr. Palmer responded. "I have given them up as a dead loss, and do not believe that we shall ever discover the thief."

Ray looked very sober.

"I am very sore over that affair, father," he said, gravely. "If I had not allowed my head to be turned by that fascinating woman, I never should have lost them. She just smiled and talked all the sense out of me. I ought never to have removed my hand from that package, even to prevent a dozen tailor-made dresses from being torn, and then she could not have stolen it."

"Don't grieve over it, Ray, for it will not avail," his father returned, kindly. "Experience is the best teacher, and no one will ever rob us in the same way again."

"I do not think that is likely, and yet I cannot get over it; I cannot bear to consider the gems irretrievably lost, even yet."

"You may as well, for I am sure we shall never see any of them again," said Mr. Palmer, calmly.

"Who is this lady approaching us?" Ray asked, after a moment. "You were talking to her when I motioned to you."

Mr. Palmer glanced up.

"That is a Mrs. Montague——"

"Montague!" interrupted Ray, in a startled tone. "Can she be anything to Mona?"

"No, nothing. I asked the question upon learning her name," his father answered.

Ray sighed heavily; then, as his glance still lingered upon the beautiful woman, he exclaimed:

"Isn't she lovely? I believe she is the purest blonde I have ever seen. Her hair is like spun gold, her features are faultless, and her neck and arms are as perfect as if sculptured from marble."

"Take care, Ray," said his father, with a sly smile; "people say that she is a perfect siren. I have myself been warned against her to-night."

"Pshaw!" retorted the young man. "Where is her husband?"

"She has none, and therein lies the danger."

"Ah! a widow! How old is she?"

"Not more than twenty-eight or thirty, I judge— at least, she does not look it in full dress, and she is very charming in manner. Merrill says that all the men, both old and young, are making fools of themselves over her."

"Well, then, you and I will not help to swell the list," said Ray, curtly, a trifle irritated that his staid and dignified father should have so much to say about the gay society woman; and turning on his heel, he moved away, with the purpose of approaching the one whose diamonds had attracted so much attention. He meant to seek an introduction, and get an opportunity to examine the stones more closely.

Fifteen minutes later he stood bowing before her, as a friend presented him, and he was long in recovering from the shock which went through him as he caught the name by which she was introduced:

"Mrs. Vanderbeck, allow me to present my friend, Mr. Palmer."

"Pardon me. Did I understand the name—Mrs. Vander*beck?*" Ray said, trying to control the rapid throbbing of his pulses, and putting a slight emphasis upon the last syllable of the name.

He was sure that the lady started and changed color as he did so, for he was watching her closely.

"No," she said; "you haven't it quite right; we spell it *h-e-c-k*."

But she seemed strangely ill at ease during the few moments that Ray stood conversing with her, while from time to time he caught her regarding him curiously. He did not, however, get any satisfaction from his examination of her ornaments; for among such a blazing array of diamonds it was impossible to tell if he had ever seen any of them before.

"I believe she was connected in some way with that strange affair. She *may* be the woman who called upon Doctor Wesselhoff to arrange for my imprisonment," he said to himself, after he had left her. "At all events," he added, resolutely, "I am

going to lay the matter before Detective Rider, and
see what he thinks about it."

He was more strongly confirmed in his suspicions
a few minutes later, when he saw Mrs. Vanderheck
bidding her host and hostess good-night, and then
withdraw from the company.

About ten o'clock supper was served, and, strangely
enough, after the company was seated, Ray found that
his left-hand neighbor was no other than the fascinating Mrs. Montague, while, glancing beyond her, he
saw that his father had acted as her escort to the
table.

It annoyed him exceedingly to see them together,
and to observe the gallantry with which his father
was attending to the fair widow's wants.

During all the years that had elapsed since the
death of his mother, Mr. Palmer had not manifested
the slightest desire for the society of ladies, and Ray
had never thought of such a thing as his marrying
again.

But now it suddenly flashed across him: "What if
this gay woman of the world, with her beauty and
powers of fascination, should tempt him to make her
the mistress of his home and wealth?"

The thought was far from agreeable to him, and
yet he could not have told why.

He could find no fault with Mrs. Montague personally; she was beautiful in face and figure; she was
delightful in manner. Why, then, did he shrink from
the thought of having her come into the family?

Was he jealous? Was he selfish? Did he be-
grudge his father the comfort and enjoyment of a
more perfect domestic life? Was he unwilling to
have any one come between them? Was he fearful

that his own prospects—his expectations of wealth
—would be affected by such a union?

All these questions darted through his mind, and
he felt shamed and humiliated by them. He could
not analyze his feelings; he only knew that the
thought was not pleasant to him.

Mr. Palmer soon espied his son, and leaning back
in his chair, asked, with his usual genial smile:

"Well, Ray, who have you for a companion?"

"Miss Grace Merrill," he briefly responded.

"Ah! a pleasant girl; but allow me to make you
acquainted with your left-hand neighbor also; Mrs.
Montague, my son, Mr. Raymond Palmer."

Mrs. Montague turned to the young man with her
most brilliant smile, though a gleam of amusement
illuminated her lovely eyes, as she remarked the conscious flush upon the elder gentleman's face, as he
performed the ceremony of introduction.

"I am delighted to meet you, Mr. Palmer," she
said: "but I could hardly believe that you were the
son when your father pointed you out to me."

Ray could not have been ungracious beneath the
charm of her manner, even had he been naturally so,
and he soon found himself disarmed of all his disagreeable reflections and basking with delight in the
sunshine of her presence, her bright wit and repartee,
and her sweet, rippling laugh. By the time supper
was over it would have been difficult to tell who was
the more ardent admirer of the fascinating widow—
the father or the son.

Later in the evening she ran across him again by
accident(?), and another half-hour spent in her society completed the glamour which she had thrown
around him at supper, and, in spite of his assertion

to the contrary, it really seemed as if Raymond Palmer was likely to help swell the "list of fools" who blindly worshiped at her shrine.

———

CHAPTER XIV.

LOUIS HAMBLIN IS INTERESTED IN MONA.

Mrs. Richmond Montague had a purpose in honoring Mr. Palmer and his handsome son with so much of her society on the evening of Mr. Merrill's reception.

When Mr. Palmer had mentioned the name of Mona Montague, inquiring if she was a relative of the young girl, a sudden shock had thrilled through her nerves, for it was a name which, for certain reasons, with her whole heart, she *had hated,* although, as she believed, she had never seen the young lady.

Before the evening was over, however, she had learned why the diamond merchant was so anxious to find the ex-heiress of Walter Dinsmore.

She discovered, by adroit references and questions, by putting this and that together, that Ray Palmer was in love with the girl; that the old gentleman favored his suit in spite of her poverty, and would willingly have sanctioned an immediate marriage if she could have been found.

"So much for this evening, and now I wish that I could find the girl," she mused, as she stood before her mirror and removed her ornaments, after returning from the reception. "So she is beautiful! I wonder if she looks like her mother—my hated rival!

Ah! Mona Montague, I vowed that I would have vengeance, and I had it. You dared to come between me and the man I loved, and I swore I would crush you—I did, and now I mean to crush your child also, if I can find her. True, I won your husband after you were dead and gone, but he never loved me as he loved you, in spite of my blind idolatry for him."

She had become greatly excited over these reflections, and, sweeping into a heap the laces and jewels which she had removed from her person, she began pacing the floor with swift, angry steps.

"I wish now," she began again, after a time, "that I had gone to Walter Dinsmore's funeral, if for nothing more than to get a glimpse of the girl; but he bore me no good-will, and somehow I could not make up my mind to enter his house. I am sorry I didn't, for then I should have known this pretty little lady-love of Mr. Ray Palmer, if ever I met her again. Now I may have a long hunt for her. It was a great oversight on my part; but I never thought of her disappearing in such a mysterious way."

After a while she removed her rich evening costume, then donning a warm flannel wrapper, she seated herself before the glowing grate, clasped her hands around her knees, and, gazing upon the bed of red-hot coals, she fell to musing.

"So young Palmer is bound to marry Richmond Montague's fair daughter," she murmured, with curling lips and a bitter laugh; "and his father is only too willing, provided she can be found. Ha! ha! ha!" a soft, rippling laugh of intense amusement and scorn bursting from her red lips. "I wonder what they would say if they knew all that I know? I'd give a great deal if I could ascertain just how much the girl

knows about herself. She could make a great deal
of trouble for me if——"

She broke off suddenly just here, but after a few
moments of thought resumed, in another strain:

"I believe I shall have to cultivate my new acquaintances. I think I can play the father against the
son, and, *vice versa,* for it was evident to-night that
both, with very little encouragement, would become
my willing slaves. I imagine that the senior Palmer
might make a very agreeable companion. He is reported to be rich—a diamond merchant, and I am
fond of diamonds. He is certainly very gallant and
not bad-looking. Yes, I think I must cultivate him;
and then, if the junior member should discover his
inamorata by and by, a word in the ear of the father
might be sufficient to blast Miss Mona's hopes, and
thus complete the work I began so successfully—at
least in some respects—so many years ago. Ah,
Madame Mona, you did not realize the strength of
the spirit which you defied that day in Paris. I made
you *believe* that your marriage was all a sham, but
if I could have made it really so I should have been
better pleased with my work, for then I should have
had nothing to fear, at this late day, from your child."

It is impossible to describe the venom and hatred
that were concentrated in the voice of this beautiful
woman, as she thus reviewed this portion of her history, which, as can plainly be seen, had left a keen
sting in her heart, notwithstanding her boasted victory over her rival.

It did not seem possible that she could be the same
person, with her dark, revengeful face, her contracted
brow, fiercely gleaming eyes, and that cruel, bitter
curl upon her lips, who, in all the glory of her beauty

and powers of fascination, had been the centre of attraction in Alexander Merrill's elegant residence less than two hours previous.

It almost seemed as if she must be possessed of a dual nature, similar to that so cleverly represented in the story of "Doctor Jekyll and Mr. Hyde." Then, she had been all smiles, and sweetness, and graciousness, a vision of delight, a presence that charmed and pleased every one with whom she came in contact; now, she was transformed into a beautiful fiend, with a nature of spite and fury, and cruel revenge written upon every delicate feature.

She sat there in the glow of the firelight until the gilded clock on the mantel chimed the hour of two; then, with passion and pain showing themselves in her every movement, she arose, and without undressing, threw herself upon her bed, and wept herself to sleep.

*　　*　　*　　*　　*　　*

Mona was gradually becoming accustomed to her new life, although it was so very different from the almost charmed existence which she had hitherto led, and had it not been for her grief for her uncle and on account of Ray's seeming neglect and indifference, she would not have been unhappy in her position.

Mrs. Montague was not unreasonable—she did not overwork her, although there was always plenty of sewing to be done. She rather enjoyed being busy, on the whole, while she experienced a great deal of satisfaction in knowing that she could be independent; she even felt something of pride, in thus rising above the adverse circumstances that had so unexpectedly overtaken her.

She was very careful about her health, for she knew

that this sudden change from her previous active care-free life to such sedentary habits, must be a great tax upon her constitution, and so she persisted in taking exercise in the open air every day, although often she would have preferred to remain in the house.

A couple of days after her encounter with Mr. Louis Hamblin upon the steps of Mrs. Montague's residence, she was returning from her usual stroll, when the young man again suddenly appeared around the corner of a street she was passing, and almost ran into her.

"I beg your pardon, Miss Richards," he exclaimed, stopping short, and regarding her with apparent surprise, while he lifted his hat to her with great politeness, "I hope I did not startle you."

"Oh, no; and you are quite excusable," Mona responded, but somewhat astonished that he should address her by her name; but she imagined that he must have asked Mrs. Montague who she was.

She was about to hasten on, when he remarked:

"Since we are both going the same way, perhaps you will allow me to walk with you."

Mona would have preferred to proceed on her way alone, but she had not quite the courage to say so, since he appeared so courteous, so she made no reply at all.

The young man took her silence for consent, and, falling into step with her, began chatting as freely as if they had been old acquaintances.

His manner was very respectful, while there was nothing in what he said to which she could in the least object—indeed, she found him rather entertaining at first, and almost forgot, for the time, that she was Ruth Richards, the seamstress, instead of Mona

Montague, the heiress, and social equal of any high-toned young man whom she might meet.

"Have you lived long in New York, Miss Richards?" Mr. Hamblin inquired, after he had rattled on about various matters, and Mona had hardly spoken. He desired to hear her talk, that he might judge of her mental caliber.

"Yes, thirteen or fourteen years," Mona replied.

Louis Hamblin frowned; he had hoped that she was a stranger there.

"Ah! Then of course New York is very familiar to you," he remarked. "Do your friends reside here?"

"No—I have no friends," Mona said, flushing and with starting tears.

"Indeed," returned her companion, in a tone of sympathy. "I noticed that you were in mourning— I am very sorry."

Mona had heard so few words of sympathy of late that she came near losing her self-control at this, and she found herself unable to make any reply, lest her tears should fall.

"You look very delicate, too," her companion continued, bending a curious glance upon her. "I am sure you have not always lived as you are living now; it must be very hard to sit and sew all day. I hope you find my aunt considerate, Miss Richards."

Mona was astonished at this last remark which she thought was in very bad taste, and she turned a cold, questioning glance upon him.

"If at any time you should not," he went on, flippantly, "just let me know, Miss Richards, and I will see what I can do for you, for I have considerable influence with Aunt Marg."

Mona looked amazed, and wondered what he could mean by speaking in such a way of Mrs. Montague.

He had made a grand mistake in assuming that she should make a confidant of him—an entire stranger—in the event of her being overworked by his aunt.

"Mrs. Montague has been very good," she said, icily, and drawing her slight, graceful figure haughtily erect, "but—if at any time I *should* find my duties heavier than I could perform faithfully, I should tell *her* so and seek some other position."

Mr. Hamblin flushed hotly—not with embarrassment, although he had seldom had such a rebuff, but with anger and chagrin that a poor sewing-girl whom he had seen fit to patronize, should dare to give him such a set-back.

But he had no intentions of being beaten at his game, and so curbed his ire for the time.

"Pardon me," he humbly responded, "I did not mean to offend you nor to interfere, 'pon my word I didn't; only you seem so delicate and unfit for such a life; and fashionable ladies have such oceans of work to be done that they sometimes crowd their help—I——"

"Excuse me—I must leave you here; my work is waiting for me," Mona interposed, coldly, and cutting him short as they reached Mrs. Montague's residence.

She ran lightly up the steps and rang the bell before he could offer to admit her with his latch-key as before.

A servant let her in immediately, and she went directly up stairs, without deigning her would-be escort another word or look, while she carried herself with

so much hauteur that he knew she resented his presumptuous familiarity.

"Hoity toity!" he muttered, with a crimson face;
"our pretty seamstress hath the manner of a princess!
One would almost suppose that she had been born and
bred in a palace and was the mistress of millions, instead of being only a common working-girl and dependent upon the skill of her own dainty fingers for
her living. But she is wonderfully interesting, aside
from her beauty, and I must change my tactics or I
shall never get into her good graces. Who would
have dreamed that she would have the sense to resent my offer. Most girls would have blushed, sim-
pered, and thanked me, feeling flattered with my con-
descending interest.

Mr. Hamblin did change his tactics.

The next morning, when Mona went into the sewing-room, she found a tiny vase filled with choice
flowers upon her table.

She suspected that Mr. Hamblin might have been
the donor, and she was annoyed that he should presume to take such a liberty upon so slight an acquaintance. Still, she was not sure that he had put them
there, and the pretty things made a bright spot in
the room, while their fragrance was not without its
charm for her; so she did enjoy them in a measure.

"Where did you get your flowers, Ruth?" Mrs.
Montague inquired, when she came in later to inquire
regarding a wrap that was being mended, and espied
them.

"My flowers!" Mona said, determined that she
would not claim them; "they are not mine, and I do
not know who put them here. I found them on the
table when I came down this morning."

Mrs. Montague frowned, but said nothing more.

She suspected who had made the floral offering, however, and secretly resolved that Louis should not be guilty of continuing such attentions to her seamstress.

She gave orders to Mary to go into the sewing-room every morning before breakfast, and if she found flowers there to take them down to the dining-room and put them upon the table.

The girl found a bouquet on Mona's table three mornings in succession.

She carried out her mistress' instructions to the letter, and Mr. Louis Hamblin, observing the disposition of his expensive gifts, imagined that the pretty seamstress herself had taken this way to reject them.

The measure angered him, and only made him more resolute to conquer Mona's indifference and pride.

"By Jove!" he said to himself, as he gazed frowningly upon the discarded blossoms, "I believe I am really becoming interested in the proud little beauty, and I must find some other way to bring her around. It is evident that she recognizes the social distance between us, and wishes me to understand it. Perhaps, however, with a little judicious coaxing of a different character, I may win her to a more friendly mood."

He waylaid Mona several times after that, while she was out walking, but, though she never forgot to conduct herself in the most lady-like manner she plainly indicated by her coldness and reserve that she did not care to cultivate Mr. Hamblin's acquaintance.

This opposition to his wishes only made him the more persistent, and added zest to his pursuit of her.

The girl's exquisite beauty and grace—her high-bred self-possession and polished manner—impressed him as he had never been impressed before, even by the society girls whom he was in the habit of meeting, and Kitty McKenzie's charms grew pale and dim beside the brighter and more perfect loveliness of this dainty sewing-girl.

When Mona found that the young man persisted in following her and forcing his society upon her, she changed the time of her daily walk to an hour when she knew he would be down town, and she also took care to go in different directions, thus successfully avoiding him for some time.

But fortune favored him later on.

One morning Mrs. Montague came into the sewing-room all animation, and beaming with smiles.

"Ruth, I am going to ask a great favor of you," she said: "I wonder if you will oblige me."

"Certainly, Mrs. Montague, I shall be very glad to do so, if it is within my power," Mona readily responded.

"Well, then," continued the lady, "I am invited to spend a week at the residence of a friend who lives near Rhinebeck, a little way up the Hudson. Quite a party are going also, and great preparations have been made for us. In fact, it is to be a sort of carnival, on a small scale, and is to wind up with a grand ball. Now, I want you to go with me, Ruth, to help arrange my different costumes, and to act as a kind of dressing-maid—you have such good taste and judgment. Will you go? You will, of course, be relieved from your regular work, while, perhaps, you will find the rest and change agreeable."

Mona thought a few moments before replying.

Her only objection to going with Mrs. Montague
was she feared she might meet people whom she had
known and associated with before her uncle died.
She dreaded to be ignored or treated rudely by old
acquaintances. She could not forget her recent experience at Macy's.

But she reasoned that she might not see any one
whom she knew; she had never met Mrs. Montague
in society, and her circle of friends might be entirely
different from those with whom she had mingled. She
longed for a respite from ceaseless stitching, and for
some change of scene, and she finally resolved to go."

"Why, yes, I am perfectly willing to attend you if
you wish," she said at last.

"Thank you—you have relieved my mind of quite
a burden, for I feared you might decline my request,"
Mrs. Montague returned, and then went away to do
her packing.

They were to leave New York that afternoon, but
Mona had not once thought that Louis Hamblin
would be likely to be one of the party, until he joined
Mrs. Montague at the station.

There were a dozen or fifteen people in the party,
and the young man was devotedly attentive to a pretty
dark-eyed girl, who was addressed as Kitty Mc-
Kenzie.

His eyes lighted with a flash of pleasure, however,
the moment he caught sight of Mona, although he betrayed no other sign that he had ever seen her before.

The fair girl flushed with indignation at this slight.

Not because she was at all anxious to have him
take notice of her, but because he failed to treat her,
in the presence of his friends and social equals, with

the courtesy which he had always been so eager to show her elsewhere.

It was a very gay party, and, as a drawing-room car had been chartered for their especial use, there was nothing to impose any restraint upon them, and mirth and pleasure reigned.

Two-thirds of the company were young people, and Kitty McKenzie was one of the merriest of the group, and apparently a great favorite, while it could be readily seen that the attentions of Louis Hamblin were very acceptable to her—her every look and smile, when conversing with him, indicating that he was far more to her than an ordinary acquaintance.

When they arrived at their destination carriages were found to be in waiting to take the party to Hazeldean, the residence of Mr. Wellington, who was to entertain the company for the ensuing week.

A drive of a mile brought them to the fine estate, where an imposing mansion stood in the middle of a beautiful park. The interior of the dwelling was in perfect keeping with its exterior—luxury and beauty prevailed on every hand, and it was really an ideal place in which to entertain a numerous company.

The wide, mammoth hall ran the whole length of the house, while numerous rooms opened into it, with wide doors sliding upward, so that almost the whole of the lower floor could be made into one grand room. The floors were of hard wood, and polished to the last degree of brightness, and were, as Kitty McKenzie merrily remarked, while she executed a gay pirouette on entering, "just capital for dancing."

The upper stories were equally spacious, and luxuriously furnished—it really seemed like a great hotel, only far more home-like and comfortable.

The guests were soon assigned to their apartments, and Mona was gratified to find that, instead of being consigned to some remote corner of the great house, she had a cozy room opening directly into the one occupied by Mrs. Montague.

CHAPTER XV.

A GAY COMPANY AT HAZELDEAN.

The week that followed was one never to be forgotten. Such feasting and merry-making, such excursions, and card parties, and dancing parties Mona had never witnessed.

She had read of such scenes occurring in the great manor-houses of England, and had often thought that she should like to witness something of the kind; but she did not imagine that Americans had yet attained the art of displaying such magnificent hospitality. It was a carnival, indeed, from the evening of their arrival until the morning of their departure.

It was the month of February, there was no snow on the ground, and the weather was very mild and more like early spring, than winter, so that every morning there was planned an excursion of some kind —either a drive or a canter on horseback to different points of interest in that picturesque section, which everybody appeared to enjoy as well as if all nature had been at the height of its glory in midsummer.

Mona, of course, was never invited to join these excursions; she was regarded as nothing but a seamstress or a maid, and most of the company would have

scorned the idea of thus associating with her upon
equal terms.

Her heart often swelled with bitter pain as she
watched a gay cavalcade ride away through the park,
for she dearly loved horseback riding, and she well
knew that six months previous she would have been
most cordially welcomed by every member of that
merry company.

She wondered what had become of her pretty sad-
dle-horse, Jet, and her uncle's proud steed, Banquo,
and sighed regretfully as she reviewed the happy past,
when they four—for the horses had seemed almost
human—had roamed over the country together. She
sometimes even longed to be back in New York among
her piles of sewing, for she had not enough to do
now to occupy her time, and it often hung heavily on
her hands, thus allowing painful memories to depress
her.

The third morning after their arrival, just as a gay
party was on the point of starting off, Mona, being
at liberty, thought she would slip down to the library
and try to find an entertaining book to pass away the
long hours before lunch.

She was half-way down stairs, when Kitty McKenzie came running breathlessly back, looking flushed
and exceedingly disappointed over something.

"Oh, dear!" she cried, as she was passing Mona;
"I tripped in my riding-habit, and have ripped the facing so badly that I must change it and go in the
carriage with mamma.   It is too bad, for I had the
loveliest pony to ride."

"Have you ripped it too badly to have it repaired?"
Mona asked, sorry to have the gay girl deprived of
her coveted pleasure.

"Yes, for it takes me forever to mend anything. I am a wretched bungler with my needle," she confessed, with engaging frankness, but with a conscious blush.

"Let me see it," and Mona stooped to examine the rip. "This is not so bad, after all," she continued, cheerfully. "Just come to my room, and I will catch it up for you; I can do it in less time than it would take to change your dress."

"*Can* you? Oh, that will be so good of you!" and, delighted that she was not to be deprived of her ride, Miss Kitty followed Mona, with a bright face and an eager step.

Five minutes sufficed for our young seamstress to make the garment wearable, and then she told Miss McKenzie that if she would bring the habit to her upon her return, she would repair it more thoroughly.

The kind-hearted girl was very grateful.

"How kind you are to do it!" she cried, as Mona smoothed the heavy folds into place, then, with a sudden impulse and a sympathetic look into the fair face of the seamstress, she added: "What a pity it is that you have to stay here all by yourself, while the rest of us are having such delightful times! Why cannot you come with us, Miss Richards? I will make mamma let you go with her—there is an extra seat in that carriage."

"Thank you; you are very good to suggest it, Miss McKenzie, but I cannot go," Mona answered, with a flush, but touched that the girl should wish her to share her pleasures.

"I am sure you would enjoy it, for you are young, and it is too bad to be obliged to stay indoors this delightful weather, and I imagine, if the truth were

known, you could be as gay as anybody, while truly,"
with an arch, winsome glance, "I believe you are the
prettiest girl here. Do you know how to dance?"

"Yes."

"Then I think I can manage it—if you would like
it, Miss Richards—to have you join the german this
evening; will you?"

"You are very thoughtful, Miss McKenzie," Mona
replied, appreciatively, "but I should feel out of place,
even if others were as kindly disposed as yourself."

"You have had trouble—you have lost friends,"
Miss Kitty remarked, glancing at her black dress.

"Yes—all that I had in the world," Mona returned,
with a quivering lip and a sigh that was almost a sob;
for the sweet girl's kindly interest moved her deeply.

"I am sorry," said her companion, simply, but sincerely. Then she continued, with heartiness: "But
let me count myself your friend after this—will you?
I think you are very nice, and I believe it would be
very easy to love you—you poor, lonely child!" and
before Mona realized her intention, she had stooped
and kissed her softly on the cheek.

She did not give her any opportunity to reply, but
tripped away, flushing over her own impulsive familiarity.

She looked back over her shoulder as she reached
the door and added:

"Good-by, Miss Richards; remember, you and I
are to be friends; and thank you ever so much for
mending my dress."

She was gone before Mona could answer, even to
tell her that she was very welcome, but her heart
warmed toward the bright, genial maiden, and she
stood listening, with a smile on her lips, to the sound

of her little feet pattering down the stairs, and the next moment she caught her merry laugh as some one swung her lightly into her saddle.

Then Mona went down to the library, where she selected a book, and then, finding the room empty, she decided to remain where she was for a while.

Rolling a great easy-chair into a deep bay-window, she nestled, with a feeling of pleasure, in its cozy depths, and was soon deeply absorbed in the contents of her book.

She must have been reading half an hour when a slight sound in another portion of the room startled her. Turning to see what had caused it, she saw Louis Hamblin standing between the parted portieres of an archway, and gazing upon her, a smile of triumph on his handsome face.

Mona sprang from her chair, looking the surprise she felt, for she did not suppose he was in the house.

"Do not rise, Miss Richards," said the young man, as he came forward. "It is really a great pleasure to find you here, but I pray that you will not allow me to disturb you."

"I thought you had gone with the party," the young girl said, hardly knowing how to reply to him, but deeply annoyed by his presence.

"No; I had a raging toothache all night, so had to make up my rest this morning and have but just eaten breakfast. But sit down, Miss Richards; everybody has gone off and left me behind; I am lonely, and nothing would suit me better than a social little chat with yourself," he concluded, with obnoxious familiarity.

Mona drew her graceful form to its full height, while her red lips curled scornfully.

"Thank you, but it might be considered in bad taste for one in Mr. Hamblin's position to be found chatting socially with his aunt's seamstress, whom he is not supposed to know," she said, a note of sarcasm in her tone.

The young man laughed out lightly.

"Ah! you resent it because I did not recognize you the day we came to Hazeldean," he returned; "but you will forgive me, I know, when I tell you that I avoided betraying the fact of our previous acquaintance simply for your own good. I feared it might make you conspicuous if I saluted you, as I wished to do, and my aunt is very particular about the proprieties of life."

Mona smiled proudly. She failed to perceive how a courteous recognition could have made her conspicuous or violated in any way the most rigid laws of etiquette.

"In that case we will continue to observe the proprieties of life upon all occasions," she dryly remarked.

He read her thoughts, and was keenly stung by her words.

"Forgive me," he said, with an assumption of regret and humility, thinking thus the better to gain his end; "had I realized that you would have been so wounded I should have acted very differently. I assure you I will never offend you in the same way again."

"Pray do not be troubled," Mona coldly retorted. "I had no thought of resenting anything which you might consider proper to do. If I thought of the matter at all, it was only in connection with the generally accepted principles of courtesy and good-breeding."

Mr. Hamblin flushed hotly at this keen shaft, but he ignored it, and changed the subject.

"I am sorry to have interrupted you in your reading, Miss Richards. What have you that is interesting?"

"Victor Hugo's 'Les Miserables,'" Mona briefly replied.

"Have you?" the young man eagerly demanded, "I was searching for that book only yesterday. May I look at it one moment? McArthur and I had quite a discussion upon a point regarding Father Madelaine, and we were unable to settle it because we could not find the book."

Mona quietly passed the volume to him; but a blank look overspread his face as he took it.

"Why, it is the original!" he exclaimed, "and I do not read French readily. Are you familiar with it?"

"Oh, yes," and Mona smiled slightly.

She had been accounted the finest French scholar in her class.

Mr. Hamblin regarded her wonderingly.

"Where did you learn French to be able to read it at sight?" he inquired.

"At school."

"But—I thought——" he began, and stopped confused.

"You thought that a common seamstress must necessarily be ignorant, as well as poor," Mona supplemented: "that she would not be likely to have opportunities or ambition for self-improvement. Well, Mr. Hamblin, perhaps some girls in such a position would not, but I honestly believe that there is many a poor girl, who has had to nak· her own way in life, who is better educated than many of the so-called society belles of to-day."

"I believe it, too, if you are a specimen," her companion returned, as he gazed admiringly into Mona's flushed and animated face.

"At any rate," he added, "you are far more beautiful than the majority of society girls."

"Mr. Hamblin will please reserve his compliments for ears more eager for and more accustomed to them," Mona retorted, with a frown of annoyance.

"Why are you so proud and scornful toward me, Miss Richards?" he appealingly asked. "Can you not see that my admiration for you is genuine—that I really desire to be your friend? And why have you avoided me so persistently of late—why have you rejected my flowers?"

"Because," Mona frankly answered, and meeting his glance squarely, "I know, and you know, that it is not proper for you to offer, nor for me to accept, such attentions, even if I desired them."

"I am my own master; you are your own mistress, if, as you say, you are alone in the world; consequently, such a matter lies between ourselves, without regard to what others might consider as 'proper.' And I may as well make an open confession first as last," he went on, eagerly, and bending nearer to her, with a flushed face. "Ruth, my beautiful Ruth, I love you —I began to love you that morning when we met on the steps before our own door, and every day has only increased my affection for you."

A startled look swept over Mona's face, which had now grown very pale. She had not had a suspicion that she was destined to hear such a declaration as this; it had taken her wholly unawares, and for a moment she was speechless.

But she soon recovered herself.

"Stop!" she haughtily cried "you have no right to use such language to me; you would not presume— you would not *dare* to do so upon so brief an acquaintance, if I stood upon an equal footing with you, socially. It is only because I am poor and unprotected —because you simply wish to amuse yourself for a time. You would not dare to repeat in the presence of Mrs. Montague what you have just said to me. Now let me pass, if you please, and never presume to address me again as you have to-day."

The indignant girl looked like some beautiful princess as she stood before him and thus resented the insult he had offered her.

Her slight form was held proudly erect, her small head was uplifted with an air of scorn, her eyes blazed forth angry contempt as they met his, while her whole bearing indicated a conscious superiority which both humiliated and stung her would-be suitor.

She had never appeared so beautiful to him before. Her face was as pure as a pearl; her glossy hair, falling loosely away from her white forehead, was simply coiled at the back of her small head, thus revealing its symmetrical proportions to the best advantages. Her great brown eyes glowed and scintillated, her nostrils dilated, her lips quivered with outraged pride and delicacy.

Her dress of dead black fell in soft, clinging folds about her slender form, making her seem taller than she really was, while one hand had been raised to enforce the commands which she had laid upon him.

He thought her the fairest vision he had ever seen,

in spite of her indignation against him, and if she
had sought to fascinate him—to weave the spell of
her witchery more effectually about him, she could
have taken no surer way to do so.

He could not fail to admire her spirit—it but served
to glorify her in his sight, and made him more eager
than before to conquer her.

"Nay, do not leave me thus—do not be so bitter
against me, my peerless Ruth," he pleaded.   "Perhaps I have been premature in my avowal, but I beg
that you will not despise me on that account.   Do
not judge me so harshly.   Lay my impatience rather
to my eagerness to win you.   I would do anything in
the world to make you love me, and now, I fear, I
have only been driving you farther from me.   I love
you, honestly and sincerely, my beautiful Ruth, and I
would not only dare to confess it to my aunt, but proclaim it before the world, if that would serve to prove
it to you.   Ah! teach me how to woo you, my darling; give me but a crumb of hope upon which to
feed, and I will try to be satisfied until you can learn
to have more confidence in me."

He reached forth his arms as if he would have in-
folded her; and Mona, who for the moment had been
rendered spell-bound by the swift rush of burning
words that he had poured forth, seemed suddenly
electrified by the act.

She felt both insulted and humiliated by this premature avowal of a love that had not received the slightest encouragement from her, and she recoiled from
him with a gesture of contempt.

"I wonder how you have dared to say this to me,"
she cried, in a voice that quivered with indignation,
"when in my very presence you have shown another

attentions such as a man has a right to bestow only upon the woman whom he intends to marry. But for the respect I owe myself and my sex, I would like to brand you with a mark that would betray your disloyalty to the world, and make Miss McKenzie despise you as I do; being only a weak woman, however, I must content myself with simply manifesting my scorn, and by telling you to go!" and she pointed authoritatively toward the door with one white taper finger.

A hot, crimson flush dyed the young man's white face with a sense of shame, such as he had never before experienced in the presence of any one, while the purple veins stood out in ridges upon his forehead.

He was completely cowed before her. Conscious himself of the insincerity and unworthiness of his declaration, he knew that she also had read him like an open book, and the knowledge made him fearfully angry; while to be foiled in his purpose and browbeaten by this girl, whom he imagined to be only what she seemed, was more than his indomitable spirit could tamely submit to.

"A love like mine is not to be despised, and you shall yet find it so," he muttered between his tightly shut teeth.

Mona would not deign him a reply, but standing in the same attitude, she again motioned him to go.

Unable longer to endure the unflinching gaze of her clear, scornful eyes, he shrank back through the portieres, which instantly fell into place again, and Mona, with a smile of disdain curving her red lips, went back to her seat by the window.

But all enjoyment in her book was gone; she was much excited, for she had been greatly shaken by the interview and made to feel her position as she never yet had done; and after sitting a few moments gazing sadly out of the window she again went up to her own room.

CHAPTER XVI.

MONA LEARNS SOMETHING OF RAY.

That same evening as Mona was passing up stairs from the laundry, whither she had been to press out the ruffles of a dress, which Mrs. Montague wished to wear at the german a few hours later, she heard the hall-bell ring a resounding peal.

She hastened on, for she did not wish to be observed by strangers, but as she reached the upper landing, she caught some hearty words of welcome from Mr. Wellington, the host, and knew that another guest had arrived.

But she suddenly stopped short, and the color receded from her cheeks, while her heart beat with quick, heavy throbs as she heard the name of Palmer pronounced.

"Can it be possible that Ray Palmer is the newcomer?" she asked herself.

She leaned over the banister, curiosity and an eager longing prompting her to ascertain if he were the guest.

But no, it was not Ray.

She saw instead an elderly gentleman, of benevolent and genial appearance, who seemed to be a valued friend of the family, judging from the enthusiastic greeting which his host accorded him.

"Well, well, Palmer, you are rather late in the week, but none the less welcome on that account," remarked Mr. Wellington. "We have been having gay times, and I have only needed your presence to make my enjoyment complete. But where is that precious son of yours? How is it that Raymond did not come with you?"

Mona held her breath at this.

The question had told her that the new arrival was Ray's father, and that the young man had also been invited to join the gay company that was sojourning beneath the hospitable roof.

She leaned farther over the railing that she might not fail to catch Mr. Palmer's reply.

"Oh," answered that gentleman, as he removed his overcoat and gloves, "Ray is not yet quite as strong as we could wish, although he calls himself well, and he feels hardly equal to much dissipation as yet. Besides, he is rather depressed just now."

"Over the affair of the diamonds, I suppose?" Mr. Wellington observed.

"Yes, and—some other matter that troubles him."

"I am very sorry. I was depending upon him to help amuse some of our fair young guests," said his host. Then he added, with considerable interest: "Any new developments regarding that remarkable robbery?"

"No; and I do not imagine there ever will be," Mr. Palmer gravely returned.

"Then you have given up all hope of ever recovering them?"

"Well, almost, though I have a detective on the lookout yet, and he thinks if he can get track of the thief in this case, she will prove to be the very woman that he has been searching for during the last three years. He imagines that she is the same one who was concerned in a bold swindle in Chicago about that time."

"Well, I sincerely hope that he will be successful in finding her; such wickedness should not be allowed to prosper," said Mr. Wellington. "I am really sorry about Ray, though—he is such capital company, and there are six or eight wonderfully pretty girls here who will be deeply disappointed when they learn that he is not coming at all."

The two gentlemen passed into the drawing-room just then, and Mona heard nothing more.

She deeply sighed, and continued to stand there for some moments lost in thought.

She could not really make up her mind whether she was more disappointed than rejoiced over Ray's failure to meet this engagement.

It would have been very pleasant to see him again, but it would also have been very humiliating to have him find her there in the capacity of a servant, and ignore her on this account, as Louis Hamblin had done. She still felt most keenly his apparent neglect of her during her troubles, and of course, being entirely ignorant of what had occurred, she attributed it to the most unworthy motives, which, however, did not help to reconcile her to the loss of his friendship.

She gathered from what Mr. Palmer had said about his not being quite strong yet that Ray had been ill, and she wondered, too, what he had meant by his being depressed on account of some other matter that was troubling him.

She had also learned something new about the robbery, of which she had only had a faint hint from the little item which she had read in the paper on the day she went to Mrs. Montague's. She gleaned now that Ray had in some way been responsible for the loss—or, at least felt himself to be so to some extent.

She wished that she could have heard more about him, and she was conscious of a deeper sense of lone-liness and friendliness, from this little rift in the cloud that had shut her out of the world where once she had been so happy.

Another sigh escaped her as she slowly turned to go on to her room and almost unconsciously she cried out, with a little sob of pain and longing:

"Oh, Ray, Ray!"

"Aha!"

The ejaculation startled the young girl beyond meas-ure. She did not dream that there was any one near her. She had been so absorbed in observing Mr. Palmer and listening to what had occurred in the lower hall, and in her own sad thoughts, that she was unconscious that any one had stolen up on her un-awares, and had also been a witness to the inter-view between Mr. Palmer and Mr. Wellington, until this exclamation made her look up. She found her-self again face to face with Louis Hamblin.

"Aha!" he repeated, in a tone of triumph, but with a frown upon his brow; "that explains why my suit was so disdained this morning! So you know and—love Mr. Raymond Palmer! My pretty Ruth, pray tell me how this young Apollo managed to inspire the princess of sewing-girls with such tender senti-ments, that I may profit by his successful method."

"Let me pass!" Mona commanded, as, straight as a young palm, she confronted the insolent fellow with blazing cheeks and flashing eyes.

"It makes you wonderfully pretty to get angry," he
returned, with a gleeful chuckle; "but I am not going to let you pass until you tell me when and where
you made young Palmer's acquaintance," and he continued to stand directly in her path.

"Do you imagine that you can *compel* me to say
anything?" Mona burst forth, with stinging contempt,
her patience all gone. "Let this be the last time that
you ever waylay or persecute me with your attentions,
for, I give you fair warning, a repetition of such conduct on your part will send me straight to Mrs. Montague with a full report of it."

The young man looked decidedly crestfallen at this
spirited threat.

There was but one person in the world of whom he
stood in awe, and that was his aunt, Margaret Montague.

He well knew that it would not be for his interest
to offend her, and, of all things, he would dread most
a revelation of what had occurred in the library that
morning, notwithstanding he had affirmed to Mona
that he was willing to proclaim his affection before
her and the whole world.

Besides, if it should come to the ears of Kitty Mc-
Kenzie, his prospects of a marriage with that pretty
and wealthy young lady would be blighted, and no end
of trouble would follow, for Mrs. Montague had determined to effect a union between them, and if he
should go contrary to her wishes, she could make it
very uncomfortable for him pecuniarily.

Still, he was deeply smitten with the beautiful young
seamstress, and was rapidly becoming more so every
time he met her.

He had promised himself the pleasure of a secret

flirtation with her, while at the same time he intended
to continue his attentions to Miss McKenzie in public, and he did not like to be balked in his purpose.

He saw that he could never intimidate her into any
concessions; she was far too high-spirited and
straightforward; so he must adopt other measures if
he would win.

"Certainly you shall pass, if you wish," he said,
respectfully, as he stepped aside; "but please do not be
quite so unkind; and, by the way, can you tell me what
the old codger down below meant by his son being
upset about the diamonds?"

He knew well enough, for of course he had seen the
accounts of the affair in the papers; but he had an
object in wishing to find out how much Mona knew.

"No, I cannot," she coldly replied, as, with uplifted
head and haughty bearing, she passed him and entered
Mrs. Montague's room.

While this incident was occurring in the hall of the
second story, Mr. Amos Palmer was being introduced
to the company below.

His advent caused quite a flutter of excitement
among the young ladies; for most of them were acquainted with Ray, who for nearly two years had
been a great favorite in society, and they had been
led to expect that he was to join their company at
Hazeldean.

Great disappointment was expressed when they
learned that he was not likely to put in an appearance
at all, and Mr. Palmer began to feel sorry that he had
not insisted upon having his son come with him.

Mr. Wellington was full of wit and pleasantry, and
made merry, as he went around the room with his
friend, to introduce the strangers to him.

As they came to Mrs. Montague, he was somewhat surprised when the lady greeted Mr. Palmer with great cordiality.

"I have already the pleasure of Mr. Palmer's acquaintance," she said, with one of her most alluring smiles, as she extended her hand to him, and forthwith she entered into conversation with him, thus effectually chaining him to her side.

He seemed only too well pleased to linger there—he was, in fact, a willing captive to her wiles, a circumstance which the bright eyes of the younger portion of the company did not fail to observe and to comment upon, with something of amusement, and not a little of the matchmaking spirit of their own mammas.

"Girls!" exclaimed Alice Farwell, a gay, dashing beauty of twenty, to a group of friends whom she had coaxed into a corner, "do you know that a romance has begun here this evening?—a romance that will not be long in culminating in matrimony? Oh! don't go to pluming your feathers," she continued, as there was a general flutter, "for we *young* Americans will not figure in the story at all, though we may possibly be invited to the wedding. Oh, if it should prove to be the only match of the season!" and with a long-drawn sigh, she glanced mischievously across the room, toward the recent arrival, who was apparently oblivious of all, save the attractions of the charming Mrs. Montague.

Talk of match-making mammas!

This bevy of young girls became so engrossed in watching the progress of the romance which was then being enacted in their presence, that they forgot to flirt themselves, and took pains to help it on in every possible way.

"It will be just the nicest match in the world," said Edith Brown, delightfully. "Mr. Palmer is a fine-looking old gentleman, and Mrs. Montague, though she seems a great deal younger, will make him a lovely wife."

"It will be so suitable, too, for they are both rich, and stand high in society," whispered a third, with an eye to worldly prosperity.

"And she can have all the diamonds she wants," chimed in a little miss of sixteen, "for he is a diamond merchant, you know."

This remark caused a general laugh, and then the conversation turned upon the recent robbery, which was discussed at some length.

"Who would have thought of decoying Ray Palmer into Doctor Wesselhoff's retreat?" exclaimed Alice Farwell. "It was a very daring thing to do. By the way, I wonder what the reason *is* young Palmer did not come with his father? I can't quite believe he isn't well enough, for I saw him only the day before we left New York, and he was walking down Broadway with as much energy as any one, only he looked a trifle pale and anxious."

"I wish he would come up for the grand hop on next Monday," said Edith Brown. "He is capital company, and a delightful partner. I am going to coax Mr. Palmer to send for him. Come, girls, he has monopolized our pretty widow long enough; suppose we break up the conference and put in our petition."

The merry maidens were nothing loath to have another handsome escort added to their number, and, headed by the audacious Edith, they went in a body to make their request of Mr. Palmer.

"Well, it is too bad to have Ray miss all this," he

said, smilingly, when they allowed him an opportunity
to reply. "I believe it would do him good to come,
and he could not help enjoying himself here," he
added, as his genial eyes rested on the bright faces before him. "I believe I will telegraph him in the
morning."

The fair petitioners were satisfied with their success, and, dinner being announced just then, the subject was dropped for the time.

After dinner there was a progressive whist party
for an hour, at the end of which there was considerable fun occasioned by the awarding of the prizes,
and after that everybody was ready for the german.

But great disappointment was expressed when they
found that there was one lady lacking to enable them
all to participate in the dance.

"What shall we do?—no one wants to sit and look
on—it is very stupid, and the rest of us wouldn't enjoy it, either, to have any wallflowers about," Kitty
McKenzie regretfully remarked. "Oh! Mrs. Montague," she added, as if the idea had just occurred to
her, "there is your pretty seamstress; may she not
come, just for this once?"

Mrs. Montague hesitated.

"Please," persisted the generous-hearted Kitty; "she
is very nice and lady-like; I am sure no one could object to her, and I know she would enjoy it."

Two or three others seconded the proposal, and the
lady then gave her consent, though with evident reluctance.

Miss Kitty, all elated with the success of her pro-
ject, and never dreaming that Mona would not enjoy
it, ran away to bring her down.

She found her in her own room reading a recent magazine.

"Come," she said, with gleaming eyes, "you are to join us in the german. I have Mrs. Montague's permission, and we are all waiting for you."

"I thank you very much Miss McKenzie," Mona responded, flushing, "but I do not believe I will go down."

"Oh, do; we need just one more lady, and some of the gentlemen will have to sit it out if you do not. Miss Nellie Wellington has to play for us, or she would dance, so please come," Miss Kitty urged, looking disappointed enough over Mona's unexpected refusal.

Mona shrank from joining the dancers, or from mingling with the company, for several reasons.

She had no heart for dancing, so soon after her uncle's death; she disliked to go among people who would regard her as an inferior, and only tolerate her presence because she would help to "fill out," while last, but not least, she wished to keep out of Louis Hamblin's way.

But she did not like to appear disobliging or unappreciative of Miss McKenzie's kindness, and a bright idea suddenly occurred to her.

"I really do not care to dance, Miss McKenzie, although it is very thoughtful of you to invite me; but if it will be agreeable to the company, I will take Miss Wellington's place at the piano, and she can make up the desired number."

"Oh, *can* you play?" cried Kitty, both astonished and delighted. "That will help us out, and I am sure it is very nice of you to offer, for I think it is awfully stupid to play for dancing. Come, then, and I know everybody will be surprised as well as pleased."

And winding her arm about the slender waist of the fair seamstress, they went down stairs together, Miss McKenzie chatting away as sociably as if they had always been friends and equals.

Mrs. Montague lifted her eyebrows with well-bred astonishment when the young lady informed the company that Miss Richards preferred to preside at the piano, and a number of others appeared to share her surprise, and looked somewhat skeptical, also.

They were more amazed still when she modestly took her seat and began her duties, for Mona was perfectly at home in music, and soon made the room ring with inspiring melody for the eager dancers.

"Who is that beautiful and talented girl?" Amos Palmer asked of his host, when the young people were tired of dancing, and Mona quietly withdrew from the room.

"Her name is Ruth Richards, I believe," Mr. Wellington replied.

"You 'believe!' Isn't she a guest here?" inquired Mr. Palmer, with surprise.

"No; she is simply a maid in the employ of Mrs. Montague."

"Well, it is a great pity."

"What is a great pity?"

"That such a lovely young lady should have to serve any one in that capacity; she is beautiful and talented enough to fill any position."

And this was Amos Palmer's opinion regarding Ray's unknown lady-love.

CHAPTER XVII.

MRS. MONTAGUE QUESTIONS MONA.

"Where did you learn to play the piano, Ruth?" Mrs. Montague inquired the next morning, while Mona was engaged in assisting her to dress, and she turned a searching glance upon her as she put the question.

To conceal the flush that mounted to her brow, Mona stooped to pick up a pin.

It had not occurred to her, when she offered to play for the dancing the previous evening, that such proficiency in music would be regarded as something very unusual in a sewing-girl, and might occasion remark.

Her only object had been to oblige Kitty McKenzie and avoid dancing with the guests.

"I had a relative who gave me lessons for a while," she said, in reply to Mrs. Montague's query.

"For a while!" repeated that lady, who had not been unobservant of the flush. "You finger the piano as if you had been accustomed to diligent practice all your life, and you must have had the best of instruction, too."

"I am very fond of music, and it was never any task to me to practice," Mona remarked. Then she added, to change the topic: "Shall I baste this ruffle in the full width, or shall I set it down a trifle?"

Mrs. Montague smiled at the tact of her pretty companion, in thus attempting to draw her attention to her own affairs.

A good many things had convinced her of late that her seamstress had not been reared in poverty, and certain suspicions, that had startled her when she first saw her, were beginning to force themselves again upon her.

"You can set it down a trifle," she replied; then she asked, persistently returning to the previous question: "Why do you not give music lessons, since you play so well, instead of sewing for your living? I should suppose it would be a much more congenial occupation."

"There are so many music teachers, and one needs a reputation in order to obtain pupils; besides, people would doubtless regard me as too young to have had much experience in teaching. There, I have finished this—is there anything else I can do for you?" and Mona laid the dress she had been at work upon on a chair, and stood awaiting further orders.

"Yes; the buckle on this slipper needs to be more securely fastened. It is true that there are legions of music teachers. Was this relative of yours a teacher?"

"Oh, no; he simply bore the expense of my instruction."

"I suppose he cannot be living, or you would not be sewing for me," Mrs. Montague remarked, with another searching glance.

"No," was the brief reply, and hot tears rushed to Mona's eyes, blinding her so that she could hardly see where to put her needle.

She then made some remark to the effect that she needed some stronger silk, and left the room to hide the grief which she found so hard to control.

"Aha! this relative must be the friend for whom she is in mourning—he cannot have been dead very long, for the girl is unable to speak of him without tears," muttered Mrs. Montague, thoughtfully, a heavy frown settling on her brow. "There is some mystery about her which I am bound to ferret out; she is exceedingly reticent about herself—I wonder if my suspicions can be correct?" she continued, her face settling into hard, revengeful lines. "She certainly looks enough like that girl to be her child. If I were sure, I would not spare her; I would crush her, for the hate that I bore her mother, notwithstanding she is so useful to me. Ha, ha!" and the laugh was exceedingly bitter, "it would seem like the irony of fate to have her child thrown thus into my power. But if she is Mona Montague why does she call herself Ruth Richards? what can be her object? Can it be possible," she added, with a startled look, "that she has been told her history, and she has engaged herself to me with the purpose of trying to obtain the proofs of it? Is she deep enough for that? or has she been advised to adopt such a course? She seems to be very frank and innocent, intent only upon doing her work well and pleasing me. Yet, if she should get hold of any of those proofs, she could make a great deal of trouble for me. I believe I shall have to destroy them, although I always feel as if a ghost were haunting me whenever I touch them. I shall never be satisfied until I learn Ruth's history. I'll attack her about the Palmers; if she is Mona Montague—the girl that Ray Palmer loves— she certainly will betray herself if I take her unawares; although she did not appear to know Mr. Palmer, last evening."

Mona returned at this moment, and Mrs. Montague's musings were cut short.

The young girl had recovered her self-control, and

was as calm and collected as usual; even more so, for she had told herself that she must be more on her guard or she would betray her identity.

Mrs. Montague appeared to have forgotten all about their recent conversation, and chatted sociably about various topics for a while. But suddenly she asked:

"Did you observe the new arrival last night, Ruth?"

"Do you mean that portly gentleman, who is slightly bald, and with whom you went out for refreshments?" Mona inquired, lifting a frank, inquiring look to her companion, though her heart beat fast at this reference to Ray's father.

"Yes; he is very fine-looking, don't you think so?"

"Perhaps so—rather," replied Mona, reflectively.

"That is 'rather' doubtful praise, I am afraid," observed Mrs. Montague, with a light laugh. "I think he is a very handsome old gentleman, and he is certainly a decidedly entertaining companion. You know who he is, I suppose."

"I do not think that I heard anybody address him by name while I was in the drawing-room; of course I was not introduced to any one," Mona evasively answered.

"His name is Palmer," Mrs. Montague remarked, as she bent a searching look upon the young girl.

But Mona had herself well in hand now, and she made no sign that the name was a familiar one to her.

"He has a son who is strikingly good looking, too," Mrs. Montague continued. "I met them both at a reception in New York a little while ago, and was greatly attracted to them, though just now the young man is rather unhappy—in fact, he is wearing the willow for some girl whom he imagines he loves."

Mrs. Montague paused to note the effect of this con-

versation, but Mona had finished fastening the buckle
on the slipper, and quietly taken up some other work,
though her pulses were beating like trip-hammers.

"It seems," the woman resumed, her keen eyes never
leaving the fair face opposite to her, "that he has long
been very fond of a girl whose surname is the same
as mine—a Miss Mona Montague. She was a niece
of that wealthy Mr. Dinsmore, who died so suddenly
in New York a short time ago."

It seemed to Mona that her heart must leap from
her bosom as she listened to this reference to herself;
but, with every appearance of perfect composure, she
measured off some ribbon that she was making into
bows, and severed it with a sharp clip of her scissors.

"Perhaps you do not know whom I mean," said
Mrs. Montague, and paused, determined to make the
girl speak.

"Oh, yes, I have heard of him, and I remember reading the notice of his death in a paper," Mona compelled herself to say, without betraying anything of
the pain which smote her heart in recurring thus to
her great loss.

Mrs. Montague frowned.

She was not progressing as well as she could have
wished in her "pumping" operation; but she meant to
probe the matter as far as she dared.

"Well," she went on, "this niece was supposed by
everybody to be Mr. Dinsmore's heiress; but a discarded wife suddenly made her appearance, after his
death, and claimed the whole of his property, and the
girl was left without a penny. She must have been
terribly cut up about it, for she suddenly disappeared,
and cannot be found, and it is this that has so upset
young Palmer. He had not committed himself, his

father informed me, but was just on the point of declaring his love when Mr. Dinsmore died; and the girl, evidently crushed by her loss, has hidden herself so securely that no one can find her."

It was fortunate for Mona that her recent troubles had taught her something of self-control, or she must have betrayed herself at this point.

She realized that Mrs. Montague must have a purpose in relating all this to her, and feared it was to verify some suspicion regarding herself.

She now believed that the woman must know all her mother's history, and certain facts regarding her own birth, which she felt that Mr. Dinsmore had, for some reason, withheld from her. This conviction had grown upon her ever since she had been a member of her family, and she hoped, by some means, if she remained long enough with her, to learn the truth. Still she feared that if Mrs. Montague should discover that she was her husband's daughter she might be so prejudiced against her she would at once dismiss her from her employ, and she would then lose her only chance to solve the questions that puzzled her. But she found it very hard to conceal the great and sudden joy that went thrilling through her as she listened to these facts regarding Ray Palmer's affection for and his loyalty to her.

He had not been unworthy and faithless, as she had imagined; there had been some good reason why he had not come to her during the early days of her trouble. He might have been called suddenly away from New York on business and not been able to return until her home was broken up; and now he was grieving—"wearing the willow," as Mrs. Montague expressed it—because he could not find her. He loved

her! he had been upon the point of telling her so, and
this blissful knowledge made the world seem suddenly
bright again to the hitherto depressed and grieving
girl.

But it would never do to betray anything of this, for
then Mrs. Montague would know at once that *she* was
Mona Montague; so she made no sign that she was
any more interested in this little romance regarding
Ray Palmer's love, than she would have been in that
of any stranger. She even forced herself to ignore
him altogether, and ask, in a matter-of-fact way:

"Is it not strange, if Mr. Dinsmore had a wife living, that he did not make some provision for his niece,
by will?"

"The girl *isn't* Mona Montague after all, or she
never would have asked such a question with that innocent air," said Mrs. Montague to herself, with some
disappointment; "the strange resemblance must be
only a coincidence, striking though it is. But I would
really like to know where Walter Dinsmore's niece is.
I feel as if I had an enemy in ambush all the time, for
she would have it in her power to do me a great deal
of harm if she could prove her identity. I am half
sorry that Ruth doesn't prove to be she, for having
her here, under my eye, I could manage her capitally."

"Why, the papers discussed all that at the time,"
she remarked aloud, with some surprise. "There was
considerable excitement over the affair, and sympathy
was very strong for the niece. Didn't you read about
it?"

"No, I was very much engaged just then, and I did
not read any account of it. There, these bows are
ready, and I will sew them to the dress," Mona con-

cluded, rising to get the garment, but trembling with nervous excitement in every limb.

"Ah!" she added, glancing at her fingers, three of which were stained with blood. "I have pricked myself with my needle; I hope I have not soiled the ribbon. No, fortunately, I have not," as she carefully examined it, "but I will step into the bath-room to wash my hands. I will not be long," and she immediately left the room again. She had purposely run the needle into her delicate flesh to obtain this respite, for she felt as if she could no longer endure the trying conversation.

"Oh, how she has tortured me!" she sobbed, as she swung the door to after her, and dashed from her eyes the tears which she could no longer restrain. "I could not bear it another moment, and I must not give way, even now, or she will see that I am unnerved, but I cannot be wholly wretched now that I know that *Ray loves me!*"

A vivid blush mounted to her brow as she whispered the sweet words, and she dashed the cold water over her burning cheeks to cool them.

"Ah!" she continued; "I judged him wrongfully, and I am sorry. It will be all right if we can but meet again. It must be true that he loved me; he must have confessed it, or his father would not have told Mrs. Montague so."

She hastily dried her face, and hands, then composing herself, returned to Mrs. Montague's room to find her with her dress on and looking very fair and lovely in the delicately tinted blue cashmere, with the soft ruching in the neck and sleeves and the shining satin bows at her waist.

The woman glanced sharply at Mona as she entered.

but, for all that she could see, the sweet face was as
serene as if she were intent only upon her duties as
waiting-maid, instead of thrilling with joy over the
knowledge of being beloved by one whom, until that
hour, she had believed lost to her.

"I will submit her to one more test, and if she can
stand it I shall be satisfied," she said to herself, as
she fastened a beautiful pin at her throat, and then
turned smilingly to Mona, but with the most innocent
air in the world.

"Am I all right, Ruth? Is the dress becoming?"
she asked.

"Exceedingly," Mona returned; "the color is just
suited to you."

"Thank you, I wonder if Mr. Palmer will also think
so. Do you know," with a conscious laugh and forced
blush, but with a covert glance at the girl, "I am becoming very much interested in that gentleman. I
like the son, too, but chiefly for his father's sake. By
the way, young Mr. Palmer is to be here for the ball
on Monday evening; at least his father is going to
telegraph him to come."

"Is he?" said Mona, absently, while she appeared to
be engrossed with something which she had suddenly
discovered about the new morning robe. But the
statement that Ray was coming to Hazeldean had
given her an inward start that made every nerve in
her body bound as if an electric current had been applied to them. "This skirt does not seem to hang just
right," she added, dropping upon her knees, as if to
ascertain the cause. "Ah! it was only caught up—it
is all right now."

She smoothed the folds into place and arose, while,
the breakfast-bell ringing at that moment, Mrs. Mon-

tague passed from the room, very nearly if not quite
satisfied that Ruth Richards was an entirely different
person from Mona Montague.

Poor over-wrought Mona, however, fled into her
own chamber, and locked the door the moment she
was alone.

She sank into the nearest chair, buried her face in
her hands, and fell to sobbing nervously.

"How can I bear it?" she murmured. "It is perfectly dreadful to have to live such a life of deception.
I never would have been guilty of it if I had not been
caught just as I was; but I could not give her my real
name, for she would have known at once who I am;
and I do so want to find out just why my father deserted my mother, and what there was between him
and Uncle Walter that was so terrible. Perhaps I
never shall, but I mean to stay with her for a while
and try. She is a strange woman," the young girl
went on, musingly. "Sometimes I think she is kind
and good, then again she seems like a designing and
unprincipled person. Can it be possible that she is
contemplating an alliance with Mr. Palmer? She certainly received his attentions last evening with every
appearance of pleasure, and he seemed to be equally delighted with her society. I wonder if Ray will like
it? Somehow the thought of it is not agreeable to
me, if—if——"

A vivid blush suffused Mona's cheeks as she reached
this point in her soliloquy, as if she was overcome at
having allowed her thoughts to run away with her to
such an extent.

"So Ray is coming to Hazeldean for the ball on
Monday evening," she continued, after a while.
"Shall I see him? Yes, I shall try to," with an air

of resolution. "If he loves me as well as I love him, why should any foolish sensitiveness prevent my allowing him to make it manifest, if he wishes? I do not believe I have any right to ruin both our lives by hiding myself from him. I will prove him in this way; but I must see him alone, so that no one will know that I am Mona Montague, instead of Ruth Richards, the sewing-girl. What if *he* should ignore me?" she added, with sudden fear and growing very white; then, with renewed confidence: "He will not; if he has been noble enough to confess his feelings to his father, he will not hide them from me. He is noble and true, and I will not doubt him."

CHAPTER XVIII.

"MY DARLING, I LOVE YOU!"

Mr. Palmer, true to his promise to the fair young guests at Hazeldean, telegraphed to Ray the next morning requesting him to come up for the ball on Monday. Later in the day he received a reply from the young man stating that he would do so, although he did not mention the hour when he should arrive.

Thursday, Friday, and Saturday were gay and busy days, for the ball was to be a grand affair, and everybody was anxious to do all possible honor to the occasion and made preparations accordingly.

Mrs. Montague, however, was not so busy but that she managed to spend a good deal of her time with Mr. Palmer, who seemed to renew his youth in her presence, and was so gallant and attentive that the young people, who were exceedingly interested in

watching the progress of this middle-aged romance,
were kept in a constant flutter of amused excitement.
Mr. Wellington and his wife were also considerably
diverted by the affair.

"I'm afraid Palmer is a 'gone goose,'" the gentleman laughingly remarked to his spouse, after they had
retired to their room on Saturday evening.

"It looks like it," the lady returned; "and really,"
she added, with some impatience, "there is something
almost ridiculous to me in seeing an old man like him
dancing attendance upon a gay young widow like Mrs.
Montague."

"*Young!* How old do you imagine her to be?" inquired Mr. Wellington.

"She cannot be much over thirty, and she dresses in
a way to make her look even younger than that," the
lady responded. "At all events, she seems like a mere
girl beside portly, bald-headed Mr. Palmer, and I am
afraid that he will regret it if he allows himself to become entangled in her net."

"I see that you are not in favor of the match," replied Mr. Wellington, much amused over his wife's
earnestness.

"No, Will; I confess I am not," she said, gravely.
"I knew Amos Palmer's first wife, and she was a devoted, care-taking, conscientious woman, never spar-
ing herself when she could add to the comfort and
happiness of her family. But this woman is entirely
different—she cares very little for anything but society. I admit she is very delightful company—a
charming person to have in the house at such a time
as this; but I doubt her ability to make Mr. Palmer
happy, and I never would have believed that he could
have had his head so thoroughly turned by any

woman. I thought he was bound up in making money, to leave to that handsome son of his."

"Well, it appears that Cupid can make fools of the best of us," Mr. Wellington returned, with a roguish glance at his wife; "and we do not discover the fact until the noose is irrevocably knotted about our necks. By the way, speaking of accumulating money makes me remember that Palmer had a telegram to-day, telling him that the detective whom he employed on that affair of the diamonds thinks that he is on the track of the thief at last."

"Is that so?" said Mrs. Wellington, with surprise. "Do you imagine that he will ever recover the stones?"

"He may—some of the larger ones, for they had been submitted to an expert; but I doubt if he ever sees many of them again," her husband replied.

*　　*　　*　　*　　*　　*

During these last two days Mona had been kept steadily employed in performing various duties for Mrs. Montague.

That lady's costume for the ball was to be of great elegance and beauty.

The material was a rich garnet velvet, brocaded in white and gold, with point-lace garniture.

It had not been quite finished before they left New York, and Mona found no little difficulty in setting the many last stitches, for she had had but small experience in finishing garments of any kind, and Mrs. Montague was very particular.

It was quite late in the evening when she completed her task, and, with a sigh of relief, laid the beautiful costume upon the bed, ready for Mrs. Montague's inspection when she should come up stairs for the night.

There was something of regret also mingled with
her feeling that she, too, could not join the festivities
on Monday evening. She had dearly loved society
during the little while she had mingled with it, and
the pleasurable excitement of the last few days, which
kept all the young ladies in a constant flutter, made her
long to be one among them.

It was about half-past two when Mrs. Montague
made her appearance, looking flushed and elated, for
she had just parted from Mr. Palmer, who had begged
her to attend service at the village church with him
the next morning. The request was so impressively
expressed that she imagined her conquest was nearly
complete, and she was therefore in high spirits.

She caught sight of her ball-dress immediately upon
entering the room.

"How lovely it is, Ruth," she remarked, "and you
have arranged the lace very tastefully upon the corsage. I believe it will be exceedingly becoming. I
only wish I could see myself as others will see me on
Monday night, and know just how I am going to look.
Ruth," she added, suddenly, as if inspired with a
bright idea, "you are about my height; suppose you
put on the dress and let me get just the effect; that
is, if you are not too tired and do not mind being made
a show figure, here all by ourselves."

Mona smiled slightly over the woman's vanity, but
she was willing to oblige, and so signified her readiness to put the dress on, and in less than ten minutes
she had metamorphosed herself from the quiet, retir-
ing sewing-girl into a brilliant society belle.

The dress was a trifle loose for her, yet it was not
a bad fit, while her pure neck and arms were as white
as the costly lace, which fell in soft folds over them.

Mrs. Montague marveled at the exquisite fairness of her skin, and told herself that she had never realized, until that moment, how very beautiful her young seamstress was.

"You must put everything on, even to the jewels that I shall wear," she said, bringing a large case from one of her trunks, and exhibiting an almost childish eagerness to get the full effect of her costume.

She opened the case, and taking a diamond necklace of great beauty and value from it, clasped it about the girl's milk-white neck. Then she fastened some fine solitaires in her small ears; three or four pins, each having a blazing stone for its head, were tucked amid the glossy braids of her hair, and two glittering snakes were wound about her beautifully rounded arms.

"Now for the fan, and you will be complete," cried Mrs. Montague, as she brought an exquisite affair composed of white ostrich tips, with a bird of Paradise nestling in its center, and handed it to Mona.

Then she stood off to admire the *tout ensemble,* and just at that moment there came a tap upon her door.

She went immediately to open it, and found her nephew standing outside.

"I've come for the money, Aunt Margie," he said. "I thought I'd better have it to-night, since I am going to town on the early train, and did not like to disturb you in the morning."

"Very well, I will get it for you, and I hope that Madame Millaise will have the mantle ready for you, for I must have it on Monday evening to throw over my shoulders after dancing," Mrs. Montague responded, as she turned back to get her purse.

She was on the point of closing the door, for she

did not care to have her nephew know what was going
on within the room. But Mr. Louis Hamblin was very
keen. He knew from her manner that something unusual was occurring, and so he boldly pushed on after
her, and entered the chamber before she was aware
of his intention.

He stopped suddenly, however, the moment he had
crossed the threshold, stricken with astonishment, as
his glance rested upon Mona.

He had known that the girl was unusually lovely, but
he was not quite prepared to see such a vision of
beauty as now greeted his eyes.

"Jove! Aunt Marg, isn't she a stunner?" he cried,
under his breath. "You won't see one at the ball
Monday night that can hold a candle to her!"

Mona had flushed a vivid scarlet when he had so
unceremoniously forced his way into the room; but
at his bold compliment she turned haughtily away
from his gaze with the air of an offended queen.

Her bearing, though full of scorn, was replete with
grace and dignity, while the voluminous train of the
rich dress made her slender form seem even taller and
more regal than it really was.

Mrs. Montague had been no less impressed with the
young girl's beauty, but it would have affected her
no more than that of a wax figure would have done
had no one else been present to remark it. Now, however, at Louis' high praise, a feeling of envy sprang
up in her heart, and a frown of annoyance gathered
on her brow.

"I wish you would go out, Louis," she said, sharply.
"It is very rude of you to thus force yourself into my
room."

"Come now, Aunt Marg, that's a good one, when

all my life I have been in the habit of running in and out of your room, to do your bidding like a lackey," the young man retorted, mockingly. "But really this is an unexpected treat," he added, wickedly. "Miss Richards, in these fine togs, is the most beautiful woman that I have ever seen. And—'pon my word, Aunt Marg, I really believe she looks like——"

"Louis!" came in a sharp, warning cry from Mrs. Montague's lips, as she wheeled around upon him, her blazing eyes having a dangerous gleam in them.

"Like—a *picture* that I have seen somewhere," he quietly finished, but with a meaning smile and intonation. "How you do snap a fellow up, Aunt Margie! Here, give me the money, and I will clear out before another blast!"

Mrs. Montague handed him a roll of bills, telling him in an icy tone to be sure and get back as early as possible on Monday; and then, as he beat a retreat before her offended looks, she sharply shut the door upon him.

"Take off that dress!" she abruptly commanded of Mona.

Deeply wounded by her ungracious tone, as well as indignant at what had just occurred, the fair girl quickly divested herself of the costly apparel, and then, wishing the woman a quiet good-night, withdrew to her own room.

But nothing could make her very unhappy with the glad refrain that was continually ringing in her heart:

"Ray is coming! I shall see him!" she kept saying over and over. All other emotions were swallowed up in the joy of this, and she was soon sleeping the sweet, restful sleep of youth and dreaming of the one she loved.

But Mrs. Montague was terribly excited when she found herself alone.

"I should never have thought of it if Louis had not spoken, I was so absorbed in the costume," she muttered, as she stood in the middle of the floor and tried to compose herself. "I could almost swear that she was Mona come back to life. She looked almost exactly as she did that night in Paris—shall I ever forget it?—when I *told* her, and she drew herself up in that proud way; and *she* had a garnet dress on, too. She *does* look wonderfully like that picture! Louis was quick to see it, and I will have it destroyed when I return to New York. I can't imagine why I have kept it all these years. Ugh! I feel almost as if I had seen a ghost."

She shook herself, as if to dispel these uncanny thoughts, and then disrobing, retired to rest.

Sunday was a lovely day—more mild and springlike even than the previous ones had been.

Some of the guests at Hazeldean went to Rhinebeck to attend the morning service, Mr. Palmer and Mrs. Montague among the number; but most of them remained within doors until evening, when Mr. Wellington, their host, requested, as a favor, that all would attend a special service at one of the village churches, where a college friend was to preach, and he wished to give him as large an audience as possible. He also hinted, with a gleam of mischief in his eyes, that they would do well to take their pocket-books along, as a collection would be taken to help to pay for a new organ which the society had just purchased.

It was a glorious evening, and, everybody appearing to partake of the enthusiasm of the host, the whole party set out to walk to the church.

No one thought of asking Mona to go, and thus the young girl was left entirely alone in the house, except for the servants, who were by themselves in the basement.

She was very lonely, and felt both sad and depressed, as she saw the party pass out of sight down the avenue, and for a moment she was tempted to rebel against her hard lot, and the neglect of others, who might at least have remembered that she had a soul to be benefited by Sabbath services as well as they.

She even shed a few tears of regret, for she was young and buoyant, and would dearly have loved to join that gay company of youths and maidens, if she could have done so as an equal.

But after a few moments she bravely wiped away the crystal drops, saying:

"I will not grieve; I will not give up to *anything* until I have seen Ray. If *he* is true, the world will be bright, though everybody else gives me the cold shoulder—and he will be here to-morrow. But I *am* a trifle lonely, all by myself in this great house. I believe I will run down to the music-room and play for a little while. No one is here to be disturbed by it, and I shall not be afraid of critics."

So she went slowly down the dimly lighted stairs to a room on the right of the hall, where, without even turning up the gas, she seated herself at the piano.

The "dim religious light" was rather pleasant to her, in her tender mood, and she could see well enough for her purpose.

She ran her skilled fingers lightly over the keys of the sweet-toned instrument, and almost immediately her whole soul began to wake up to the rich harmony which she evoked.

She played a few selections from Beethoven's "Songs Without Words," sang a ballad or two, and was just upon the point of getting up to look for a book of Sabbath hymns, when a step behind her caused her to turn to ascertain who was intruding upon her solitude.

She saw standing in the doorway leading from the hall, a tall form clad in a long overcoat and holding his hat in his hand.

She could not distinguish his features, but courteously arose to go forward to see who the stranger was, when he spoke, and his tones thrilled her instantly to the very center of her being.

"Pardon me," he began. "I rang the bell, but no one answered it, and, the door being ajar, I ventured to enter. Can you tell me—— Ah!—*Mona!*"

The speaker had also advanced into the room as he spoke, but the light was too dim for him to recognize its occupant until he reached her side, although she had known him the instant he spoke.

His start and exclamation of surprise, the glad, almost exultant tone as he uttered her name, told the fair girl all she needed to know to prove that Ray Palmer was loyal to her, in spite of all the reverses of fortune, of friends, of position, and to prove him the noble character she had always believed him to be.

He stretched forth an eager hand, and grasped hers with a fervor which told her how deeply he was moved to find her, even before his words confirmed it.

"Oh! I *have* not made a mistake, have I?" he asked, bending his luminous face closer to hers, eager to read a welcome there. "I *have* found you—*at last?*

If you knew—if I could tell you—— But first tell *me* that you are glad to see me," he concluded, somewhat incoherently.

Mona's hand lay unresisting in his clasp, and a feeling of restful peace filled her heart, as she lifted her glad face to him.

"No, you have made no mistake—it is I, Mona Montague, and I am very"—with a little sob of joy, which she could not control—"very glad to see you again, Mr. Palmer."

"My darling!" he said, made bold by her look, her tone, but more by the little sob, which his own heart told him how to interpret. "Tell me yet more—I cannot wait—I have been so hungry for the sight of your dear face, for the sound of your voice, and I thought that I had lost you. I love you, Mona, with all my heart and strength, and this unexpected meeting has so overcome me that the truth must be told. Are you still 'glad'?—will you make *me* glad by telling me so?"

"But—Mr. Palmer——" Mona began, tremulously, hardly able to credit her ears, hardly able to believe that this great and almost overwhelming joy was a reality, and not some illusive dream. "I am afraid you forget——"

"What have I forgotten?" he gently asked, but without releasing her hand.

"That my uncle is gone. I have no home, friends, position! Do you know——"

"I know that you are Mona Montague—that I *love* you, and that I have *found* you," he interrupted, his own voice quivering with repressed emotion, his strong frame trembling with eager longing, mingled with something of fear that his suit might be rejected.

"Then I *am* glad," breathed Mona, and the next

moment she was folded close to Raymond Palmer's manly bosom, where she could feel the beating of the strong, true, loyal heart of her lover while with his lips pressed upon her silken hair he murmured fond words which betrayed how deep and absorbing his affection was for her—how he had longed for her and how bitterly he had suffered because he could not find her.

CHAPTER XIX.

MONA IS JOYFULLY SURPRISED.

"Then you do love me, Mona?" Ray whispered, fondly, after a moment or two of happy silence. "I must hear you say it even though you have tacitly confessed it and my heart exults in the knowledge. I cannot be quite satisfied until I have the blessed confirmation from your own lips."

"You certainly can have no reason to doubt it after such a betrayal as this," Mona tried to say playfully, to shield her embarrassment, as she lifted her flushed face from its resting-place, and shot a glad, bright look into his eyes. Then she added in a grave though scarcely audible voice: "Yes I *do* love you with all my heart!"

The young man smiled; then with his arm still infolding her he led her beneath the chandelier and turned on a full blaze of light.

"I must read the glad story in your eyes," he said, tenderly, as he bent to look into them. "I must see it shining in your face. Ah, love, how beautiful you are still! And yet there is a sad droop to these lips"

—and he touched them softly with his own—"that pains me; there is a heaviness about these eyes which tells of trial and sorrow. My darling, you have needed comfort and sympathy, while I was bound hand and foot, and could not come to you. What did you think of me, dear? But you knew, of course."

"I knew—I hoped there was some good reason," faltered Mona, with downcast eyes.

"You 'hoped!' Then you *did* think—you *feared* that I, like other false friends, had turned the cold shoulder on you in your trouble?" he returned, a sorrowful reproach in his tone. "Surely you have known about the stolen diamonds?"

"Yes, I knew that your father had been robbed."

"And about my having been kidnapped also—the papers were full of the story."

Mona looked up, astonished.

"Kidnapped!" she exclaimed. "No; this is the first that I have heard of that."

"Where have you been that you have not seen the papers?" Ray inquired, wonderingly.

"As you doubtless know," Mona replied, "Uncle Walter died very suddenly the day after I attended the opera with you, and for a fortnight afterward I was so overcome with grief and—other troubles, that I scarcely looked at a paper. After that, one day, I saw a brief item referring to the robbery, and it is only since I came here that I had even a hint that you had been ill."

"Come, then, dear, and let me tell you about it, and then I am sure you will absolve me from all willful neglect," Ray said, as he led her to a *tête-à-tête* and seated himself beside her. "But first tell me," he

added, "how I happen to find you nere.   Are you one
of the guests?"

"No," Mona said, blushing slightly.   "You know,
of course, that I lost home and everything else when
I lost Uncle Walter, and now I am simply acting as
seamstress and waiting maid to a Mrs. Montague,
who is a guest here."

"Ah!" exclaimed the young man, with a start, as
he remembered how Mrs. Montague had denied all
knowledge of Mona.   "I have met the lady—is she
a relative of yours?"

"No; at least, I never saw her until I entered her
house to serve her."

"My poor child! to think that you should have to
go out to do such work," said Ray, with tender regret.   "But of course, as you say, I can understand all
about it, for that, too, was in the papers; but it was
very heartless, very cruel in that Mrs. Dinsmore not
to make you any allowance, when she could not fail
to know that your uncle wished you to inherit his
property.   She must be a very obnoxious sort of person, isn't she?"

"I do not know," said Mona, with a sigh; "I have
never seen her—at least, not since I was a child, and
too young to remember anything about her."

"Do you mean that you did not meet her during the
contest for Mr. Dinsmore's fortune?" questioned Ray
in surprise.

"No, she did not appear at all personally; all her
business was transacted through her lawyer, as mine
was through Mr. Graves," Mona answered.

"Well, it was an inhuman thing for her to do, to
take everything and leave you penniless, and obliged
to earn your own living.   But that is all over now,"

the young man said, looking fondly into the fair face beside him. "Isn't it, darling? You have told me that you love me, but you have not yet promised me anything. You are going to be my wife, are you not, Mona?"

"I hope so—if you wish—some time," she answered, naively, yet with crimson cheeks and downcast eyes.

He laughed out gladly as he again embraced her.

"'Some time, if I wish,'" he repeated. "Well, I do wish, and the some time must be very soon, too. Ah, my sweet, brown-eyed girlie! how happy I am at this moment! I did not dream that I was to find such a wealth of joy when I came hither at my father's earnest request. I was grieving so for you I had no heart for the gayeties which I knew I should find here; now, however, I shall not find it difficult to be as gay as any one. How glad I am, too, that I came to-night to find you here alone. My father does not expect me until to-morrow; but I had a matter of importance to talk over with him, so ran up on the evening train. But I am forgetting that I have a thrilling story to tell you."

He then related all that had occurred in connection with the bold diamond robbery and his imprisonment and subsequent illness in Doctor Wesselhoff's retreat for nervous patients, while Mona listened with wonder-wide eyes and a paling cheek, as she realized the danger through which her lover had passed.

"What an audacious scheme!" she exclaimed, when he concluded. "How could any woman dare to plan, much less put it into execution! No wonder that you were ill, and you must have been very sick, for you are still thin and pale," Mona said, regarding him anxiously.

"I shall now soon outgrow that," Ray responded, smiling. "It was chiefly anxiety and unhappiness on your account that kept me thin and pale. You will see how quickly I shall recover my normal condition now that I have found you and know that you are all my own. Now tell me all about your own troubles, my darling. Do you know, it seems an age to me since we parted that night at your uncle's door, and you gave me permission to call upon you? My intention then was to seek an interview with Mr. Dinsmore within a day or two, tell him of my love for you, and ask his permission to address you. But, even had no misfortune overtaken me, I could not have done so, since he was stricken that very night; but at least I could have come to you with words of sympathy."

Mona then gave him a detailed account of all that had happened during those dark days, when her only friend lay dead and she felt as if all the world had forsaken her.

"Mona," the young man gravely said, when she had finished her story, "I shall tell my father to-night of this interview—he already knows that I love you—and ask his sanction to our immediate marriage, for I cannot have you remain here among my friends and acquaintances another day in the capacity of a seamstress or waiting-maid."

"But, Ray——" Mona began, then she stopped short, blushing rosily at having thus involuntarily called him by his Christian name. She had always thought of him thus, and it passed her lips before she was aware of it.

He laughed out, amused at her confusion.

"There, dear, you have broken the ice almost without knowing it," he said; "now we shall get on nicely if you do not let it freeze over again; but what were you going to say?"

"I was going to ask you not to speak of—of our relations to each other to any one just yet," Mona returned, with some embarrassment.

"Why not?" Ray demanded, astonished, and looking troubled by the request.

"There are reasons why I must remain for a while longer with Mrs. Montague," said the young girl.

"Not in the capacity of waiting-maid," Ray asserted, decidedly; "I cannot allow that."

"Indeed I must, Ray," Mona persisted, but with an appealing note in her voice; "and I will tell you why. I told you that Mrs. Montague was no relative; she is not really, and yet—she was my father's second wife."

"Mona! you astonish me," cried her lover, regarding her wonderingly.

"It is true, and there is some mystery connected with my own mother and my early history which I am exceedingly anxious to learn. Uncle Walter told me something of it only the day before he died; but I am very sure that he kept back certain portions of the story which I ought to know, and which he was also anxious to tell me when he was dying, and could not. I have no means even of proving my identity; if I had, I suppose that I could claim some of this wealth of which Mrs. Montague appears to have abundance, and I am sure that she has some proof in her possession. I want to get it, and that is why I am anxious to remain with her a little longer. Let me tell you everything," Mona went on, hurriedly, as Ray seemed about to utter another protest to her wish. "As I understand the story, my father was dependent upon a rich aunt who wished him to marry the present Mrs.

Montague; but he, being in love with my mother, was opposed to so doing, although he was anxious to secure the fortune. As he was about to start on a European tour he married my mother and took her with him, none of his friends apparently suspecting the union.

"Now comes a part of the story which I cannot understand. They traveled for several months; but, while in Paris, my father suddenly disappeared, and my mother, believing herself deserted, in her pride and humiliation, immediately left the city, doubtless with the intention of returning to America. She was taken ill in London, however, and there, a few months later, I was born, and she died only a few hours afterward. Uncle Walter heard of her sad condition, and hastened to her, but was three days too late, and found only a poor weak infant upon whom to expend his love and care. It seems very strange to me that she did not write to him at the time she fled from Paris; but I suppose, since she had eloped with and been secretly married to my father, she was too proud and sensitive to appeal to any one. Later, my father married this Miss Barton to please his aunt and secure the fortune which he so much desired. I do not know anything about his after-life. I questioned Uncle Walter, but he would not talk about him—the most that he would tell me was that he was dead, but how, or when he died, I could never learn, and I do not know as there even exists any proof of his legal marriage with my mother, although my uncle confidentially asserted that she was his lawful wife. I believe, however, that such proofs do exist and that they are in Mrs. Montague's possession."

Mona then proceeded to relate how she had happened to secure the position she now occupied.

"It seems very strange," she said, "that fate should have thrown me thus into her home, and somehow I have a suspicion that she must have been concerned in the great wrong done my mother—that it was because of her influence that my father never owned nor provided for me. And now," Mona continued, flushing a deep crimson, "I am obliged to confess something of which I am somewhat ashamed. When I found myself in Mrs. Montague's home, and had resolved to remain, I knew that she would instantly suspect my identity if I should give her my true name. This, of course, I did not wish her to do, and so when she asked me what she should call me, I told her 'Ruth Richards.' The name Ruth really belongs to me, but Richards is assumed. Now, Ray, you can understand why I do not wish to have Mrs. Montague undeceived regarding my identity, as she must be if you insist upon at once proclaiming our relations. I am very strongly impressed that she knows the secret of my father's desertion of my mother, and also that she could prove, if she would, that I am the child of their legal marriage."

Ray Palmer had grown very grave while listening to Mona's story, and when she spoke of her assumed name it was evident, from the frown on his brow, that he did not approve of having her hide herself from the world in any such way.

"Why not ask her outright, then?" inquired this straightforward young man, as the young girl concluded.

"That would never do at all," said Mona. "Uncle Walter told me that she hated my mother, and me a hundred-fold on her account, and she would not be very likely to put any proofs into my hands, especially when they would be liable to be very detrimental to her own interests."

"True, I did not think of that," returned Ray, thoughtfully. "But how do you expect to obtain possession of these proofs, even if she has them, and how long must I wait for you?" he gloomily added.

"I do not know, Ray," she answered, with a sigh. "I do not see my way very clearly. I keep hoping, and something seems to hold me to this position in spite of myself. Let me remain three or six months longer; then if I do not succeed——"

"I will concede three months, but no more," Ray interposed, decidedly; then added: "What does it matter whether you know all this history or not? It cannot be anything of vital importance, or that will affect your future in any way. I wish you would let me speak to my father and announce our engagement at once, my darling."

"Nay, please, Ray, let me have my way in this," Mona pleaded, with crimson cheeks. She could not tell him that she felt sensitive about becoming his wife until she could have absolute proof of the legal marriage of her father and mother.

He bent down and looked earnestly into her face.

"Mona, is that the only reason why you wish to wait? You do not shrink from our union from any doubt of your own heart—of your love for me, or mine for you?" he gravely asked.

"No, indeed, Ray," and she put out both her hands to him, with an eagerness that entirely reassured him even before she added: "I cannot tell you how glad, how restful, how content I am since your coming to-night. I was so lonely and sorrowful, the future looked so dark and cheerless because I feared I had lost you; but now all is bright."

She dropped her face again upon his breast to hide the blushes this confession had called up, and the happy tears also that were dropping from her long lashes.

He gathered her close to his heart, thrilling at her words.

"Then I will try to be patient for three months, love," he murmured, "and meantime I suppose you will have to be Ruth Richards to me. as well as to others."

"Yes, it will not do to have my real name known— that will spoil all," Mona replied, with a sigh, for her truthful soul recoiled with as much aversion from all deception as he possibly could do.

"And am I not to see you during all this time?" Ray ruefully asked.

"Oh, yes; not to see you would be unbearable to me," Mona responded quickly. "Can you not manage to have some one introduce me to you as Miss Richards while you are here? then neither Mrs. Montague nor any one else would think it strange if you should seek me occasionally; only——"

"Only what?" inquired the young man, wondering to see her color so vividly and appear so embarrassed.

"Perhaps I should not tell you," Mona said, with some hesitation, "and yet you must learn the fact sooner or later from some other sources; but Mrs. Montague appears to be growing quite fond of your father, who is very attentive to her, and she might not exactly like——"

"She might not like to have the son of the man for

whom she is angling to pay attention to her seamstress, is what you were going to say?" Ray interposed, laughing, yet with a look of annoyance sweeping over his fine face.

"Something like it, perhaps," Mona responded,
flushing again.

"Well, I do not believe she is going to land her
fish, if you will pardon the slang phrase," said the
young man, confidently. "My father has successfully
resisted the allurements of the gentler sex for too
many years to succumb at this late day; so you and
I need give ourselves no uneasiness upon that score.
Does he know you as Ruth Richards?"

"Yes, if indeed he knows me at all. I have received
no introduction to him, and I only knew him from
hearing Mr. Wellington greet him and inquire regarding the lost diamonds," Mona explained. Then
she added: "Do you expect to recover them, Ray?
have you any clew?"

"Yes, we have a slight one, we think, and that is
one reason why I am here to-night. The detective
in our employ sent a telegram to my father yesterday mentioning the fact, but he thought it best for
me to come up to-night and talk the matter over more
fully with him, and hurry him back to New York
early on Tuesday morning. A woman is being shad-
owed upon the suspicion of having committed a bold
swindle in Chicago, and Mr. Rider thinks, without
any doubt, that she is the same person who so cleverly
did us out of our diamonds."

"Hark! please," said Mona, as just then she caught
the sound of voices in the distance, "the party is returning from evening service, and I must not be
found here with you."

"I am loath to let you go, my brown-eyed sweet-heart," Ray tenderly responded.

"And I to go," Mona answered softly, "but it is best that I should; we must both be judicious for a while—we must not be too exacting when we have had this great new happiness come to us so unexpectedly," and she lifted her luminous eyes to him.

He clasped her to him again.

"Good-night, my darling," he said; then with one lingering kiss upon her lips, he let her go, and she stole softly up stairs, with a joyous heart and step, while Ray drew a paper from his pocket, and was apparently deeply absorbed in its contents when the party entered the house.

A good deal of surprise was expressed when his arrival was discovered, and he was accorded a warm welcome by the host and hostess as well as by every guest.

CHAPTER XX.

MR. RIDER MAKES AN ARREST.

While the festivities were in progress at Hazeldean, some incidents of a somewhat singular character were occurring in New York.

It will be remembered that Mr. Palmer and his son met Mrs. Montague for the first time at the reception given by Mrs. Merrill; also that their attention was attracted to a lady who wore a profusion of unusually fine diamonds—a Mrs. Vanderheck.

We know how Ray was introduced to her, and repeated her name as Vander*beck,* with an emphasis on

the beck; how she started, changed color, and glanced
at him curiously as he did so, and seemed strangely
ill at ease while conversing with him afterward, and
a little later abruptly took her leave.

The next day, the young man communicated these
suspicious circumstances to the private detective whom
his father had employed to look up his stolen diamonds, and from that time Mrs. Vanderheck had been
under close surveillance by that shrewd official.

Mr. Rider was a very energetic man, and, by dint
of adroit inquiries and observations, learned that she
was a woman who devoted most of her time to social
life—was very gay, very fond of dress and excitement of every kind. She did not, however, resemble
in any way the Mrs. Vanderbeck who had conducted
the robbery of the Palmer diamonds, although, he
argued, she might easily enough be an accomplice.

The detective interviewed Doctor Wesselhoff, who
was now as eager as any one to assist in the discovery
of those who so imposed upon him, and obtained a
minute description of the other woman who had arranged for Ray Palmer to become an inmate of his
institution, and he thought that possibly by the aid
of a clever disguise, Mrs. Vanderheck might have
figured as Mrs. Walton, the pretended mother of the
pretended monomaniac.

Consequently, energetic Mr. Rider had followed
close upon her track, bound to discover her real character.

She resided in a fine brown-stone mansion up town;
sported an elegant carriage and a spanking pair of
bays, and, to all appearances, possessed an unlimited
bank account.

She was sometimes attended on her drives by a

gentleman, many years older than herself, who appeared to be something of an invalid, and who, as far as the detective could learn, was engaged in no business whatever.

These latter facts increased his suspicions, for the reason that the woman who had robbed Mr. Palmer had wished to submit her selections to the sanction of an invalid husband.

Disguised as a spruce young coachman, Mr. Rider managed to ingratiate himself with a pretty, but rather vain young servant-girl in Mrs. Vanderheck's employ, and by means of well-turned compliments, re-enforced now and then with some pretty gift, he managed to keep himself well posted regarding the mistress' movements and her social engagements, and then he diligently followed up his espionage by frequenting the many receptions and balls which she attended.

At these places she was always magnificently attired and seldom wore any ornaments except diamonds, of which she appeared to possess an endless store, and all were of great beauty and value.

It was at a Delmonico ball, which was given in honor of a person of royal descent, and on the Friday evening preceding Ray Palmer's visit to Hazeldean, that Mr. Rider found his plans ripe for action and accomplished his great *coup de grâce*.

He had learned, through the pretty servant-girl, that Mrs. Vanderheck was to grace the occasion with her presence and was to be attired in a costume of unusual richness and elegance—"with diamonds enough to blind you," the lively and voluble Fanny had boasted to her admirer.

Consequently the detective got himself up in elab-

orate style, obtained a ticket for the ball by some
means best known to himself, and, when the festivities were at their height, slipped in upon the brilliant
scene.

He was not long in "spotting" his prey, who was
conspicuous in white brocaded velvet and white ostrich
tips, while her person was literally ablaze with diamonds.

"Great Scott!" the man muttered, as he ran his keen
eye over her gorgeous attire; "it is a mystery to me
how any woman dare wear such a fortune upon her
person; she is liable to be murdered any day. Why,
she—— Aha!"

His heart gave a sudden leap, and for a moment,
as he afterward described his sensations, it seemed
as if some one had struck him on the head with a
club, for he actually saw stars and grew so dizzy and
confused that he could scarcely stand; for—*in the
woman's ears he caught sight of a gleaming pair of
crescents!*

He soon recovered himself, however, and took a
second look. He had, as we know, been looking for
those peculiar ornaments for more than three years,
and now he had found them, as he had always believed he should, upon a gay woman of fashion in the
midst of fashionable admirers.

It did not take him long to decide upon his course
of action, and he was now again the cool and collected detective, although the fierce glitter in his eyes
betrayed some relentless purpose in his mind.

He made his way quietly into a corner, where he
stood covertly watching the brilliant woman, and
comparing her appearance with a description that was

written in cipher upon some tablets which he took from his pocket.

"'Very attractive, about twenty-eight or thirty years, rather above medium height, somewhat inclined toward *embonpoint*, fair complexion, blue eyes, short, curling red hair,'—Hum!" he softly interposed at this point, "she answers very well to all except the red hair; but drop a red wig over her light-colored pate, tint her eyebrows and lashes with the same color, and I'll wager my badge against a last year's hat we'd have the Bently widow complete. There can be no doubt about the crescents, though, and that cross on her bosom looks wonderfully like the one that Palmer described to me. I suppose she thought no one would be on the lookout for it here, and she could safely wear it with all the rest. I always said the same woman put up both jobs," he interposed, with a satisfied chuckle. "Guess I'll take a nearer look at the stones, though, before I do anything desperate."

He put up his tablets, and began to move slowly about the rooms; but his eagle eye never once left the form of the woman in white brocaded velvet.

Three hours later, Mrs. Vanderheck, wrapped in an elegant circular of crimson satin, bordered with ermine, and attended by her maid and a dignified policeman as a body-guard, swept down the grand stair-way leading from the ball-room to the street, on her way to her carriage.

As she stepped out across the pavement and was about to enter the vehicle, a quiet, gentlemanly looking person approached her and saluted her respectfully.

"Madame—Mrs. Vander*beck*," with an intentional emphasis on the last syllable, "you are my prisoner!"

The woman gave a violent start as she caught the

name, and darted a keen glance of inquiry at him, all of which Mr. Rider was quick to note.

Then she drew herself up haughtily.

"Sir, I do not know you, and my name is not Vander*beck;* you have made a mistake," she said, icily.

"I have made no mistake. You are the woman I have been looking for, for more than three years, whether you spell your name with a *b,* an *h,* or in a different way altogether; and I repeat—you are my prisoner."

Mr. Rider laid his hand firmly but respectfully on her arm, as he ceased speaking, to enforce his meaning.

She shook him off impatiently.

"What is the meaning of this strange proceeding?" she demanded, indignantly; then turning to the policeman who attended her, she continued, in a voice of command: "I appeal to you for protection against such insolence."

"How is this, Rider?" now inquired the officer, who recognized the detective, and was astonished beyond measure by this unexpected arrest.

"She has on her person diamonds that I have been looking for, for over three years, and I cannot afford to let them slip through my fingers after such a hunt as that," the detective quietly explained.

"It is false!" the woman stoutly and indignantly asserted. "I wear no jewelry that is not my own property. Everything I have was either given to me or purchased with my husband's money."

"I trust you will be able to prove the truth of your assertions, madame," Mr. Rider quietly returned. "If you can do so, you will, of course, have no further trouble. But I must do my duty. I have been employed to search for a pair of diamond crescents which properly belong to a person in Chicago. I have seen such a pair in your ears to-night. You also wear a cross like one that I am searching for, and I shall be obliged to take you into custody until the matter can be properly investigated."

Mrs. Vanderheck was evidently very much startled and upset by this information, yet she behaved with remarkable fortitude, considering the trying circumstances.

"What am I to do?" she inquired, again appealing to the policeman attending her. "The crescents he mentions are *mine*—I bought them almost three years ago in Boston. Of course, I know that I must prove my statement, and I think I can if you will give me time, for I believe I still have the bill of sale in my possession. I will look it up, and if"—turning to the detective—"you will call upon me some time to-morrow you shall have it."

Mr. Rider smiled, for the unsophisticated suggestion amused him immensely.

"I cannot lose sight of you, madame," he said, courteously. "What you have said may be true; I shall be glad, on your account, if it proves so; but my duty to others must be rigidly enforced, and so I am obliged to arrest you."

"But *I* cannot submit to an *arrest;* you surely do not mean that I—a woman in *my* position—am to be imprisoned on the charge of *theft!*" exclaimed the woman, growing deadly white.

"The law is no respecter of persons or position, madame," laconically responded the detective.

"What *can I* do?" Mrs. Vanderheck cried, in a tone of despair.

"Rider, I am afraid you have made a mistake," the policeman now remarked, in a low tone; "the woman is all right. I've acted as escort for her on such occasions as these for the last two years."

The detective looked astonished and somewhat perplexed at this statement.

If Mrs. Vanderheck had led a respectable life in New York for two years, and was as well known to this officer as he represented, he also began to fear that he might have made a mistake.

"You are willing to defer the arrest if she can furnish ample security for her appearance when wanted?", the policeman asked, after a moment of thought.

"Ye-es; but responsible parties must vouch for her," Mr. Rider answered, with some hesitation.

The woman seized the suggestion with avidity.

"Oh, then, I have a dozen friends who will serve me," she cried, eagerly. "Come back to the ball-room with me and you shall have security to any amount," and with a haughty air she turned back and entered the brilliantly lighted building which she had recently left.

The policeman conducted them into a small reception-room, and Mrs. Vanderheck sent her card, with a few lines penciled on it, to a well-known banker, who was among the guests in the ball-room, requesting a few moments' personal conversation with him.

The gentleman soon made his appearance, and was greatly astonished and no less indignant upon being informed of what had occurred.

But he readily understood that the matter in hand must be legally settled before the lady could be fully acquitted. He therefore unhesitatingly gave security for her to the amount required by the detective, but politely refused to receive, as a guarantee of her integrity, the costly ornaments which Mrs. Vander-heck offered him then and there for the service so kindly rendered.

She, then, without a murmur, delivered over to the detective, in the presence of her friend, the police-man, and her maid, the contested crescents and cross, and was then allowed to take her departure, with her attendants, without further ceremony.

Early the next morning the following message went flashing over the Western wires to Chicago, addressed thus:

"To JUSTIN CUTLER, ESQ.:—Crescents found. Come at once to identify. Bring bogus ones.
"RIDER."

The detective then sought Mr. Palmer, but upon being informed that he was out of town, and would not return until the early part of the coming week, he related to Ray what had happened on the previous evening, and advised him to communicate the fact as soon as possible, to his father, and notify him that an examination would take place at ten o'clock on the following Tuesday.

Ray had already telegraphed, in answer to his fa-ther's message, that he would come to Hazeldean on Monday for the ball, and at first he thought he would make no change in his plans. The news was good news, and would keep for a day or two, he told himself.

But the detective's enthusiasm over the arrest was so contagious, he found himself wishing that his fa-ther could also know what had occurred.

He had an engagement for that evening—which was Saturday—so he could not go to Hazeldean that day, and finally contented himself by commissioning Mr. Rider to drop Mr. Palmer a message, giving him a hint of the arrest, and then arranged to go himself to explain more fully, by the Sunday evening train.

It almost seemed as if fate had purposely arranged it thus, that he might find Mona alone as he did, to declare his love, and win in return the confession of her affection for him.

The moment his father entered the house and met him, on his return from the evening service at the village, he realized that some great change had come over him; he was very different from the depressed, anxious-eyed son whom he had left only a few days previous.

He could hardly attribute it entirely to the news of the arrest of the supposed thief of the diamonds, and yet he could think of nothing else, for he firmly believed that Walter Dinsmore's niece had left New York after her uncle's death, and he had no reason to believe that Ray had found trace of her.

But whatever had caused the change—whatever had served to bring back the old light to his eyes, the old smile to his lips, and all his former brightness and energy of manner, he was grateful for it, and he hailed the result with a delight that made itself manifest in the hearty grip of his hand and his eager-toned:

"How are you, Ray, my boy? I am glad to see you."

CHAPTER XXI.

MONA AND RAY HAVE ANOTHER INTERVIEW.

Mona was very happy as she went up to her room after her interview with Ray that eventful Sunday evening, during the early part of which life had seemed darker than usual to her.

The man whom she loved was true, in spite of the doubt and sorrow she had experienced over his apparent neglect. She had not after all built her hopes upon shifting sand; she had not reared an idol in her heart only to have to hurl it from its shrine as false and worthless. Oh, no; her lover was a man to be reverenced—to be proud of, and to be trusted under all circumstances.

She exulted in these facts almost as much as in the knowledge of his love for her, and she dropped to sleep with joy in her heart, smiles on her lips, and tears of gratitude flashing like diamonds on her long brown lashes.

The next morning she seemed almost like a new creature. The world had suddenly acquired a wonderful brightness and beauty, and it was a delight even to exist.

It was no hardship to be a seamstress or even a waiting-maid, so long as she was blessed with Raymond Palmer's love and with the prospect of becoming his wife in the near future.

Involuntarily a gay little song rippled from her lips while she was dressing, and the unusual sound catching Mrs. Montague's ear caused a look of sur-

prise to sweep over her face, for she had never heard
Ruth Richards sing so much as a note before.

"The girl has a sweet, flexible voice. I wonder
if she is going to surprise me, every now and then,
with some new accomplishment! Maybe I have an
embryo *prima-donna* in my employ!" she muttered,
with a scornful smile.

Her surprise was not diminished when she saw the
happy girl with her bright and animated manners and
the new love-light shining on her face, making it
almost dazzling in its intensified loveliness.

"What has come over you, Ruth?" Mrs. Montague
inquired, regarding her curiously. "One would almost
imagine you were going to the ball yourself to-night,
you appear to be so happy and elated."

"I believe there must be something unusually ex-
hilarating in the atmosphere," Mona replied, a gleeful
little laugh rippling over her smiling lips, although she
blushed beneath the woman's searching look. "Don't
you think that excitement is sometimes infectious?—
and surely everybody has been active and gay for
days. I like to see people happy, and then the morning is perfectly lovely."

Truly the world was all *couleur de rose* to her since
love's elixir had given a new impetus to her heart-
pulses!

Mrs. Montague frowned slightly, for somehow the
girl's unusual mood annoyed her.

She could not forget her exceeding loveliness on
Saturday evening, when she had been arrayed in the
festal robe which she herself was to wear at the ball,
and the memory of it nettled her.

Perhaps, she thought, Ruth remembered it also, and
was secretly exulting over the fact of her own beauty.

Exceedingly vain herself, she was quick to suspect
vanity in others, and this thought only increased her
irritation.

"I'd give a great deal if she wasn't so pretty; and
—and that style of beauty always annoys me," she
said to herself, with a feeling of angry impatience.

And giving a sudden twitch to a delicate ruffle,
which she had begun to arrange upon the corsage of
a dress, to show Mona how she wanted it, she made
a great rugged tear in the filmy fabric, thus completely ruining the frill.

This only served to increase her ill humor.

"There! now I cannot wear this dress at dinner
to-day," she cried, flushing angrily over the mishap,
"for the frill is ruined."

"Haven't you something else that you can use in
its place?" Mona quietly asked.

"No; nothing looks as well on this corsage as these
wide, fleecy frills of *crape lisse*. It is the only dress,
too, that I have not already worn here, and I was
depending upon it for to-day," was the irritable response.

Mona thought she had plenty of laces and ruffles
that would have answered very well, and which might
easily have been substituted, but she did not think it
best to make any further suggestions to her in her
present mood.

"I know what I can do," Mrs. Montague continued,
after a moment, in a milder tone. "I saw some ruf-
fling very nearly like this in a milliner's window at
Rhinebeck, when I was out riding on Saturday.
There are some other little things that I shall want
for this evening, and you may take a walk by and by
to get them for me."

Rhinebeck was a full mile away, and Mrs. Montague could easily have arranged to have Mona ride, for a carriage was sent every morning for the mail; but it did not occur to her to do so, or if it did, she evidently did not care to put herself to that trouble.

Mona, however, did not mind the walk—indeed, on the whole, she was rather glad of the privilege of getting out by herself into the sunshine which was so in harmony with her own bright mood. Still she could not help feeling that it was rather inconsiderate of Mrs. Montague to require her to walk two miles simply to gratify a mere whim.

It was about nine o'clock when she started out upon her errand, and as she ran down the steps and out upon the broad avenue, her bright eyes went glancing eagerly about, for Mona had secretly hoped that she might catch a glimpse of and perhaps even secure a few words with her lover.

But Ray was nowhere visible, being just at that moment in the smoking-room with several other gentlemen.

Mr. Palmer, the senior, however, was walking in the park, and evidently deeply absorbed in the consideration of some important matter, for his hands were clasped behind him, his head was bowed, and his eyes fixed upon the ground.

But he glanced up as Mona passed him, and his eyes lighted as they fell upon her beautiful face.

He lifted his hat and bowed as courteously to her as he would have done to Mrs. Montague herself, and Mona's heart instantly warmed toward him for his politeness as she returned his salute.

"She is the prettiest girl in the house if she *is* only a waiting-maid," he muttered, as he turned for a second to look at the graceful figure after Mona had passed him. "How finely she carries herself—how elastic her step!"

Another pair of observing eyes had also caught sight of her by this time, and mental comments of a far different character were running through a younger brain.

The smoking-room at Hazeldean was in the third story of the south wing of the house, and overlooked the avenue and park, as well as a broad stretch of country beyond, and Ray Palmer, sitting beside one of the windows—apparently listening to the conversation of his companions, but really thinking of his interview with Mona the previous evening—espied his betrothed just as she was leaving the grounds of Hazeldean and turning into the main road.

He knocked the ashes from his cigar, took another whiff or two, then laid it down, and turned to his host, who was sitting near him.

"I believe I would like a canter across the country this bright morning, Mr. Wellington," he remarked. "May I beg the use of a horse and saddle for a couple of hours?"

"Certainly, Mr. Palmer—whatever I have in the stable in the form of horses or vehicles is as the disposal of my guests," was the courteous reply. "It is a fine morning for a ride," the gentleman added, "and perchance," with an arch smile, "you may be able to find some bright-eyed maiden who would be glad to accompany you."

Ray thanked him, and then hastened away to the stable to select his horse—his companion he knew he would find later on. In less than fifteen minutes from the time he had seen Mona leave the grounds he was cantering in the same direction; but she was a rapid walker, and he did not overtake her until she had nearly reached the village.

She caught the sound of a horse's hoofs behind her, but did not like to look back to see who was approaching, and it was only when the equestrian was close beside her that she glanced up to find the fond, smiling eyes of her lover resting upon her.

The glad look of welcome which leaped into her own eyes and flashed over her face told him how well he was beloved far better than any words could have done.

"*Ray!*" she exclaimed, in a joyous tone, as he drew rein beside her, and unhesitatingly laid her hand within the strong palm which he extended to her.

"My darling!" he returned, as he leaped to the ground, "this is an unexpected pleasure! I hardly dared to hope that I should see you alone to-day. How does it happen that you are so far from Hazeldean and walking?"

"Mrs. Montague had a few errands which she wished me to do for her in the village," Mona explained.

"Could she not have arranged for you to ride?" Ray asked, with a frown, and flushing to have his dear one's comfort so ignored.

"Oh, I do not mind the walk in the least," she hastened to say. "The morning is very lovely, and I am glad, on the whole, for I should have missed you if I had ridden."

"True, I saw you just as you were leaving Hazeldean, and so came after you," Ray returned, smiling.

They were just entering Rhinebeck now, and Mona looked anxiously up and down the street.

She feared that some of the other guests at Hazel-dean might be about and see her with Ray if they should go through the place together.

He was quick to note the anxiety, and to understand its cause.

"How long will it take you to make your purchases, Mona?" he inquired, looking at his watch.

"Half an hour, perhaps," she replied.

"Well, then, I will leave you here, for a little trot about the country, and meet you again at this spot at the end of thirty minutes. I cannot resist the temptation to have a little chat with you on the way home," Ray returned, and, with another fond pressure of the hand, he leaped again upon his horse and galloped away.

With a rapidly beating heart and flushed cheeks, Mona hurried on her way. She made her purchases with all possible dispatch, then, as she had a few minutes to spare, she slipped into a hot-house, where flowers were cultivated for the city market, and bought a bunch of white violets, and a few sprays of heliotrope, then she turned her footsteps back toward Hazeldean.

She had hardly reached the spot where she had parted from Ray, when she heard him coming in the distance.

He joined her in another moment, and springing from the saddle, he threw the bridle-rein over his arm and walked beside her, leading his horse.

They had not proceeded far when they came to a place where another road appeared to branch off from the road they were on.

"Let us turn here," Ray said. "I have been exploring while you were in the village, and I found that this is a kind of lane, hedged on either side with a thick growth of pines, and leads back to the main road farther on. It is a little roundabout, but we shall not be likely to meet any one whom we know, and we shall feel far more freedom."

Mona was very glad to adopt this plan, and wandering slowly along beneath the shadows of the heavy pines, the lovers soon forgot that there was any one else in the world except themselves.

They talked over more fully the incidents of the weeks of their separation, but Ray dwelt a good deal upon the story of the stolen diamonds, and Mona could not fail to observe that he was very much troubled about the affair.

"It is a great loss," he remarked, with a sigh, "and though I cannot feel that I am culpably blamable, yet I do not cease to reproach myself for having been so thoroughly fooled by that woman. If I had only retained my hold upon the package, she never could have got it."

"But you may recover the diamonds, even now," Mona remarked. "You say that the detective arrested a woman on Friday evening as the suspected party."

"Yes, he suspects her in connection with another case, which he has been at work upon for over three years," and Ray related the story of the stolen crescents, then continued: "At the Delmonico ball he saw this Mrs. Vanderheck with them in her ears, and a cross like one that we lost, so he arrested her upon suspicion of both robberies, but somehow I am not very sanguine that we shall recover the stones."

"Did you not see the cross?" Mona asked.

"No; Mr. Rider had deposited it somewhere for

safe keeping. It will be produced at the examination to-morrow. But, really, Mona," Ray interposed, with a nervous laugh, "I feel worse over the fact of having been so taken in by this pretended Mrs. Vanderbeck, than over the pecuniary loss."

The poor fellow felt very much as Justin Cutler felt when he learned how he had been tricked into paying a large price for the pair of paste crescents.

"How did the woman look, Ray? Describe her to me," Mona said.

She experienced a strange fascination in the story with all its curious details.

Ray gave a vivid word-picture of the beautiful woman, her dress, her carriage, and even her driver, for everything connected with that unexampled experience was indelibly stamped upon his mind.

"You say her dress was badly torn," Mona musingly observed, when he had concluded the account of the discovery, and what had followed their getting out of the carriage and entering Doctor Wesselhoff's office.

"Yes, there was quite a rent in it, and I imagine this circumstance was not premeditated in the plan of her campaign, for she certainly was annoyed to have the beautiful cloth torn, although she tried to make light of it," Ray replied, then added: "And later in the day I found a piece of the goods adhering to my clothing."

"Did you?" questioned Mona, eagerly.

"Yes, and if I should ever see that dress again I could easily identify it, for I have the piece now and could fit it into the rent. But doubtless my lady has disposed of that costume long before this. Here is the piece, though—I have kept it, thinking it might possibly be of use some time."

Ray drew forth his pocket-book as he spoke, opened it, took out a folded paper, and handed it to Mona.

She opened it, and found carefully pinned within, a scrap of mauve colored ladies' cloth, in the form of a ragged acute angle.

"It is almost like broadcloth—very fine and heavy," she exclaimed. "It is a lovely color, too, and must have been a very beautiful costume."

"It was, and dangerously so," said Ray, dryly. "I admired it exceedingly, especially the fit and make of it."

"I imagine it might have been found in some dye-house shortly after, if you had only thought of it and known where to look, Mona thoughtfully observed.

"That is a bright idea," said Ray, quickly. "I honestly believe that women would make keener and better detectives than men. But," with a sigh, "I'm afraid it is too late now to put your theory to the test, and perhaps I have brushed against its folds on the street a dozen times since in a different color. Well, I suppose I must try to reconcile myself to the inevitable and make up my mind that the stones are gone beyond recovery, unless this Mrs. Vanderheck should prove to be the thief. I have not much faith in the detective's theory, that the Chicago adventuress and our diamond thief are one and the same."

"There seems to be a singular coincidence about the name of the lady who so imposed upon you, and that of the one who is now under arrest," Mona remarked.

"Yes, the only difference is in one letter, and if Mrs. Vanderheck does not prove to be my charmer,

or connected with her in any way, I shall be tempted
to believe that she purposely took a name so similar
in order to throw suspicion upon this woman," said the
young man, thoughtfully.

"That may be; and is it not a little suspicious, too,
that Mrs. Vanderbeck should have mentioned an invalid husband when Mrs. Vanderheck really has one?"
Mona inquired.

"I had not thought of that before," Ray replied.
"Still another singular circumstance comes to my mind
just at this moment. At the time I was introduced to
Mrs. Vanderheck, at Mrs. Merrill's reception, I repeated the name as if it was spelled with a 'b,' and
emphasized the last syllable. The woman started,
glanced at me curiously, and changed color a trifle,
while she did not seem to quite recover her self-
possession throughout our conversation."

"That does seem rather strange, considering all
things," said Mona. "Perhaps, after all, she may
prove to be your adventuress; and yet she must be a
very bold one to flaunt her plunder so recklessly and
in the very presence of people who would be sure to
recognize it."

They changed the subject after that, and chatted
upon topics of a more tender and interesting nature.

It was a delightful walk in the mild February air,
and a pleasant interview, and both were loath to part
when they suddenly found themselves at the other
end of the pine-shadowed lane where it curved into the
main road again.

Ray took a tender leave of his dear one, then
mounting his horse, rode back over the way they had
just traversed, while Mona went on to Hazeldean.

CHAPTER XXII.

MONA ATTENDS THE BALL AT HAZELDEAN.

Mona found considerable excitement and confusion prevailing upon her return, for carpenters and decorators were busy about the house; flowers and plants were being carried in from the conservatory; the caterer and his force were arranging things to their minds, in the dining-room and kitchen, and everybody, guests included, was busy and in a flutter of anticipation over the approaching festivities.

"It seems to me that you were gone a long while," Mrs. Montague curtly remarked, as Mona entered her room.

"Was I?" the young girl asked, pleasantly; then she added: "Well, two miles make quite a walk."

Mrs. Montague flushed at the remark.

She was well aware that she had been unreasonable in requiring so much, just to secure a few articles which she might have very well done without, and this thought did not add to her comfort.

She made no reply, but quietly laid out some work for Mona, whom she kept busily employed during the remainder of the day.

The young girl cheerfully performed all that was required of her, however; her interview with Ray had served to sweeten every task for that day, while she hoped that she might secure another opportunity, before it was over, for a few more words with him.

But after dinner Mrs. Montague came up stairs

better-natured than she had been all day, and turning to Mona, as she entered the room, she asked:

"Have you none but mourning dresses with you? nothing white, or pretty, for evening?"

"No; my dresses are all black; the only thing I have that would be at all suitable for evening is a black net," Mona answered, wondering, with rising color, why she had asked the question.

"That might do with some white ribbons to liven it up a bit," said Mrs. Montague, thoughtfully. Then she explained: "Mr. Wellington has arranged a balcony in the dancing hall for some friends who are coming to the ball, just to look on for a while, and he has just said to me that there would be a seat for you, if you cared to see the dancing."

Mona looked up eagerly at this.

She dearly loved social life, and she had wished, oh, so much! that she might have the privilege of witnessing the gay scenes of the evening.

"That is very kind of Mr. Wellington," she gratefully remarked.

"Get your dress, and let me look at it," continued Mrs. Montague, who would not commit herself to anything until she could be sure that her seamstress would make a respectable appearance among Mr. Wellington's friends.

He had requested as a favor that Miss Richards might be allowed this privilege in return for having so kindly relieved his daughter at the piano a few evenings previous.

Mona brought the dress—a rich, heavy net, made over handsome black silk, which had been among her wardrobe for the previous summer, when she went to Lenox with her uncle.

"That will be just the thing, only it needs something to relieve its blackness," said Mrs. Montague, while she mentally wondered at the richness of the costume.

"I have some narrow white taste in my trunk, which I can perhaps use to make it a little more suitable for the occasion, if you approve," Mona quietly remarked.

"Yes, fix it as you like," the lady returned, indifferently, adding: "that is if you care about going into the pavilion."

"Thank you; I think I should enjoy watching the dancers for a while," the young girl returned.

Perhaps, she thought, she might be able to snatch another brief interview with Ray. At all events she should see him, and that would be worth a great deal.

Her nimble fingers were very busy after that running her white ribbons into the meshes of her dress.

She wove three rows of the narrow, feather-edged taste into each of the flounces, and the effect was very pretty. Then she did the same between the puffs of the full sleeves, tying some dainty bows where she joined them, and finished the neck to correspond.

This was hardly completed when she was called to assist Mrs. Montague in dressing, and by the time she was ready to descend her good humor was thoroughly restored, for she certainly was a most regal looking woman in her elegant and becoming toilet.

"I do not believe there will be another dress here this evening as beautiful as this," Mona remarked, as she fastened the last fold in place, her pretty face flushing with genuine admiration for the artistic costume.

"It *is* handsome, and I look passably young in it, too; how old should you take me to be Ruth?" Mrs. Montague asked, with a smiling glance at her own reflection in the mirror.

"A trifle over thirty, perhaps," Mona replied, and the little exultant laugh which broke from her companion told her that she felt highly flattered by that estimate of her years.

"There!" she remarked, as she drew on her gloves, "you need do nothing more for me; go now and get ready yourself, or you will miss the opening promenade."

Mona hastened away to her own room, where she had everything laid out in the most orderly manner, ready to put on, and if Mrs. Montague could have seen the dainty undergarments and skirts spread upon her bed; the costly kid boots and silken hose for her pretty feet, she might have arched her eyebrows more than ever over the extravagant taste of her seamstress.

Mona arranged her hair with great care, as she had worn it on the evening when she attended the opera with Ray, and this done she was soon ready.

She looked lovely. The black net, with its dainty white trimmings, was very becoming to her delicate complexion. The lining to the corsage had been cut low, and her pure white neck gleamed like marble through the meshes of the dusky lace. There was no lining, either, to her sleeves and her beautifully rounded arms looked like bits of exquisite sculpture. She had turned the lace away in the shape of a V at her throat, and now finished it by pinning to her corsage the cluster of white violets which she had purchased in the morning.

She regretted that she had no gloves with her suitable for the occasion, but since she was only to sit in the balcony, she thought it would not matter much if she wore none, and her small white hands, with their rose-tinted finger-tips, were by no means unsightly objects.

She was very happy and light-hearted, as she turned for one last look in her mirror before leaving her room.

She smiled involuntarily at her own loveliness, and gave a gay little nod at the charming reflection as she turned away.

Then she went out and softly down a back stair-way to avoid the crowds of people who were going up and down the front way.

But, on reaching the lower floor, she was obliged to cross the main hall and drawing-room in order to reach the pavilion, which Mr. Wellington had caused to be erected outside on the lawn for dancing, and which was connected with the house by a covered passage leading from one of the long windows of the drawing-room.

Mona stood in the door-way a moment, feeling slightly embarrassed at the thought of going unattended to search for her seat in the balcony.

Just then a round, white arm was slipped about her waist, and a gay, girlish voice cried in her ear:

"Oh, Miss Richards! how perfectly lovely you look! Are you coming to the ball?"

Mona turned and smiled into the bright face of Kitty McKenzie, who was radiant in pink silk and white tulle.

"No, only as a spectator," she replied, with an answering smile. "Mr. Wellington has kindly offered me a seat in the balcony, where I shall enjoy watching the merrymakers."

"But do you not *like* to dance yourself?" questioned the girl.

"Oh, yes, indeed. I used to enjoy it very much," Mona replied, with a little sigh.

"Then I think it is a great pity that you cannot join us to-night," returned Miss Kitty, regretfully, for she had caught the sigh; "only," she added, with sudden thought, "being in mourning, perhaps you would rather not."

"No, I should not care to dance to-night," Mona returned, and then she became conscious that a familiar form was approaching the spot where they stood.

It was not an easy matter for her to keep back her color as Ray drew near, and try to appear as if she had never seen him before. She knew that he was choosing this opportunity to be formally introduced to her.

But the voluble Miss McKenzie saluted him in her frank outspoken manner.

"Oh, Mr. Palmer," she cried, "are not the rooms lovely?—the flowers, the lights, indeed *all* the decorations?"

"They are, truly, Miss McKenzie; and," he added, with a merry smile, as he glanced at her bright face and figure, and then turned his gaze upon Mona, "there are some other lovely adornments about the rooms, besides those so skillfully used by the professional decorator."

"Thank you—of course that was intended as a compliment to ourselves," the quick-witted little lady returned, as she dropped him a coquettish courtesy; "and," turning to Mona, "perhaps you would like an

introduction to my friend. Miss Richards, allow me
to present you to Mr. Palmer."

Ray bowed low over the white hand which Mona
mechanically offered him, and which he clasped in a
way to send a thrill leaping along her nerves that made
the violets upon her bosom quiver, as if a breath of
wind had swept over them.

She barely had time to acknowledge the presentation, however, when an icy voice behind her remarked:

"Miss Richards, Mr. Wellington is looking for you
to conduct you to your seat in the balcony."

Turning, Mona saw Mrs. Montague regarding her
with a look of cold displeasure, and she knew that she
must have witnessed her introduction to Ray, and dis-
approved of it.

But she was secretly glad that she had been so near,
for now she could feel free to recognize her lover
whenever they met, without the fear of being questioned as to how she happened to know him.

"Mr. Wellington looking for Miss Richards, did
you say, Mrs. Montague?" Ray inquired, quickly improving his opportunity, and looking about him in
search of that gentleman. "Ah! I see him yonder—
Miss Richards, allow me to conduct you to him."

He offered his arm in a ceremonious way, as any
new acquaintance might have done, and led her
slowly toward the spot where Mr. Wellington was
standing, while Mrs. Montague watched them, with a
frown upon her brow.

"I believe I was a fool to allow her to come down;
she is far too pretty to appear in public with me; any
one would suppose her to be an equal," she muttered,
irritably. "Who would have believed," she added,
"that she could have gotten herself up in that bewitch-

ing style, with only a few bits of white ribbon and not a single ornament! I wonder where she got her violets? She has exquisite taste, anyhow."

But Ray and Mona were unconscious of these jealous remarks. They were oblivious of everything just then, except the presence of each other and the fortunate circumstances which had thrown them together.

"My darling," Ray said, under his breath, "that was very cleverly managed, was it not? Don't you think I am quite a tactician? I caught sight of you the moment you appeared; then that bright fairy, Kitty McKenzie, arrived upon the scene, and I knew that my opportunity had come."

"But you almost took my breath away, Ray, when you bore me off so unceremoniously before Mrs. Montague's disapproving eyes," Mona murmured in response.

"Unceremonious!" the young man retorted, with assumed surprise, and a roguish smile. "Why, I thought I was excessively formal."

"Yes, in your manner to me; but you did not ask the lady's permission to conduct me to the host."

"How was I supposed to know that Miss Richards, to whom I had just been introduced, was not a guest as well as the more gorgeous, but less lovely, Mrs. Montague?" questioned the young lover, lightly. "But," he continued, with a sigh, "I cannot bear this sort of thing a great while. When I see you looking like some beautiful young goddess, I find it very difficult to assume an indifferent exterior. I nearly forgot myself a moment ago."

Perhaps it would have been better if I had remained quietly in my own room," Mona archly returned, as

she gave him a mischievous glance out of her bright
eyes.

He drew the hand that lay on his arm close to his
side with a fond pressure.

"Indeed, no!" he said, tenderly; "it is better to meet
you thus than not at all. But must I give you up to
Mr. Wellington?" he continued, in a wistful tone, as
they drew near the gentleman. "No; I will ask him
to direct me to the balcony, and I will conduct you
there myself."

"Ah, Miss Richards, I have been looking for you,"
Mr. Wellington remarked, as his eye fell upon the
fair girl. "It is almost time for the opening promenade, and you ought to be in your seat, so as not to
miss anything. But wait a moment; I must speak to
this gentleman first," he concluded, as some one approached him.

"Pray, Mr. Wellington, since you are so engaged,
let me conduct Miss Richards to the balcony," Ray
here interposed, as if the thought had just occurred
to him.

Mr. Wellington, with a look of relief, readily as-
sented to the proposition, and Ray and his companion were thus permitted to enjoy a little more of each
other's society.

They easily found their way to the balcony, where
Ray secured a good position for his *fiancée*.

"I suppose I will have to leave you now," he whispered in her ear; "I am engaged to Miss Wellington
for the promenade; but, by and by, Mona, I shall steal
away and come to you again."

"Do not leave the dancing on my account, Ray,"
Mona pleaded; "it is all so bright and lovely down
there. I know you will enjoy it."

"I should, if I could have you with me," he interrupted, fondly; "but, as I cannot, I would much prefer to remain quietly here with you—only that would not do, I suppose."

"No, indeed," she returned, decidedly. "Now you *must* go, for the orchestra is beginning to play."

He left her, with a fond hand-clasp that brought a happy smile to her red lips, and went below to seek his host's daughter.

Mona was very glad, later on, that she was not below with the dancers, for she saw quite a number of people from New York, whom she knew, and she would not have cared to be recognized by them—or rather snubbed by them.

It was a brilliant scene when the grand procession formed.

The pavilion had been very tastefully decorated, and one would hardly have believed that there were only bare, rough boards behind the artistically draped damask silk and lace, which had been used in profusion to conceal them. The spacious room was brilliantly lighted; flowers and potted plants were everywhere, making the place bright with their varied hues, and sending forth their fragrance into every nook and corner, while the fine orchestra was concealed behind a screen of palms, mingled with oleanders in full bloom.

There must have been at least two hundred people present, the gentlemen, of course, in full evening dress, while the ladies' costumes were of exceeding richness and beauty, yet among them all, it is doubtful if there was one so happy as the lovely girl who sat so quietly in the balcony and watched the gay scene in which she could not mingle.

There were a good many people sitting there with her, and not a few regarded her with curious and admiring interest, and judged from her dress that she was in mourning, and that she was thus debarred, by the customs of society, from appearing in a ball-room as one of the dancers. That she was a lady no one doubted for a moment, for her every look and movement betrayed it.

Now and then Ray's fond glances would seek her, and, catching her eye, a little nod or smile plainly told her how he longed to be with her.

Mona saw Mrs. Montague conspicuous among the dancers, and she appeared to enter into the spirit of the occasion with almost the zest of a young girl during her first season; while it was noticed that Mr. Palmer was her companion more frequently than any other person.

She had come in with him for the grand march, and when the procession for supper was formed she was again upon his arm.

But Mona could not see Ray anywhere among this crowd, and the occupants of the balcony also going below for refreshment, she found herself almost alone in the pavilion.

But it was not for long, for presently she caught the sound of a quick, elastic step, and the next moment her lover was beside her.

"Come back a little, dear, where we can sit in the shadow of the draperies, and we will have a precious half-hour all by ourselves," he said, in a low tone; "then in a few moments a servant will bring us up some supper."

"How thoughtful you are, Ray! But, truly, I do not care for anything to eat," Mona returned, as she arose and followed him to a cozy nook, where the draperies would partially conceal them from observation.

"I do, my brown-eyed lassie," Ray responded, emphatically; "after the violent exercise of the last two hours I am quite sure my inner man needs replenishing. Ah, James, you're a good fellow," he continued, as a tan-colored son of the South now made his appearance, bearing a tray of tempting viands. "Here, take this and drink my health by and by; but come back and get your tray in the course of half an hour."

The darky showed two rows of brilliant teeth as Ray slipped a silver dollar into his hand; then with a cheerful "Yes, sir—thank'ee, sir," and a low bow he disappeared as suddenly as he had come.

Mona was hungry, in spite of her assertion to the contrary, and she enjoyed the rich treat that Ray had so thoughtfully provided for her, while he was full of fun and gayety, and they had a merry time up there all by themselves.

When the dancers began to return, Ray quietly remarked:

"My darling, I am not going down to the company again; I feel guilty to have you sit moping here, while I am playing the gallant cavalier to other girls."

Mona laughed out softly, but gleefully, at this speech.

"I trust you will always be as conscientious and dutiful, my loyal knight," she roguishly retorted.

"You will never have cause to question my loyalty, my own," he whispered, with a look that brought a bright color into her cheeks.

"But I have not been moping," Mona resumed. "I

have enjoyed being here and watching the dancers very much, and you know I could not join them even if my present position did not debar me," she tremulously concluded.

"True; I had not thought of that," the young man said, gravely, as his eye swept over her black dress.

"So, then, if you feel that your duty is below, do not hesitate about leaving me," Mona urged.

"I am not going," he firmly reiterated. "I have been formally introduced to 'Miss Richards,' and I have a perfect right to cultivate her acquaintance if I choose."

Mona did not urge him further; she saw that he really wished to stay, and she was only too happy to have him there by her side; and so the lovers passed two delightful hours, watching the gay throng below, now and then exchanging fond looks or a few low spoken words, and only one pair of eyes among the multitude espied and recognized them.

These belonged to Louis Hamblin, whose eyes lighted with sudden triumph, while an evil smile played over his face as he saw them.

"I thought so," he muttered, as he noticed Ray Palmer's attitude of devotion. "That would prove the truth of my suspicions, if nothing else did so."

CHAPTER XXIII.

LOUIS HAMBLIN IS JEALOUS OF RAY.

It was after one o'clock when Mona told Ray that she must go to her room, so as to be in readiness to assist Mrs. Montague when she came up from the pavilion.

Ray was loath to let her go; he longed to keep her there with him until the last moment, but he felt that she was the best judge of her duty, and he would not interfere with it, since he had conceded the point of her remaining with Mrs. Montague for the present.

He arose to accompany her through the pavilion and drawing-room to the hall.

"Will it not be better for me to go alone?" asked Mona, fearing that she might be made conspicuous by this attention.

"Through all that crowd!" exclaimed her lover, surprised. "No, indeed; I would not allow any lady whom I knew to go unattended, and since it is known that I have been formally presented to Miss Richards, why should I not treat her with becoming politeness?"

Mona made no further objection, but quietly took his arm and allowed him to have his way. She was proud and happy to know that Ray was noble-minded enough to have no fear of being seen publicly showing courtesy to a simple seamstress.

As they were passing through the drawing-room Mona caught sight of Mrs. Montague and Mr. Palmer sitting in an alcove by themselves.

Both glanced up, for the young couple were obliged to pass near them, and Mrs. Montague frowned as she saw her waiting-maid, for the second time that evening, upon the arm of Ray.

Mr. Palmer flushed and appeared somewhat embarrassed as he met his son's eye, although he nodded and smiled in his usual genial way.

Reaching the main hall, Ray led Mona to the foot of the stairs, and held out his hand for a parting clasp.

"Good-night, my darling," he said, bending over her and speaking in a low tone. "Do you know that you are all the world to me, and I shall impatiently count the days until I can claim you—three months hence at the farthest! I must say good-by, too," he added, "as we leave for New York early in the morning; but I shall try to see you again in a few days."

Mona smiled, a delicate flush suffusing her face at his fond words; then, responding to his good-night, she went quickly up stairs and sought her room, firmly believing that she was the happiest person at Hazeldean, and that her lover was the noblest man in the world.

Louis Hamblin had seen the young couple leave the pavilion, and following them at a distance, had watched them with a jealous eye as they took leave of each other.

Another pair of eyes were also peering at them over the banister in the upper hall, and a beautiful face clouded over with anger and jealousy when Ray bent, with that earnest, luminous look, to whisper his parting in Mona's ear.

They belonged to a brilliant society belle, Miss Josephine Holt, who had long entertained a secret affection for Ray.

She also knew Mona, having met her in society earlier in the season, and had been jealous of the young man's attentions to her.

She wondered at finding her there at Hazeldean, for she knew of her loss of fortune. She slipped out of sight into a dressing-room as Mona came up stairs, and, finding Miss Merrill there, asked her, in an in-

different tone, as Mona passed the door, who the
young lady was.

"Oh, that is Ruth Richards——Mrs. Montague's
waiting-maid," was the reply.

A smile of scorn leaped to Miss Holt's proud lips
as she heard the name.

"Ruth Richards," she repeated to herself. "So this
is how she disappeared so suddenly out of the knowledge of everybody. A common waiting-maid, and too
proud to sail under her own name! I wonder if she is a
relative of Mrs. Montague? If she is, perhaps that
lady objected to having it known, and so called her
Ruth Richards. Can it be possible that Ray Palmer
is attentive to her *now?* Does he know that she is
sailing under false colors? I think I will look into
this state of affairs a little!"

The young lady donned her wraps and took her
departure from Hazeldean, but with an angry frown
upon her brow, for her enjoyments of the evening had
been entirely spoiled by the little scene which she
had just witnessed.

After Ray left Mona he drew his outside coat on
over his evening dress and went out into the grounds
for a quiet smoke and to think, for he felt troubled
and nervous.

His father's flush and embarrassment, as he caught
his eye while passing through the drawing-room, were
a revelation to him.

Mona had spoken to him of his attentions to Mrs.
Montague, and he had also observed them, since coming to Hazeldean, but he had hoped that they were
only temporary, and would not amount to anything
serious.

But to-night it was only too evident that the beautiful and dashing widow had acquired a strong influence over his father, and he began to fear that he was seriously contemplating making her his wife.

He was startled and shocked—not because of any unreasonable jealousy, or a selfish aversion to the thought of having his father take a congenial companion into his home; but he feared she was not a woman to make him happy. She was gay and worldly; she lived for and in the excitement of society, while Mr. Palmer was more quiet and domestic in his tastes.

Besides, he had somehow became imbued with the idea that she was lacking in principle. Perhaps what Mona had told him about her, in connection with her mother's history, might have given him this impression; but, whatever had caused it, he shrank with the greatest repugnance from having her become the wife of his father.

Still he felt helpless to prevent it; he experienced great delicacy about making any objections if his father should intimate a wish to change his condition, and he could readily see that by so doing he would not only deeply wound him, but be likely to make an enemy of Mrs. Montague.

So these were the things he wished to think over by himself, and that sent him out into the grounds after he had left Mona.

The night was a beautiful one. There was not a cloud in the sky, and the full moon was sailing in matchless majesty through the star-studded vault above, while the brilliantly lighted house and park, with the entrancing music from the pavilion floating out to him on the still air, added their charm to the scene.

Ray lighted his cigar and strolled down the avenue,

his heart filled with conflicting emotions. He was very happy in his new relations with Mona, yet strangely uneasy and depressed regarding his father's prospects.

There was a line of great Norway spruce trees along one side of the avenue, not far from the main road, and as Ray, deeply absorbed in his own thoughts, was passing these, a figure suddenly stepped out from among them and accosted him.

It was Louis Hamblin.

"Ah, Palmer," he said, affably, "out for a smoke? Give me a light, will you?"

"Certainly," Ray responded, cordially, and politely extended his cigar to him.

The man made use of it, then returned it, with thanks, remarking, as he turned to walk along with him:

"Glorious night, this!"

"Indeed it is—we seldom have so perfect an evening," Ray heartily responded.

"Quite a blow-out, too," added Mr. Hamblin, who was somewhat given to slang. "Wellington is a generous old codger, and has done things up in fine style."

"Yes, I should say the ball has been a great success, at least everybody has appeared to enjoy it," Ray politely replied.

He was not very well pleased with the young man's enforced companionship; he would have much preferred to be left to his own reflections.

"That is so, and there were lots of pretty girls on the floor," Mr. Hamblin went on, in his free-and-easy style, "and the costumes were exceptionally fine, too. By the way," with a covert look at Ray, "that Miss Montague is a remarkably beautiful girl."

Ray felt a great inward shock go through him at this observation, and he was on his guard in an instant.

"Miss Montague!" he repeated, bending a keen glance upon his companion, "was there a *Miss* Montague here this evening?"

"I beg ten thousand pardons, Palmer," the young man broke forth, with well-assumed confusion, "I don't know why I used that name, 'pon my word I don't, unless it was because of association. I'd heard, you know, that you were attentive at one time to a Miss Montague, niece to that rich old chap, Dinsmore, who died recently. The name I should have spoken, however, was Miss Richards, with whom I saw you talking a while ago."

Louis Hamblin had at once suspected Mona's identity, upon discovering the lovers sitting together in the balcony. He was confirmed in this suspicion when he followed them from the pavilion and observed their tender parting in the hall, and so he had dogged Ray's steps, when he went out for a walk, with the express purpose of pumping him, and had thus tried to take him off his guard by speaking of Mona in the way he did.

"Ah, yes," Ray quietly responded, for he had seen through the trick at once; "Miss Kitty McKenzie introduced me to Miss Richards early in the evening. She is an interesting girl, and she informs me that she is in the employ of your aunt, Mrs. Montague."

"Yes, she's seamstress, or something of that sort," Mr. Hamblin returned, knocking the ashes from his cigar. "Deuced shame, isn't it, that a pretty, lady-like girl like her should have to work at such a trade for her living? I—I believe," with a sly glance at Ray, "if I wasn't dependent on Aunt Margie—that is, if I had a fortune of my own—I'd like nothing better than to marry the girl and put her in a position more befitting her beauty."

It was fortunate, for Mona's sake, that they were walking in the shadow of the tall spruces, or Louis Hamblin must have seen the look of wrath that kindled on Ray's face at the presumptuous speech.

His first impulse was to hurl the conceited puppy to the ground for daring to speak of his betrothed in that flippant manner; but such a demonstration he knew would involve serious consequences, and at once betray Mona's identity and make it impossible for her to learn anything from Mrs. Montague regarding her mother's history.

He had a terrible struggle within himself for a moment before he could control his anger sufficiently to make any reply. But after two or three vigorous puffs at his Havana, he managed to say, with some degree of calmness, though with an undertone of sarcasm, which he could not restrain, and which did not fail to make itself felt:

"Really, Hamblin, your philanthropic spirit is a great credit to you, and doubtless Miss Richards would appreciate it if she could know of your deep interest in her. But, if I am not mistaken, I have heard that you are contemplating matrimony in another quarter—that Miss McKenzie is the bright, particular star in your firmament; and she is really a charming young lady in my estimation."

"Oh, Kitty is well enough," returned Mr. Hamblin, with a shrug of his shoulders, "but a fellow doesn't quite relish having a girl thrust upon him. Aunt Marg is set upon my marrying her, and it's human nature, you know, never to want to do anything under compulsion, but to be inclined to do just what you know you must not. Eh, Palmer?"

What could the fellow mean? Ray asked himself. Did he still suspect, in spite of his efforts to conceal the fact, who Ruth Richards really was? And did he mean to imply, by his moralizing, that he knew how Ray longed to thrash him for his insolence, and yet knew he must not, for fear of compromising the girl he loved?

Then, too, he could not help despising him for the slighting and insulting way in which he had spoken of Kitty McKenzie, who, he felt, was far too true and lovely a girl to throw herself away upon such a flippant and unprincipled fellow.

He knew that he could not tamely submit to much more conversation of such a nature, so he merely replied in an absent tone.

"Perhaps." Then tossing away his cigar, he added: "I believe I heard a clock strike two a few moments ago. I think I shall go in and retire, as I have important business to attend to in the morning."

"Sure enough! I heard something about the case of the diamond robbery coming off to-morrow," responded Mr. Hamblin, in an eager tone. "That was a queer affair throughout, wasn't it?—and the story about the Bently woman is another—it got into the papers in spite of all old Vanderheck's efforts to bribe the reporters to silence. Do you credit the theory that the same woman was concerned in both swindles?"

"I hardly know what to think about it," Ray answered. "We do not even know yet whether the cross belongs to us; but Mr. Rider is confident that Mrs. Bently, of the Chicago affair, and Mrs. Vanderbeck, or 'heck'—whatever her name may be—are one and the same person."

"Well, it is certain that Mrs. Vanderheck, of New York, who figures so conspicuously in society, has an enormous store of diamonds, however she came by them," Louis Hamblin remarked.

Then, having reached the house, Ray bade him a brief good-night, and went immediately up to his room.

He found his father there before him and walking up and down the floor in an unusually thoughtful mood.

"Ah, Ray!" he said, as his son entered, "I have been waiting for you. I want to have a little talk with you before we go to bed."

"About the examination of to-morrow?" Ray inquired, with a keen glance.

"No—about—Ray, how would you like it if I should—well, to out with it at once—if I should marry again?" and the embarrassed old gentleman grew crimson even to the bald spot upon his head, as he then blundered through his question.

Ray sat down before he allowed himself to reply.

Now that the crisis had really come, he found he had less strength to meet it than he had anticipated.

"Well, father," he gravely said, after a moment of thought, "if you think that a second marriage is essential to your comfort and happiness, I should not presume to oppose it."

Mr. Palmer bent an anxious look upon his son.

"And yet you do not exactly approve of the plan?" he observed.

Ray looked up and frankly met his father's eye.

He believed it would be better to speak his mind freely than to dissemble in any way.

"I cannot fail to understand your meaning, for, of course, I have not been blind of late," he remarked. "I have seen how agreeable the society of Mrs. Montague is to you, and, judging from appearances, yours is no less so to her. I am bound to confess that she is a very handsome woman and very charming also in company. Still it is plain to be seen that she is a thorough society woman, and the question in my mind is, would you, with your more quiet tastes and disposition, enjoy sharing the kind of life that she leads?"

"But—I think—I hope that she would enjoy quiet home life and—my companionship, more than society, after our marriage," Mr. Palmer remarked, with some confusion.

Ray smiled slightly, for he saw that his father was very far gone, and he doubted if any argument would convince him that the fascinating widow would not be satisfied to settle down to the quieter joys of domestic life, even after she had succeeded in capturing the wealthy diamond merchant.

Still he resolved that he would say all that he had to say now, and then leave the matter with him to decide as his heart and judgment dictated.

"I hope that you will not deceive yourself, father," he said. "Mrs. Montague's nature is one that craves excitement and admiration, and she has been so long accustomed to this kind of life I imagine it would be impossible for her to resign it, cheerfully, for any one. Of course I know but very little of her personally, and I do not wish to judge her unfairly; but I should be very sorry to have you take any step which you would be likely to hereafter regret."

Mr. Palmer looked grave. His judgment, his common sense told him that Ray was right; that the gay woman of the world would not be willing to sacrifice her pleasures to his wishes, would never meet the wants of his more quiet and home-loving nature.

But he had been blinded and captivated by Mrs. Montague's wiles and preference for his society; he had, in fact, been led on so far that he saw no way of maintaining his dignity and honor except by making her a formal offer of his hand.

"You have no personal objection to her, I hope, Ray," he said, without replying to his remarks. "I assure you," he added, "the change shall not affect your prospects in any way. I will make handsome settlements upon you, and turn over the business to you before I take any important step."

"Thank you, sir," Ray heartily responded, but realizing that the matter was as good as settled, and it would be useless to discuss it any further. "Of course I should not feel at liberty to oppose you, were I so inclined, in a matter which concerns you so exclusively; as I said before, if you feel that such an alliance will be for your comfort and happiness, I would not wish to lay any obstacle in your way."

"You are very good, my son," Mr. Palmer returned, and yet he felt far from comfortable over the very doubtful approbation of his choice.

He had made up his mind to marry Mrs. Montague; he had indeed been almost upon the point of offering himself to her, just as Ray and Mona had passed through the drawing-room, when he had suddenly resolved to wait and consult his son, before taking the irrevocable step. He felt that he owed it to him to do so, for they had been good friends and confidants for so many years.

"I must be looking out for number one, you know," he added, trying to speak playfully; "for you will be getting married yourself one of these days, and the old home would be very lonely without you."

Ray wondered, with a twinge of bitterness, if his father could have forgotten how often he had told him that he "could never bear to be separated from him, and that when he found a wife to suit him, he must bring her home to brighten up the house and help to take care of him."

Now, it was evident, from what he had just said, that he would be expected to make a home for himself and his bride elsewhere.

"I wish you could find the girl you love, Ray," he went on, wistfully, as he did not reply. "It is rather hard on you that she should have disappeared so unaccountably. By the way, who was that lovely maiden with you a while ago?"

"She was introduced to me as Miss Richards," Ray responded, evasively, and flushing slightly.

Mr. Palmer looked up, surprised.

"So it was!" he exclaimed; "but I did not recognize her; and yet I thought there was something familiar about her. I suppose it was because she was in evening dress. Well, she is a charming little girl, anyhow. I only hope your Mona is as pretty, and that you'll find her soon. But suppose we go to bed," he said, with a weary sigh; "I'm tired, and we must be off early to-morrow morning."

The conclusion of this story, and what fortunes be-

fell Mona, are fully told in the sequel to this volume
entitled "True Love's Reward," which is published in
a handsome cloth bound edition, uniform with this
volume.

THE END.

MONA

PART 2

(TRUE LOVE'S REWARD)

CHAPTER I.

A NEW DISCOVERY DEEPENS A MYSTERY.

When Mrs. Montague entered her room, an hour after Mona went up stairs, there was a deep frown upon her brow.

She found Mona arrayed in a pretty white wrapper, and sitting before the glowing grate reading a new book, while she waited for her.

"What are you sitting up for, and arrayed in that style?" she ungraciously demanded.

"I thought you would need help in undressing, and I put on this loose wrapper because it was more comfortable than any other dress," Mona answered, as she regarded the lady with some surprise, for she had never before quite so curtly addressed her.

Mrs. Montague did not pursue the subject, and Mona patiently assisted her in taking off her finery, hanging the rich dress carefully over a form, folding her dainty laces, and arranging her jewels in their cases.

"Can I do anything more for you?" she asked, when this was done.

"No."

"At what time shall I come to you in the morning?"

3

the fair girl inquired, without appearing to heed the uncivil monosyllable.

"Not before nine o'clock; but you can mend that rip in my traveling suit before that, as we shall go back to New York on the eleven o'clock express."

"Very well; good-night," Mona said, with gentle politeness, as she turned to leave the room.

"Stop a moment, Ruth," Mrs. Montague commanded.

Mona turned back, flushing slightly at the woman's imperiousness.

"I have not been at all pleased with your deportment this evening," the woman continued. "You have been exceedingly forward for a person in your position."

Mona's color deepened to a vivid scarlet at this unexpected charge.

"I do not quite understand you——" she began, when her companion turned angrily upon her, thus arresting her in the midst of her speech.

"I do not see how you can fail to do so," was her icy retort. "I refer to your acceptance of Mr. Palmer's attentions. One would have supposed that you regarded yourself as his equal by the way you paraded the drawing-room with him to-night."

Mona could hardly repress a smile at this attack, and she wondered what Ray would have thought if he could have heard it. Yet a thrill of indignation shot through her at this unreasonable abuse.

"You witnessed my introduction to Mr. Palmer this evening," she quietly replied; "you heard him offer to conduct me to Mr. Wellington, and so know how I happened to accept his attentions."

"You should have rejected his offer," was the quick retort.

"I could not do so without appearing rude—you yourself know that no young lady would have done so under the circumstances."

"No young *lady*—no, of course not," interposed Mrs. Montague, with significant emphasis; "but you must not forget that your position will not admit of your doing what might consistently be done by young ladies in society. You received Mr. Palmer's attentions as a matter of course—as if you considered yourself his equal."

"I do so consider myself," Mona returned, with quiet dignity, but with a dangerous sparkle in her usually mild eyes. The woman's arrogance was becoming unbearable, even to her sweet spirit.

"Really!" was the sarcastic rejoinder. "Your vanity, Ruth, would be odious if it were not so ridiculous. But you should not allow your complacency, over a merely pretty face, to lead you into such presumption as you have been guilty of to-night. I blame myself somewhat for what has occurred; if I had not accorded you permission to witness the dancing, you would not have been thrown into such temptation; but I did not dream that you would force yourself upon the notice of any of Mr. Wellington's guests."

"You are accusing me very unjustly, Mrs. Montague," Mona began, with blazing eyes, but the woman cut her short.

"I consider myself a competent judge in such matters," she insolently asserted. "At all events, however, you are to receive no more attentions from Mr. Palmer. He—is the son of the gentleman whom I expect to marry, and I have no intention of allowing my seamstress to angle for my future step-son."

"Madame——" began Mona, indignantly.

"We will not discuss the matter further," Mrs. Montague interposed, imperiously; "you can go now, but be sure to have my traveling dress ready by nine o'clock in the morning."

Mona went out, and forced herself to shut the door after her without making the slightest sound, although every nerve in her body was tingling with indignation and resentment, to which she longed to give some outward expression.

But for one thing, she would have faced the coarse, rude woman, and proclaimed that she was already the promised wife of Raymond Palmer, and had a perfect right to receive his attentions whenever and wherever she chose.

That secret of the desertion of her mother haunted her, however, and she was bound to curb herself and bear everything for three months longer, while she would diligently apply herself to the task before her.

She retired immediately, but she could not go to sleep until she had relieved her overcharged heart of its bitterness and passion in a burst of weeping.

The next morning early Ray and his father were on their way to New York, and ten o'clock found them seated in the private court-room, where Mrs. Vanderheck was to answer the charges against her.

Money will accomplish a great deal, and in this case it had secured the privilege of a private examination, before a police justice, who would decide whether the suspected culprit should be held for the grand jury.

Immediately upon the arrival of the Palmers, Detective Rider came to them, accompanied by a gentleman whom he introduced as Justin Cutler, Esq., of Chicago.

They all took seats together, and presently a door

opened to admit Mrs. Vanderheck, who was attended by her husband and counsel, and who was richly attired in a close-fitting black velvet robe, and wore magnificent solitaires in her ears, besides a cluster of blazing stones at her throat.

If she was the adventuress whom the officials were searching for, she was certainly bringing a bold front to the contest in thus parading her booty before their very eyes.

Her husband was an elderly gentleman, who appeared to be in feeble health, but who conducted himself with dignity and self-possession.

The case was opened by Mr. Cutler's counsel, who told the story of the purchase of the spurious crescents in Chicago, and affirmed that they had been found upon the person of the party under arrest.

Mrs. Vanderheck listened with intense interest throughout the recital, while a look of astonishment overspread her face as the narrative proceeded.

The crescents were produced and Mr. Cutler brought forth the bogus ones, which he still had in his possession, and the two pairs appeared to be exact counterparts of each other.

The magistrate examined them with interest and care, after which he placed them on the desk before him.

Mrs. Vanderheck's counsel then said that his client would like to relate how the contested jewels came in her possession.

Permission being given for her to do so, the lady took the stand and began:

"Three years ago the coming month, which, according to the dates just given by the prosecuting counsel, was about three months after the gentleman in Chi-

cago was defrauded, I was boarding at the Revere
House, in Boston. While there I became acquainted
with a lady—a widow who called herself Mrs. Bent,
and her appearance corresponds with the description
given of Mrs. Bently. I was very much pleased with
her, for she seemed to be a lady of very amiable character, and we became quite intimate. She appeared to
have abundant means, spent her money very freely, and
wore several diamonds of great beauty and value—
among them the crescents which were taken from me
last Friday evening. About two months after becoming acquainted with her, she came to me one day in
great distress and said that the bank, in which she
was a large stockholder, had suspended payment, and
all her available funds were locked up in it. She said
she had considerable money invested in Western land,
which she might be able to turn into cash later, but
until she could do so she would be absolutely penniless
—she had not even enough ready money to defray
her hotel bill, which had been presented that day. Then
with apparent reluctance and confusion she remarked
that she had often heard me admire her diamond
crescents, and so she had ventured to come and ask me
if I would purchase them and thus relieve her in her
present extremity, while she offered them at a price
which I considered a great bargain. I said I would
consult my husband.

"I have a weakness for diamonds—I confess that I
am extravagantly fond of them," Mrs. Vanderheck
here interposed, a slight smile curling her lips, "and
my husband has generously gratified my whims in this
respect. He approved of the purchase of the crescents,
provided some reliable jeweler would warrant that
they were all right. I reported this decision to Mrs.

Bent, and we went together to an expert to submit the stones to his verdict.

"He pronounced them exceedingly fine, and valued them far above the price which my friend had put upon them, and I told her I would take them. We returned to our hotel and went directly to my rooms, where my husband drew up a check for a hundred dollars more than the stipulated price, Mrs. Bent giving a receipt for the amount, while she was profuse in her expressions of gratitude for our kindness in relieving her from pecuniary embarrassment. 'I shall go immediately to pay my bill,' she said, looking greatly pleased that she was able to do so, as she handed me the case containing the diamonds, and then she immediately left the room. Half an hour later she came to me again, her eyes red and swollen from weeping, an open telegram in her hand. Her mother was dying, and had sent for her, and she was going immediately to her. She took an affectionate leave of me and soon after left the hotel. This, your honor, is how I came to have the crescents and"—taking a folded paper from her elegant purse—"here is the receipt for the money paid for them."

The lady took her seat after giving this testimony, while the receipt was examined by the police justice and Mr. Cutler's counsel.

"I hope the lady has not been a victim to the same cunning scheme that served to defraud the gentleman from Chicago," he gravely observed.

"You do not mean to imply that my stones are not genuine!" exclaimed Mrs. Vanderheck, with sudden dismay.

"I am not able to say, madame," his honor courteously replied, "but I should like to have them examined by an expert and proved."

Mr. Palmer here stated that he could settle the question if he were allowed to examine them.

Both cases were passed to him, and after closely inspecting the crescents for a moment or two, he returned them, with the remark:

"The stones are *all* paste, but a remarkably good imitation. I should judge that they had been submitted to a certain solution or varnish, which has recently been discovered, and is used to simulate the brilliancy of diamonds, but which, if the stones are dropped in alcohol, will dissolve and vanish."

"Impossible!" Mrs. Vanderheck protested, with some warmth. "It *cannot* be that I have worn paste ornaments for more than three years, and never discovered the fact."

"It is not strange that you were deceived," the gentleman replied, glancing at the glittering gems, "for I think that only an expert could detect the fact, they are such a clever imitation of genuine gems."

"I cannot believe it," the lady persisted, "for Mrs. Bent was not out of my sight a moment, from the time the expert in Boston pronounced his verdict, until they were delivered to me in my room at the hotel."

"Nevertheless," Mr. Palmer positively affirmed, "the woman must have adroitly managed to change the crescents on the way back, substituting the bogus for the real ones, for these are certainly paste."

Mr. Cutler's counsel here stated that his client had an important statement to make, whereupon that gentleman related that Mr. Arnold, the Chicago expert to whom the real crescents had been submitted, had made a private mark upon the setting, with a steel-pointed instrument, and if such a mark could be discovered upon Mrs. Vanderheck's ornaments they were doubtless real.

He produced the card which Mr. Arnold had given him, and the crescents were carefully examined, but no mark of any kind could be found upon them, and the general conclusion was that they were but a skillful imitation of genuine diamonds, and that Mrs. Vanderheck had only been another victim of the clever adventuress, whose identity was still as much of a mystery as ever.

Mr. Palmer and Ray now began to feel quite uncomfortable regarding the cross which Mr. Rider had also taken in charge. They consulted a few moments with Mrs. Vanderheck's counsel, and then the cross was quietly submitted to Mr. Palmer's examination.

He at once said it did not belong to him, although it was very like the one that had been stolen, for he also was in the habit of putting a private mark upon his most expensive jewelry; and he further remarked that he very much regretted that Mrs. Vanderheck should have been subjected to so much unpleasantness in connection with the unfounded suspicion.

The case was then dismissed without further discussion, and the lady behaved in the most generous and amiable manner toward both Mr. Cutler and Mr. Palmer.

She said it was not at all strange that she should have been suspected, under the circumstances, and she bore them no ill-will on account of the arrest. She was only annoyed that any publicity had been given to the matter. She even laughingly accused Ray of having suspected her on the evening of Mr. Merrill's reception, and then she explained the cause of her own

strange behavior on that occasion. She had read of
the Palmer robbery and the circumstances of his being kidnapped, and she realized at once, upon being
introduced to him when he had mispronounced her
name, that his suspicions had fastened upon her.

She shook hands cordially with Mr. Cutler, and remarked that, while she experienced some vexation and
mortification over the discovery that the crescents were
spurious, the imposition had taught her a lesson, and
she should henceforth purchase her diamonds of a reliable dealer in such articles.

"But," she added, gayly, "I shall never see a diamond crescent after this without asking the owner to
allow me to examine it. I believe I shall turn detective myself and try to ferret out the original ones if
they are still in existence."

She bowed smilingly to the three gentlemen, and
passed out of the room, leaning upon the arm of her
husband.

"Well, Ray," Mr. Palmer remarked, as they wended
their way to the store, "we may as well give up our
diamonds once for all; I have not the slightest hope
that we shall ever see them again. If we ever do find
them," he added, with an arch glance, "I'll present
them to your wife on her wedding day—that is, if they
come to light before that event occurs."

"Then my wife is to have no diamonds unless the
stolen ones are found?" Ray responded, in a tone of
laughing inquiry.

"I did not mean to imply that, my boy," Mr. Palmer responded. "I will present your wife with diamonds, and fine ones, too, when I am introduced to
her."

"Then I will give you three months in which to

make your selection," Ray retorted, with animation.

"Whew! you are hopeful, my son, or else you have had good news of your lady-love," the elder gentleman exclaimed, with surprise. "You are a sly dog, and I thought you seemed happier than usual, when you came to Hazeldean. You must tell me more about it when you have time. But three days will be time enough for my selections for your wife, and she shall have the stolen ones also, if they are ever recovered."

Mr. Rider was the most disappointed one of the whole party, for he had been so sure of his game; while he had been doggedly persistent for over three years in trying to hunt down the tricky woman, who had imposed upon Justin Cutler, and it was a bitter pill for him to swallow, to discover, just as he believed himself to be on the verge of success, that he was only getting deeper into the mire.

"She is the keenest-witted thief I ever heard of," he muttered, moodily, when the case was dismissed, "but if I could only get track of some of the Palmer diamonds there might be some hope for me even now, for I firmly believe that the same woman is at the bottom of all three thefts."

He would not take anything from Mr. Cutler for what he had done or tried to do, although the gentleman offered to remunerate him handsomely for his labor.

"I've earned nothing, for I've accomplished nothing," he said, dejectedly. "I feel, rather, as if I ought to pay your expenses on from the West, for it's been only a wild-goose chase."

"I had other business, aside from this, which called me to New York, so don't feel down at the mouth about the trip," Mr. Cutler kindly replied. "I am going to remain in the city for a few weeks, then I go to Havana to meet my sister, who has been spending the winter in Cuba for her health."

The same week Mrs. Vanderheck appeared at a select ball, wearing more diamonds than any one had ever before seen upon her at once; but after that one brilliant appearance it was remarked that she was becoming more subdued in her tastes, for she was never again seen in New York with such an expensive display of gems.

CHAPTER II.

A STORMY INTERVIEW.

After their return from Hazeldean, Mrs. Montague seemed to forget her spite against Mona. Indeed, she was even kinder than she had ever been. Mona quietly resumed her usual duties, and was so faithful and obliging that the woman apparently regretted her harshness on the night of the ball, and was very considerate in her requirements, and verified what Mary, the waitress, had once said, that she was a kind mistress if she wasn't crossed.

On the morning after their arrival in New York, Mona wrote a note to Ray, related something of what had occurred, and suggested that it might be as well not to antagonize Mrs. Montague further by being seen together while she remained in her employ. She told him where she would attend church the following Sabbath, and asked him to meet her so that they could talk over some plan by which they might see each other from time to time without exciting suspicion regarding their relations.

Mr. Amos Palmer called by appointment upon Mrs. Montague on Wednesday evening, following the return from Hazeldean, when he formally proposed, and was accepted.

When, on Thursday morning, the triumphant widow announced the fact to her nephew, he flew into a towering passion, and a bitter quarrel ensued.

"You have promised me that you would never marry," he cried, angrily; "you have pledged your word that I should be your sole heir, and I swear that you shall not give me the go-by in any such shabby fashion."

"Hush, Louis; you are very unreasonable," said his aunt. "I believe that it will be for your interest as well as mine that I marry Mr. Palmer, and because I simply change my name, it does not follow that you will not be my heir. You know that I have no other relative, and I mean that you shall inherit my fortune. If *you* will marry Kitty McKenzie immediately, I will settle a hundred thousand upon you outright."

"But I don't like the idea of your marrying at all —I vow I won't stand it!" the young man reiterated, and ignoring the subject of his own marriage. "I suppose you have reasons for wishing to change your name," he added, with a sneer, "but you must not forget that I know something of your early history and subsequent experiences, and I have you somewhat in my power."

"And you are no less in mine, young man," his companion sternly retorted. "It will not be well for you to make an enemy of me, Louis—it will be far better for you to yield to my plans gracefully, for my mind is fully set on this marriage. Can't you understand that as the wife of a man in Mr. Palmer's position, nothing that has ever been connected with my previous history will be liable to touch me. Mrs. Richmond Montague," with a sneering laugh, "will have vanished, or become a myth, and Mrs. Palmer will be unassailable by any enemies of the past."

"Yes; I can fully understand that," her nephew thoughtfully replied, "and perhaps——" Well, if I withdraw my objections, will you let me off from any supposed obligations to Kitty McKenzie? Truly, Aunt Marg," with unusual earnestness, "I don't want to marry the girl, and I do want to marry some one else; give me the hundred thousand and let me choose my own wife, and we will cry quits."

"Louis Hamblin, I believe you will drive me crazy!" cried Mrs. Montague, growing crimson with sudden anger. "What new freak has got into your head now? Who is this some one else whom you wish to marry?"

"That girl up stairs—Ruth Richards, she calls herself," the young man answered, flushing, but speaking with something of defiance in his tone.

"Good gracious, Louis! you cannot mean it!" she exclaimed, aghast. "I told you I would have no nonsense in that direction. Does she, Ruth, suspect your folly?"

"Only to toss her head and turn the cold shoulder on me. She is in no way responsible for my folly, as you call it, except by being so decidedly pretty. You'd better give in, Aunt Marg—it'll be for your interest not to make an enemy of me," he quoted, in a peculiar tone, "and it will make a man of me, too, for I vow I love the girl to distraction."

Mrs. Montague uttered a sigh of despair.

"I was afraid you'd make a fool of yourself over her, and now I shall have to send the girl away. It is too bad, for she is the only expert seamstress I have had for a year," she said, tears of vexation actually rushing to her eyes.

"No, you don't," the young man retorted, flaming up angrily; "don't you dare to send her away, or I swear I will do something desperate. Besides, the girl doesn't care a rap for me, but she is dead gone on young Palmer; and if you drive her away, the next you'll know she will forestall you in the Palmer mansion."

Mrs. Montague grew pale at this shaft, and sat for several moments absorbed in thought.

"I thought that he was in love with Walter Dinsmore's *protégée,* Mona Montague," she at last remarked, with a bitter inflection.

A peculiar smile flitted over Louis Hamblin's lips at this remark. But he quickly repressed it, and replied:

"So I heard and thought at one time; but he was deeply smitten with Ruth the night of the Hazeldean ball, and never left her side after refreshments; they sat in the balcony, half concealed by the draperies, until after one o'clock."

"You don't mean it!" Mrs. Montague exclaimed, with a start and frown. "Then the girl is more artful than I thought; but, on the whole, I'm not sure but that I should prefer to have Ray Palmer marry Ruth Richards rather than Mona Montague—it might be better for me in the end. I wonder where she is. I am almost sorry——"

She broke off suddenly, but added, after a moment:
"I don't know, Louis—I am somewhat perplexed.

If, as you say, Ray Palmer is so deeply smitten with
Ruth he must have gotten over his penchant for the
other girl. I will think over your proposition, and
tell you my conclusion later."

An expression of triumph swept over Louis Hamblin's face, but quickly assuming a grateful look, he
remarked:

"Thank you, Aunt Margie—if you'll bring that
about I'll be your loyal slave for life."

Mrs. Montague's lips curled slightly at his extravagant language, but she made no reply to it.

Presently, however, she asked:

"When are you going to attend to that matter of
business for me? I do not think it ought to be delayed any longer."

"Blast it! I am tired of business," responded her
dutiful nephew impatiently, adding: "I suppose the
sooner I go, though, the quicker it will be over."

"Yes, I want everything fixed secure before my
marriage, for I intend to manage my own private affairs afterward, the same as before," his companion
returned.

Louis laughed with some amusement.

"You ought to have been a man, Aunt Marg; your
spirit is altogether too self-reliant and independent
for a woman," he said.

"I know it; but being a woman, I must try to make
the best of the situation in the future, as I have done
all my life," she returned, with a self-conscious smile.

"Well, I will look after that matter right away—
get your instructions ready and I will be off within
an hour or two," said the young man, as he rose and
went out, while Mrs. Montague proceeded directly to
her own room.

CHAPTER III.

MONA FORESTER.

While Louis Hamblin and Mrs. Montague were engaged in the discussion mentioned in the preceding chapter, below stairs Mona sat in the sewing-room reading the paper of the previous evening. She was waiting for Mrs. Montague to come up to give her some directions about a dress which she was repairing before she could go on with it.

She had read the general news and was leisurely scanning the advertisement columns, as people often do without any special object in view, when her eye fell upon these lines:

WANTED—INFORMATION REGARDING A PERSON named Mona Forester, or her heirs, if any there be. Knowledge to her or their advantage is in the possession of CORBIN & RUSSEL, No. —— Broadway, N. Y.

Mona lost all her color as she read this.

"Can it be possible that there is any connection between this Mona Forester and my history?" she murmured thoughtfully; "Mona is a very uncommon name —it cannot be that my mother's surname was Forester, since she was Uncle Walter's sister. Perhaps this Mona Forester may have been some relative for whom she was named—possibly an aunt, or even her mother, and thus I may be one of the heirs. But," she interrupted herself and smiled, "what a romantic creature I am, to be weaving such a story out of a mere advertisement! Still," she added, more thoughtfully, "this woman's heirs cannot be very numerous or it would not be necessary to advertise for them."

She carefully cut out the lines from the paper, slipped the clipping into her pocket-book, then took up her work just as Mrs. Montague entered the room.

She gave instructions regarding the alterations she wished made, and then left Mona by herself again. All day long Mona's mind kept recurring to the advertisement she had cut from the paper, while she had an instinctive feeling that she might be in some way connected with Mona Forester, although how she could not comprehend.

"It would be useless for me to go to Corbin & Russel to make inquiries, for I could give them no reliable information about myself," she said, while considering the matter. "Oh, why could not Uncle Walter have told me more? I could not even prove that I am Mona Montague, for I have no record of my parents' marriage or of my birth. Perhaps, if I could find that woman—Uncle Walter's wife—she might be able to tell me something; but I do not know where to find her. Possibly Mrs. Montague would know whether this Mona Forester is a relative, if I dare ask her; but I do not—I could not—without betraying myself and perhaps spoil all my other plans. Oh, dear, it is so dreadful to be alone in the world and not really know who you are!" she concluded, with a sigh.

About the middle of the next forenoon Mrs. Montague asked her if she would come with her to look over a trunk of clothing preparatory to beginning upon spring sewing.

Mona readily complied with her request, and together they went up to a room in the third story. There were a number of trunks in the room, and unlocking one of these, Mrs. Montague threw back the lid and began to lay out the contents upon the floor. Mona was astonished at the number and richness of the costumes thus displayed, and thought her income must be almost unlimited to admit of such extravagance.

She selected what she thought might do to be remodeled, and then she began to refold what was to be replaced in the trunk.

Among other things taken from it, there was a large, square pasteboard box, and Mrs. Montague had just lifted it upon her lap to examine its contents to see if there was anything in it which she would need, when Mary appeared at the door, saying that Mr. Palmer was below and wished to see her.

Mrs. Montague arose quickly, and in doing so, the box slipped from her hands to the floor and its contents, composed of laces, ribbons, and gloves, went sliding in all directions.

"Oh dear! what a mess!" she exclaimed, with a frown of annoyance. "You will have to gather them up and rearrange them, Ruth, for I must go down. Just lay the dresses nicely in the trunk, and I will lock it when I return."

She went out, leaving Mona alone, and the latter began to fold the ribbons and laces, laying them in the box in an orderly manner.

When this was done she turned her attention again to the trunk into which Mrs. Montague had hastily tumbled a few garments.

"She has disarranged everything," the girl murmured. "I believe I will repack everything from the bottom, as the dresses will be full of wrinkles if left like this."

She removed every article, and noticing that the cloth in the bottom was dusty, took it out and shook it.

As she was about to replace it, she was startled to find herself gazing down upon a large crayon picture of a beautiful girl.

A low, startled cry broke from her lips, for the face looking up into hers was so like her own that it almost seemed as if she were gazing at her own reflection in a mirror, only the hair was arranged differently from the way she wore hers, and the neck was dressed in the style of twenty years previous.

"Oh, I am sure that this is a picture of my mother," she murmured, with bated breath, as, with reverent touch, she lifted it and gazed long and earnestly upon it.

"If you could but *speak* and tell me all that sad story—what caused that man to desert you in the hour of your greatest need!" she continued, with starting tears, for the eyes, so life-like, looking into hers, seemed to be seeking for sympathy and comfort. "Oh, how cruel it all was, and why should those last few weeks of your life have been so shrouded in mystery?"

She fell to musing sadly, with the picture still in her hands, and became so absorbed in her thoughts that she was almost unconscious of everything about her, or that she was neglecting her duties, until she suddenly felt a heavy hand upon her shoulders, and Mrs. Montague suddenly inquired:

"Ha! where did you get that picture? Why don't you attend to your work, and not go prying about among my things?" and she searched the girl's face with a keen glance.

Mona was quick to think and act, for she felt that now was her opportunity, if ever.

"I was not prying," she quietly responded. "I thought I would pack everything nicely from the bottom of the trunk, and as I took out the cloth to shake and smooth it, I found this picture lying beneath it. I was very much startled to find how much it resembles me. Who can she be, Mrs. Montague?" and Mona lifted a pair of innocently wondering eyes to the frowning face above her.

For a moment the woman seemed to be trying to read her very soul; then she remarked, through her set teeth:

"It is more like you, or you are more like it than I thought. Did you never see a picture like it before?"

"No, never," Mona replied, so positively that Mrs. Montague could not doubt the truth of her statement. "Is it the likeness of some relative of yours?" she asked, determined if possible to sift the matter to the bottom.

"A *relative? No, I hope* not. The girl's name was Mona Forester, and—I *hated* her!"

"Mona Forester!" repeated Mona to herself, with a great inward start, though she made no outward sign, while a feeling of bitter disappointment swept over her heart.

It could not then have been a picture of her mother, she thought, for her name must have been Mona Dinsmore, unless—strange that she had not thought of it when she read that advertisement in the paper—unless she had been the half-sister of her Uncle Walter.

"You hated *her?*" Mona murmured aloud, with her tender, devouring glance fastened upon the beautiful face.

The tone and emphasis seemed to arouse all the passion of the woman's nature.

"Yes, with my whole soul!" she fiercely cried, and before Mona was aware of her intention, she had snatched the picture from her hands, and torn it into four pieces.

"There!" she continued, tossing the fragments upon the floor, "that is the last of that; I am sure! I don't know why I have kept the miserable thing all these years."

Mona could have cried aloud at this wanton destruction of what she would have regarded as priceless, but she dared make no sign, although she was trembling in every nerve.

"Is the lady living?" she ventured to inquire, as she turned away, apparently to fold a dress, but really to conceal the painful quivering of her lips.

"No. You can finish packing this trunk, then you may take these dresses to the sewing-room. You may begin ripping this brown one. And you may take the pieces of that picture down and tell Mary to burn them. I came up for a wrap; I am going for a drive."

Mrs. Montague secured her wrap, then swept from the room, walking fiercely over the torn portrait, looking as if she would have been glad to trample thus upon the living girl whom she had so hated.

Mona reverently gathered up the fragments, her lips quivering with pain and indignation.

She laid them carefully together, but a bitter sob burst from her at the sight of the great ragged tears across the beautiful face.

"Oh, mother, mother!" she murmured, "what an insult to you, and I was powerless to help it."

She finished her packing, then taking the dresses that were to be made over, and the torn picture, she went below.

She could not bear the thought of having that lovely face, marred though it was, consigned to the flames, yet she dare not disobey Mrs. Montague's command to give it to Mary to be burned.

She waited until the girl came up stairs, then she called her attention to the pieces, and told her what was to be done with them.

She at once exclaimed at the resemblance to Mona.

"Where could Mrs. Montague have got it?" she cried; "it's enough like you, miss, to be your own mother, and a beautiful lady she must have been, too. It's a pity to burn the picture, Miss Ruth; wouldn't you like to keep it?"

"Perhaps Mrs. Montague would prefer that no one should have it; she said it was to be destroyed, you know," Mona replied, but with a wistful look at the mutilated crayon.

"You shall have it if you want it, and I'll fix it all right with her," said the girl, in a confidential tone, as she put the pieces back into Mona's hands. She had become very fond of the gentle seamstress, and would have considered no favor too great to be conferred upon her.

That same afternoon, when Mona went out for her walk, she took the mutilated picture with her.

She made her way directly to the rooms of a first-class photographer, and asked if the portrait could be copied.

Yes, she was assured; there would be no difficulty about getting as good a picture as the original, only it would have to be all hand work.

Mona said she would give the order if it could be done immediately, and, upon being told she could have the copy in three days, she said she would call for it at the end of that time.

She did so, and found a perfect reproduction of her mother's face, and upon her return to Mrs. Montague's she gave the pieces of the other to Mary, telling her she believed she did not care to keep them—they had better be burned as her mistress had desired.

This relieved her mind, for she did not wish the girl to practice any deception for her sake, and she feared that Mrs. Montague might inquire if her orders had been obeyed.

The following day she took the fresh portrait with her when she went out, and proceeded directly to the office of Corbin & Russel, who had advertised for information regarding Mona Forester or her heirs.

A gentlemanly clerk came forward as she entered, and politely inquired her business.

She asked to see a member of the firm, and at the same time produced the slip which she had cut from the paper.

The clerk's face lighted as he saw it, and his manner at once betrayed deep interest in the matter.

"Ah, yes," he said, affably; "please walk this way. Mr. Corbin is in and will be glad to see you."

He led the way to a private office, and, throwing open the door, respectfully remarked to some one within:

"A lady to see you, sir, about the Forester business." Then turning to Mona, he added: "This is Mr. Corbin, miss."

A gentleman, who was sitting before a desk, at once arose and came eagerly forward, scanning Mona's face with great earnestness.

"Have a chair, if you please, Miss ——. Be kind enough to tell me what I shall call you."

"My name is Mona Montague," the young girl replied, a slight flush suffusing her cheek beneath his keen glance.

The gentleman started as she spoke it, and regarded her more closely than before.

"Miss Mona Montague!" he repeated, with a slight emphasis on the last name; "and you have called to answer the advertisement which recently appeared in the papers. What can you tell me about Miss Mona Forester?"

"She was my mother, sir," Mona replied, as she seated herself in the chair offered her. "At least," she added, "my mother's name was Mona Forester before her marriage."

"Well, then, young lady, if you can prove that the Mona Forester, for whom we have advertised, was your mother, there is a snug little sum of money awaiting your disposal," the gentleman smilingly remarked.

Mona looked astonished. She had scarcely given a thought to reaping any personal advantage, as had been hinted in the advertisement, from the fact of being Mona Forester's child. Her chief desire and hope had been to prove her mother's identity, and to learn something more, if possible, of her personal history.

She was somewhat excited by the information, but removing the wrapper from her picture, she arose and laid it before Mr. Corbin, remarking:

"This is a portrait of Mona Forester, and she was my mother."

Mr. Corbin took the crayon and studied the beautiful face intently for a few moments; then turning his glance again upon his visitor, he said, in a tone of conviction:

"There can be no doubt that you and the original of this picture are closely united by ties of consanguinity, for your resemblance to her is very striking. You spoke in the past tense, however, so I suppose the lady is not living."

"No, sir; she died at the time of my birth," Mona answered, sadly.

"Ah! that was very unfortunate for you," Mr. Corbin remarked, in a tone of sympathy. "You gave your name as Mona Montague, so, of course, Miss Forester must have married a gentleman by that name. May I ask—ah—is he living?"

"No, sir, he is not."

"Will you kindly give me his whole name?" Mr. Corbin now asked, while his eyes had a gleam of intense interest within their dark depths.

"Richmond Montague."

Again the lawyer started, and a look of astonishment passed over his features.

"Where have you lived, Miss Montague, since the death of your parents?" he inquired.

"Here in New York, with my uncle."

"Ah! and who was your uncle, if you please?" and the man seemed to await her reply with almost breathless interest.

"Mr. Dinsmore—Walter Dinsmore."

The lawyer sat suddenly erect, and drew in a long breath, while his keen eyes seemed to be trying to read the girl's very soul.

He did not speak for nearly a minute; then he said, with his usual composure:

"So, then, you are the niece of Walter Dinsmore,

Esq., who died recently, and whose property was claimed by a—a wife who had lived separate from him for a good many years."

Mona flushed hotly at this remark. It seemed almost like a stain upon her uncle's fair name to have his domestic affairs spoken of in this way, and she had been very sore over the revelation that he had had a discarded wife living.

"Yes, sir," she briefly responded, but with an air of dignity that caused a gleam of amusement to leap to the lawyer's eyes.

"Well—it is very queer," he remarked, musingly, while his eyes traveled back and forth between the picture he held in his hands and the face of the beautiful girl before him.

Mona looked a trifle surprised—she could not understand what was "queer" in the fact that she was Walter Dinsmore's niece.

"I suppose," resumed Mr. Corbin, after another season of reflection, during which he looked both grave and perplexed, "that you have the *proofs* of all that you claim? You can prove that you are the daughter of Mona Forester and—Richmond Montague?"

Again Mona blushed, and hot tears of grief and shame rushed to her eyes, as, all at once, it flashed into her mind that her errand there would be a fruitless one, for she was utterly powerless to prove anything, while the peculiar emphasis which Mr. Corbin had almost unconsciously used in speaking of her father made her very uncomfortable. She had hoped to learn more than she had to reveal, and that her strong resemblance to her mother's picture would be sufficient to prove the relationship between them; but now she began to fear that it would not.

"What proofs do I need?" she asked, in a voice that was not quite steady.

"The marriage certificate of the contracting parties, or some witness of the ceremony, besides some reliable person who can identify you as their child," was the business-like response.

"Then I can prove nothing," Mona said, in a weary tone, "for I have no certificate, no letters, not even a scrap of writing penned by either my father or my mother."

A peculiar expression swept over Mr. Corbin's face at this statement, and Mona caught sight of it.

"What could it mean?" she asked herself, with a flash of anger that was quite foreign to her amiable disposition. "Did the man imagine her to be an impostor, or did he suspect that there might have been no legal bond between her parents?"

This latter thought made her tingle to her finger-tips, and aroused all her proud spirit.

"I can at least prove that I am Walter Dinsmore's niece," she added, lifting her head with a haughty air, while her thoughts turned to Mr. Graves, her uncle's lawyer. He at least knew and could testify to the fact. "He took me," she continued, "three days after mother's death, and I lived with him from that time until he died."

"Ah! and your mother was Mr. Dinsmore's sister?" questioned Mr. Corbin.

"Yes. I always supposed, until within a few days, that she was his own sister," Mona said, thinking it best to be perfectly open in her dealings with the lawyer; "that her name was Mona Dinsmore; but only this week I learned that it was Mona Forester, so, of course, she must have been a half-sister."

"Well, if you can prove what you have stated it may lead to further developments," said Mr. Corbin, kindly. "Let me examine your proofs, and then I shall know what to do next."

A sudden fear smote Mona—a great shock made her heart almost cease its beating at the lawyer's request.

What proofs had she for him to examine? How could she establish the absolute fact?

It was true that her uncle had authorized a will to be made leaving all his property to his "beloved niece," but he had not been able to sign it, and it of course amounted to nothing. Must even this relationship be denied her in law? Oh, why had he not been more careful in regard to her interests? It was very hard—it was very humiliating to have her identity thus doubted.

"Mr. Horace Graves was my uncle's lawyer; he will tell you that I am his niece," she faltered, with white lips.

"My dear young lady, I know Mr. Graves, and that he is a reliable man," Mr. Corbin observed; "but a hundred people might assert that you were Mr. Dinsmore's niece, and it would not prove anything. Don't you know that to satisfy the law upon any point there must be indisputable proof forthcoming; there must be some written record—something tangible to demonstrate it, or it amounts to nothing? You may be the niece of Mr. Dinsmore; you may be the daughter of Mr. and Mrs. Richmond Montague; this may be the portrait of Miss Mona Forester; but the facts would have to be established before your claim could be recognized and the property bequeathed to Miss Forester made over to you."

"Oh," cried Mona, in deep distress, "what, then,

shall I do? I do not care so much about the property as I do about learning more about my mother. I will tell you frankly," she went on, with burning cheeks and quivering lips, "that I know there is some mystery connected with her married life; my uncle told me something, but I have reason to believe that he kept back much that I ought to know," and Mona proceeded to relate all that Mr. Dinsmore had revealed to her on her eighteenth birthday, while the lawyer listened with evident interest, his face expressing great sympathy for his fair young visitor.

"I am very glad to have you confide in me so freely," he remarked, when she concluded, "and I will deal with equal frankness with you so far as I may. Our reason for advertising for information regarding Miss Mona Forester was this: I received recently a communication from a lawyer in London, desiring me to look up a person so named, and stating that a certain Homer Forester—a wool merchant of Australia—had just died in London while on his way home to America, and had left in his lawyer's hands a will bequeathing all that he possessed to a niece, Miss Mona Forester, or her heirs, if she was not living. The date and place of her birth were given, but further than that Homer Forester could give no information regarding her."

"Where was she born?" Mona here interposed, eagerly. "Oh, sir, it is strange and dreadful that I should be so ignorant of my own mother's history, is it not?"

"Miss Forester, according to the information given in her uncle's will, was born in Trenton, New Jersey, March 10th, 1843, but that is all that I can tell you about her," bestowing a glance of sympathy upon the agitated girl. "You say that she died at the time of your birth. I wish you could bring me proof of this, and that you are her daughter; but of course your mere assertion proves nothing, nor your possession of this picture, which may or may not be her. Believe me, I should be very glad to surrender this property to you if it rightly belongs to you."

"Of course I should like to have it, if I am the legal heir," Mona said, thoughtfully; "but," with a proud uplifting of her pretty head, "I can do without it, for I am able to earn my own living."

"Is there no one to whom you can appeal? How about Mr. Dinsmore's wife, who succeeded in getting all his property away from you—could she prove anything?" and Mr. Corbin regarded his companion with curious interest as he asked the question.

"I do not know—I have never even seen her," said Mona, thoughtfully; "or, at least, if I have, it must have been when I was too young to remember anything about her; besides, I should not know where to find her. There is only one person in the world, I believe, who really knows anything about me."

"And who is that?" interposed Mr. Corbin, eagerly.

"Mrs. Richmond Montague, my father's second wife."

Mr. Corbin suddenly arose from his chair, and began to pace the floor, while, if she had been watching him closely, Mona might have seen that his face was deeply flushed.

"Hum! Mrs. Richmond Montague—is—— Where is Mrs. Richmond Montague?" he questioned, somewhat incoherently.

"Here, in this city."

"Then why do you not appeal to her?" demanded

the lawyer, studying the girl's face with some perplexity.

"Because—there are reasons why I do not wish to meet her just at present," Mona said, with some embarrassment, "and I do not know that she would be able to prove anything. To be frank," she continued, with increasing confusion, "the present Mrs. Montague entertained a strong dislike, even hatred, against my mother. Doubtless her animosity extends to me also, and she would not be likely to prove anything that would personally benefit me."

"You have not a very high opinion of Mrs. Richmond Montague, I perceive," Mr. Corbin remarked, with a curious smile.

"I have nothing special against her personally, any further than that I know she hated my mother, and I do not wish to meet her at present. Why," with sudden thought, "could not you try to ascertain from her some facts regarding my mother's marriage?"

"I might possibly," said Mr. Corbin, gravely, "but that would not benefit you; you would be obliged to meet her in order to be identified as Mona Forester's child."

"I had not thought of that," replied Mona, with a troubled look, "and," she added, "she could not even identify me to your satisfaction, for she never saw me to know me as Mona Montague."

"As Mona Montague!" repeated the quick-witted lawyer; "does she know you by any other name? Are you not keeping something back which it would be well for me to know?"

"Yes; I will tell you all about it," Mona said, flushing again, and resolving to disclose everything. She proceeded to relate the singular circumstances which led to her becoming an inmate of Mrs. Montague's home, together with the incident of finding her mother's picture in one of her trunks.

"Ah! I think this throws a little light upon the matter," Mr. Corbin said, when she concluded. "If you had told me these facts at first we should have saved time. And you never saw this woman until you met her in her own house?" he asked, in conclusion, and regarding Mona searchingly.

"No, never; and had it not been for the hope of learning something about my mother's history, I believe I should have gone away again immediately," she replied.

"I should suppose she would have recognized you at once, by your resemblance to this picture," remarked her companion.

"She did notice it, and questioned me quite closely; but I evaded her, and she finally thought that the resemblance was only a coincidence."

"Well, I must confess that the affair is very much mixed—*very* much mixed," said the lawyer, with peculiar emphasis, "but I believe, now that I know the whole story, that the truth can be ascertained if right measures are used; *and*," he continued, impressively, "if we can prove that you are what you assert, the only child of Richmond Montague and Mona Forester, you will not only inherit the money left by Homer Forester, but, being the child of the first union—provided we can prove it legal—you could also claim the bulk of the property which your father left. Mrs. Montague, if she should suspect our design, would, of course, use all her arts to conceal the truth; but I imagine, by using a little strategy, we may get at it. Yes, Miss Montague, if we can only work it up it will be a

beautiful case—a *beautiful* case," he concluded, with
singular enthusiasm.

Mona gave utterance to a sigh of relief. She was
more hopeful than ever that the mystery, which had
so troubled her, would be solved, and she was very
grateful to the kind-hearted lawyer for the deep interest he manifested in the matter.

"You are very good," she said, as she arose to take
her leave; "but really, as I have said before, I am not
so anxious to secure property as I am to know more
about my parents. Do you suppose," she questioned,
with some anxiety, "that the enmity between my uncle
and my father was so bitter that—that Uncle Walter
was in any way responsible for his—my father's—
death?"

"Poor child! have you had that terrible fear to contend against with all your other troubles?" asked Mr.
Corbin, in a tone of compassion. "No, Miss Montague," he added, with grave positiveness, "I do not believe that Walter Dinsmore—and I knew him well—
ever willfully committed a wrong against any human
being. Now," he resumed, smiling, to see the look of
trouble fade out of her eyes at his assurance, "I am
going to try to ferret out the 'mystery' for you. Come
to me again in a week, and I believe I shall have something definite to tell you."

Mona thanked him, after which he shook hands cordially with her, and she returned to West Forty-ninth
street.

"Well, well!" muttered the lawyer, after his fair
client had departed, "so that is Dinsmore's niece, who
was to have had his fortune, if he could have had his
way about it! I wonder what Madame Dinsmore
would say if she knew that I had taken her husband's

protégée as a client! It is a burning shame that she could not have had his money, if it was his wish—or at least a share of it. Poor little girl! after living in such luxury all her life, to have to come down to such a humdrum existence as sewing for a living! I will do my best for her—I will at least try to secure Homer Forester's money to her. It's strange, too, that I should happen to have dealings with the brilliant Mrs. Montague, also. It's a very queer case and there is a deep scheme behind it all! I believe——"

What he might have believed remained unsaid, for the office-boy entered at that moment and announced another client, and the astute lawyer was obliged to turn his attention, for the time, in another direction.

CHAPTER IV.

MR. CORBIN MAKES A CALL.

On the evening of the same day that Mona visited the office of Corbin & Russel, attorneys at law, and shortly after Mrs. Montague had finished her lonely dinner—for her nephew was away on business—there came a sharp ring at the door of No. — West Forty-ninth street.

Mary answered it, and, after ushering the gentleman into the reception-room, went to her mistress to inform her that a caller was waiting below.

"Erastus Corbin," Mrs. Montague read, as she took the neat card from the salver, and her face lighted with sudden interest.

"Perhaps he has sold that property for me," she

murmured. "I hope so, for I wish to turn all my real
estate into money, if possible, before my marriage."

She made some slight change in her costume, for
she never allowed herself to go into the presence of
gentlemen without looking her best, and then hastened
below.

She greeted the lawyer with great cordiality, and
remarked, smilingly:

"I hope you have good news for me. Is that property sold yet?"

"I cannot say that it is sold, madame," Mr. Corbin returned; "but I have had an offer for it, which,
if you see fit to accept, will settle the matter very
shortly."

"Tell me about it," said the lady, eagerly.

Mr. Corbin made a statement from a memorandum
which he drew from his pocket, upon the conclusion of
which Mrs. Montague authorized him to sell immediately, saying that she wished to dispose of all her
real estate, even if she had to sacrifice something in
doing so, remarking that a bank account was far less
trouble than such property; and, having discussed and
decided some other points, the lawyer arose as if to
take his leave.

"Pray do not hasten," Mrs. Montague smilingly remarked.

She happened to have no engagement for the evening, and, being alone, was glad of even the companionship of a prosy attorney.

"Thank you," Mr. Corbin politely returned; "but I
have other matters on hand which ought to be attended to."

"Surely you do not work evenings as well as during the day?" Mrs. Montague observed, with some surprise.

"Not always; but just now I seem to have some very knotty cases on hand—one, in particular, seems to baffle all my skill with its mystery. Indeed, it bids fair to develop quite a romance."

"Indeed! you pique my curiosity, and we women are dear lovers of romance in real life, you know," said the charming widow, with an arch smile. "Would it be betraying confidence to tell me a little about it?" she added, persuasively.

"Oh no; the matter is no secret, that I know of, and really you are so cozy here," with an appreciative glance about the attractive room as he resumed his seat, "I am tempted to stay and chat a while. I recently received a communication from an English lawyer who desired to turn a case over to me, as it related to American parties, and he had no time to come here to look them up. A man who was on his way home from Australia, was taken ill in London and died there; but before his death he made his will, leaving all his property to a niece, although he did not know whether she was living or not. All the information he could give regarding her was her name, with the date and place of her birth. In case she should not be living, her heirs are to inherit the money. I have made every effort to find her—have been to the place where she was born—but can get no trace of her—no one remembered such a person, and I could not even learn whether she had ever married. I am afraid that the case will prove to be a very complicated and vexatious one."

"I should think so," responded Mrs. Montague, who

appeared to be deeply interested in the story. "What was the girl's name?"

"Mona Forester."

"Mona Forester!" repeated the woman, in a startled tone, and growing as white as her handkerchief. "I didn't know she had a relative in the world, except——"

She abruptly paused, for she had been thrown entirely off her guard, and had committed herself, just as the wily lawyer intended and suspected.

A flash of triumph gleamed in his eyes for an instant at the success of his ruse.

"Ah! did you ever know of such a person?" he demanded, eagerly, and with well-feigned surprise.

"I—I knew of—a girl by that name before I was married," Mrs. Montague reluctantly admitted, and beginning to recover her composure.

"Where did she reside?"

"She was born in Trenton, New Jersey, I believe," was the evasive reply.

"Yes, my papers so state—and she must be the same person," said Mr. Corbin, in a tone of conviction. "But that is very meager information. Was Trenton your home also?"

"No, I lived in New York until my marriage."

"Was Miss Forester ever married?"

"Yes."

"Ah! how fortunate that I happened to mention this circumstance to you this evening!" exclaimed the lawyer, with great apparent satisfaction, but ignoring the evident reluctance of his companion to give him information. "Perhaps you can give more particulars. Whom did the lady marry?"

"Don't ask me anything about her, Mr. Corbin,"

Mrs. Montague cried, excitedly, and with an angry gesture. "The girl ruined my life—she loved the man I loved and—I hated her accordingly."

"But surely you can have no objection to telling me what you know of her history," returned Mr. Corbin, with assumed surprise. "I have this case to settle, and I simply wish to find the woman or her heirs, in order to do my duty and carry out the instructions of the will. It would assist me greatly if you could tell me where I might find her," he concluded, in an appealing tone.

"She is dead—she died more than eighteen years ago."

"Ah! where did she die?"

"Abroad—in London."

"Did she leave any heirs?"

"She died in giving birth to her only child."

"Did the child live?"

"I—believe so."

"Was it a son or a daughter?"

"The latter."

"What became of her—where is she now?"

"I do not know—I do not care!" were the vicious words which burst from the woman's white lips, and Mr. Corbin saw that she was greatly excited, while everything that she had said thus far went to corroborate the statements Mona had made to him regarding her mother.

"But, my dear madame," Mr. Corbin said, soothingly, "while I do not like to trouble you, or recall painful memories, cannot you see that it is my duty to sift this matter and avail myself of whatever information I can get? If Miss Forester was married and had a child, that child, if living, is Homer Forester's heir, and I must find her. Now, if you know anything about these people that will assist me in my search, it becomes your duty to reveal it to me."

"I cannot; I do not know of anything that will assist you," sullenly returned Mrs. Montague, who was mentally reproaching herself in the most bitter manner for having allowed herself to be taken so unawares and to betray so much.

"Whom did the lady marry?" persisted Mr. Corbin.

"I will not tell you!" passionately exclaimed his companion. "Oh, why have I told you anything? Why did I acknowledge that I even knew Mona Forester? I should not have done so, but you surprised the truth from me, and I will tell you nothing more. I hated the girl, and though I have never seen her, I hate the child on her account, and I would not lift even a finger to help her in any way."

"Are you not unreasonably vindictive, Mrs. Montague?" mildly asked Mr. Corbin.

"Unreasonable or not, I mean what I say, and Homer Forester's money may be scattered to the four winds of heaven for any effort that I will make for Mona Forester's child," was the dogged response.

"Do you not see that I must learn the truth?" the lawyer asked, with some sternness, "and though I am averse to using threats to a lady, if you will not tell me voluntarily I shall be obliged to use means to compel you to reveal what you know."

"Compel me!" repeated Mrs. Montague, confronting him with haughty mien. "You cannot do that."

"But I can, Mrs. Montague," Mr. Corbin positively asserted. "Since you have acknowledged so much, and it is evident that you could reveal more, you can be compelled, by law, to do so under oath."

"You would not dare to adopt such stringent measures with me, after all the business that I have thrown into your hands," the woman said, sharply, but growing white about the mouth.

"My duty is just as obligatory to one client as to another. I am under as much obligation to carry out the conditions of Homer Forester's will as I am to be faithful to your interests," the lawyer replied, with inflexible integrity.

"Then you will no longer be faithful to me—you will transact no more business for *me*," Mrs. Montague asserted, with angry brow and compressed lips.

"Very well, if that is your decision I must submit to it," was the imperturbable response. "And now, madame, I ask you, once for all, to tell me the name of the man whom Mona Forester married?"

"I will not."

"Then let *me* tell *you* what conclusion I have drawn from what I have learned during this interview," said Mr. Corbin, as he leaned forward and looked straight into the woman's flashing eyes. "You have said you hated her because she ruined your life—because she loved the man you loved. You have refused to tell me the name of that man. You can have but one reason in thus withholding this information—that motive is fear; therefore, I infer that Mona Forester was the *first wife of your husband—her child was your husband's daughter.*"

"Prove it, then!" cried his companion, with a scornful, though nervous, laugh. "Find the marriage certificate—find the witnesses who saw them married, the clergyman who performed the ceremony, the church register where their names are recorded, if you can."

"I believe they will be found in good time," confidently asserted Mr. Corbin, as he arose the second time to leave; "and, madame, if such proofs are found do you comprehend what the result will be? Not only will Mona Forester's child inherit the fortune left by Homer Forester, but also the bulk of your deceased husband's property."

"Never! for no one in this world can prove that Mona Forester was ever legally married, and—I defy you to do your worst," hoarsely cried Mrs. Montague, with lips that were almost livid, while she trembled visibly with mingled excitement, fear, and anger.

But the gentleman had no desire to discuss the matter further. He simply bade her a courteous good-evening, and then quietly left the house.

"It is the strangest affair that I ever had anything to do with," he muttered, as he walked briskly down the street. "The girl's story must be true, for it tallies exactly with the woman's admissions this evening. There must be proof somewhere, too. Can it be possible," he went on, with a start, "that they are in Mrs. Montague's hands? If so, she is liable to destroy them, and thus plunge my pretty little client into endless trouble. It is strange that her uncle, Dinsmore, could not have been more sensible and left some definite information regarding the child. But I am going to do my best for her, and though I never had quite so mysterious a case before, I believe the very obscurity which invests it only adds interest to it."

Mrs. Montague was in a terrible passion after her lawyer had left. She sprang to her feet and paced the floor from end to end, with angry steps, her face almost convulsed with malice and hatred.

"Can it be possible that I am going to have that

battle to fight over again, after all these years?" she muttered; "that the child is going to rise up to avenge the wrongs of her mother? What if she does? Why need I fear her? I have held my own so far, and I will make a tough fight to do so in the future. Possession is said to be nine points in law and I shall hold on to my money like grim death. I never could—I never will give up these luxuries," she cried, sweeping a covetous glance around the exquisitely furnished room. "I plotted for them—I sold my soul for them and him, now they are mine—mine, and no one shall take them from me! Mona Forester, how I hated you!—how I hate your daughter, even though I have never seen her!—how I almost hate that girl up stairs for her strange resemblance to you. I would have sent her out of the house long ago for it, if she had not been so good and faithful a seamstress, and needful to me in many ways. She, herself, saw the resemblance to that picture—— By the way," she interposed, with a start, "I wonder if she obeyed me about that crayon the other day! If she didn't—if she kept it I shall be tempted to believe—— I'll find out, anyhow."

With a somewhat anxious look on her face, the woman hurried up stairs to her room.

Upon reaching it she rang an imperative peal upon her bell.

Mary presently made her appearance, and one quick glance told her that something had gone wrong with her mistress.

"Bring me a pitcher of ice-water," curtly commanded Mrs. Montague. "And, Mary——"

"Yes, marm."

"Did Miss Richards give you a torn picture the other day?"

"Yes, marm," answered the girl, flushing, "she said you wanted it burned."

"Did you burn it?"

"N-o, marm, somehow I couldn't make up my mind to put it in the fire; it was such a pretty face, and so like Miss Richards, and I've been wanting a picture of her ever since she came here, only I thought maybe she'd resent it if I asked her for one; and so I pasted it together as well as I could, and tacked it up in my room," the girl explained, volubly, and concluded by meekly adding: "I hope there was no harm in it, marm."

"You may bring it to me," was all the reply that Mrs. Montague vouchsafed her attendant; and Mary, looking rather crestfallen, withdrew to obey the command.

"It is a shame to burn it," she muttered, as she took down the defaced picture, and slowly returned down stairs; "but I'm glad Miss Ruth gave it to me before she asked for it."

Mrs. Montague sprang up the moment the girl entered the room, and snatching the portrait from her hands, dashed it upon the bed of glowing coals in the grate.

"When I give an order I want it obeyed," she said, imperiously. "Now go and bring me the water."

Mary withdrew again, wondering what could have happened to make her mistress so out of sorts, and finally came to the conclusion that the lawyer must have brought her bad news.

"There! that is the last of that!" Mrs. Montague said, as she watched the flames curl about the beautiful face in the grate. "I'm glad the girl didn't keep the picture herself; I believe that all my previous suspicions would have been aroused if she had. It *can't* be that *she* is Mona's child, for she has always been so indifferent when I have questioned her. Possibly she may be a descendant of some other branch of the family, and does not know it. My only regret is that I did not try to see that other girl before Walter Dinsmore died; then I should have been sure. I wonder where she can be? And to think that Mona Forester should have had an uncle to turn up just at this time! I didn't suppose she had a relative in the world besides the child."

Her musings were cut short at this point by the return of Mary with the water. She poured out a glassful for her mistress, and then was told that she might go.

The lady set down the glass without even tasting its contents; then rising, went to the door and locked it, after which she walked to a small table which stood in a bay-window, and removed the marble top, carefully laying it upon the floor.

This act revealed instead of the usual skeleton stand where a marble top is used a polished table of solid cherry, with what appeared to be a lid in the top, and in which there was a small brass-bound key-hole.

Drawing a bunch of keys from her pocket, Mrs. Montague selected a tiny one from among the others, inserted it in the lock, and the next moment the lid in the table was lifted, thus revealing a secret compartment underneath.

This was filled with various things—paper boxes, packages of various forms and sizes, together with some documents and letters.

Drawing a chair before the table, the woman sat down and began to examine the letters.

There was an intensely bitter expression on her face—a frown on her brow, a sneer on her lips— which so disfigured it that scarcely any one would have recognized her as the brilliant and beautiful woman of the world who so charmed every one in society.

There were perhaps a dozen letters in the package which she took out of the table, and these, as she untied the ribbon that bound them together, and slipped them through her fingers, were all addressed in a delicate and beautiful style of penmanship.

She snatched one from the others, and passionately tore it across, envelope and all. Then she suddenly dropped them on her lap, a shiver running over her, her cheek paling with some inward emotion.

"Ugh! they give me a ghostly feeling! My flesh creeps! I feel almost as if Mona Forester herself were standing beside me, and had laid her dead hand upon me. I cannot look them over—I will tie them up again and burn them all at once," she muttered, in a hoarse tone.

She gathered them up, and hastily wound the ribbon about them, laying them upon the table beside her, then proceeded with her examination of the other contents of the secret compartment.

CHAPTER V.

MONA DECLINES A PROPOSAL.

Mrs. Montague next took a square pasteboard box from the secret compartment in the table, and opened it.

On a bed of pure white cotton there lay some exquisite jewelry. A pearl and diamond cross, a pair of unusually large whole pearls for the ears, and two narrow but costly bands for the wrists, set with the same precious gems.

"Pearls!" sneered the woman, giving the box, with its contents, an angry shake. "He used to call her his 'pearl,' and so, forsooth, he had to represent his estimate of her in some tangible form. There is nothing of the pearl-like nature about me," she continued, with a short, bitter laugh. "I am more like the cold, glittering diamond, and give me pure crystallized carbon every time in preference to any other gem. He wasn't niggardly with her on that score, either," she concluded, lifting the upper layer of cotton, and revealing several diamond ornaments beneath.

"She was a proud little thing, though," she mused, after gazing upon them in silence for a moment, "to go off and leave all these trinkets behind her. I'd have taken them with me and made the most of them. They haven't done me much good, however, since they came into my possession. I never could wear them without feeling as I did just now about the letters. I might have sold them, I suppose, and I don't know why I haven't done so, unless it is because they are all marked."

She covered them and threw the box from her with a passionate gesture, and then searched for a moment in silence among the remaining contents of the table.

She finally found what she wanted, apparently, for a look of triumph swept over her face.

It was a folded document, evidently of parchment.

"Ha, ha! prove your shrewd inferences, my keen-witted lawyer, if you can," she muttered, exultantly, as she unfolded it, and ran her eyes over it. "Mona Forester's child the heir to the bulk of my husband's property, indeed! Perhaps, but she will have to prove it before she can get it. How fortunate that I helped myself to these precious keepsakes when he was off his guard; even he did not dream that I had this," and she shook the parchment until it rattled noisily through the room; then refolding it, she put it carelessly aside, and turned once more to what remained to be examined.

"Here is that exquisite point-lace fan," she said, lifting a long, narrow box, and removing the lid. "I never had a point-lace fan until I bought it for myself; and here is that picture; I never had his likeness painted on ivory and set in a frame of rubies! Ha! Miss Mona, you were a favored wench, but your triumph was of short duration."

It is impossible to convey any idea of the bitterness of the woman's tone, or the vindictiveness of her look, as she took from a velvet case the picture of a handsome young man, of perhaps twenty-five years, painted on ivory, and encircled with a costly frame of gold set with rubies.

"You loved her," she cried, fiercely, as she gazed with all her soul in her eyes upon that attractive face, while her whole frame shook with emotion. "Nothing was too costly or elegant for your petted darling; her slightest wish was your law, while for me you had scarcely a word or a look of affection; you were like ice upon which not even the lava-tide of my idolatry could make the slightest impression. Is it any wonder that I hated her for having absorbed all that I craved? Is it strange that I exulted when they drove her from her apartments in Paris, believing her to be a thing too vile to be tolerated by respectable people. Well, she had his love, but I had him—I vowed that I would win, and—I did."

But, evidently, the memory of her triumph was not a very comforting one, for she suddenly dropped her face upon the hands that still clasped the picture, and burst into a torrent of tears, while deep sobs shook her frame, and she seemed utterly overwhelmed by the tempest of her grief.

Surely in this woman's nature there were depths which no one, who had seen her the center of attraction in the thronged and brilliant drawing-rooms in high-life, would have believed possible to her.

Suddenly, in the midst of this unusual outburst, there came a knock upon the door.

The sound seemed to give her a terrible start in her nervous state.

She half sprang from her chair, a look of guilt and fear sweeping over her flushed and tear-stained face, the table before her gave a sudden lurch, and before she could put out her hand to save it, it went over and fell to the floor with a crash, spilling its contents, and snapping the lid to the secret compartment short off at its hinges.

"What is it?—who is there?" Mrs. Montague demanded, as she went toward the door, while she tried to control her trembling voice to speak naturally.

"What has happened?—I thought I heard a fall," came the response in the anxious tones of Mona's voice.

"Nothing very serious has happened," returned Mrs. Montague, frowning, for the girl, who so closely resembled the rival she hated, coming to her just at that moment, irritated her exceedingly. "I simply upset something just as you knocked. What do you want?"

"I only came to ask if I should finish your tea-gown in the morning, or do the mending, as usual," Mona replied.

"Finish the tea-gown. I shall need it for the afternoon."

"Very well; I am sorry if I disturbed you, Mrs. Montague. Good-night," and Mona turned away from the door wondering what could have caused such a clatter within the woman's room.

Mrs. Montague went back to the bay-window, righted the table, rearranged its contents, and fitted the broken lid over them with hands that still trembled with her recent excitement.

"What a pity that the lid is broken," she muttered, impatiently, "for now it will do no good to lock it. I cannot help it, however, and perhaps no one will suspect that there is a secret compartment beneath the slab."

She carefully replaced the heavy marble, moved the table to its usual position, and then, worn out with the conflict she had experienced, retired for the night.

But she did not sleep well; she was nervous, and tossed uneasily upon her bed until far into the small hours of the morning, when she finally dropped into a fitful slumber.

She was aroused from this about eight o'clock the following day by Mary, who came as usual to bring her a cup of coffee, which she always drank before rising. There also lay upon the tray a yellow official-looking envelope.

"What is this?" Mrs. Montague demanded, as she seized it and regarded it with some anxiety.

"A telegram, marm. A messenger brought it just as I was coming up stairs," the girl replied.

Her mistress tore it open and devoured its contents with one sweeping glance.

Instantly her face flushed a deep crimson, and she crushed the message hastily within her hand, while she began to drink her coffee, but seemed to become deeply absorbed in her own thoughts while doing so.

A few moments later she arose and dressed herself rapidly, but all the time appeared preoccupied and troubled about something.

"I believe I shall let Louis marry her if he wants to. I could settle the hundred thousand on him, and stipulate that they go West, or somewhere out of the State, to live. I believe I'll do it," she murmured once, while thus engaged, "that is, if——"

She did not finish the sentence, but, with a resolute step and air, went down to her breakfast.

She had no appetite, however, and after dallying at the table for half an hour or so, she went up stairs again and entered the sewing-room.

She found Mona busy at work upon the tea-gown —a beautiful robe of old-rose cashmere, made up with a lighter shade of heavy armure silk.

"Can you finish it in season?" she inquired.

"Oh, yes, easily. I have about an hour's more work to do upon it," the young girl answered.

"That is well, for I want you to go down town to do some shopping for me. I cannot attend to it, as I wish to keep fresh for my high-tea this afternoon," Mrs. Montague returned, flushing slightly. Then she added: "I will make out a list of what I need, and you may go as soon as the dress is done."

Mona was pleased with the commission, for the

morning was lovely, and she had felt unusually weak and weary ever since rising. The close application to which she had been subjected since her return from Hazeldean—for she had been hurried with spring sewing—had worn upon her.

A feeling of discouragement had also taken possession of her, for she seemed no nearer learning the truth about her mother than when she had first come there.

She was confident that Mrs. Montague had been her father's second wife, and she fully believed that she must have in her possession papers, letters, or some other documents that would reveal all that she wished to know regarding Richmond Montague's first marriage, and give her some information regarding the great sorrow that had so blighted the life of his beautiful young wife.

She had promised that she would give herself to Ray at the end of three months; he still held her to that promise, and six weeks of the time had already elapsed, and she seemed to be no nearer the attainment of her desires than when she had made it.

True, she had found the picture of her mother, and learned that her name was Mona Forester. She had also discovered that a relative had been seeking for her with the desire of leaving her all that he possessed.

But all this was very unsatisfactory, for she had not gained the slightest clew by which to prove herself to be the child of Mona Forester, or any one else.

It was all a wearisome and harrowing tangle, and it wore both upon her spirits and her strength.

It was true, too, that she had found Ray, and learned that he loved her. This was a great comfort, and she knew she had but to tell him that she was ready to go to him, and he would at once make her his wife; but—a flush of shame flooded her face every time she thought of it—she was continually haunted by the fear that her mother might never have been Richmond Montague's wife—that possibly she might have no legal right to the name she bore, in spite of her uncle's assurance to the contrary, and she shrank from marrying Ray if any such stigma rested upon her.

She had never breathed these fears to him—she kept hoping that some accident, or some remark from Mrs. Montague, would throw light on the perplexing mystery.

But Mrs. Montague never referred in any way to her past life in her presence. She had never once mentioned her husband, and, of course, Mona had not dared to ask her any questions upon these subjects.

"I can never marry Ray until I know," she had told herself over and over in great distress, "for I love him too well ever to bring any blight upon his life."

She had had a dim hope that Mr. Corbin might in some way manage to unravel the mystery, and yet she could not see that he had anything more tangible to work upon than she herself had.

Mona finished the dress and carried it to Mrs. Montague, who seemed very much pleased with it.

"You are a lovely seamstress, Ruth, and a good, faithful girl," she said, as she carefully examined the neatly made garment. "But for one thing," she added, as she covertly searched the girl's fair face, "I believe I should grow really fond of you."

This remark put Mona on her guard in a moment,

though it also set her heart to beating with a vague hope.

"Thank you for your praise of my work, Mrs. Montague," she quietly said, "but," lifting a wondering glance to her face, "what is the one thing that I lack to win your esteem? If I am at fault in any way I should be glad to know and correct it."

"You lack nothing. It is because you so much resemble a person whom I used to detest—I am unaccountably antagonized by it," said the woman, frowning, for the clear eyes, looking so frankly into hers, were wondrously like Mona Forester's.

"Oh, I suppose you refer to the person whose picture I found up stairs a while ago," said Mona.

"Yes," and Mrs. Montague looked slightly ashamed of her confession; "I imagine you think I am somewhat unjust to allow my prejudice to extend to you on that account, and I know I am; but the power of association is very strong, and I did hate that girl with all my heart."

Mona was trying to acquire courage to ask what reason she could have for hating any one who looked so gentle and inoffensive, when the woman resumed, with some embarrassment:

"Louis scolded me for the feeling when I mentioned it to him—he is not tainted in any such way, I assure you. Do you know, Ruth," with a little laugh of assumed amusement, "that he is very fond of you?"

Mona's face was all ablaze in an instant—her eyes likewise, although she was greatly surprised to learn that the young man had betrayed his liking for her to his aunt.

"I trust that Mr. Hamblin has not led you to believe

that I have ever encouraged any such feeling on his part," she coldly remarked.

"I know that you have been very modest and judicious, Ruth; but what if I should tell you that the knowledge of his preference does not displease me; that, on the whole, I rather approve of his regard for you?" questioned Mrs. Montague, observing her closely.

"From what you told me a moment ago, I should suppose you would feel anything but approval," Mona replied, without being able to conceal her scorn of this sanction to Louis Hamblin's presumption.

"What do you mean?" demanded her companion, with some sharpness.

"I refer to the prejudice which you confessed to entertaining against me."

"But did I not acknowledge that it was unjust? And when one confesses wrong and is willing to correct it, credit should not be withheld," Mrs. Montague retorted, with some warmth. "But seriously, Ruth," she continued, with considerable eagerness, "Louis is very much in earnest about this matter. He has dutifully asked my permission to address you, and I believe it would be for his happiness and interest to have a good wife, such as I am confident you would make. I know that he has betrayed something of this feeling to you, or I should not presume to speak to you about it; but my reason for so doing is that I thought perhaps you might feel more free to accept his suit if you knew that I approved of the union."

Mona was trembling now with mingled excitement and indignation. Excitement over the discovery that Louis Hamblin had really been in earnest when he had made love to her at Hazeldean, and indignation that he should still presume to think that she would marry him after the decided rebuff she had given him at that time. She was also astonished that Mrs. Montague should propose such a thing after what she had said, on the night of the ball, about her "angling for Ray Palmer, and imagining herself to be his equal in any respect."

Then she grew very pale with a sudden suspicion. Perhaps Mrs. Montague had discovered who she was, possibly Mr. Corbin had been to her to question her, and had aroused her suspicions that she was Mona Montague, and she was plotting to marry her to her nephew in order to keep her fortune in the family, and thus tie Mona's hands to render her incapable of mischief.

These thoughts inspired her with fresh hope and courage, for she told herself that if this was the woman's object, there must be some proofs in existence that her mother's marriage with Richmond Montague had been legal.

But Mrs. Montague was waiting for some answer, and she could not stop to consider these points very fully now.

"I thank you," she said, trying hard to curb the scorn that was surging fiercely within her, "but I shall be obliged to decline a union with Mr. Hamblin—I could never become his wife."

"Why not, pray?" sharply demanded her companion.

"Because I believe that marriage should never be contracted without mutual love, and I do not love Mr. Hamblin," Mona returned, with cold positiveness.

"Really?" Mrs. Montague sneered, with a frowning brow, "one would suppose that a person in your position—a poor seamstress—would be only too glad to marry a handsome young man with Louis' prospects —for he will eventually inherit my fortune if he outlives me."

"Then, perhaps, it will be a surprise to you to learn that there is one poor seamstress in the world who does not regard marriage with a rich young man as the most desirable end to be achieved in life," Mona responded, with quiet sarcasm.

Mrs. Montague grew crimson with anger.

"Then you would not marry my nephew if he should offer himself to you?" she indignantly inquired.

"No, madame; I could not. With all due appreciation of the honor intended me, I should be obliged to decline it."

The girl spoke with the utmost respect and courtesy, yet there was a slight inflection upon certain words which irritated Mrs. Montague almost beyond endurance.

"Perhaps you are already in love with some one else—perhaps you imagine that you may win young Palmer, upon whom you so indelicately forced your society at Hazeldean," she snapped.

Mona could not quite conceal all emotion at this unexpected attack, and a lovely color stole into her cheeks, at which the watchful woman opposite her was quick to draw her own conclusions, even though the fair girl made no reply to her rude speech.

"Let me disabuse your mind at once of any such hopes and aspirations," Mrs. Montague continued, with increased asperity, "for they will never be realized, since Ray Palmer is already engaged."

This statement was made upon the strength of what she had learned from Mr. Palmer regarding Ray's affection for Mr. Dinsmore's niece, and his own approval of the union if the young lady could be found.

Poor Mona's powers of endurance were tried to the utmost by this thrust, and she longed to proclaim, there and then, that she knew it—that she was the young man's promised wife.

But the time for such an avowal was not yet ripe; a few weeks longer, if she could have patience, and then she hoped there would be no occasion for further secrecy.

She put a strong curb upon herself, and simply bowed to show that she had heard and understood Mrs. Montague's statement.

The effort, however, drove every atom of color from her face, and seeing this, Mrs. Montague believed that she had planted a sharp thorn in her bosom.

She did not wish to antagonize her, however, and she was almost sorry that she had said so much; but she was a creature of impulse when her will was thwarted, and did not always stop to choose her words.

She had, for certain reasons, yielded her objections to Louis marrying her, and now this unexpected opposition on Mona's part only served to make her determined to carry the point, for the sake of conquering her, if for no other.

"Well, we will not quarrel over the matter, Ruth," she said, in a conciliatory tone. "Of course I have no right to coerce you in such a matter, and you are too useful to me to be driven away by contesting the point. So we will drop the subject; and now if you will take this memorandum and go about the shopping I shall be obliged to you. I shall need all my strength for this evening, because I am to have a large company to entertain, and——"

She abruptly paused, and seemed a trifle confused for a moment. Then she asked, with unusual consideration:

"Shall I send you in the carriage?"

"No, I should prefer to take a car down town and then walk about to the different stores. I sit so much I shall be glad of the exercise," Mona replied, as she turned to leave the room, but wondering what Mrs. Montague had been going to add when she stopped so suddenly.

CHAPTER VI.

RAY MAKES AN IMPORTANT DISCOVERY.

Mona hastened to her own chamber, after leaving Mrs. Montague, where she hastily exchanged her house dress for a street costume, and then started out upon her errands.

She had a great deal to think of in connection with her recent conversation with Mrs. Montague, but, although much had been said that had annoyed her greatly, on the whole she had been inspired with fresh hope that the mystery enshrouding her mother's life would eventually be solved.

She therefore quickly recovered her spirits, and her face was bright and animated as she tripped away to catch the car at the corner of the street.

She had several errands to do, and she very much enjoyed the freedom of running about to the different stores, to buy the pretty things regarding which Mrs. Montague had discovered she possessed excellent taste and judgment.

She had nearly completed her purchases—all but some lace, which that lady wished to add to the ravishing tea-gown which was to be worn that evening, and to get this she would have to pass Mr. Palmer's jewelry store.

Her heart beat fast as she drew near it, for she had been hoping all the way down town that she might see Ray and have a few minutes' chat with him.

She glanced in at the large show-window, as she went slowly by, and, fortunately, Ray was standing quite near, behind the counter, talking with a customer.

He caught sight of her instantly, but indicated it only by a quick flash of the eyes, and a grave bow, and quietly continued his conversation.

Mona knew, however, that having seen her, he would seek her at the earliest possible moment, and so slowly sauntered on, looking in at the different windows which she passed.

It was not long until she caught the sound of a quick step behind her, and the next moment a firm, strong hand clasped hers, while a pair of fond, true eyes looked the delight which her lover experienced at the unexpected meeting.

"My darling!—I was thinking of you the very moment you passed, and wishing that I could see you. I have something very important to tell you," he said, eagerly, but his fine face clouded as he uttered these last words.

"It is something that troubles you, I am sure, Ray," said Mona, who was quick to interpret his every expression.

"Yes, it is—I am free to confess," he admitted, then added: "Come in here with me—there will not be many people about at this hour—where we can talk more freely, and I will tell you all about it."

They were passing the Hoffman House at that moment, and the young man led the way inside the *café*.

They proceeded to a table in a quiet corner, where, behind some palms and tall ferns, they would not be likely to be observed, and then gave an order for a tempting lunch, the preparation of which would require some time.

While waiting for it, Ray confided his trouble to Mona.

"My father is really going to marry Mrs. Montague," was the somewhat abrupt communication which he made with pale lips and troubled brow.

"I have known it for some time, but did not like to speak of it to you," Mona quietly replied.

"You have known it for some time?" Ray exclaimed. "For how long, pray?"

"Ever since we were at Hazeldean."

"Impossible! for my father did not make his proposal until after our return to New York."

"But she certainly told me the night of the ball, when she came up stairs to retire, that she expected to marry Mr. Palmer," Mona returned, and flushing at the memory of that conversation, which, however, she had been too proud to repeat to her lover.

"Well, she may have expected to marry him, and I imagine that his own mind was pretty well made up at that time," said Ray, gloomily, "but the matter was not settled until after our return, as I said before, and the engagement is to be formally announced this afternoon at the high-tea given by Mrs. Montague."

Ah! this explained to Mona what had puzzled her just before leaving home—why Mrs. Montague had once or twice appeared embarrassed during their conversation, why she had abruptly paused in the midst of that last sentence, and why, too, she had been so unusually particular about her personal appearance for a home-reception.

She mentioned these circumstances to Ray, and asked, in conclusion, if he were also invited to the high-tea.

"Yes; but, really, I am so heart-sick over the affair I feel as if I cannot go. I am utterly at a loss to understand this strange infatuation," he continued, with a heavy sigh. "My father, until this meeting with Mrs. Montague, has been one of the most quiet and domestic of men. He went occasionally into society, but never remained late at any reception, and never bestowed especial attention upon any lady. He has been a dear lover of his home and his books. We have seldom entertained since my mother's death, except in an informal way, and he has always appeared to have a strong antipathy to gay society women."

"How strange! for Mrs. Montague is an exaggerated type of such a woman; her life is one continual round of excitement, pleasure, and fashion," Mona remarked, "and I am sure," she added, with a glance of sympathy at her lover's downcast face, "that Mr. Palmer would soon grow very weary of such an existence."

"I am certain of it, also," Ray answered, "and more than that, from what I have learned of the woman through you—of her character and disposition—I fear that my father is doomed to a wretched future, if he marries her."

"I have similar forebodings," Mona said, thoughtfully, as her mind recurred to the conversation of the morning. "How would it do for you to tell your father what you know? It might influence him, and I shall not mind having my secret revealed if he can be saved from future unhappiness."

"I fear it is too late for that now. He is so thoroughly infatuated and has committed himself so far, I doubt the wisdom of seeking to undeceive him," Ray responded, with a sigh. "What powers of fascination that woman has!" he exclaimed, with some excitement. "She charms every one, young and old. I myself experienced something of it until you opened my eyes to her real character."

"Such women are capable of doing a great deal of harm. Oh, Ray, I believe that society ruins a great many people. Perhaps it was well that my career in it was so suddenly terminated," Mona remarked, gravely.

Ray smiled fondly down upon her.

"I do not believe it could ever have harmed you very much," he said, tenderly; "but I believe very many young people are unfitted for the higher duties of life where they give themselves up to society to such an extent as they do here in New York; it is such a shallow, unreal kind of life. We will be social— you and I, Mona, when we make a home for ourselves; we will be truly hospitable and entertain our friends for the good that we can get and give, but not merely for the sake of show and of being 'in the swim.'"

The smile and look which concluded these observations brought the quick blood to the cheeks of the fair girl, and made another pair of eyes, which were peering at them through the palms and ferns, flash with malicious anger and jealousy.

"I have so few friends now, Ray, I fear we shall not

have many to entertain," Mona replied, a little sadly.

"I do not believe you know how many you really have, dear. You disappeared from social life so suddenly, leaving everybody in the dark regarding your whereabouts, that very few had an opportunity to prove their friendship," Ray said, soothingly. "However," he added, his fine lips curling a trifle, "we shall know how to treat those who have met and ignored you. But have you heard anything from Mr. Corbin since I saw you last?"

"No, and I fear that I shall not," Mona replied, with a sigh. "I do not see any possible way by which he can prove my identity. As you know, I have not a single item of reliable evidence in my possession, although I firmly believe that such evidence exists, and is at this moment in Mrs. Montague's keeping."

She then related how her suspicions had been freshly aroused by the conversation of that morning, and Ray was considerably excited over the matter.

"Why did you not tell me before that Louis Hamblin made himself obnoxious to you at Hazeldean?" he questioned, flushing with indignation, for Mona had also told him of her interview with the young man in the library, in connection with the story of Mrs. Montague's more recent proposal to her.

"Because I believed that I had myself thoroughly extinguished him," Mona answered, smiling; "and besides," she continued, with a modest blush, "I believe that no true, considerate woman will ever mention her rejection of a suitor to a third party, if she can avoid doing so."

Ray gave her an admiring glance.

"I wish there were more women in the world of the same mind," he said. "But mind, dear, I will not have you annoyed about the matter further. If, after what you have told Mrs. Montague to-day, young Hamblin should presume to renew the subject again, you are to tell me and I will deal with him as he deserves. It certainly is rather suspicious her wanting you to become his wife. Why, it is in everybody's mouth that she has been trying for months to make a match between him and Kitty McKenzie," he concluded, thoughtfully.

"Kitty McKenzie is far too good a girl for such a fate; but I am afraid she is really quite fond of him," said Mona, with a regretful sigh. "But shall you come up to Forty-ninth street this afternoon, Ray?"

"I suppose I must, or people will talk," he replied, dejectedly. "If my father is determined to marry the woman it will create gossip, I suppose, if I appear to discountenance it; so all that remains for me to do is to put the best possible face upon the matter and treat my future step-mother with becoming deference."

"What do you suppose she will say when she learns the truth about us?" Mona inquired, with an amused smile. "I imagine there will be something of a breeze about my ears, for she informed me this morning that I need have no hopes or aspirations regarding you upon the strength of any attention that you bestowed upon me at Hazeldean, for—you were already engaged," and a little ripple of merry laughter concluded the sentence.

Ray smiled, delighted to see the sunshine upon his dear one's face, and to hear that musical sound. Yet he remarked, with some sternness:

"I think she is overstepping her jurisdiction to meddle in your affairs to such an extent. But here comes our lunch," he interposed, as the waiter appeared, bearing a well laden tray of tempting viands.

"Then let us drop all unpleasant topics, and give ourselves up to the enjoyment of it," said Mona, looking up brightly. "A light heart and a mind at ease greatly aid digestion, you know."

She would not allow him to refer to anything of a disagreeable nature after that, but strove, in her bright, sweet way, to banish the cloud from his face, and succeeded so well that before their meal was ended they had both apparently forgotten Louis Hamblin and his aunt, and the unsuitable engagement about to be announced, and were only conscious that they were there together, and all in all to each other.

But time was flying, and Mona knew that she must get back to assist Mrs. Montague with her toilet for the high-tea.

"It was very nice of you, Ray, to bring me here for this delightful lunch," she said, as they arose from the table, with a regretful sigh that they must separate, and began to draw on her gloves.

"We shall take all our lunches together before long, I hope, my darling," he whispered, fondly; "half the stipulated time is gone, Mona, and I shall certainly claim you at the end of another six weeks."

Mona flushed, but she did not reply, and her heart grew heavy, for she knew she should not be willing to become Ray's wife until she could prove the circumstances of her birth.

She longed to tell him how she felt about it—she longed to know how he would feel toward her if they should discover that any stain rested upon her.

But she dare not broach the subject—a feeling of

shame and humiliation kept her silent, and she resolved to wait and hope until the six weeks should pass.

They went out together, but still followed by that pair of malignant eyes, which had, however, been cautiously veiled, as was also the face in which they were set.

Ray walked with his betrothed to a corner, where he helped her aboard a car, and then returned to his store.

Later, on that same day, a gay company of gentlemen and ladies filled Mrs. Montague's spacious and elegant rooms, where she, in her elaborate and becoming costume, entertained in her most charming manner.

Mr. Palmer had come very early and secured a private interview, previous to the arrival of the other guests, and it was noticeable that, as the lady received, a new and magnificent solitaire gleamed upon the third finger of her left hand.

People surmised, very generally, what this meant, even before it was whispered throughout the rooms that the engagement of Mr. Palmer and the beautiful widow was formally announced. It was not very much of a surprise, either, as such an event had been predicted for some time.

Ray did not arrive until late, for he had little heart for the gay scene, and less sympathy in its object. But for his respect and love for his father, he would not have set foot in the house at all.

"Gentlemen's dressing-room on the left of the hall above," said the polite colored man, who attended the door, and Ray slowly mounted the stairs, hoping that he might catch a glimpse, if not secure an opportunity for a word with Mona.

But there was no such treat in store for him, for she was at that moment assisting Mary, who had met with a mishap in running up stairs, having stepped upon her dress and torn it badly.

Ray found the room indicated, which proved to be Mrs. Montague's boudoir, deposited his hat, gloves, and cane where he could conveniently get them again —for he did not intend to remain long—and then descended to the drawing-room.

He made his way at once to where Mrs. Montague was standing with her captive beside her, for he desired to get through with the disagreeable duty of offering congratulations, with all possible dispatch.

Poor Mr. Palmer! Ray pitied him, in spite of his aversion to the engagement, for he looked heated and flushed, and somewhat sheepish as his son approached, although he tried to smile and look happy, as if he enjoyed the glitter and show and confusion reigning all about him.

Ray politely shook hands with his hostess, making some general remark upon the occasion and the brilliant assembly, as he did so.

"And—I hope I am to have your congratulations," Mrs. Montague archly remarked, as she glanced from him to his father.

"You certainly can have no doubt that I sincerely hope the arrangement may be for your mutual happiness," the young man gravely replied, as he bowed before them both.

"Then show yourself a dutiful son by drinking a cup of tea with me," laughingly returned the lady, as she slipped her white hand within his arm, and led him toward the great silver urn, where several charming "buds" were dispensing the fragrant beverage to the numerous guests.

Ray had no alternative, and he well knew that the wily widow had adroitly taken this way to make it appear to her guests that the son heartily approved his father's choice.

She possessed infinite tact, and chatted away in the most brilliant manner, making him wait upon her so assiduously that Ray was sure, from the looks of those about them, that every one was admiring his devotion (?) to his future step-mother.

She released him at last, however, and returned to her position beside his father, and watching his opportunity he stole unobserved from the room, and up stairs, intending to get away from the house as soon as possible.

Reaching Mrs. Montague's boudoir, he walked to the bay-window, and looked out upon the street. He was nervous and excited, and wished to regain his accustomed composure before going down stairs again.

He stood there a moment absorbed in unpleasant reflections, then turned to get his coat and hat.

As he did so, one of his feet caught in the heavy damask draperies, and in trying to disengage it, something crackled sharply beneath it, and he stooped to ascertain what it was.

Sweeping aside the heavy curtains, he saw a long, narrow document lying upon the floor beneath its folds.

He picked it up, and saw that it was a piece of parchment with something apparently printed upon it.

Not supposing it to be anything of importance, he mechanically unfolded it and began to read.

"Why, it is a marriage certificate!" he exclaimed, in surprise, under his breath.

Not caring to read the whole form, he simply glanced at the places where the names of the contracting parties were written, and instantly a mighty shock seemed to shake him from head to foot.

"Ha! what can this mean?" he exclaimed, in a breathless voice.

His face grew deathly pale. A blur came before his eyes. He rubbed them to dispel it, and looked again.

"It cannot be possible!" he said, in a hoarse whisper, and actually panting as if he had been running hard. "I cannot believe my sight, and yet it is here in black and white! and Mona—Mona, my darling! the mystery will be solved, and you will be righted at last."

The certificate, as will be readily surmised, was the very one which Mrs. Montague had examined the previous evening.

When Mona had knocked upon the door, it will be remembered that she was greatly startled and had upset the table. The accident had caused the certificate to be thrown upon the floor, with the other things, and by some means it was pushed beneath the heavy damask curtain and had escaped Mrs. Montague's eye and memory, when she hastily gathered up the scattered treasures and rearranged them in the secret compartment of the table.

Thus it had come into Ray's possession just at a time when it was most needed and desired.

Regaining his composure somewhat, he read it carefully through from beginning to end.

"How could it have come to be in such a strange place, and to fall into my hands?" he said, the look of wonder still on his face. "She—that woman must have had it in her possession, even as Mona suspected, and by some mistake or oversight dropped and forgot it. Shall I tell her I have found it? Shall I return it and then demand it from her?" he questioned, his innate sense of honor recoiling from everything that seemed dishonorable. "No," he continued, sternly, "it is not hers—she has no right whatever to it; it belongs to Mona alone, for it is the proof of her birthright. I will take it directly to Mr. Corbin, and I will not even tell Mona until I have first confided in him."

With a resolute purpose written on his fine face, Ray carefully put the document away in an inner pocket; then donning his coat and hat, quietly left the house.

The last postal delivery of that same evening brought to Mrs. Richmond Montague the following anonymous letter:

"MADAME:—The girl in your employ, who calls herself Ruth Richards, is not what she pretends to be. Her true name is Mona Montague, and she is compromising herself by secret meetings with a gentleman in high life. She lunched this morning at the Hoffman House Café with Mr. Raymond Palmer, the son of a worthy gentleman whom you intend to marry. You perhaps will best know whether she has any hidden purpose in figuring as a seamstress, and under the name of Ruth Richards, in your house."

Unfortunately for our young lovers, Miss Josephine Holt had also been taking an early lunch in the Hoffman House Café that morning, and had seen Ray and Mona the moment they had entered.

Ever since she had discovered Mona at Hazeldean

she had been trying to think of some way by which
she could separate them, and now, knowing that Mrs.
Montague was bent upon marrying Mr. Palmer, and
feeling sure that there was some secret which Mona
wished to preserve by becoming a seamstress in the
woman's house under an assumed name, she believed
she could the best achieve her purpose by disclosing
her identity and setting Mrs. Montague against her.

How well she succeeded will be seen later on.

CHAPTER VII.

MONA MAKES A SURPRISING DISCOVERY.

It was now the third week in April, and the season
was unusually early. The grass had become quite
green, the trees were putting forth their leaves, and
the weather was very warm for the time of the year.

On the morning after the high-tea and the announcement of the engagement, Mrs. Montague
sought Mona and informed her that a party of friends
had arranged for a pleasure trip through the South
and down the Mississippi, and asked her if she would
accompany her, since Louis had business to attend to,
and could not act as her escort.

Mona did not exactly like to go, but there was
really no good reason why she should refuse; the
rush of sewing was nearly over, and if she were left
behind, she would have to be idle the greater portion
of the time; besides, she had worked very steadily, and
she knew that she needed rest and relaxation.

She inquired how long Mrs. Montague intended

to be gone, and the lady replied that she expected to return within two weeks.

"Of course you can please yourself about the matter, Ruth," she remarked. "I suppose I could take Mary, but she is not companionable—she would not appreciate the journey, and I really wish you would go. I should regard it as quite a favor," the woman concluded, appealingly.

If Mona had been more observing, she might have seen that she was being closely watched, and that her answer was anxiously awaited. Mona considered the subject a few moments before replying. Her greatest objection was leaving Ray for so long—two weeks would seem almost interminable without seeing him.

But, on the other hand, perhaps while in such close companionship with Mrs. Montague as there would have to be on such a journey, something might be dropped about her former life which would enlighten her regarding what she was so eager to ascertain. It would be a delightful trip, too, and Mona knew that she should enjoy seeing the country, as she had never been South.

"When do you start?" she inquired, before committing herself.

"I want to get off in the evening express," Mrs. Montague returned, watching every expression of the young girl's face.

"In *this* evening's express?" asked Mona, in surprise.

"Yes. It is short notice, I know," the woman said, smiling; "but I, myself, only knew of the plan yesterday, and, as you know, I was too busy to make any arrangements for it. Will you go, Ruth? We have nothing to do but to pack our trunks."

"I suppose there is no reason why I should not," the young girl returned, musingly, while she told herself that she could send a note to Ray, informing him of her intention. She was not quite sure that he would approve of it, and she wished that she could have known of it the previous day, so that she could have consulted him.

"That is nice of you," Mrs. Montague quickly responded, and assuming that her remark was intended as an assent to the trip; "and now we must at once go about our preparations. How long will it take you to pack?"

"Not long," Mona answered; "I have only my dresses to fold, and my toilet articles to gather up. I have not really unpacked since I came here," she said, smiling; "for I have needed so few things."

"Well, then, get yourself ready; then you may come to help me," Mrs. Montague said, as she arose to go to her own room, and breathing a sigh of relief that this vital point had been gained with so little trouble.

Mona was as expeditious as possible, but, somehow, now that she had given her consent to go, her heart grew unaccountably heavy, and she began to feel a deep aversion to leaving New York.

She wrote a hasty note to Ray, telling him of the intended journey, and how she regretted not being able to consult him, but could not, under the circumstances. She also wrote, as she did not know the route they were to take, she could not tell him where to address her, but would write to him again when she learned where they were to be.

Then she packed what she thought she would need to take with her, after which she went to assist Mrs. Montague. She found that she had been very expeditious, for she had one trunk already packed and locked, ready to be strapped, and was busily engaged filling another.

Their arrangements were all made and they were ready to start by the time dinner was served, and this meal Mrs. Montague insisted they should eat together, as they must leave immediately afterward.

She was very chatty and agreeable, treating Mona more as an equal than she had ever done before. She seemed in excellent spirits, and talked so gayly and enthusiastically about the trip that the young girl really began to anticipate it with considerable pleasure.

Mary and the cook were to have a holiday during their absence; the house was to be closed, and the coachman alone would remain about the premises to look after the horses and see that nothing happened to the place.

At seven o'clock they left the house, and an hour later were seated in a luxurious Wagner, and rolling rapidly Southward.

They arrived in St. Louis on the morning of the second day, and drove directly to the Southern Hotel, where Mrs. Montague said they would remain for a day or two, to rest, and where the friends who were going down the Mississippi to New Orleans with them would join them.

The following morning Mrs. Montague dressed herself with great care, and told Mona that she was going out to make some calls, adding that she might amuse herself as she chose, for there was nothing to be done, and she might get lonely to remain alone in the hotel.

The young girl resolved to improve the opportunity and look about the city a little on her own account.

She donned her hat and jacket, and running down

to the street, hailed the first car that came along, with
the intention of riding as far as it would take her.

She changed her purpose, however, as the car was
about passing a street leading down to the great bridge
across the Mississippi.

She had heard and read a great deal about the
grand structure, and she determined to walk across
and see how it would compare with the wonderful
Brooklyn Bridge.

She was feeling very well, the morning was bright,
and she enjoyed her walk immensely. By the time
she returned her cheeks were like wild roses, and her
whole face glowing from exercise.

She was a little weary, however, and glad to get
seated again in a car going back toward her hotel.

The car had proceeded only about half a block, however, when it stopped again, and two people, a man
and a woman, stepped aboard, and seated themselves
next to her.

They seemed to be absorbed in earnest conversation,
and did not appear to notice any one about them.

The woman was an elderly person, rather fine looking, with a good figure, and an erect, graceful bearing. Her hair was almost white, and there were deep
wrinkles in her forehead, at the corners of her eyes,
and about her mouth, although they were somewhat
concealed, or softened, by the thickly spotted black lace
veil which she wore; but on the whole she was an
agreeable looking person, and her manner was full of
energy and vitality.

. Her companion was a rather rough-appearing per-
sonage and dressed like a Western farmer or miner,
rather coarsely handsome, and with an easy, off-hand

manner that was quite attractive, and he might have been thirty or thirty-five years of age.

"What a dark skin—what black hair and beard, with blue eyes!" was Mona's mental comment, as she observed this peculiarity about him. He also had very white teeth, which contrasted strikingly with the intense blackness of his mustache and beard.

He appeared to be quite disturbed about something, and talked to his companion rapidly and excitedly, but in low tones.

"You were very imprudent to try to dispose of so many at one place," Mona overheard his companion say, in reply to some observation which he had previously made, and then a great shock went tingling through all her nerves as her glance fell upon the dress which the woman wore.

It was a fine, heavy ladies' cloth, of a delicate shade of gray—just the color, Mona was confident, of that tiny piece of goods which Ray had shown her at Hazeldean, and which had been torn from the dress of the woman who had trapped him into Doctor Wesselhoff's residence, and stolen his diamonds.

She was very much excited for a few moments, and her heart beat with rapid throbs.

Could it be possible that this woman had been concerned in that robbery?

That woman had had red hair, and according to Ray's description, was much younger; but she might possibly be the other one, who had made arrangements with the physician for Ray's treatment. At all events, Mona was impressed that she had found the dress in which the fascinating Mrs. Vanderbeck had figured so conspicuously.

Her face flushed, her fingers tingled with the rapid

coursing of her blood, and she felt as if she could hardly wait until the woman should rise, so that she might look for a place that had been mended in the skirt of her dress.

She resolved that she would ride as long as they remained in the car, and when they left it, she would follow them to ascertain their stopping place.

She could not catch anything more that they said, although she strained her ears to do so.

Those few words which she had overheard had also aroused her suspicions—"you were very imprudent to try to dispose of so many in one place," the woman had said, and Mona believed she had referred to diamonds; her vivid imagination pictured these people as belonging to the gang of robbers who had been concerned in the Palmer robbery, and now that the excitement attending it had somewhat subsided, they had doubtless come to St. Louis to dispose of their booty; while it was the strangest thing in the world, she thought, that she should have happened to run across them in the way she had.

They were drawing very near the Southern Hotel, where Mona and Mrs. Montague were stopping; but the excited girl resolved that she would not get out— she would ride hours rather than lose sight of these two strangers, and the chance to ascertain if that gray cloth dress was mended—"on the back of the skirt, near the right side, among the heavy folds." Ray had told her that was where the tear was.

But what if she should find it there? What should she do about the matter? were questions which arose at this point to trouble her. What could she, a weak girl, do to cause the arrest of the thieves? how was she to prove them guilty?

At that moment the man signaled the conductor to stop the car, and Mona's heart leaped into her throat, for they were exactly opposite her own hotel.

The couple arose to leave the car, and Mona slowly followed them.

As the woman was about to step to the ground she gathered up her skirts with her right hand, to prevent them from sweeping the steps of the car, and Mona looked with eager eyes, but she could detect no mended rent.

She kept a little behind them as they crossed the sidewalk and made straight for the entrance of the hotel, when, as they were mounting the steps, the woman suddenly tripped and almost fell.

In the act, her skirts were drawn closely about her, and Mona distinctly saw a place, where the plaits or folds were laid deeply over one another, that had been mended, and not nicely, either, but hastily sewed together on the wrong side. It would hardly have been noticed, however, unless one had been looking for it as Mona was, because it lay so deeply in among the folds.

The couple entered the hotel, and both gave Mona a quick, sharp glance as she followed; but she quietly passed them with averted eyes, and went into a reception-room on the left of the hall.

"Go and register, Jake, and I will wait here for you," Mona heard the woman say, and the man immediately disappeared within the clerk's office opposite, while his companion walked slowly back and forth in the hall.

Presently the man rejoined her, remarking:

"It's all right; they had a room next yours which

they could give me. Come," and both passed directly up stairs.

Mona waited a few minutes, to be sure they were well out of the way, then she quietly slipped across the hall to the office.

"Will you allow me to look at the register?" she asked of the gentlemanly clerk.

"Certainly," and with a bow and smile he placed it conveniently for her.

She thanked him, and glanced eagerly at the last name written on the page.

"J. R. Walton, Sydney, Australia," she read, in a coarse, irregular hand, as if the person writing it had been unaccustomed to the use of the pen.

Running her eye up the page, Mona also read, as if the name had been signed earlier in the day:

"Mrs. J. M. Walton, Brownsville, Mo."

"It would appear," mused Mona, as she left the office, "as if they are mother and son—that he had just returned from far Australia, and she had come here to meet him. But—I don't believe it! Walton—Walton! Where have I heard that name before?"

She could not place it, but she was so sure that these people were in some way connected with the Palmer robbery, she was determined to make an effort to establish the fact, and immediately leaving the hotel again, she sought the nearest telegraph office, and sent the following message to Ray:

"Send immediately piece of the ladies' cloth torn from dress."

This done she retraced her steps, and went directly up to her own room.

She found that Mrs. Montague had returned from making her calls, and was dressing for dinner.

She seemed a little disturbed about something, and finally it came out that the trip down the Mississippi would have to be delayed for a day or two longer than she had anticipated, as one of her friends was not quite well enough to start immediately.

Mona was very glad to learn this, for she was sure that she should hear from Ray and receive the piece of dress goods; her only fear was that the Waltons might not remain at the hotel long enough for her to find an opportunity to fit the piece into the rent, to ascertain if it belonged there.

The earnestly desired letter reached her the next evening. Ray had been very expeditious. Receiving Mona's dispatch just before the southward mail closed, he had hastily inclosed the piece of cloth, with a few words, in an envelope, and so there was no delay.

She was certain, as she examined it, that it was exactly the same color as the dress she had seen the day before, and reasonably sure regarding the texture; but the great question now to be answered was: Would it fit the rent?

"Now I must find the dress, if possible, when the woman is wearing something else," Mona mused, with a troubled face, and beginning to think she had undertaken a matter too difficult to be carried out. "Perhaps she has no other dress here; how, then, am I going to prove my suspicion true, or otherwise?"

She knew that she could go to the authorities, tell her story, and have the woman and dress forcibly examined; but she could not bear to do anything that would make herself conspicuous, and it would be very disagreeable to carry the affair so far and then find she had made a lamentable mistake.

"If Ray were only here he would know what to do,"

she murmured, "but he isn't, and I must do the best I can without him. I must find out where the woman rooms. I must examine that dress!"

Fortune favored her in an unexpected way the very next morning.

The chambermaid who had charge of the floor on which their rooms were located, came, as usual, to put them in order, but with a badly swollen face, around which she had bound a handkerchief.

"Are you sick?" Mona asked, in a tone of sympathy, for the girl's heavy eyes and languid manner appealed very strongly to her kind heart.

"I have a toothache, miss," the girl said, with a heavy sigh. "I never slept a wink last night, it pained me so."

"I am very sorry, and of course you cannot feel much like work to-day, if you had no sleep," Mona said, pityingly.

"Indeed I don't—I can hardly hold my head up; but the work's got to be done all the same," was the weary reply.

"Cannot you get some one to substitute for you while you have your tooth taken out and get a little rest?" Mona kindly inquired.

"No, miss; the girls are all busy—they have their own work to do, and I shall have to bear it as best I can."

"Then let me help you," Mona said, a sudden thought setting all her pulses bounding.

Perhaps she might come across that dress!

"You, miss!" the girl cried, in unfeigned astonishment. "A young lady like you help to make beds in a hotel where you are a guest!"

Mona laughed.

"I have often made beds, and—I am not regarded as a 'young lady' just now; I am only a kind of waiting-maid to the lady with whom I am traveling," she explained, thinking she might the more easily gain her point if the girl was led to think the difference in their positions was not as great as she had imagined. "Come now," she added, "I am going to help you, for I know you are not able to do all this work yourself," and she immediately began to assist in putting her own chamber to rights.

They went from room to room, Mona chatting pleasantly and trying to take the girl's mind from her pain; but she saw that it was almost more than she could do to keep about her work.

Finally she made her sit down and let her work alone.

"How many rooms are there yet to be cared for?" she asked, as she began to spread up the bed where they were.

"Only four more, miss—just what are left in this hall," said the girl, as her head fell wearily back against the high rocker which Mona had insisted upon her taking.

Mona went on with the work she had volunteered to perform, and when she returned to look at the girl again, she found that she was sleeping heavily.

"Exhausted nature has asserted itself, and I will let her rest," the young girl murmured; "there can be no possible harm in my doing this work for her, although I suppose it would not be thought just the thing for a stranger to have access to all these rooms."

She put everything there as it should be, then she went out, softly closing the door after her, that no one might see the girl sleeping.

She proceeded to do the four remaining apartments without finding what she sought until she came to the very last one.

As she entered it she picked up a card that had been dropped upon the floor, and a joyful thrill ran through her as she read the name, "Mrs. J. M. Walton."

She knew, then, that she had found the room occupied by the woman who had worn the gray dress.

Would she find the garment?

A trunk stood in one corner of the room, and her eyes rested covetously upon this. Then she went to the wardrobe and swung the door open.

Joy! the robe she sought was hanging on a peg within!

With trembling hands she sought for the rent which she had seen the day but one before.

She found it, and with fluctuating color and a rapidly beating heart, she took hold of the knot of the silk, which had been used to mend it, and deliberately pulled it out, when the ragged edges fell apart, revealing a triangular-shaped rent.

Mona drew her purse from her pocket, found the precious piece of cloth that Ray had sent to her, and laid it over the hole in the skirt.

It fitted perfectly into the tear, and she knew that the dress which the beautiful Mrs. Vanderbeck had worn, when she stole the Palmer diamonds, was found.

But the woman!

Mona was puzzled, for surely the woman whom she had seen wearing the dress was much older than the one whom Ray had described to her. She was wrinkled and gray; and then—the name! But stay! All at once light broke in upon her. Walton had been the name of the person who had so cleverly deceived

Dr. Wesselhoff. She had been old and wrinkled, and now, without doubt, she had come to St. Louis to dispose of her share of the stolen diamonds, and had worn the other woman's dress, thinking, perhaps, it would be safe to do so, and would not be recognized under such different circumstances.

"But what shall I do?" seemed now to be the burden of her thought. At first she felt impelled to telegraph Ray to come and attend to the matter; then she feared the man and woman would both disappear before he could arrive, and she felt that some immediate action should be taken.

"I believe my best way will be to go directly to a detective, and tell him my story; he will know what ought to be done, and I can leave the matter in his hands," was her final conclusion.

She sped to her own room, secured a needleful of silk, then hastened back to Mrs. Walton's room and sewed the rent in the dress together once more, taking care not to fray the edges, lest the piece she had should not fit when it was examined again.

CHAPTER VIII.

MR. RIDER BECOMES ACTIVE AGAIN.

After hanging the dress again in its place, Mona quickly finished her work in the room, then went back to the girl whom she had left sleeping in one of the adjoining chambers, and awoke her.

She had slept nearly an hour, and, though Mona knew that she needed many hours more of rest, she was sure that she would be the better for what she had secured.

"You are very good, miss," she said, gratefully; "the pain is all gone from my tooth, and I feel ever so much better."

"Your sleep has quieted your nerves; but I advise you to see a dentist and have the tooth attended to," Mona returned; then hastened away to her room, where she dressed herself for the street and went out.

Mrs. Montague had been out for a long time driving with some friends.

Mona inquired of an elderly, respectable policeman, whom she found standing upon a corner, where she should go to find a detective.

He directed her to the headquarters of the force, although he looked surprised at the question coming from such a source, and she repaired thither at once.

As she entered the office, a quiet-looking man, who was the only occupant at that time, arose and came forward, bowing respectfully; but he also appeared astonished to see a young and beautiful girl in such a place.

"I wish to see a detective," said Mona, flushing hotly beneath the man's curious glance.

"The men connected with this office are all out just at this moment, miss. I am a stranger, and only sitting here for a half-hour or so, just to oblige the officer in charge," the man courteously replied.

"I am very sorry," said the young girl, with a sigh, "for I have come upon business which ought to be attended to immediately."

"I am a detective, miss, although I do not belong here. I'm an officer from New York; but if you see fit to tell me your business, perhaps I might advise you," said the officer, kindly, for he saw that she was greatly troubled.

"You are from New York!" Mona exclaimed, eagerly; "then perhaps it will be better for me to tell you, rather than a St. Louis detective; for the robbery happened in New York."

The detective's eyes flashed with sudden interest at this.

"Ah!" was all he said, however, and this very quietly.

"Yes, it was a diamond robbery. A dress worn by one of the persons connected with it was torn; a small piece was entirely cut out of it. I have found the dress; I have fitted the piece into the rent, and now I want the woman who owns it to be arrested and examined," Mona explained, in low, excited tones, but very comprehensively.

"Ah!" said the detective again, in the same quiet tone; "you have reference to the Palmer robbery."

Mona lifted a pair of very astonished eyes to his face.

"Yes," she responded, breathlessly; "but how did you know?"

"Because I am looking after that case. I am in St. Louis upon that very business," replied the man, with a twinkle in his eyes.

"Are *you* Detective Rider?" questioned the young girl, wonderingly, and trembling with excitement.

Her companion smiled.

"What do you know about Detective Rider?" he inquired. Then, as she flushed and seemed somewhat embarrassed, he continued: "And who are *you,* if you please?"

"I am—I am acquainted with Raymond Palmer,"

Mona answered, evasively; "he has told me about the robbery and——"

"Ah! yes. I understand," interposed the quick-witted officer, as he comprehended the situation. "But sit down and tell me the whole story as briefly as possible, and I can then judge what will be best to do."

He moved a chair forward for her, then sat down himself, where he could watch her closely, as she talked, and Mona related all that we already know regarding the two people whom she had seen upon the street-car, together with all that followed in connection with the discovery of the rent in the gray cloth dress, the sending for the fragment that Ray had preserved, and which had fitted so exactly into the tear.

The detective listened with the closest attention, his small, keen eyes alone betraying the intense interest which her recital excited.

When she had concluded, he drew forth a set of tablets and made notes of several items, after which he said:

"Now, Miss —— What shall I call you? Whom shall I ask for at the hotel, if I should wish to see you again upon this business?"

"Miss Richards. I am traveling with a Mrs. Montague, of New York," Mona replied.

"Well, then, Miss Richards, you go back to your ·hotel, and of course conduct yourself as if you had nothing unusual on your mind; but hold yourself in readiness to produce that important bit of cloth, if I should call upon you to do so within the next few hours. By the way," he added, with sudden thought, "if you have it with you, I might as well take a look at it."

Mona took the paper containing it from her purse and gave it to him.

"You are *sure* this matches the dress?" he asked, examining it closely. "We don't want to make any awkward mistakes, you know."

"It is identical. I believe that every thread in this piece can be matched by a corresponding thread in the garment," the fair girl asserted, so positively that he seemed to be entirely satisfied.

He returned the piece to her and then arose in a brisk, business-like way, which told that he was ready for action.

Mona also rose, and, bidding him a quiet good-day, went quickly out of the office, and hastened back to the hotel.

*   *   *   *   *   *   *

In order to understand more fully some of the incidents related, we shall have to go back a few days.

It was a bright, clear morning when a rather rough-looking, yet not unattractive person, entered a large jewelry establishment located on one of the principal streets of St. Louis.

He might have been thirty-five years of age, for there was a sprinkling of silver among his coarse, intensely black hair, which he wore quite long, and also in his huge mustache and beard. His face was bronzed from exposure; there were crow's feet about his eyes, and two deep wrinkles between his brows, and his general appearance indicated that he had seen a good deal of the rough side of life.

He wore a coarse though substantial suit of clothes, which hung rather loosely upon him; a gray flannel shirt with a turn-over collar, which was fastened at the throat by a flashy necktie, rather carelessly knot-

ted; a red cotton handkerchief was just visible in one
of his pockets; there were coarse, clumsy boots on his
feet, and he wore a wide-brimmed, slouch hat.

He inquired of the clerk, who came forward to wait
upon him, if he could see the "boss of the consarn,"
as he had a little private business to transact with him.

The clerk smiled slightly at his broad vernacular,
as he replied that he would speak to the proprietor, and
presently an elderly gentleman appeared from an inner
office, and inquired the nature of the man's business.

"I'm a miner," he said. "I'm just home from Australia, where I've been huntin' di'monds for the last
ten years. I've made a pretty good haul, and sold
most of 'em in London on my way home. I had a
few dandy ones cut there, though, to bring back to my
gal; but—but—well, to tell the plain truth," he said,
with some confusion, "she's gone back on me; she
couldn't wait for me, so married another fellar; and
now I want to sell the stones. D'ye want to buy?"

There was something rather attractive, as well as
amusing, in the man's frankness, and the merchant
smiled, as he kindly remarked that he would examine
the stones.

The miner thereupon pulled out a small leather bag
from one of the pockets of his trousers, unwound the
strong thong at its throat, and rattled out upon the
counter several loose glittering diamonds of various
sizes.

The merchant could hardly repress a cry of astonishment, for they were remarkable for their purity
and brilliancy, while there were two among the collection of unusual size.

He examined them critically, and took plenty of
time about it, while the miner leaned indifferently

against the counter, his hands in his pockets, and gazed absently out of the window.

"What do you value these stones at?" the merchant finally inquired, as he removed the glass from his eye and turned to the man.

"Wall, I don't suppose it would make much difference what my price might be," he drawled; "I know they're about as good ones as anybody would care to see, and you know about what you'd be willin' to give."

"Yes; but I would like to know what value you put upon them before I make an offer," responded Mr. Cohen, shrewdly.

"Wall, before I found out about the gal, I wouldn't a' sold 'em at any price," was the rather gloomy response, "fur I'd promised 'em to her, ye know; but now—so's I get what's reasonable, I don't care much what becomes on 'em. What'll ye give? I'll trust to yer honor in the matter."

The jeweler had been watching the man closely while he was speaking, although he appeared to be thinking deeply of the purchase of the gems.

"I— do not think that I am prepared to set a price on them just at this moment," he at length thoughtfully remarked. "As far as I can judge, they are very fine stones and well cut; still, I am not an expert, although a dealer in such things, and I should like to submit them to one before making you an offer."

"All right," was the hearty and unhesitating reply, "that's fair, and I'm agreeable. Bring on your expert."

"Are you going to be in the city long?" asked the merchant.

"Wall, no; I didn't calkerlate on staying any long-

er'n I could turn the stones into money," the man said.
"My old mother lives up to Brownsville, and I thought
of goin' up to make her a little visit—han't seen her
fur ten years. Then I'm going back to the mines,
since I han't no reason to hang around these parts
now," with a bitter emphasis on the last word.

"This is Tuesday," said Mr. Cohen, reflectively;
"the expert to whom I wish to subject the stones is out
of town, but will be here to-morrow evening; suppose
you come in again on Thursday morning."

"All right," responded the miner, as he began to
gather up his glittering pebbles, though there was a
look of disappointment in his eyes. "I'd ruther have
got rid of 'em, fur they're kind o' ticklish things to
be carrying about. Wonder if I couldn't leave 'em
in your safe till Thursday?"

"Certainly, if you are willing to trust them with
me," said Mr. Cohen, looking rather surprised at the
man's confidence in him: "still you would have to do
so on your own responsibility. I should not be willing to be held accountable for them in case of a robbery."

"Wall, then, perhaps I'd better take them along,"
the miner returned, as he tied the mouth of his leather
pouch, and shoved it into one of his pockets.

Then drawing forth a plug of tobacco from another, he bit off a generous quid, remarking, as he
did so:

"I'll be on hand Thursday mornin', I reckon. Good-
day."

The merchant politely returned his salutation, and
watched him thoughtfully after he shut the door and
went swaggering down the street, looking in at every
window he passed, in regular country fashion.

A few moments after, the merchant took his hat and also went out.

A few hours later, Mr. Amos Palmer received the following dispatch:

"Send expert and detective at once to examine suspicious stones.   EZRA COHEN."

Ezra Cohen had for years had business relations with Amos Palmer, going to New York several times every twelve months to purchase diamonds and other jewels, for the St. Louis trade.

On his last visit thither Mr. Palmer had mentioned the bold robbery, which had resulted in his losing such valuable diamonds, and had described some of the most costly stones, saying, that possibly they might some time fall into his hands.

Mr. Cohen was not sure, but he was impressed that the two larger stones of the collection which the miner had brought to sell him, on that morning, resembled, in some points, the ones described by Mr. Palmer; and so he thought it worth while to have the matter proved, if possible, although he felt some compunctions regarding his suspicions, because the miner had appeared so frank and ingenuous.

If he had only left the stones with him as he had proposed doing, the matter of testing them could have been attended to during his absence. He hoped that he had not acted too hastily in telegraphing to Mr. Palmer; but he had done as his best judgment had prompted, and could only await the result with patience.

It was with no little nervousness, however, that he awaited Thursday morning, especially after receiving a reply to his message to the effect that "Tom Rider, the detective, and a diamond expert, would **arrive** on an early train of that day."

They did so, and presented themselves at Ezra Cohen's establishment soon after the store was opened for business that morning.

The merchant was already there, awaiting them, and received the two gentlemen in his private office, where they held a confidential conversation regarding the matter in hand.

The expert was quite confident, after listening to Mr. Cohen's description of the diamonds, that they would prove to be the ones they were seeking, but the detective was not quite so hopeful; he had been disappointed so many times of late that he looked upon the dark side, while he was somewhat skeptical about the supposed miner making his appearance again.

About nine o'clock, however, the man swaggered into the store, an enormous quid of tobacco inside his cheek.

"*He* has never been in Australia," said Detective Rider, in a low tone, but with sudden energy, as he and his companion watched him approach the counter, where Mr. Cohen was quietly examining a case of watches.

"Wall," he remarked, in his broad, drawling tone, "got yer expert on hand this mornin'? I'd like to close up this 'ere business before I go up to Brownsville."

"Yes, I think I can settle about the diamonds to-day," Mr. Cohen politely remarked. "James," to a clerk, "please ask Mr. Knowlton to step this way."

James disappeared, and presently an elderly gentleman in spectacles issued from the private office.

"Mr. Knowlton," said the merchant, "this is **the**

man who wished to dispose of some diamonds. Will you examine them, and give your opinion of their value?"

The miner darted a quick, searching look at the newcomer; but apparently the man was intent only upon the business in hand.

Drawing forth his leather pouch, the miner untied it and emptied its contents upon the square of black velvet which had been laid upon the show-case to receive them.

Mr. Knowlton examined each stone with careful scrutiny through a powerful glass, never once speaking until he had looked the collection through.

"They are quite valuable," he remarked, as he laid the last one down. "These," indicating the two large ones, "are especially so; you have been very fortunate, sir, to make such a collection, for there is not one poor one in the lot."

The miner gave a slight start at this observation, and the color deepened on his face; but he replied, with his habitual frankness:

"Well, I've had poor ones—plenty on 'em; but these were saved for a special purpose," and he winked knowingly at Mr. Cohen: Then he added, as he shot a sweeping look around the store and out through the window upon the sidewalk: "Jest give us their value in round figgers, and we'll soon settle this matter."

The expert quietly made a memorandum upon a card and laid it before the jeweler, then immediately withdrew to the private office.

"Well?" demanded Tom Rider, his keen little eyes gleaming with repressed excitement, as Mr. Knowlton shut the door after him.

"The two large stones belong to Amos Palmer, the

others I never saw before, and you'd better hook your man as soon as possible, because he is beginning to smell powder," said the gentleman, in a low tone.

"I'm ready for him," muttered the detective, as he grabbed his hat, crushed it upon his head, and vanished out of the back door with a good deal more of elasticity in his step than when he had entered.

Going around to the front entrance he sauntered into the store and up to the counter, where Mr. Cohen was apparently trying to drive a close bargain for the Australian(?) diamonds, but really waiting for some sign from the men closeted in his office.

He paused at the entrance of the newcomer, bowed gravely, and politely inquired:

"What can I do for you, sir?"

"I'm sorry to give you any trouble," the detective returned, in quick, sharp tones, "but it is my duty to arrest this man! You are my prisoner, sir," he concluded, laying his hand on the shoulder of the supposed miner.

A startled oath broke from the man's lips, and he made an agile spring for the door.

But the detective was too quick for him, and deftly placed a pair of twisters about his wrists, with such force as to wring a howl of agony from him.

"None of that, my fine fellow," Mr. Rider said, sternly, as he slyly tried to slip his other hand underneath his coat, and he gave the twisters another forcible turn. "Just you let that revolver alone."

"All right," said the miner, apparently yielding; "but what's the charge? Ye can't expect a fellar to submit very tamely to this kind o' thing without knowing what he's nabbed for."

"I arrest you for robbery. These diamonds are

stolen property," was the brief reply of the detective.

"You don't say!" drawled the man, in a tone of sarcastic wonder. "Perhaps ye'll be good enough to prove what ye assert."

The detective could but admire, the cool effrontery of the fellow, but he quietly responded:

"It has already been proved—those large diamonds have just been identified."

"Ah!"

The miner said no more, but quietly submitted to have a pair of handcuffs snapped on his wrists.

The diamonds were secured, and the prisoner was marched off to the station-house, while Ezra Cohen gave utterance to a sigh of relief over the fact that he had made no mistake.

CHAPTER IX.

MR. RIDER RECEIVES ANOTHER SET-BACK.

Jake Walton, as the supposed miner gave his name, was thoroughly searched by Detective Rider, after reaching the station-house, but nothing suspicious was found upon him except a revolver. He had considerable money, but nothing to indicate that he had ever been concerned in any robbery, or to confirm the belief that he was other than he pretended to be.

He submitted to being searched with the utmost indifference, but drawlingly remarked during the operation, he "supposed they'd take bail—he wasn't used to bein' shut up, and it would come pretty tough on him."

"Of course the magistrate will accept suitable bail," said Rider, not imagining that the prisoner could find any one to go security for him to the large sum likely to be asked.

The miner requested that a lawyer might be sent to him at once, after which he coolly sat down, drew out a morning paper, and began to read.

Later in the day a legal gentleman presented himself in his cell, and there followed a long consultation between the two, and toward evening the lawyer, after consulting with a police justice, called at the Southern Hotel and inquired for a lady by the name of Mrs. J. M. Walton.

Yes, there was such a person stopping there, the clerk informed him, whereupon the lawyer sent up his card to her with the request that she would grant him a private interview.

The messenger returned in about fifteen minutes, saying the lady would receive him in her private parlor. Upon being conducted thither, he found a handsome elderly woman awaiting him, and immediately explained his business, relating the circumstances of the arrest of Jake Walton, and concluded by telling her that he had been employed as counsel for the young man, who had sent him to her to arrange for bail.

Mrs. Walton appeared to be greatly disturbed by these disagreeable tidings. She said she had come there expecting to meet her son, who had just returned from Australia, and it was very trying to be told that he had been arrested for theft. Then she inquired what amount would be required for security.

The counsel named the sum fixed by the police justice, whereupon Mrs. Walton appeared to be considerably agitated for a moment.

"I am an entire stranger in the city," she remarked, recovering herself somewhat. "I know no one to whom I could appeal to become bound for so large a sum. What can I do?"

"Have you plenty of means at your disposal, madame?" her companion inquired.

"Yes, I could give bail to almost any reasonable amount, only being a stranger here, I fear it would not be accepted from me," the lady returned, with a look of anxiety.

"No; but I think I can suggest a way out of that difficulty," said the lawyer, with a crafty smile.

"Then do so," said Mrs. Walton, quickly; "I am willing to pay handsomely to secure the release of my son from his uncomfortable position."

"Very well. Then if you can command the sum named you can deposit it in one of the city banks and I will attend to all other formalities for you. Of course, the money will be returned to you after the trial of your son."

"Could such arrangements be made?" Mrs. Walton eagerly inquired.

"Certainly. All that is required is sufficient security to insure the young man's appearance at his trial, and then he will be released."

"Then I can arrange it," the woman said, apparently greatly relieved; and after discussing ways and means a while longer, the lawyer took his leave.

A few hours served to arrange matters satisfactorily to all parties. The sum required was deposited in one of the city banks, and the cashier was empowered to pay it over to the city treasurer, if Jake Walton failed to appear at the time named to answer to the charge of complicity in the Palmer diamond robbery. He was then released, the lawyer was handsomely remunerated for his efficient services, and Mrs. Walton and her son returned to the Southern Hotel.

It was on their way thither that they entered the car in which Mona was also returning to the hotel, and when she made the discovery that the woman had on the very dress which the charming Mrs. Vanderbeck had worn on the day of the Palmer robbery.

We know what followed—how she immediately sent on to Ray for the scrap of cloth, and how, later, she found that it exactly fitted the rent in the dress.

We know, also, how, immediately following this discovery, she sought the headquarters of the detective force, where she opportunely encountered Mr. Rider, and related to him the discoveries which she had made.

Mrs. Walton had not appeared personally in connection with the formalities regarding the release of her son.

Everything had been conducted by the shrewd lawyer, so Detective Rider had not met her at all; but he felt confident, when Mona described her, together with her dress, that she was not the mother of Jake Walton at all, but one of the "gang" who had so successfully robbed different parties during the last two or three years.

The moment the young girl disappeared from the office, after her interview with him, the detective executed a number of antics which would have done credit to a practiced athlete.

"The girl is a cute little body," he muttered, with a chuckle, as he sat down to rest a moment, and plan his course of action, "and it is lucky for me that she happened to be in St. Louis just at this time and stopping at that very hotel. I wonder," he added, with a frown, "that I didn't think that the woman who gave bail, might be one of the gang. By Jove!" with a sudden start, "I believe that money, which she deposited in the bank as security, is only a blind after all, and *they both intend to skip!* What a wretched blunder it was to accept bail anyway! But I'll cage both birds this time, only what I do must be done quickly. They must have done a smashing big business in diamonds," he went on, musingly; "and there are evidently two women and one man associated. This Mrs. Walton is doubtless the old one who tricked Doctor Wesselhoff, and that red-headed Mrs. Vanderbeck, I am still confident, is none other than the Widow Bently, who did Justin Cutler and Mrs. Van-der*heck* out of their money. I'd just like to get hold of all three! Tom Rider, if you only could, it would be a feather in your cap such as doesn't often wave over the head of an ordinary detective, not to mention the good round sum that would swell your pocketbook! But half a loaf is better than no bread, and so here goes! I'll arrest them both, and shall object to anybody going bail for them."

Highly elated over the prospect before him, the man brushed his neat suit until there wasn't an atom of dust upon it, polished his boots until he could see his own face reflected in them, rearranged his necktie in the last new style, then ran lightly down stairs, and hastened, with quick, elastic tread, toward the Southern Hotel, where he expected to accomplish such great results.

*   *   *   *   *   *   *

"Where have you been, Ruth?" exclaimed Mrs.

Montague, in an irritated tone, as Mona entered that lady's parlor upon her return from the detective's office. "I wish you wouldn't go out without consulting me. I've been waiting here for a long time for you to mend these gloves."

"I am very sorry," Mona returned, flushing, "but after you went out to drive I assisted the chambermaid, who was nearly crazy with the toothache, to put some of the rooms in order; then, as you had not returned, I went out for a little walk."

"Well, I don't mind about the walk, but I didn't bring you with me to do chamber-work in every hotel we stop at," sharply retorted the much annoyed lady. You can go at the gloves right away," she added; "then I shall want you to help me pack, for we are to leave on the first boat to-morrow morning. And," she concluded, thus explaining to Mona her unusual irritability, "we've got to make the trip alone, after all, for my friend is worse this morning, and so the whole family have given it up."

"I am sorry that you are to be disappointed. I should suppose you would wish to give it up yourself. I am afraid you will not enjoy it at all," Mona replied, wondering why she did not at once return to New York instead of keeping on.

"Of course, I shall not enjoy it," snapped the woman, but bestowing a searching glance upon her companion, "and I would not go on, only Louis was to join us at New Orleans, and it is too late now to change his plans."

Mona's face fell at this unexpected and disagreeable intelligence.

The last thing she desired was Louis Hamblin's

companionship, and she would have been only too glad
to return at once to New York.

"Could you not telegraph to him?" she suggested.

"No; for I suppose he has already left New York,"
Mrs. Montague curtly replied.

Mona was quite unhappy over the prospect before
her; then it suddenly occurred to her that perhaps
Detective Rider would need her as a witness, if he
should arrest the Waltons, and in that case she would
be compelled to return to New York.

Still she felt very uncomfortable even with this
hope to encourage her, and but for the discovery of
that morning, she would have regretted having consented to accompany Mrs. Montague upon her trip.

She sat down to mend the gloves, with what composure she could assume, although her nerves were in
a very unsettled state, for she was continually looking for a summons from Mr. Rider.

When they were finished she helped about the packing of Mrs. Montague's wardrobe, and then repaired
to her chamber, to get her own in readiness to leave;
but still no word from the detective, and she thought
it very strange.

It might have been an hour after Mona's return to
the hotel, when that official sauntered into the office,
where he picked up a paper and looked it over for a
few minutes. Then he went to the counter, pulled the
register before him, and began to glance up and down
its pages.

He finally found the names he was searching for,
then turning to the clerk, he requested that a boy might
take a note from him to Mrs. J. M. Walton's room.

"Mrs. Walton?" repeated the clerk, with some surprise.

"Yes; I have a little matter of business with her," said Mr. Rider, who intended to make his arrest very quietly.

"I am sorry you did not come earlier, then," regretfully responded the clerk, "for Mrs. Walton and her son left the hotel about two hours ago."

The detective's heart sank with a sudden shock.

Gone! his birds flown when he had them so nearly captured!

"Are you sure?" he sharply demanded, while in spite of his long and severe training, he turned very white, and his under lip twitched nervously.

"Certainly, or I should not have so stated," returned the clerk, with some dignity. "When young Mr. Walton settled his bill, he ordered a carriage to be in waiting at eleven o'clock, and both he and his mother left the house at that time. I regret your disappointment, sir, in missing them."

This was almost more than Mr. Rider could bear; but he could not doubt the man's word, and he feared the thieves had escaped him again. They must have left while Mona was telling him her story at the detective headquarters.

They had been very sharp. Finding themselves in a bad box, they had planned their movements with great cunning. He believed that Mrs. Walton had deposited the amount required for bail in the bank, with the deliberate intention of forfeiting it, rather than have her accomplice brought to trial; doubtless he was too useful to her to run any risk of his being found guilty, and imprisoned for a term of years, and thus put an end to their successful career.

The detective berated himself soundly again for not objecting to the acceptance of bail at all, but it was too late now to remedy the matter. Regrets were useless, and he must bestir himself, strike a fresh trail, if possible, and hope for better results.

He wondered why they had not skipped immediately after Jake Walton's release, but finally concluded that they had remained in the city for a day or two to disarm suspicion.

"Where did they go?" he inquired, as soon as he could command his voice to speak calmly.

"To the Grand Union Station. I believe they were going North, for I heard the young man say something about purchasing tickets, at reduced rates, for Chicago," the clerk replied.

"Had they baggage with them?" Mr. Rider questioned.

"Yes, a trunk and a good-sized grip," said the man.

The detective thought a moment.

Then he called for writing materials, hastily wrote a few lines, which he sealed, and directed to "Miss Richards."

"There is a young lady by that name stopping here, I believe," he remarked, as he laid the envelope before the clerk.

"Yes; she is with a Mrs. Montague."

"That is the lady," said the detective. "Will you see that this letter is given into her own hands, and *privately?* It is a matter of importance."

"Yes, sir, I will myself attend to the matter," responded the obliging clerk.

Mr. Rider deposited a piece of silver upon the envelope, touched his hat, and walked briskly from the hotel.

He jumped into a carriage that was waiting before the door.

"To the Grand Union Station," he ordered. "Be quick about it, and you shall have double fare."

The man was quick about it, but the train for Chicago had been gone some time.

Mr. Rider had of course expected this, but he at once sought an interview with the ticket agent, and made earnest inquiries regarding those who had purchased tickets for Chicago that morning; but he could learn of no persons answering to the description of the miner and his supposed mother.

If he could have obtained any intelligence regarding them, he had intended to telegraph ahead, and order their arrest when they should arrive at the end of their journey. But of course it would be of no use to put this plan into execution now, as he doubted very much their having gone to Chicago at all.

He was very much disheartened, and retraced his steps to his hotel, with a sickening sense of total defeat.

"Tom Rider," he muttered, fiercely, as he packed his own grip to take the first train back to New York, "you might as well give up the business and take up some trade; you've been hoodwinked by these clever thieves often enough."

But there was a very dogged, resolute expression on his plain face, nevertheless, as he turned it northward, which betrayed that he did not mean to give up his search quite yet.

That afternoon when Mona went down to dinner, the clerk of the hotel waylaid her and quietly slipped an envelope into her hand.

"Thank you," she said, in a low tone, and hastily concealed it in her pocket.

When she was alone again she broke it open and

read, with almost as much disappointment as the detective himself had experienced, when he found that his birds had flown, these words:

"Gone! They gave us the slip about eleven o'clock. Save the scrap of cloth—it may be needed later. R."

"Oh, dear!" sighed Mona, regretfully; "and the Palmer robbery is still as much of a mystery as ever."

CHAPTER X.

THE PLOT AGAINST MONA THICKENS.

The next morning Mrs. Montague and her young companion left the Southern Hotel and proceeded directly on board one of the palatial steamers which ply between St. Louis and New Orleans.

Mrs. Montague secured one of the best staterooms for their use, and immediately made herself comfortable for the trip.

The weather was very fine, the season advanced, for the foliage was rapidly developing to perfection, and the sail down the broad tortuous river was delightful.

Mona enjoyed it, in spite of her dread of meeting Louis Hamblin at the end of it, and her anxiety to get back to New York and Ray.

Mrs. Montague had entirely recovered her good nature; indeed, she had never been so kind and gracious toward her seamstress as during this portion of their trip. She appeared to exert herself to make her enjoy it—was more free and companionable, and an observer would have regarded them as relatives and equals.

Mrs. Montague made many acquaintances, as she always did everywhere, and entered most heartily into every plan for amusing and entertaining the party on board the steamer.

The days were mostly spent in delightful intercourse and promenades on deck, where Mona was put forward and made to join in the pleasures; while the evenings were devoted to tableaux, charades, music, and dancing, as the passengers desired.

It seemed almost like a return to her old life before her uncle's death, and could she have obliterated all sadness and painful memories, Mona would have enjoyed it thoroughly.

They had barely touched the levee at New Orleans when they espied Louis Hamblin, dressed with great care and in the height of style, awaiting their arrival.

Mrs. Montague signaled to him from the upper deck; and he, with an answering wave of his hand, sprang aboard, and quickly made his way to her side.

He greeted her with evident pleasure, remarking that it seemed an age since he had seen her, and then he turned to Mona, with outstretched hand and smiling eyes.

"How well you are looking, Miss Richards," he remarked; "your trip has done you a great deal of good."

Mona bowed, but without appearing to notice his extended hand, and then she turned away to gather their wraps and satchels, preparatory to going ashore.

Mr. Hamblin frowned at her coldness, but a pecu-

liar smile curved his lips as he whispered in Mrs.
Montague's ear:

"We'll soon bring your proud beauty to better
terms."

"Don't be rash, Louis," she returned; "we must be
very wary if we would accomplish our purpose. You
say you love the girl, and I have consented to let you
have your way, but, since she is not inclined to accept
your advances, you will have to play your cards very
shrewdly if you expect to win."

"All right; I will be circumspection personified, if
you will only help me to make that girl my wife," the
young man said earnestly. "I do love her with all
my heart; and, Aunt Margie, I'll quit sowing wild
oats, turn over a new leaf, and be a good man if I
succeed in this."

Mrs. Montague regarded him somewhat skeptically,
as he made this eager avowal, but it was almost immediately followed by a look of anxiety.

"I hope you will—you certainly owe me that much
after all that I have done for you," she returned.
"Mind you," she added, "I never would have yielded
this point if I had not been driven to it.'

"Driven to it! How?" inquired her nephew, regarding her searchingly.

"Driven to it, because I have found out that she is
Mona Montague, and I'm afraid that she has an eye
to her father's property. I believe she is very keen
—doubtless she knows that she has a legal claim upon
what he left, and means to assert it, or she never would
have so cunningly wormed herself into my family. Of
course it will be difficult for her to prove her position,
since I have that certificate of marriage; still she may
have some other proof that I know nothing about

which she is secretly working. Of course I'd rather you would marry her," Mrs. Montague gloomily observed, "and thus make our interests mutual, than run any risk of losing the whole of my money. Still, I did want you to marry Kitty McKenzie: I wanted you to fortify yourself with additional wealth."

"I have suspected that the girl was Mona all along," Louis quietly remarked.

"Oh, have you?" sharply retorted his aunt, as she studied his face with suspicious eyes. "Perhaps you have been plotting to marry her for the sole purpose of getting this fortune wholly under your control."

"Pshaw! Aunt Margie, how foolish you are! Haven't I always worked for your interests? More than that, haven't you always assured me that the fortune would be mine eventually? Why, then, should I plot for it?" the young man replied, in soothing tones, but coloring beneath her glance. "I tell you," he went on, a note of passion in his voice, "I love the girl; I would even be willing to marry her without a dollar in prospect, and then go to work to support her. Now come, do not let us quarrel over imaginary troubles, but unite our forces for our mutual benefit. It will be far safer for you if she becomes my wife, for then you will have nothing to fear, and I shall have won the desire of my heart."

"Well, it will have to be, I suppose," said Mrs. Montague, moodily. "I wonder how I was ever so deceived though, when she looks so like Mona Forester. I can understand now why Ray Palmer was so attentive to her at Hazeldean. Strange it never occurred to me, when I saw him waiting upon her, that she was Mona Montague, and they must have had a quiet laugh by themselves over having so thoroughly hoodwinked us."

"They didn't hoodwink me," Mr. Hamblin affirmed, with a sly smile; "I knew all the time who she was."

"I don't see how you knew it," Mrs. Montague retorted, impatiently.

"I will tell you. I was in Macy's one day when the girl ran across some acquaintances. She bowed and smiled to them, as I suppose she had always been in the habit of doing; but the petted darlings of *le bon ton* drew themselves up haughtily, stared rudely at her, and passed on, while the poor child flushed, then paled, and looked ready to drop. A moment later, the two proud misses shot by me, one of them remarking with curling lips and a toss of her head, 'Do you suppose that Mona Montague expects that we are going to recognize her now?'"

"Why didn't you tell me this before?" Mrs. Montague angrily demanded.

"Because I knew that, if you suspected her identity, you would turn her out of the house forthwith, and then I should have hard work getting into her good graces."

"You are a sly one, Louis."

"One must look out for one's own interests in some respects," he coolly responded.

"Does she know that you suspect her identity?"

"No, not yet; but I mean she soon shall."

"Ah!" said Mrs. Montague, with sudden thought, "maybe you can use this knowledge to aid your suit —only don't let her know that I am in the secret until you are sure of her."

"That has been my intention all along—for I have

meant to marry her, by hook or crook," and the young man smiled complacently.

"Look out, Louis; don't overreach yourself," said his companion, bending forward, and looking warningly into his face. "If you make an enemy of me, I warn you, it will be the worse for you."

"My dear aunt, I have no intention of making an enemy of you—you and I have been chums too long for any ill-will to spring up between us now. But," he concluded, looking about him, "we must not remain here talking any longer; most of the passengers have already left the boat. I will go for a carriage and we will drive directly to the St. Charles, where I have rooms engaged for you."

Mrs. Montague turned to call Mona, who was standing at some distance from them, watching the men unload the boat.

"Come," she said, "we must go ashore."

Mona followed her from the boat, and into the carriage, utterly ignoring Louis Hamblin's assistance as she entered. She shrank more and more from him, while a feeling of depression and foreboding suddenly changed her from the bright, care-free girl, which she had seemed ever since leaving St. Louis, into a proud, reticent, and suspicious woman.

Upon reaching the St. Charles Hotel, Mrs. Montague informed Mona that dinner would be served shortly, and she would need to be expeditious in making her toilet.

"I should prefer not to go to the dining-room," Mona began, flushing.

"But I wish you to, for we are going to drive afterward to some of the points of interest in the city," Mrs. Montague returned.

"If you will excuse me——"

"Nonsense," retorted her companion, again interrupting her; "don't be a goose, Ruth! I want you with me, and we will not discuss the point any further."

Mona hesitated a moment, then turned away, but with a dignity which warned Mrs. Montague that it might not be well to enforce her commands too rigorously, or she might rebel outright.

Mona went down to the dining-room, but to her great relief received no disagreeable attentions from Mr. Hamblin, who sat on the right, while her seat was on the left of his aunt. He did not address her during the meal, except to ascertain if she was properly waited upon by the servants.

Afterward they went for a drive out on the shell road, which proved to be really delightful, for the city was in its prime, while, rain having fallen early in the day, the streets were not in the least dusty.

Mrs. Montague and Louis monopolized the conversation, thus leaving Mona free to look around about her.

The only thing that occurred to annoy her was on their return to the hotel. Louis, in assisting her to alight, held her hand in a close, lingering clasp for a moment, and, looking admiringly into her eyes, remarked, in a low tone:

"I hope you have enjoyed your drive, Miss—Richards."

What could he mean, Mona asked herself, by that significant pause before and that emphasis on her name?

She forcibly wrenched her hand from his, and deigning him no reply, walked with uplifted head into the hotel, and up to her own room.

The next day she politely, but firmly, declined to go out driving, and remained by herself to write a long letter to Ray; thus she avoided the hated companionship of the man, who became more and more odious to her.

The third evening after their arrival Mrs. Montague went to a concert with some people whose acquaintance she had made while on the steamer, and Mona congratulated herself that she could have a long quiet evening in which to read a book in which she had become deeply interested.

She had not a thought of being interrupted, for she supposed that Lewis had accompanied his aunt, and she was sitting contentedly by the table in Mrs. Montague's private parlor, when she heard the door behind her open and close.

She looked up surprised, but the expression was quickly succeeded by one of dismay when she saw Louis Hamblin advancing toward her.

She arose, regarding him with cold displeasure.

He bowed politely as he remarked:

"Do not rise. I simply came to get some letters that Aunt Margie wished me to mail for her."

Mona resumed her seat, greatly relieved at this assurance, and went on with her reading, while the young man took up his aunt's writing-pad, which lay upon the table, as if to search for the letters.

He took out a couple and slipped them into his pocket; then selecting a pen, began himself to write.

Mona felt very uncomfortable, sitting there alone with him, but she kept hoping that he would soon go out again, and so went on with her reading.

Presently, however, he laid down his pen, and, glancing across the table at her, asked:

"What book have you that is so interesting?"

" 'The Senator's Bride,' " Mona briefly responded.

"Ah! I have never read it. What do you think of it?"

"It is quite entertaining," was the brief, cold reply.

"Pray, do not be so cold and proud—so exceedingly laconic," the young man said, with a smile, which was intended to be persuasive.

Instantly the young girl arose again, stately and frigid as an iceberg.

She attempted to pass him and go to her own room, but he threw out his hand, seized her arm, and stopped her.

"*Please* do not go!" he urged, in an imploring tone. "I have something which I want very much to say to you."

Mona's blood began to boil, and her eyes flashed dangerously at his presumption in daring to touch her.

She was too proud to struggle with him, and she could not shake off his hold upon her arm.

"Release me, Mr. Hamblin!" she said, in ominously quiet tones.

"Nay, *do* not treat me so!" he pleaded. "Be kind to me for once, and let me open my heart to you."

Her red lips curled.

"*Will* you let me pass?" she icily demanded.

He colored hotly at her tone; a flash of anger gleamed in his eyes.

"*No*. Be seated, *Miss Mona Montague;* I have something important to say to you," he said, in a tone that struck terror to her heart, while the utterance of her real name so startled and unnerved her that, almost involuntarily, she sank back into her chair, her face as white as her handkerchief, and trembling in every limb.

"Ah! that surprises you, doesn't it?" he remarked, with a smile of triumph; "and now I imagine you will be more tractable.

"What do you mean?" demanded Mona, recovering her composure somewhat, and determined not to commit herself, if she could avoid it.

"What do I mean?" he repeated, with a light laugh. "I mean to have a little private and serious conversation with Miss Mona Montague; and when I have finished, I do not believe that she will treat me quite so cavalierly as she has been doing of late."

"I do not wish to hold any conversation with you, Mr. Hamblin," Mona began, haughtily.

"Perhaps not, but you will, nevertheless," he interposed; "and, let me tell you, to begin with, it will be useless for you to ignore the name by which I have addressed you. I have discovered your identity in spite of your clever efforts to represent some one else—or rather to conceal your personality. I know that you are Mona Montague, the daughter of my aunt's husband and a girl named Mona Forester——"

"Stay!" cried Mona, starting again to her feet, her eyes blazing. "I will not hear my mother spoken of with any disrespect."

"I beg your pardon; I had no intention of wounding you thus," said the young man, regretfully, and flushing. "I simply wished you to understand that I had discovered your identity; and since you have now virtually acknowledged it, by asserting that Mona Forester was your mother, I beg you will be rea-

sonable, and talk the matter over calmly with me, and
hear what I have to propose to you.

Mona sank weakly back.

She saw that it would be worse than useless to deny
what he had asserted; she had indeed betrayed and
acknowledged too much for that.

"Very well. I will listen to what you wish to say,
but be kind enough to be brief, for I have no desire
to prolong this interview beyond what is absolutely
necessary for your purpose," she said, with freezing
dignity.

"Well, then," Louis Hamblin began, "I have known
who you were ever since you came into Aunt Margie's
house as a seamstress."

Then he went on to explain how he learned it, and
Mona, remembering the incident but too well, saw that
it would be best to quietly accept the fact of his knowledge.

"Does Mrs. Montague also know?" she asked, with
breathless eagerness.

"She suspected you at first," he evasively answered,
"but you so diplomatically replied to her questions—
you were so self-possessed under all circumstances, and
especially so when one day you found a picture of your
mother, that she was forced to believe your strange resemblance to Mona Forester only a coincidence."

CHAPTER XI.

MONA IN A TRYING POSITION.

Mona breathed more freely, for she believed from
his evasive reply that Mrs. Montague did not now believe her to be Mona Forester's child.

"I beg you will not tell her," she said, impulsively, and then instantly regretted having made the request.

The young man's face lighted.

If they could have a common secret he believed that he should make some headway in his wooing.

"That will depend upon how kind you are to me," he said, meaningly.

Mona's head went up haughtily again. His presumption, his assurance, both annoyed and angered her.

He affected not to notice her manner, and asked:

"What was your object, Miss Montague, in coming into my aunt's family under an assumed name?"

Mona thought a moment before replying; then she felt that since he already knew so much, it would do no harm to tell him the truth.

"I had no intention at first of going anywhere under an assumed name," she said, gravely. "I applied at an employment bureau for a situation as seamstress, and this position was obtained for me. I did not even know the name of the woman who had engaged me, until I entered Mrs. Montague's house. When I learned the truth, I was tempted to leave at once; but the desire to learn more than I already knew regarding my parentage made me bold to brave discovery, and remain at least for a while, and so upon the spur of the moment I gave the name of Ruth Richards—Ruth is my middle name, and Richards very nearly like that of the man who married my mother——"

"Who married your mother?" questioned Louis Hamblin, in a mocking tone.

"Yes; they were legally married. I at least know that much," said Mona, positively, determined to make him think she fully believed it.

"How did you learn so much?"

"My uncle assured me of the fact only the day before he died."

"Your uncle? You mean Walter Dinsmore, I suppose?"

"Yes; of course."

"How much of your history did he reveal to you?" questioned the young man, eagerly.

"I do not feel under any obligation to tell you that," Mona coldly answered.

"Now, Miss Montague," Louis said, with well assumed frankness and friendliness, "why will you persist in treating me as an enemy? Why will you not have confidence in me, and allow me to help you? I know your whole history—I know, too, from what you have said, that you are ignorant of much that is vital to your interests, and which I could reveal to you, if I chose. Now forget any unpleasantness that may have arisen between us, tell me just what you hoped to learn by remaining in my aunt's family, and, believe me, I stand ready to help you."

Mona lifted her great liquid brown eyes, and searched his face.

Oh, how she longed to know the truth about her mother; but she distrusted him—she instinctively doubted his sincerity.

He read something of this in her glance, and continued, hoping to disarm her suspicions:

"Of course you know that Aunt Margie is, or was, Richmond Montague's second wife——"

"Ah! by that statement you yourself virtually acknowledge that my mother was his first wife," triumphantly interposed Mona. "As I said before, my uncle assured me of the fact, but your admission is worth something to me as corroborative evidence. All that I desire now is tangible proof of it; if you can and will obtain that for me, I shall have some faith in your assertion that you wish to help me."

"Are you so eager to claim, as your father, the man who deserted your mother?" Louis Hamblin asked, with a sneer, and wishing to sound her a little further.

"No; I simply want proof that my mother was a legal wife—I have only scorn and contempt for the man who wronged her," Mona replied, intense aversion vibrating in her tones. "I regard him, as my uncle did, as a knave—a brute."

"Did Walter Dinsmore represent him as such to you?" inquired her companion, in a mocking tone.

"He did; he expressed the utmost contempt and loathing for the man who had ruined his sister's life."

The young man gave vent to a short, derisive laugh.

"I cannot deny the justness of the epithets applied to him," he said, with a sneer, "but, that such terms should have fallen from the immaculate lips of the cultured and aristocratic Walter Dinsmore, rather amuses me, especially as the present Mrs. Dinsmore might, with some reason, perhaps, bring the same charges against him."

"Did you know my uncle?" Mona questioned, with some surprise.

"Not personally; but Mrs. Montague knew him very well years ago."

"Oh! I wonder if you could tell me——" Mona began, greatly agitated, as she recalled the dreadful suspicion that had flashed into her mind regarding her uncle, in connection with her father's death.

"If I could tell you what?" Louis inquired, while he wondered what thought could have so suddenly blanched her face, and sent that look of terror into her beautiful eyes.

"Oh, I want to know—did he—how did my father die?" the young girl cried, in faltering, trembling tones.

Louis Hamblin regarded her with unfeigned astonishment at the question.

"How did your father die?" he repeated. "Why, like any other respectable gentleman—in his own house, and of an incurable disease."

"Oh! then he did die a natural death," breathed Mona, with a sigh of relief that was almost a sob.

"Certainly. Ah!" and her companion appeared suddenly to divine her thoughts, "so you imagined that Walter Dinsmore killed Richmond Montague for the wrong done your mother! Ha! ha! I have no doubt that he felt bitter enough to commit murder, or almost any other act of violence, to avenge her; but let me assure you, Miss Montague, that that high-toned gentleman never soiled his hands with blood; and if that was your thought——"

"It is no matter what I thought," Mona hastily, but coldly, interposed, for she had no intention of confessing any such suspicion; but she was greatly relieved to learn that it had no foundation, and she now bitterly reproached herself for having even momentarily entertained a thought of anything that had been so foreign to her uncle's noble nature.

"To go back to what we were speaking of before," she continued, gravely, "will you furnish me with tangible proof of my mother's marriage? I know that she eloped with Richmond Montague, that they lived together for several months, when he suddenly deserted her, and that there is some mystery connected with that event—something which my uncle hesitated or feared to tell me. I know, too, that he was very anxious to reveal something more to me when he lay dying, and could not, because he had been stricken speechless. But for that fact, I believe I should not now be obliged to ask this favor of you," she concluded, flushing.

"Does it gall you so much, to ask a favor of me?" he inquired, bitterly. "But why," he went on, without waiting for a reply, "are you so exceedingly anxious to obtain this proof? Do you expect by the use of it to secure to yourself the property left by your father? Was that your object in remaining in my aunt's family under an assumed name?"

"No!" Mona vehemently returned. "I would not touch one dollar of his money. I would scorn to profit by so much as a penny of the fortune left by the man who deserted his wife in her sad extremity. and then, when death freed him from the tie which bound him to her, married a woman whom he did not love; who possessed so little of fatherly instinct in his nature, that he never acknowledged his child, nor betrayed the slightest interest in or affection for her. I would never own him for such a purpose; while, were it not for the sake of establishing my mother's honor, I would even repudiate the name I bear," she concluded, looking so proud and beautiful in her righteous scorn that the young man gazed upon her with admiration.

"You are very proud-spirited," he remarked; then, with a sly smile, "but as for the name you affect to so despise, it would be an easy matter to change it."

Mona colored at this observation, not because she gave a thought to his meaning, but because she hoped it would not be so very long before she would change the hated name of Montague for the honored one of Palmer.

Her companion noticed the flush, and an eager look flashed into his eyes, while his lips trembled with the torrent of burning words which he longed to pour into her ears. But he controlled himself for the moment, and continued:

"You ask me if I will give you the tangible proof of your mother's marriage. I have told you that I can do so; that I know the whole story of the elopement and the desertion. I can produce absolute proof that Mona Forester was a legal wife."

"Then give it to me—give it to me and I will believe that you are my friend," Mona cried, appealingly, and trembling with excitement at his statement.

"I will do so gladly," the young man said, a smile of triumph curling his lips, "but I can only do so conditionally."

"Conditionally?" repeated Mona, her great eyes flashing up to his face with a startled look.

"Yes. I can produce the certificate proving your father's and mother's honorable marriage. I can give you letters that will also prove it, and prove, too, that your father was not quite so disreputable and heartless as you have been led to believe. There is also a picture of him, painted on ivory, and set in a frame of gold, embellished with costly stones, which he had made for his wife, and there are valuable jewels and other keepsakes which he bestowed upon her with lavish hands, and which now rightly belong to you. All these I will give you if—if you will marry me—if you will be my wife, Mona."

The girl sprang to her feet, every atom of color

now gone from her face, and confronted him with haughty mien.

"*Your wife!*" she began, pantingly. But he would not let her go on—he meant at least to explain himself more fully before allowing her to reject him.

"Yes, why not?" he asked, throwing into his tone all the tenderness he could command, "for I love you, Mona, with all my heart. I have told you so once before, but you would not believe me. You taunted me with unworthy motives, and asserted that I would not dare to confess my affection to my aunt; but I have confessed it, and she is willing that I should win you. I know that I have paid devoted attention to Kitty McKenzie, as you also twitted me of doing, and Aunt Margie wanted me to marry her; but when she found that I had no love to give her, that my heart was set upon you, she yielded the point, and I now have her full and free consent to make you my wife. Do not scorn my suit, Mona; I cannot think of you as Ruth Richards any longer; do not curl your proud lips and flash your glorious eyes upon me with scorn, as you did that day at Hazeldean, for I offer you a warm and loyal heart. I know that I am not worthy of you," he went on, flushing and speaking humbly for once, for he was terribly in earnest; "I have been guilty of a great many things which I have learned to regret, since I have known you; but I can conquer everything if you will give me your love as an incentive, and I will be a better man in the future. I will even *work* for you, if you so despise the fortune which your father left and which I have expected to inherit from my aunt. Oh, Mona, do not despise my love for you, for it is the purest attribute of my nature, and——"

"Pray cease," Mona here interposed, for she felt

unable to hear any more of this passionate avowal, while she was greatly surprised and really moved by the depth of feeling which he evinced. "I would be the last one," she continued, in kind, grave tones, but with averted eyes and trembling lips, "to despise the true affection of any man. If I said anything to wound you that day at Hazeldean, I regret it now, although I felt at the time that you showed some disrespect in your manner of approaching me. But I cannot be your wife; if you make that the condition" —and her lips curled a trifle here—"of my learning the mystery regarding my father's desertion of my mother, and securing the proof of their marriage; then I must forever relinquish all such hopes, for I could never marry a man——"

"But," he interrupted, excitedly.

"Let me finish," she persisted, lifting her hand to stay his words. "No woman should ever become the wife of a man she cannot love. I do not love you, Mr. Hamblin, and knowing this, you would not respect me if I should yield to your suit. Let me assure you that I honor you for some things you said to-day—that you would be willing to work for one whom you loved; that you would even relinquish a fortune for her sake. Believe me, I respect you and appreciate such an avowal, and only regret that your regard could not have been bestowed upon some one who could return such devotion. I cannot, but, Mr. Hamblin, I feel more friendly toward you at this moment than I have ever felt before. I beg, however," she concluded, sadly, "that you will never address me thus again, for it gives me pain to know that any one's life should be marred through me; put this affection away from you—crush it in your heart, and seek some dear, good

girl who will love you and make you happier than I
possibly could, if I should yield to your suit without
any heart to give you."

"Put this love out of my heart! crush it!" burst
forth the young man, with pale lips. "Could you do
that, Mona Montague, if the man you loved should
stand coldly up before you and bid you to do so?"

Mona flushed, and hot tears sprang into her eyes.
She knew, but too well, that she could never crush
out of her heart her love for Raymond Palmer.

If Louis Hamblin had bestowed but a tithe of such
affection upon her there was indeed a sad future in
store for him, and the deepest sympathies of her nature were aroused for him.

"I am sorry—" she began, falteringly, as she lifted
her swimming eyes to his face, and both look and
tone stirred him to hot rebellion, for he knew well
enough of what she had been thinking.

"How sorry are you?" he cried, in a low, intense
tone; "sorry enough to try to do for me what you have
bidden me do for another? Will you crush your love
for Ray Palmer, and bestow it upon me?"

Mona recoiled beneath these fierce, hot words, while
she inwardly resented the selfishness and rudeness of
his question.

Still she tried to make some allowance for his bitter
disappointment and evident suffering.

"I do not think you have any right to speak to me
like that," she said, in tones of gentle reproof, though
her face was crimson with conscious blushes.

"Have I no right to say to you what you have said
to me?" he demanded. "You have said that no
woman should marry a man whom she does not love,
while, in the very next breath, you bid me go 'seek

for some dear, good girl,' and ask her to marry me, who can never love any woman but you. Are you considerate—are you consistent?"

"Perhaps not," she returned, sorrowfully, "but I did not mean to be inconsistent or to wound you—I could hardly believe that you cared so deeply! I hoped you might be mistaken in your assertion that no other affection could be rooted in your heart."

"There may be other natures besides your own that are capable of tenacious affection," he retorted, with exceeding bitterness.

"True," Mona said, sighing heavily, "but," driven to desperation, and facing him with sudden resolution, "I cannot respond to your suit as you wish; I can never be your wife, for—perhaps, under the circumstances, I ought to make the confession—I am already pledged to another."

CHAPTER XII.

THE SECRET OF THE ROYAL MIRROR.

Mona's eyes were averted and she was greatly embarrassed as she made the acknowledgment of her engagement, therefore she could not see the look of anger and evil purpose which suddenly swept every expression of tenderness from Louis Hamblin's face.

He could not speak for a moment, he was so intensely agitated by her confession.

"Of course, I cannot fail to understand you," he remarked, at last. "You mean that you are engaged to Ray Palmer, and that accounts for the attentions which he bestowed upon Ruth Richards at Hazeldean.

You two were very clever, but even then I had read between the lines and knew what you have just told me."

"You knew, and yet presumed to make this avowal? You dared to ask another man's promised wife to marry you!" Mona exclaimed, all her embarrassment now gone, her scornful eyes looking straight into his.

"Well, perhaps I should not say I knew, but I surmised," he confessed, his glance wavering beneath hers.

"That is but a poor apology," she retorted, in the same tone as before; "you certainly have betrayed but very little respect for me if you even 'surmised' the truth, and would ask me to regard my plighted troth so lightly as to break it simply to gratify your own selfishness."

"And your respect for me has waned accordingly, I suppose you would be glad to add," Louis Hamblin interposed, with a sneer.

Mona made him no answer. She began to think that she had overestimated the purity of his motives— that all her recent sympathy had been expended upon an unworthy object.

"You will not forget, however, that I made the promise to surrender certain proofs and keepsakes conditional upon your yielding to my suit," he added, with cold resoluteness.

"No honorable man would make such conditions with the woman he professed to love," retorted Mona, with curling lips.

"A man, when he is desperate, will adopt almost any measure to achieve his object," her companion responded, hotly.

'We will not argue the matter further, if you

please," Mona said, frigidly, as she took up her book, which she had laid upon the table when she arose, and started to leave the room.

"Mona, do not go away like this—you shall not leave me in such a mood!" the young man cried, as he placed himself in her path. "Do you not see that I am filled with despair——that I am desperate?"

"I am sorry," she answered, gravely, "but I can tell you nothing different—my answer is final, and your own sense of what is right should make you realize and submit to it."

"Then you do not care for the marriage certificate and other proofs?" he said.

Again the young girl's lips curled with infinite scorn.

"Did you suppose that my love and my hand were, like articles of merchandise, to be bought and sold?" she asked, with scathing sarcasm. "Yes, I do care for —I do want the proofs; but they are not to be mentioned in connection with such sacred subjects," she went on, with dignity. "If you were really my friend you would never have suggested anything of the kind; you would have been glad to help me to any proof that would relieve my mind and heart from the harassing doubts regarding the history of my parents. If such proofs exist, as you claim, they rightly *belong* to me, and you are uncourteous, not to say dishonorable, in keeping them from me."

"People are not in the habit of resigning important documents simply for the sake of preserving themselves from the charge of discourtesy," Louis laconically observed.

"I am to understand from that, I suppose, that you will not give them to me," Mona remarked. "Well,

since I *know* that there was no blame or shame at-
tached to my mother—since I know that she was only
a victim to the wickedness of others—it will not matter
so very much if I do not have the tangible proofs you
possess, and I must try to be content without them."

She made another attempt to leave the room, but
he still stood in her way.

"I cannot—I will not give you up," he said, between
his tightly locked teeth.

"You will be kind enough to let me pass, Mr. Hamblin," Mona returned, and ignoring his excited assertion.

"No, I will not," he fiercely replied.

She lifted her eyes, and met his angry glance with
one so proudly authoritative that he involuntarily
averted his own gaze.

"I beg that you will not cause me to lose all faith
in you," she quietly remarked.

A hot flush surged to his brow, and he instantly
stepped aside, looking crestfallen and half-ashamed.

Without another word, Mona passed from the room
and entered her own chamber.

As soon as she had closed and locked the door, she
sat down, and tried to think over all that had been
said about her mother; this one subject filled all her
mind to the exclusion of everything else.

But for Louis Hamblin's last remarks, and the betrayal of his real nature, and his selfish, ignoble
purpose, she would have been grieved on his account,
but she saw that he was unworthy of her regard, of
even one sorrowful thought.

"These papers and keepsakes of which he has told
me are mine," she said to herself; "they belong by
right to me, and I must—I will have them. That cer-

tificate, oh! if I could get but that, I could give myself
to Ray without a scruple, and besides I could secure
this property which Homer Forester has left to my
mother, and then I need not go to Ray quite penniless.
These things must be in either Louis Hamblin's or
Mrs. Montague's possession—doubtless they are even
now somewhere in the house in West Forty-ninth
street. I shall tell Mr. Corbin immediately upon my
return, and perhaps he will know of some way by
which they can be compelled to give them up."

She fell to musing over the matter, little suspecting that the most important treasure of all—the contested marriage certificate—had already fallen into
her lover's hands, and was at that moment safely
locked in Mr. Corbin's safe, only awaiting her own
and Mrs. Montague's return from the South to set
her right before the world, both as to parentage and
inheritance.

Louis Hamblin remained in Mrs. Montague's parlor until her return from the concert, brooding over
the failure of his purpose, and trying to devise some
scheme by which he could attain the desire of his
heart.

He then gave her a faithful account of his interview with Mona, and they sat far into the night and
plotted how best to achieve their object.

Mrs. Montague was now as eager to have Louis
marry Mona as she had previously been determined
to oppose it.

"I am bound that she shall never go into the Palmer
family, if I can prevent it," she said, with a frowning
brow. "If I am to be mistress of Mr. Palmer's home,
I have no intention of allowing Mona Forester's child
to be a blot on my future happiness."

"You are complimentary, Aunt Marg, in your remarks regarding my future wife," Louis sarcastically observed.

"I can't help it, Louis. I bear the girl no goodwill, as you have known from the first, and you must make up your mind to accept matters as they are. You are determined to have her and I have given my consent to the marriage from purely selfish motives," Mrs. Montague returned, in a straightforward, matter-of-fact tone. "I would never have consented," she added, with a frown "if I had not feared that there is proof—besides what we possess—of Mona Forester's legal marriage, and that through it we might some time lose our fortune. I should be in despair to be obliged to give it up—life without plenty of money is not worth living, and I consider that I was very shrewd and fortunate in getting possession of that certificate and those other things."

"Did you bring them with you when you left home?"

"No; I never thought of them," Mrs. Montague responded, with a start and a look of anxiety. "It is the first time I ever came away from home without them; but after I received that telegram and letter I had plenty on my mind, I assure you—my chief aim was to get that girl out of New York, and away to some safe place where we could work out our scheme."

"But you ought never to leave such valuables behind," said her nephew; "the house might take fire, and they would be all destroyed."

"That would be but a small loss," the woman retorted. "I have thought a hundred times that I would throw them all into the fire, and thus blot out of existence all that remained of the girl I so hated; but whenever I have attempted to do so I have been unaccountably restrained. But I will do it as soon as we get home again," she resolutely concluded.

Louis Hamblin's eyes gleamed with a strange expression at this threat; but he made no reply to it.

"But let us settle this matter of your marriage," she resumed, after a moment of thought. "The girl shall marry you—I have brought her here for that purpose, and if she will not be reasoned into compliance with our wishes, she shall be compelled or tricked into it. But how, is the question."

"I will agree to almost anything, so that I get her," remarked her nephew, with a grim smile.

The clock on the mantel-piece struck two before they separated, but they had decided on their plan of action, and only awaited the coming day to develop it.

Meanwhile strange things had been happening in Mona's room.

We left her musing over her recent interview with Louis, and deeply absorbed in making plans to obtain possession of the proofs of her mother's marriage, which he had asserted he could produce.

The more she thought of the matter the more determined she became to accomplish her purpose, and she began to grow very anxious to return to New York to consult with Ray and Mr. Corbin.

"I wonder how much longer Mrs. Montague intends to remain here," she murmured. "She said she should return within a fortnight, but nearly that time has expired already. I cannot understand her object in prolonging her stay, since she was disappointed about coming with the party. I believe I will ask her to-morrow how soon we are to go back."

Mona felt very weary after the unusual excitement

of the evening; her nerves were also considerably un-strung, and she resolved not to wait for Mrs. Montague's return, but retire at once.

She arose and began to prepare for bed, but having sent some clothing away to be washed that morning, she found that her night-robe had gone with the other articles, and unlocking her trunk, she began to look for another.

"I thought I put an extra one in the tray," she mused, as she searched for but failed to find it.

This obliged her to remove the tray and to unpack some of the contents beneath.

While thus employed she took out a box, and without thinking what it contained, carelessly set it across a corner of the trunk.

She finally found the garment she needed, and then began to replace the clothing which she had been obliged to remove during her search.

While thus engaged she turned suddenly to reach for something that had slipped from her grasp, and in the act she hit her elbow against the box setting on the corner of her trunk, and knocked it to the floor.

"Oh! my mirror!" she cried, in a voice of terror, and hastily gathering up the box, uncovered it to see if the precious relic had been injured.

To her great joy she found that it had not been broken by the fall; but as she lifted it from the box, to examine it still further, the bottom of the frame dropped out, and with it the things which Mr. Dinsmore had concealed within it.

"Mercy!" Mona excitedly exclaimed; "it looks like a little drawer, and here are some letters and a box which some one has hidden in it! Can it be that these things once belonged to Marie Antoinette, and have been inclosed in this secret place all these long years?" she wonderingly questioned.

"No, surely not, for they would be yellow with age," she continued, as she began to examine them.

"Ah!" with a start, and growing pale, "here is a letter addressed to me—*For Mona*—and in Uncle Walter's handwriting! He must have known about the secret of this mirror, and put these letters here with some special object in view. What can it mean?"

She grew dizzy—almost faint with the excitement of her discovery, and the things dropped from her nerveless fingers upon her lap.

"There is some secret here!" she whispered, as she gazed down at them, an expression of dread in her startled eyes. "Perhaps it is the secret which I have so long wanted to know! Can it be that the mystery of my mother's sad fate is about to be solved—that Uncle Walter had not the courage to tell me all, that never-to-be-forgotten morning, but wrote it out and hid it here for me to find later? Ah!" and she lifted her head as if suddenly recalling something, "this was what he tried to make me understand the day he died! He sent me for the mirror, not to remind me to keep it always, as I thought at the time, but to explain the secret of it, so that I could find what he had hidden here. Oh, how he suffered because he could not show me! Why could I not have understood?" and her tears fell thick and fast, as she thus lived over again that painful experience.

She soon brushed them away, however, and lifting the mirror, examined it carefully.

She found that the tiny drawer would shove smoothly in and out, and she pushed it almost in, but took care not to quite close it.

"There must be a spring somewhere to hold it in place," she murmured, regarding it curiously. "Ah! now I feel it! But how is it operated? How can the drawer be opened again if I shut it entirely?"

She looked the mirror over most carefully, both on the back and front, but at first could detect nothing. But at length, as she still continued to work the drawer in and out, she noticed that the central pearl and gold point at the top of the frame moved slightly as she pressed the drawer close upon the spring, and she believed that she had discovered the Secret of the Royal Mirror.

With a resolute air she shut it entirely and heard the click of the spring as it shot into its socket. Her reason told her that pressure applied to that central point of pearl and gold would at once release the drawer again.

She tried it, and instantly it dropped out upon her lap.

"It is the strangest thing in the world. I feel almost as if I had opened a grave," she murmured, a shiver running along her nerves. "My heart almost fails me when I think of examining its contents—this letter addressed to me, this package of letters, and the tiny box. I wonder what there is in it?"

She looked strangely beautiful as she sat there upon the floor, her face startlingly pale, her eyes seeming larger than ever, with that wondering expression in their liquid depths, while she turned that little box over and over in her trembling hands, as if she tried to gather courage to untie the string that bound its cover on and look within it.

At last she threw up her head with a determined air, gathered up all the things she had found in the secret drawer, and rising, drew a chair to her table, where she sat down to solve the mystery.

CHAPTER XIII.

"I SHOULD THINK WE WERE OUT AT SEA!"

Mona's curiosity prompted her to examine the contents of the little box first.

She untied the narrow ribbon that was bound about it, lifted the cover and a layer of cotton, and discovered the two rings which we already know about.

"My mother's wedding and engagement-ring!" Mona breathed, seeming to know by instinct what they were. "They must have been taken from her fingers after she was dead, and Uncle Walter has kept them all these years for me. Oh, why could he not have told me about them? I should have prized them so." She lifted them from their snowy bed with reverent touch, remarking, as she did so, the size and great beauty of the diamond in the engagement-ring.

"My dear, deeply wronged mother! how I should have loved you!" she murmured. "I wonder if you know how tenderly I feel toward you; if you can see me now and realize that I, the little, helpless baby, for whose life you gave up your own, am longing for you with all my heart and soul."

She touched the rings tenderly with her lips, tears raining over her cheeks, while sob after sob broke from her.

She wiped **away her tears** after a little, and tried

the rings upon her own fingers, smiling sadly to see
how perfectly they fitted.

"Mamma's hand must have been about the size of
mine," she said.   "I think I must be very like her in
every way."

She slipped the heavy gold band off and bent nearer
the light to examine the inside, hoping to find some
inscription upon it.

She found only the date, "June 6th, 1861."

"The date of her marriage," she whispered, a little
smile of triumph lighting her face, then removing the
other ring from her hand, she laid them both back in
the box and put it one side.   "Now for the letters,"
she said, taking up the one addressed to herself and
carefully cutting one end across the envelope with a
little knife taken from her pocket.

She unfolded the closely written sheets, which she
drew from it, with hands that trembled with nervous
excitement.

The next moment she was absorbed in their contents, and as she read a strange change came over her.

At first there was a quick start, accompanied by a
low exclamation of surprise, then a look of wonder
shot into her great brown eyes.   Suddenly, as she
hungrily devoured the pages, her color fled, even her
lips became white, and an expression of keen pain
settled about her mouth, but she read on and on with
breathless interest, turning page after page, until she
came to the last one, where she found her uncle's name
signed in full.

"Now I know!" burst from her trembling lips, as
the sheets fell from her nerveless hands and her voice
sounded hollow and unnatural.   "How very, very

strange! Oh! Uncle Walter, why didn't you tell me? why didn't you—tell me?"

Her lips only formed those last words as her head fell back against her chair, all the light fading out of her eyes, and then she slipped away into unconsciousness. When she came to herself again she was cold, and stiff, and deathly sick.

At first she could not seem to remember what had happened, for her mind was weak and confused. Then gradually all that had occurred came back to her.

She shivered and tried feebly to rub something of natural warmth into her chilled hands, then suddenly losing all self-control, she bowed her face upon them, and burst into a passion of tears.

"Oh, if I had only known before," she murmured over and over again, with unspeakable regret.

But she was worn out, and this excitement could not last.

She made an effort to regain her composure, gathered up the scattered sheets of her uncle's letter, restoring them to the envelope, and then took up the other package which was bound with a scarlet ribbon.

There were half a dozen or more letters and all superscribed in a bold, handsome hand.

"They are my father's letters to my mother," Mona murmured, "but I have no strength to read them to-night."

She put them back, with the other things, into the secret drawer in the mirror, which she restored to its box, and then carefully packed it away in her trunk, with all her clothing except what she wished to put on in the morning.

"I shall go back to New York to-morrow," she said, with firmly compressed lips, as the last thing was laid in its place. "I cannot remain another day in the service of such a woman; and, since I have now learned everything, there is no need; I must go back to Ray and—happiness."

A tender smile wreathed her lips as she prepared to retire, but she could not sleep after she was in bed, even though she was weak and exhausted from the excitement of the last few hours, for her nerves throbbed and tingled with every beat of her pulses, and it was not until near morning that slumber came to her relief.

She was awake long before the gong for breakfast sounded, however, and rising immediately dressed herself for traveling, after which she finished packing, and then went down to breakfast with a grave, resolute face, which betrayed that she had some fixed purpose in her mind.

Mrs. Montague regarded her with some surprise as she noticed her dress, but she made no remark, although she looked troubled and anxious.

As soon as they arose from the table Mona went directly up stairs again, and waited at the door of Mrs. Montague's parlor until that lady made her appearance.

Louis was with her, but Mona ignored his presence, and quietly asked:

"Can I see you alone for a few moments, Mrs. Montague?"

"Certainly," she replied, giving the girl a sharp, curious glance, and immediately preceded her into the room. "Well?" she inquired, turning and facing her, the moment the door was closed, as if already she suspected what was coming.

"I simply wanted to tell you that I am going to return to New York to-day," Mona said, in a tone which plainly indicated that no argument would serve to change her determination.

"Aren't you somewhat premature in your movements? What is your reason for wanting to go home in such a hurry?" Mrs. Montague demanded, with some asperity.

"There are a number of reasons. I have some business to attend to, for one thing," Mona answered.

Mrs. Montague appeared startled by this unlooked-for reply. She had expected that she would complain of Louis' persecution of the previous evening.

"Do you think it just fair, Ruth, to leave me at such short notice?" she inquired, after thinking a moment.

"I am very sorry if my going will annoy you," Mona said, "but you will have Mr. Hamblin for an escort, and so you will not be left alone. I have made up my mind to go, and I would like to leave at as early an hour as possible."

Mrs. Montague saw that it would be useless to oppose her, but a look of cunning leaped into her eyes as she returned, with an assumption of graceful compliance:

"Then we will all go. A few days will not matter much with me; I have been disappointed in almost everything since leaving home, and I am about ready to go back myself. I am sure I do not wish to keep you if you are unhappy or discontented, and so we will take the afternoon boat if you like. I feel a certain responsibility regarding you, and could not think of allowing you to return alone and unprotected," she interposed, a curious smile curving her lips; then she added: "I will have Louis go to secure staterooms immediately, and you can do your packing as soon as you like."

"It is all done. I am ready to go at any hour, but," and Mona flushed, "I should prefer to go by rail, as we could reach New York much more quickly than by boat."

Mrs. Montague frowned at this remark.

"Pray do not be in such an unnecessary hurry, Ruth," she said, with some impatience. "It is much pleasanter traveling by boat than by rail at this season of the year, and I enjoy the water far more. I think you might oblige one by yielding that much," and the woman watched her anxiously as she awaited her reply.

"Very well," Mona said, gravely, though reluctantly. "I will do as you wish. At what hour does the steamer leave?"

"I don't know. I shall have to ask Louis, and I will tell you later. Now, I wish you would baste some fresh ruching on my traveling dress, then you may hem the new vail that you will find upon my dressing-case," and having given these directions, Mrs. Montague hurried from the room to find her nephew.

She met him in the hall, where he had been walking back and forth, for he surmised what the nature of Mona's interview would be, and knew that the time had come for him to act with boldness if he hoped to win the prize he coveted.

"Come into your room, where we shall not be overheard," Mrs. Montague whispered, and leading the way thither, they were soon holding an earnest consultation over this unexpected interruption of the scheme which they had arranged the night before.

They talked for half an hour, after which Mrs.

Montague returned to her parlor and Louis at once left the hotel.

He did not return until nearly lunch time, when, in Mona's presence, he informed his aunt that the state-rooms were secured, and the boat would leave at seven that evening.

"If you will get your trunks ready I will send them aboard early, and then I shall have no trouble about baggage at the last moment, and can look after your wraps and satchels," he remarked, as he glanced significantly at his aunt.

"Mine are ready to strap, and Ruth's was packed before breakfast, so they can be sent off as soon as you like," Mrs. Montague returned.

He attended to the strapping of them himself, and a little later they were taken away.

Mona wondered somewhat at this arrangement. She thought the trunks might just as well have gone with them, but concluded that Louis did not wish to be troubled with them at the last moment, as he had said.

At half-past six they left the hotel, and drove to the pier where the steamboat lay.

Louis hurried the ladies on board, and to their staterooms, telling them to make haste and get settled, as dinner would be served as soon as the boat left the landing.

He had secured three staterooms for their use, another circumstance which appeared strange to Mona, as she and Mrs. Montague had occupied one together in coming down the river.

"Perhaps," she said to herself, "she is angry because I insisted upon going home, and does not wish to have me with her. I believe, however, I shall like it best by myself."

She arranged everything to her satisfaction, and then sat down by her window to wait until the gong should sound for dinner, but a strange feeling of depression and of homesickness seemed to settle over her spirits, while her thoughts turned with wistful fondness to her lover so far away in New York, and she half regretted that she had not insisted upon returning by rail.

She wondered that she did not hear Mrs. Montague moving about in her stateroom, but concluded that she had completed her arrangements for the night and gone on deck.

Presently the last signal was given, and the steamer swung slowly away from the levee. A few moments later the gong sounded for dinner, and Mona went out into the saloon to look for her companions.

She met Louis Hamblin at the door leading to the dining-saloon, but he was alone.

"Where is Mrs. Montague?" Mona inquired, and wondering if he was going to be sick, for he looked pale, and seemed ill at ease.

"Hasn't she been with you?" he asked, appearing surprised at her question. "I thought she was in her stateroom."

"No, I did not hear her moving about," Mona replied, "so supposed she had come out."

"Perhaps she is on deck; if you will wait here I will run up to look for her," Louis remarked, and Mona sat down as he walked away.

He presently returned, but alone.

"She is not up stairs," he said; "I will go to her

stateroom; perhaps she has been lying down; she said she had a headache this afternoon."

Again he left Mona, but came back to her in a few minutes, saying:

"Yes, it is as I thought; she isn't feeling well, and doesn't care to go down to dinner. I am to send her a cup of tea, and then she will retire for the night. Shall we go down now? You must be hungry," he concluded, smiling.

Mona would have much preferred to go by herself, and have him do the same, but she did not wish to have any words with him about it, so quietly followed him to the table, and took her seat beside him.

He was very polite and attentive, supplying all her wants in a thoughtful but unobtrusive way, and did not once by word or look remind her of anything disagreeable.

The dinner was a lengthy affair, and it was after eight when they left the dining-saloon, when Mona at once retreated to her stateroom to rid herself of Louis Hamblin's companionship. On her way thither she rapped upon Mrs. Montague's door, and asked:

"Cannot I do something for you, Mrs. Montague?"

There was no response from within, and thinking she must be asleep, Mona passed on to her own room.

It was growing quite dark, and Mona, feeling both weary and sleepy from the restlessness and wakefulness of the previous night, resolved to retire at once.

She felt really relieved, although a trifle lonely to be in a stateroom by herself, but she fell asleep almost immediately, and did not awake until the gong sounded for breakfast.

She felt much refreshed, and after dressing went and knocked upon Mrs. Montague's door to inquire if she had rested well, and if she could do anything for her.

There was no reply, and thinking perhaps she was still asleep, or had already arisen, she went up on deck to get a breath of air before going to breakfast.

"Why!" she exclaimed on looking around her, as she reached the deck, "how very wide the river must be just here; I did not observe it to be so when we came down; perhaps, though, we passed this point during the night, but I did not suppose we could get out of sight of land on the Mississippi."

A storm was evidently brewing; indeed, it was already beginning to rain, the wind blew, and the vessel rolled considerably.

Mona could see nothing of either Mrs. Montague or Louis, and found that she could not walk about to search for them, for all at once she began to feel strangely dizzy and faint.

"Can it be that I am going to be sick?" she murmured. "I was not coming down, for there was not much motion to the boat, but now it rolls and pitches as if it were out on the broad ocean."

She was growing rapidly worse, and, retreating to her stateroom, she crept again into her berth, and rang for the stewardess.

She was ill all that day—so ill that she could not think of much but her own feelings, although she did wonder now and then if Mrs. Montague was prostrated like herself. She must be, she thought, or she certainly would come to her.

Once she asked the stewardess if she was ill, and the woman had briefly replied that everybody was sick, and then hurried out to answer some other call.

But during the next day Mona began to rally, and

the stewardess advised her to go up on deck, saying that the fresh air would do much toward improving her condition. She assisted her to dress, and helped her up stairs to a chair, covered her with a warm robe, and then left her alone.

Mona at first was so faint and weary from her exertions that she did not pay much attention to her surroundings. She lay with her eyes closed for a while, but finally the air made her feel better, and she began to look about her.

An expression of wonder and anxiety instantly overspread her white face.

Where were the banks of the river, so green and bright, which had made the southward trip so delightful?

The sun was shining brightly, for the storm had passed and the sky was cloudless, but, looking in every direction, she could discern no land—all about her was but a wide waste of deep blue water.

"Why!" she cried, "I should think we were out at sea!"

She looked greatly disturbed, but just at that moment she saw Louis Hamblin coming toward her, and she noticed that he also looked somewhat pale, as if he, too, had been suffering from sea-sickness.

"You are really better," he smilingly observed as he reached her side; "you have had a severe siege as well as I."

"Then you have been sick?" Mona observed, but turning away from the intense look which he bent upon her.

"Indeed, I have. I have but just ventured out of my berth," he returned, shrugging his shoulders over painful memories.

"How is Mrs. Montague? I have not seen her since we left New Orleans," Mona inquired.

A peculiar look came into Louis Hamblin's eyes.

"Well, she has been under the weather, too, and has not cared to see any one," he said. "She simply wants to be let alone, like most people who suffer from sea-sickness."

"That accounts for her absence and silence," thought Mona. Then she asked: "Is it not very strange that we do not see the banks of the river? One would almost imagine that we were far out at sea."

Again that peculiar look swept over the young man's face.

"And so we are," he quietly answered, after a momentary pause.

"What?" exclaimed Mona, in a startled tone, and turning her blanched face upon him with a look of terror.

"Do not be excited, Miss Montague," he coolly observed. "Aunt Margie simply took a sudden freak to go home by sea; she thought the voyage would be beneficial to her. She did not confide her plans to you, as she feared you would object and insist upon going home alone by rail."

Mona flushed hotly. She was very indignant that Mrs. Montague should have done such a thing without consulting her, and she deeply regretted that she had not insisted upon acting according to her own wishes.

She had no suspicion even now of the wretched deception that had been practiced upon her, but she did not now wonder so much that the woman had so persistently kept out of her way, and she felt so angry that she did not care to meet her again until they should land.

"When shall we get to New York?" she inquired, in a low, cold tone.

"We shall land some time this evening," Louis Hamblin evasively replied, but watching her with curious interest.

Mona gave utterance to a sigh of relief, but did not appear to notice how he had worded his sentence.

She believed that in a few hours more she would forever sever all connections with this bold, bad woman who had been guilty of so much wrong; that she would forever be freed from the society and attentions of her no less unprincipled and disagreeable nephew.

She resolved to go at once to Mr. Graves, then send word to Ray of her return, when she would reveal all that she had learned about herself, and all her troubles would be over. There was now no reason why she should not become his wife as soon as he desired.

She lay back in her chair and closed her eyes, thus signifying to Mr. Hamblin that she did not wish to continue their conversation.

He moved away from her, but continued to watch her covertly, smiling now and then to himself as he thought of the developments reserved for her.

When the sun began to decline Mona arose to return to her stateroom, but she was still so weak she could not walk steadily.

The young man sprang at once to her side.

"Let me help you," he cried, offering his arm to her.

She was obliged to take it, much as she disliked to do so, and he assisted her to the door of her stateroom, where, touching his hat politely, he left her.

She lay down to rest for a while before gathering up her things preparatory to going ashore, but the effort of coming down stairs had so wearied her that almost immediately she fell into a sound sleep.

CHAPTER XIV.

MONA FINDS FRIENDS.

When Mona awoke again it was dark.

The lamps were lighted in the saloon, however, and shone dimly into her stateroom through the glass in the door.

She at once became conscious that the steamer had stopped, while the confusion and bustle on deck told her that they had arrived in port and the vessel was being unloaded.

She hastily arose and dressed to go ashore, and she had hardly completed her toilet when some one rapped upon her door.

Opening it she found Louis Hamblin standing outside.

"We have arrived," he said. "How soon can you be ready to go ashore?"

"Immediately," Mona replied, then asked: "Where is Mrs. Montague?"

"Waiting for us in the carriage. I thought I would take one invalid at a time," he responded, smiling.

"What time is it, please?" the young girl asked, thoughtfully.

"Nearly ten o'clock. We are very late arriving to-night."

Mona looked blank at this reply, for she felt that it would be too late to go to Mr. Graves' that night. She would be obliged to go home with Mrs. Montague after all, and remain until morning. So she said nothing about her plans, but followed Louis above to the deck, out across the gangway to the pier, where a perfect babel prevailed, although at that moment, in the excitement of getting ashore, she did not notice anything peculiar about it.

The young man hurried her to the carriage, which proved to be simply a transportation coach belonging to some hotel, and was filled with people.

"We have concluded to go to a hotel for to-night, since it is so late and the servants did not know of our coming," Louis explained, as he assisted his companion to enter the vehicle, which, however, was more like a river barge than a city coach.

"I do not see Mrs. Montague," Mona said, as she anxiously tried to scan the faces of the passengers, and now noticed for the first time that most of them appeared to be foreigners, and were talking in a strange language.

"Can it be possible that I have made a mistake and got into the wrong carriage?" said Louis, with well-feigned surprise. "There were two going to the same hotel, and she must be in the other. She is safe enough, however, and it is too late for us to change now," he concluded, as the vehicle started.

Mona was very uncomfortable, but she could not well help herself, and so was obliged to curb her anxiety and impatience as best she could.

A ride of fifteen or twenty minutes brought them to the door of a large and handsome hotel, where they alighted, and Louis, giving her bag and wrap to the porter, who came bowing and smiling to receive them, told Mona to follow him into the house while he looked after the trunks.

Without suspecting the truth, although she was sure she had never been in that portion of the city before, the young girl obeyed, but as she stepped within the handsomely lighted entrance, she was both confused and alarmed by the fact that she could not understand a word of the language that was being spoken around her, while she now observed that the hotel had a strangely foreign air about it.

"There is something very wrong about this," she said to herself. "It does not seem like New York at all, and I do not like the idea of Mrs. Montague keeping herself so aloof from me. Even if she were sick, or angry with me, she might at least have shown some interest in me. I do not like Louis Hamblin's manner—he does not appear natural. I wish—oh, I wish I had gone home by rail. I am sure this is not New York. I am afraid there is something wrong."

She arose and walked about the room, into which the porter had shown her, feeling very anxious and trembling with nervousness. It was very strange, too, that Louis did not make his appearance.

Even while these thoughts occupied her mind he came into the room, and Mona sprang toward him.

"What does this mean?" she demanded, confronting him with blazing eyes and burning cheeks.

"What does what mean?" he asked, but his glance wavered before hers.

"This strange hotel—these foreign-looking, foreign-speaking people? Why does not Mrs. Montague come to me? Everything is very mysterious, and I want you to explain."

"Aunt Margie has gone to her room, and——"
Louis began, ignoring every other question.

"I do not believe it!" Mona interrupted, with a sinking heart, as the truth began to dawn upon her.   "I
have not seen her since we left New Orleans.   I have
seen only you.   There is some premeditated deception
in all this.   I do not believe that we are in New York
at all.   Where are we?   I demand the truth."

Louis Hamblin saw that he could deceive her no
longer; he had not supposed he could keep the truth
from her as long as he had.

"We are in Havana, Cuba," he braced himself to
reply, with some appearance of composure, which he
was far from feeling.

"Havana!—Cuba!" cried Mona, breathlessly.   "Ah!
that explains the foreign language—and I do not
know Spanish."   Then facing him again with an air
and look that made him cower, in spite of his bravado,
she sternly asked: "Why are we here?"

"We are here in accordance with Mrs. Montague's
plans," he answered.

"Mrs. Montague had no right to bring me here without consulting me," the young girl returned, passionately.   "Where is Mrs. Montague?"

"I expect that Aunt Marg is in New York by this
time," Louis Hamblin now boldly asserted.

"What?" almost shrieked Mona, smitten to the heart
with terror at this intelligence.   "Oh! you cannot
mean to tell me that you and I have come to Havana
alone!   That—that——"

A hot blush mounted to her forehead, and for a
moment she was utterly overcome with shame and
horror over the terrible situation.

"Yes, that is just what we have done," Louis returned, a desperate gleam coming into his eyes, for he began to realize that he had no weak spirit to deal with.

There was a prolonged and ominous silence after this admission, while Mona tried to rally her sinking spirits and think of some plan of escape from her dreadful position.

When she did speak again she was white to her lips, but in her eyes there shone a resolute purpose which plainly indicated that she would never tamely submit to the will of the man before her.

"How have you dared to do this thing?" she demanded, but so quietly that he regarded her in astonishment.

"I have dared because I was bound to win you, Mona, and there seemed no other way," he returned, in a passionate tone.

"And did you imagine for one moment that you could accomplish your purpose by decoying me into a strange country?"

"Yes; but, Mona——"

"Then you have yet to learn that you have made a great mistake," was the haughty rejoinder. "It is true that I am comparatively helpless in not being able to understand the language here; but there are surely people in Havana—there must even be some one in this hotel—who can speak either French or German, if not English, and to whom I shall appeal for protection."

"That will do you little good," retorted Louis, flushing with anger at the threat, "and I may as well tell you the truth first as last. Mona, you will have to give yourself to me, you will have to be my wife. Mrs. Montague and I have both decided that it shall be so, and we have taken pains to prevent any failure of our plan. You may appeal as much as you wish to people here—they cannot understand you, and you will only lay yourself liable to scandal and abuse; for, Mona, you and I came to Havana, registered as man and wife, and our names stand upon the register of this hotel as Mr. and Mrs. Hamblin, of New York, where already the story of our elopement from New Orleans has become the talk of the town."

The deadly truth was out at last, and Mona, smitten with despair, overcome by the revelation of the dastardly plot of which she was the victim, sank helplessly upon the nearest chair, quivering with shame and horror in every nerve, and nearly fainting from the shock which the knowledge of her terrible danger had sent vibrating through her very soul.

She covered her face with her hands, and tried to think, but her temples throbbed like hammers, her brain seemed on fire, and her mind was in a perfect chaos.

She sat thus for many minutes, until Louis Hamblin, who was hardly less excited than herself in view of his anxiety as to what would be the result of this critical interview, could endure the silence no longer, and quietly but kindly remarked:

"Mona, I think it is best that you should go to your room and rest; it is late, and you are both weary and excited. To-morrow we will talk this matter over again, and I hope that you will then be more reasonable."

The sound of his voice aroused all her outraged womanhood, and springing to her feet again, she turned upon him with all the courage of a lioness at bay.

"I understand you," she cried. "I know why you and that unprincipled woman have so plotted against me. You were afraid, in spite of what I told you the other night, that I would demand your fortune, if I once learned the whole truth about myself. I have learned it, and I have the proof of it also. A message came to me, after my interview with you, telling me everything."

"I do not believe you," Louis Hamblin faltered, but growing very pale at this unexpected information.

"Do you not? Then let me rehearse a little for your benefit," Mona continued, gathering courage as she went on, and in low but rapid tones she related something of the secret which she had discovered in the royal mirror—enough to convince him that she knew the truth, and could, indeed, prove it.

"Now," she continued, as she concluded this recital, "do you think that I will allow you to conquer me? You have been guilty of a dastardly act. Mrs. Montague has shown herself to be lacking in humanity, honor, and every womanly sentiment; but I will not be crushed; even though you have sought to compromise me in this dreadful way I will not yield to you. Your wife I am not, and no writing me as such upon steamer and hotel registers can ever make me so. You may proclaim from one end of New York to the other that I eloped with you from New Orleans, but it will not serve your purpose, and the one for whom I care most will never lose faith in me. And, Louis Hamblin, hear me; the moment I find myself again among English-speaking people, both you and Mrs. Montague shall suffer for this outrage to the extent of the law. I will not spare you."

"That all sounds very brave, no doubt," Louis Hamblin sneered, but inwardly deeply chagrined by her dauntless words and bearing, "but you are in my power, Miss Montague, and I shall take measures to keep you so until I tame that haughty spirit somewhat. You will be only too glad to marry me yet, for I have gone too far in this matter to be balked now. When you leave Hanava you will go as Mrs. Louis Hamblin, or you will never go."

"I would rather never go than as your wife, and I will defy you until I die!" was the spirited retort, and the man before her knew that she meant it.

He wondered at her strength of purpose and at her courage. Many girls, finding themselves in such a woeful strait, would have been entirely overcome— would have begged and pleaded in abject fear or weakly yielded to circumstances, and married him, but Mona only seemed to gather courage as difficulties closed around her.

She looked very lovely, too. She had lost a little flesh and color during her illness on shipboard, and her face was more delicate in its outlines than usual. She would have been very pale but for the spot of vivid scarlet that glowed on each cheek, and which was but the outward sign of the inextinguishable spirit that burned within her. Her eyes gleamed with a relentless fire and her slight but perfect form was erect and resolute in its bearing.

Louis Hamblin for the moment felt himself powerless to combat with such mental strength, and ignoring entirely what she had just avowed, again asked:

"Will you go to your room now?"

He did not wait for any reply, but touched a bell, and a waiter almost immediately appeared to answer the call.

Louis signified to him that his companion wished to retire, whereupon the man took her bag and wrap and motioned Mona to follow him.

With despair in her heart, but a dauntless mien, the fair girl obeyed, and crossing the wide entrance hall, mounted the great staircase to the second story.

As they were passing through a long upper hall a door suddenly opened, and a gentleman came out of one of the rooms.

Mona's heart gave a leap of joy as she saw him, for she was almost sure that he was an American, and she was on the point of speaking to him, but he passed her so quickly she had no opportunity.

She was rejoiced, however, to observe that her guide stopped before the door of a room next to the one which the stranger had just left, and she resolved that she would listen for his return, and manage to communicate with him in some way before morning.

The porter threw open the door, and stood aside to allow her to pass in.

The room was lighted, and she saw that while it was not large, it was comfortably furnished, and her trunk stood unstrapped in one corner. The next moment the door closed upon her, and she heard the key turned in the lock.

A bitter sob burst from her as she dashed the hot tears from her eyes, and a low, eager cry broke from her lips as she noticed that a door connected her room with the one from which the gentleman had issued a few moments before.

She sprang toward it, and turned the handle.

It was locked, of course. She told herself she might have known it would be, but she had acted upon an uncontrollable impulse.

But as she released her hold upon the knob she thought she heard some one moving about within the other room.

Perhaps the gentleman had his wife with him, and impelled by a wild hope, Mona knocked upon a panel to attract attention, and the next moment she was sure she caught the rustle of skirts as some one glided toward her.

Putting her lips to the key-hole, she said, in a low, appealing tone:

"Oh! can you speak English, French, or German? Pray answer me."

She thought she had never heard sweeter music than when the clear, gentle voice of a woman replied:

"I can speak English, but no other language."

"Oh! I am so glad!" almost sobbed Mona. "Please put your ear close to the key-hole, and let me tell you something. I dare not talk loud for fear of being overheard. I am a young girl, a little more than eighteen years old, and I am in a fearful extremity. Will you help me?"

"Certainly, if you are in need of help," returned the other voice.

"Oh, thank you! thank you!" cried Mona, and then in low, rapid tones she briefly told her story to the listener on the other side of the door.

When she had concluded, the woman said, wonderingly:

"It is the most dreadful thing I ever heard of. My brother, with whom I am traveling, will soon be back. We are to leave early in the morning, and he has gone down to the office to settle our bill and make necessary arrangements. I will tell him your story, and we will see what can be done for you."

Mona again thanked her, but brokenly, and then overcome by this unexpected succor she sank prone upon the floor weeping passionately; the tension on her nerves had given way and her overwrought feelings had to have their way.

Presently a hand touched the key in her door.

Startled beyond measure, she sprang to it, feeling sure that Louis Hamblin stood without.

"Do not dare to open this door," she cried, authoritatively.

"Certainly not; I simply wished to ask if you have everything you wish for the night," the young man returned, in perfectly courteous tones.

"Yes."

"Very well, then; good-night. I hope you will rest well," he said, then drawing the key from the lock, he passed on, and the next moment Mona heard a door shut across the hall.

It was scarcely five minutes later when she heard some one enter the room next to hers, and her heart leaped again with hope.

Then she heard a gentleman and lady conversing in low tones, and knew that her story was being repeated to one who had the power, if he chose to use it, to save her from her persecutor.

A little later she heard the gentleman go to a window and open it.

Then there came a gentle tap upon the door, and the lady said to the eager ear at the key-hole:

"There is a little balcony outside our window and another outside yours with only a narrow space between. My brother says if you will go out upon yours he will help you across to us, then we can talk more freely together, and decide upon the best way to help you. Turn down your light first, however, so that no one outside will see you."

"Yes, yes," breathed Mona, eagerly, and then putting out her light, she sprang away to the window.

She raised it as cautiously as she could, crept out upon the narrow iron balcony, and found a tall, dark figure looming up before her upon the other.

"Give me your hands," said the gentleman, in a full, rich voice that won the girl's heart at once, "then step upon the railing, and trust yourself entirely to me; you will not fall."

Mona unhesitatingly reached out her hands to him; he grasped them firmly; she stepped upon the railing, and the next moment was swung safely over the space between the two balconies, and stood beside her unknown friend.

He went before her through the window, and assisted her into the darkened room; the curtain was then lowered, and the gas turned up, and Mona found herself in the presence of a tall, handsome man of about thirty-three years, and a gentle, attractive-looking woman a few years his senior.

CHAPTER XV.

MONA'S ESCAPE.

The gentleman and lady both regarded the young girl with curious and searching interest as she stood, flushed and panting from excitement, in the center of the room beneath the blazing chandelier.

"Sit here, Miss Montague," said the gentleman, pulling forward a low rocker for her, "but first," he added,

with a pleasant smile, "allow me to introduce myself.
My name is Cutler—Justin Cutler, and this lady is
my sister, Miss Marie Cutler. Now, it is late—we will
waive all ceremony, so tell us at once about your
trouble, and then we will see if we cannot help you out
of it."

Mona sat down and briefly related all that had occurred in connection with her trip since she left New
York, together with some of the circumstances which
she believed had made Mrs. Montague and Louis Hamblin so resolute to force her into a marriage with the
latter.

Her companions listened to her with deep interest,
and it was plain to be seen that all their warmest
sympathies were enlisted in her cause.

Mr. Cutler expressed great indignation, and declared
that Louis Hamblin merited the severest sentence that
the law could impose, but, of course, he knew that nothing could be done to bring him to justice in that
strange country; so, after considering the matter for
a while, he concluded that the best way to release
Mona from her difficulties would be by the use of
strategy.

"We are to leave on a steamer for New York to-
morrow morning, and you shall go with us," Mr. Cutler remarked, "and if we can get you away from the
hotel and on board the boat without young Hamblin's
knowledge, you will be all right, and there will be no
disagreeable disturbance or scandal to annoy you.
Even should he discover your flight, and succeed in
boarding the vessel before she sails, he will be helpless, for a quiet appeal to the captain will effectually
baffle him. But how about your baggage?" he asked
in conclusion.

"My trunk is in my room," Mona returned.

"Of course you must have that," said Mr. Cutler; "the only difficulty will be in getting it away without exciting suspicion. We must have this door between these rooms opened by some means. I wonder if the key to ours would fit the lock."

He arose immediately and went to try it, but it would not work.

"No. I did not expect our first effort would succeed," he smilingly remarked, as he saw Mona's face fall. "There is one way that we can do if all other plans fail," he added, after thinking a moment; "you can go back to the other room and unpack your trunk, when I could easily remove it through the window, and it could be repacked in here; but that plan would require considerable time and labor, and shall be adopted only as a last resort. But wait a minute."

He sprang to his feet, and disappeared through the window, and the next moment they heard him moving softly about in the other room.

Presently he returned, but looking grave and thoughtful.

"I hoped I might find a key somewhere in there," he explained, "but the door bolts on that side. There should, then, be a key to depend upon for this side. I wonder——"

He suddenly seized a chair, placed it before the door, stepped upon it, and reached up over the fanciful molding above it, slipping his hand along behind it.

"Aha!" he triumphantly exclaimed all at once, "I have it!" and he held up before their eager gaze a rusty and dusty iron key.

A moment later the door was unlocked, and swung open between the two rooms.

Five minutes after, all Mona's baggage was transferred to Miss Cutler's apartment, the door was relocked and bolted as before, and the fair girl felt as if her troubles were over.

Overcome by the sense of relief which this assurance afforded her, she impulsively threw her arms about Miss Cutler, laid her head on her shoulder, and burst into grateful tears.

"Oh, I am so glad—so thankful!" she sobbed.

"Hush, dear child," said the gentle lady, kindly, "you must not allow yourself to become unnerved, for you will not sleep, and I am sure you need rest. I am going to send Justin away at once, then we will both retire."

"Yes, I will go directly," Mr. Cutler remarked, "but I shall call you early. I will have your breakfast sent up here, when your trunks can be removed. Then, Miss Montague, you are to put on a wrap belonging to my sister, and tie a thick veil over your face. I will come to take you to the carriage, and no one will suspect but that you are Marie. Meantime she will slip down another stairway, and out of the private entrance; then away we will speed to the steamer, and all will be well. Now, good-night, ladies, and a good sleep to you," he concluded, cheerfully, as he quietly left the room.

Miss Cutler and Mona proceeded to retire at once, but while disrobing the elder lady told her companion how it happened that she and her brother were in Havana so opportunely. She had been out of health, and had come to Cuba early in the fall to spend the winter. Her brother had come a few weeks earlier to take her home, and they had been making excursions to different points of interest on the island.

"I am so glad," she said, in conclusion, "that we decided to take rooms at this hotel during our sojourn in Havana. At first I thought I would like to go to some more quiet place, but Justin thought we would be better served here, and," with a gentle smile, "I believe it was wisely ordered so that we could help you."

Mona feared that she should not be able to sleep at all, her nerves had been so wrought upon, but her companion was so cheerful and reassuring in all that she said that before she was hardly aware that she was sleepy she had dropped off into a sound slumber.

At six o'clock the next morning a sharp rap on their door awakened the two ladies.

They arose immediately, and had hardly finished dressing when an appetizing breakfast appeared. Miss Cutler received the tray at the door, so that the waiter need not enter the room, and then was so merry and entertaining as, with her own hands she served Mona, that the young girl forgot her nervousness, in a measure, and ate quite heartily.

By the time their meal was finished another rap warned them that the porters had come for their trunks.

"Step inside the closet, dear," said Miss Cutler, in a whisper, and Mona noiselessly obeyed her.

The door was then opened, and both trunks were removed, apparently without exciting any suspicion over the fact that there were two instead of one as when Miss Cutler arrived.

A few minutes later Mr. Cutler appeared, and Mona, clad in Miss Cutler's long ulster—which she had worn almost every day during her sojourn there—and with a thick veil over her face, took her tall protector's arm, and went tremblingly out.

Her heart almost failed her as she passed through the main entrance hall, which she had crossed in such despair only a few hours previously; but Mr. Cutler quietly bade her "be calm and have no fear," then led her down the steps, and assisted her to enter the carriage that was waiting at the door.

The next moment another figure stepped quickly in after her, Mr. Cutler followed, the door was closed, and they were driven rapidly away.

Arriving at the steamer-landing, they all went on board, and after attending to the baggage, Mr. Cutler conducted his ladies directly to their stateroom.

"I will get you a room by yourself, if you prefer," he said to Mona, "but I thought perhaps you might feel less lonely if you should share my sister's."

"Thank you, but I should much prefer to remain with Miss Cutler if it will be agreeable to her," Mona returned, with a wistful glance at the lady.

"Indeed, I shall be very glad to have you with me," was the cordial reply, accompanied by a charming smile, for already the gentlewoman had become greatly interested in her fair companion.

"That is settled, then," said the gentleman, smiling, "and now you may feel perfectly safe; do not give yourself the least uneasiness, but try to enjoy the voyage—that is, if old Neptune will be quiet and allow you."

"You are very kind, Mr. Cutler, and I cannot tell you how grateful I am to both yourself and your sister," Mona said, feelingly. "But, truly," she added, flushing, "I shall not feel quite easy until we get off, for I am in constant fear that Mr. Hamblin will discover my flight, and come directly here to search for me."

"Well, even if he does, you need fear nothing," Mr. Cutler returned, reassuringly; "you shall have my protection, and should Mr. Hamblin make his appearance before we sail and try to create a disturbance, we will just hand the young man over to the authorities. The only thing I regret in connection with him," the gentleman concluded, with a twinkle in his eye, "is that I cannot have the pleasure of witnessing his astonishment and dismay when he makes the discovery that his bird has flown. Now, ladies, make yourselves comfortable, then come and join me on deck."

He left them together to get settled for their voyage, and went up stairs for a smoke and to keep his eye upon the shore, for he fully expected to see Louis Hamblin come tearing down to the boat at any moment. The reader has, of course, recognized in Justin Cutler the gentleman who, at the opening of our story, was made the victim of the accomplished sharper, Mrs. Bently, in the diamond crescent affair. It will be remembered also that he came on to New York at the time of the arrest of Mrs. Vanderheck, and that he informed Detective Rider of his intention of going to Cuba to meet his invalid sister and accompany her home, and thus we find him acting as Mona's escort and protector also.

While the three voyagers were settling themselves and waiting for the steamer to sail, we will see how Louis Hamblin bore the discovery of Mona's escape.

He did not rise until eight o'clock, and after having his bath and a cup of coffee in his own room, he went to Mona's door and knocked.

Receiving no answer, he thought she must be sleeping, and resolved that he would not arouse her just then.

He went down stairs, and had his breakfast, then strolled out to smoke his cigar, after which he went back, and again tapped upon Mona's door.

Still no answer.

He called her name, but receiving no response, he took the key from his pocket and coolly unlocking the door, threw it wide open.

The room was, of course, empty.

There were no signs that the bed had been occupied during the night, and both the girl and her trunk were gone.

With a fierce imprecation of rage, the astonished young man rushed down to the office to interview the proprietor as to the meaning of the girl's disappearance.

Although Mona had supposed there was no one in the house who could speak English, there was an interpreter, and through him Louis soon made his trouble known.

"Impossible!" the amazed proprietor asserted; "no trunk had been removed from Number Eleven, and no young lady had left the house that morning."

Louis angrily insisted that there had, and in company with the landlord and the interpreter, he returned to Mona's room to prove his statement.

At first the affair was a great mystery, and created considerable excitement, but it was finally remembered that Americans had occupied the adjoining rooms, and it was therefore concluded that the young girl had managed in some way to make her situation known to them, and they, having left that morning, had, doubtless, assisted her in her flight.

"Who were they, and where were they going?"
Louis demanded, in great excitement.

"Cutler was the name, and they had left early to
take the steamer for New York," they told him.

"What was her hour for sailing?" cried the young
man.

"Nine-thirty," he was informed.

Louis looked at his watch.

It lacked fifteen minutes of the time.

"A carriage! a carriage!" he cried, as he dashed out
of the hotel and down the steps at a break-neck pace.

He sprang into the first vehicle he could find, made
the driver understand that he wanted him to hasten
with all possible speed to the New York steamer, and
enforced his wishes by showing the man a piece of
glittering gold.

He was terribly excited; his face was deathly white,
and his eyes had the look of a baffled demon. But he
was not destined to have the satisfaction of even seeing Mona, for he reached the pier just in season to
see the noble steamer sailing with stately bearing
slowly out into the harbor, and he knew that the fair
girl was beyond his reach.

*   *   *   *   *

Meantime, as soon as she had seen Louis and Mona
safely on board the steamer, bound for Havana, Mrs.
Montague, instead of going into the stateroom that
had been engaged for her only as a blind, slipped
stealthily back upon deck, hastened off the boat, and
into her carriage, which had been ordered to wait for
her, and was driven directly to the railway station,
where she took the express going northward.

She did not spare herself, but traveled day and

night until she reached New York, when she immediately sent a note to Mr. Palmer, notifying him of her return and desire to see him.

He at once hastened to her, for she had intimated in her communication that she was in trouble, and upon inquiring the cause of it, she informed him, with many sighs and expressions of grief, that her nephew and prospective heir had eloped with her seamstress.

Mr. Palmer looked amazed.

"With that pretty, modest girl, whom you had at Hazeldean with you?" he exclaimed, incredulously.

"Yes, with that pretty, modest girl," sneered Mrs. Montague. "These sly, quiet things are just the ones to entrap a young man like Louis, and there is poor Kitty McKenzie who will break her heart over the affair."

The wily widow's acting was very good, and Mr. Palmer sympathized with her, and used his best efforts to comfort her. But all that Mrs. Montague had cared to do was to set the ball rolling so that Ray might get it, and gradually led the conversation into a more interesting channel, and they discussed at length the subject of their own approaching union.

Mr. Palmer urged an early date, and after a little strategic hesitation, Mrs. Montague finally consented to make him happy, and the wedding was set for just one month from that day. This matter settled, the sedate lover took his leave, and his *fiancée,* with a triumphant look on her handsome face, went up stairs to look over her wardrobe to see what additions would be needed for the important event.

"Whether Louis succeeds in making the girl marry him or not, she will have been so compromised by this escapade that Ray Palmer will, of course, never think of making her his wife, and my purpose will be accomplished," she muttered, with an evil smile.

She did not give a thought to the wanderers after that, but went about the preparations for her approaching marriage with all the zeal and enthusiasm that might have been expected in a far younger bride-elect.

Mr. Palmer went home feeling a trifle anxious as to how Ray would receive the news that the day was set for making Mrs. Montague his wife.

To see that he dreaded revealing the fact expresses but little of what he felt, but he had never taken any important step of late years without consulting his son, and he did not feel at liberty to now ignore him upon a matter of such vital interest.

So, after tea that evening, when they sat down to read their papers, he thought the opportunity would be a favorable one to make his confession.

Ray seemed anxious and depressed, for he had not received his usual semi-weekly letter from Mona that day, and was wondering what could be the reason, when Mr. Palmer suddenly remarked:

"Mrs. Montague has returned."

"Ah!" said Ray, and instantly his face brightened, for his natural inference was that Mona had, of course, returned with Mrs. Montague, and that accounted for his having received no letter that day.

"Yes, she arrived this morning," said his father.

"She is well, I suppose?" Ray remarked, feeling that he must make some courteous inquiry regarding his stepmother-elect.

"Yes, physically; but that scapegrace of a nephew has been giving her considerable trouble," Mr. Palmer observed.

"Trouble?" repeated his son.

"Yes, he eloped with a girl from New Orleans. They went on board a steamer bound for Havana, registered as man and wife, and that is the last she has heard of him, while she was obliged to return to New York alone," explained Mr. Palmer, wondering how he was going to introduce the subject of his approaching marriage.

"Is that possible? Who was the girl?" exclaimed Ray, astonished and utterly unsuspicious of the blow awaiting his fond heart.

"Mrs. Montague's seamstress—Ruth Richards."

CHAPTER XVI.

MONA CALLS ON MRS. MONTAGUE.

Mr. Palmer's unexpected announcement fairly stunned Ray for a moment. His heart gave a startled bound, and then sank like a lump of lead in his bosom, while a deadly faintness oppressed him.

Indeed the blow was so sharp and sudden that it seemed to benumb him to such an extent that he made no outward sign—he appeared to be incapable of either speech or motion. His face was turned away from his father, and partially concealed by his newspaper, so that Mr. Palmer, fortunately, did not observe the ghastly pallor that overspread it, and not knowing that Ruth Richards was Mona Montague, he was wholly ignorant of the awful import of his communication.

"Ruth Richards?" Ray finally repeated, in a hollow tone, which, however, sounded to his father as if he did not remember who the girl was.

"Yes, that pretty girl that Mrs. Montague had with her at Hazeldean—the one to whom you showed some attention the night of the ball—surely you cannot have forgotten her. It seems," the gentleman went on, "that young Hamblin has been smitten with her ever since she entered his aunt's service, but she has opposed his preference from the first. He followed them South, and met them at New Orleans, and it seems that the elopement was arranged there. They were very clever about it, planning to leave on the Havana steamer on the very day set for their return to New York. Mrs. Montague learned of it at almost the last moment, and that they had registered as Mr. and Mrs. Hamblin, although she did not ascertain that there had been any marriage beforehand, and, overcome by this unexpected calamity, she took the first express coming North."

It was well for Ray that his father made his explanation somewhat lengthy, for it gave him time to recover a little from the almost paralyzing shock which the dreadful announcement had caused.

He was as white as a ghost, and his face was covered with cold perspiration.

"This terrible thing cannot be true," he said to himself, with a sense of despair at his heart. "Mona false! the runaway wife of another! Never!"

Yet in spite of his instinctive faith in the girl he loved, he knew there must be some foundation for what had been told to his father. Mrs. Montague had come home alone. Louis and Mona had been left behind! What could it mean?

His heart felt as if it had been suddenly cleft in twain. He could not believe the dreadful story—he would not have it so—he would not submit to having his life and all his bright hopes ruined at one fell blow. And that, too, just as he had learned such good news for his darling—when he had been planning to give her, upon her return, the one thing which she had most desired above all others—the indisputable proof of her mother's honorable marriage; when it would also be proved that she was the heir to the property which Homer Forester had left, and could claim, if she chose, the greater portion of the fortune left by her father.

Ray had been very exultant over the finding of that certificate in Mrs. Montague's boudoir, and had anticipated much pleasure in beholding Mona's joy when he should tell her the glorious news.

But now—great heavens! what was he to think?

Then the suspicion came to him, with another great shock, and like a revelation, that it was all a plot; that Mrs. Montague had perhaps discovered Mona's identity and possibly the loss of the certificate, which, she might think, had fallen into the young girl's hands. He had felt sure, from the quizzing to which Louis Hamblin had subjected him at Hazeldean, that that young man's suspicions had been aroused, and possibly this sudden flitting to the South had been but a plot, from beginning to end, to entrap Mona into a marriage with the young man in order to secure the wealth they feared to lose.

"When did Mrs. Montague leave New Orleans?" he inquired, when his father had concluded, while he struggled to speak in his natural tone.

"On Tuesday evening."

"And you say that the Havana steamer sailed that same day?"

"Yes."

"What was the name of the steamer?"

"I do not know. I did not ask," Mr. Palmer replied. He was thinking more about his own affairs than of the alleged elopement of the young people, or he must have wondered somewhat at his son's eager questions. "And, Ray," he added, as the young man suddenly laid down his paper and arose, "there is one other thing I wanted to mention—Mrs. Montague has consented to become Mrs. Palmer on the thirtieth of next month. I—I hope, my dear boy, that you will be prepared to receive her cordially."

"You know, father, that I would never willfully wound you in any way, and when Mrs. Montague comes as your wife, I shall certainly accord her all due respect."

Ray had worded his reply very cautiously, but he could not prevent himself from laying a slight emphasis upon the adverb, for he had resolved that if Mrs. Montague had been concerned in any way in a plot against Mona's honor or happiness, he would not spare her, nor any effort to prove it to his father, and thus prevent him, if possible, from ruining his own life by a union with such a false and unscrupulous woman.

"Thank you, Ray," Mr. Palmer replied, but not in a remarkably hopeful tone, and then remarking that he had a little matter of business to attend to, Ray went out.

Late as it was, he hastened to a cable office, hoping to be able to send a night dispatch to Havana, but he found the place closed, therefore he was obliged to retrace his steps, and wait until morning.

There was not much sleep or rest for him that night. His faith in Mona's truth and constancy had all returned, but he was terribly anxious about her, for the more he thought over what he had heard, the more he was convinced that she was the victim of some cunning plot that might make her very wretched, even if it failed to accomplish its object. He knew that she was very spirited, and would not be likely to submit to the wrong that had been perpetrated against her, and this of itself might serve to make her situation all the more perilous.

He was at the cable office by the time it was opened the next morning, and dispatched the following message to the American Consul in Havana:

"Couple, registered as Mr. and Mrs. Louis Hamblin, sailed from New Orleans for Havana, April 28th. Search for them in Havana hotels. Succor young lady, who is not Mrs. Hamblin. Answer."

Ray felt that this was the very best thing that he could do.

He would gladly have gone himself to Havana, and longed to do so, but he was sure that if she should escape from her abductor—for so he regarded Louis Hamblin—Mona would be likely to return immediately to New York and to him. Thus he concluded it would be best to send the above message and await an answer from the consul, then if he could learn nothing about the couple he would go himself to search for Mona.

The day seemed interminable, and he was nearly distracted when night came, and he received no answer to his dispatch. He had not been able to apply himself to business all day, but wandered in and out of the store, looking wan and anxious, and almost ill.

This led his father to imagine that he was unhappy over his contemplated marriage—a conclusion which did not serve to make the groom-elect feel very comfortable.

On the next morning, however, Ray received the following cablegram:

"Young lady all right; sailed for New York yesterday, May 1st."

The relief which these few words afforded Ray's anxious heart can better be imagined than described.

Mona was true to herself and him, and he knew well enough that she never would have returned to New York if she had been guilty of any wrong. She would soon be with him, and then he would know all.

He ascertained what steamer left Havana on the first, and when it would be likely to arrive in New York, and as the hour drew near, he haunted the pier, that he might welcome his darling, and give her his care and protection the moment she arrived.

Meantime Mona, her mind relieved of all anxiety, was having a very pleasant passage home with Justin Cutler and his sister.

The weather was delightful, the sea was calm, and none of them was sick, so they spent most of their time together upon deck, and Mona was so attracted toward her new friends that she confided to them much more of her history than she had at first done that evening in the Havana hotel. In so doing she had mentioned the Palmer robbery and what she had discovered in connection with it while she was in St. Louis.

This led Mr. Cutler to relate his own experience with the crescents, and also the similar deception practiced upon Mrs. Vanderheck, and he mentioned that it was the opinion of the detective whom he had employed to work up the case, and whom Mona had met in St. Louis, that the same parties were concerned in all three operations.

"They are a very dexterous set of thieves, whoever they are," he remarked, while they were discussing the affair, "but though I never expect to see those crescents again, for I imagine that the stones have been unset and sold, it would afford me a great deal of satisfaction to see that woman brought to justice."

"I have the bogus crescents in my possession," Miss Cutler smilingly remarked to Mona. "Justin has given them to me to keep for him. Would you like to see them, dear?"

"Yes, indeed," Mona replied, "and I, too, hope that woman may yet be found. The affair is so like a romance, I am deeeply interested in it."

Mr. Cutler colored slightly as she spoke of the romance of the experience, for he was still quite sensitive over the cruel deception that had been practiced upon him, although he had never confessed to any one how deeply and tenderly interested he had become in the captivating widow who had so successfully duped him.

When the steamer arrived in New York, almost the first person Mona saw was Ray, who stood upon the pier searching with anxious eyes among the passengers for the face of his dear one.

A cry of glad surprise broke from her, and, snatching her handkerchief from her pocket, she shook it vigorously to attract his attention, her lovely face all aglow with joy at his unexpected appearance.

He caught sight of the fluttering signal almost immediately, and his heart leaped within him as he looked into her beaming countenance. Truth and love and purity were stamped on every expressive feature.

He sprang across the gang-plank, and in less time than it takes to tell it he was beside her, while oblivious, in his great thankfulness for her safety, to the fact that others were observing them, he caught her close to him in a quick embrace.

"My darling!" he whispered. "Oh, you can never know how thankful I am to have you safe in my arms once more! What an escape you have had!"

"Why, Ray! how did you know?—who told you?" Mona exclaimed, astonished, as, with a blushing face, she gently freed herself from his embrace, although she still clung almost convulsively to his hand.

"I will tell you all about it later," he returned, in a low tone, and now recalled to the proprieties of life. "I can only say that I learned of the plot against you, and have been nearly distracted about you."

"Ah, Mrs. Montague told you that I had eloped with her nephew," the young girl said, and now losing some of her bright color, "but," lifting her clear, questioning eyes to her lover's face, "you did not believe it; you had faith in me?"

"All faith," he returned, his fingers closing more firmly over the small hand he held.

She thanked him with a radiant smile.

"But how did you know I would come home on this steamer?" she persisted, eager to know how he happened to be there to meet her.

"I cabled the American Consul to search for you, and render you assistance. He replied, telling me that you had already sailed for New York," Ray explained.

"That was thoughtful of you, dear," Mona said,

giving him a grateful look, "but I found friends to help me. Come and let me introduce you to them."

She led him to Mr. Cutler and his sister, who had quietly withdrawn to a little distance—for, of course, they took in the situation at once—and performed the ceremony, when, to her surprise, Mr. Cutler cordially shook her lover by the hand, remarking, with his genial smile:

"Mr. Palmer and I have met before, but my sister has not had that pleasure, I believe."

Ray greeted them both with his habitual courtesy, and then in a frank, manly way, but with slightly heightened color, remarked:

"My appearance here perhaps needs some explanation, but it will be sufficient for me to explain that Miss Montague is my promised wife."

"I surmised as much, not long after making the young lady's acquaintance," Mr. Cutler remarked, with a roguish glance at Mona's pink cheeks and downcast eyes. "But," he added, with some curiosity, "it is a puzzle to me how you should know that she would arrive in New York on this steamer to-day."

Ray explained the matter to him, and then they all left the vessel together.

Mr. and Miss Cutler were to go to the Hoffman House, and invited Mona to be their guest during their stay in the city, but thanking them for their kindness, she said she thought it would be best for her to go directly to Mr. Graves, as she had business which she wished him to attend to immediately.

She also expressed again her gratitude to them for their exceeding kindness to her, and promised to call upon them very soon, then bidding them an affectionate good-by she left the wharf with her lover.

They went for a drive in Central Park before going to Mr. Graves, for Ray was anxious to learn all the story of the plot against her and to talk over their own plans for the future.

He found it very difficult to restrain his anger as she told him of her interview with Louis Hamblin in New Orleans, and how she had been decoyed upon the steamer for Havana, with the other circumstances of the voyage, and her arrival there.

"The villain will need to be careful how he comes in my way after this," he said, with sternly compressed lips and a face that was white with anger. "I will not spare him—I will not spare either of those two plotters; but you shall never meet them again, my darling," he concluded, with tender compassion in his tones, as he realized how much she must have suffered with them.

"I shall have to go to West Forty-ninth street once more, for I have a good many things there, and shall have to attend to their removal myself," Mona returned, but looking as if she did not anticipate much pleasure from the meeting with Mrs. Montague.

"Well, then, if you must go there, I will accompany you," Ray said, resolutely. "I will never trust you alone with that woman again. And now I have some good news to relate to you."

He told her then of his discovery of the marriage certificate, and what he had done with it, after which she gave him a graphic account of the discoveries which she had made in the secret drawer of the royal mirror.

"How very strange, my darling," he exclaimed, when she concluded; "how nicely your discovery fits in with mine, and now every difficulty will be smoothed out of your way, only," with an arch glance, "I am almost afraid that I shall be accused of being a fortune-hunter when it becomes known what a wealthy heiress I have won."

Mona smiled at his remark, but she was very glad that she was not to go to him empty-handed.

"And, dear," Ray continued, more gravely, "I am going to claim my wife immediately, for, in spite of the great wealth which will soon be yours, you are a homeless little body, and I feel that you ought to be under my protection."

"Ah, Ray, it will be very nice to have a home of our own," Mona breathed, as she slipped her hand confidingly into his, and then they began to plan for it as they drove down town.

Arriving at the house of Mr. Graves, they were fortunate in finding both that gentleman and his wife at home, and Mona received a most cordial welcome, while the kind-hearted lawyer became almost jubilant upon learning all the facts regarding her parentage and how comparatively easy it would now be to prove it.

It was arranged that Mona and Mr. Graves should meet Ray and Mr. Corbin at the office of the latter on the next morning, when they would all thoroughly discuss these matters and decide upon what course to pursue in relation to them.

This plan was carried out; the certificate and contents of the royal mirror were carefully examined, and then the two lawyers proceeded to lay out their course of action, which was to be swift and sure.

The third day after Mona's arrival in New York, Ray went with her to Mrs. Montague's house to take away the remainder of her wardrobe and some keepsakes which had been saved from her old home.

Mary opened the door in answer to their ring, and her face lighted with pleasure the instant she caught sight of Mona, although it was evident from her greeting that Mrs. Montague had not told her servants the story of the elopement.

"Is Mrs. Montague in?" Mona asked, after she had returned the girl's greeting.

"No, miss, she went out as soon as she had her breakfast, and said she wouldn't be home until after lunch," was the reply.

Mona looked thoughtful. She did not exactly like to enter the house and remove her things during her absence, and yet it would be a relief not to be obliged to meet her.

Ray saw her hesitation, and understood it, but he had no scruples regarding the matter.

"It is perhaps better so," he said, in a low tone; "you will escape an unpleasant interview, and since she is not here to annoy or ill-use you, I will take the carriage and go to attend to a little matter, while you are packing. I will return for you in the course of an hour if that will give you time."

"Yes, that will be ample time, and I will be ready when you call," Mona responded.

Ray immediately drove away, while she, after chatting a few moments with Mary, went up stairs to gather up her clothing and what few treasures she had that had once helped to make her old home so dear.

She worked rapidly, and soon had everything ready. But suddenly she remembered that she had left a very nice pair of button-hole scissors in Mrs. Montague's boudoir on the day they left for the South.

She ran lightly down to get them, and just as she reached the second hall some one rang the bell a vigorous peal.

"That must be Ray," she said to herself, and stopped to listen for his voice.

But as Mary opened the door, she heard a gentleman's tones inquiring for Mrs. Montague.

"No," the girl said, "my mistress is not in."

"Then I will wait, for my errand is urgent," was the reply, and the person stepped within the hall.

Mona did not see who it was, but she heard Mary usher him into the parlor, after which she went to obey a summons from the cook, leaving the caller alone.

Mona went on into Mrs. Montague's room to get her scissors, but she could not find them readily. She was sure that she had left them on the center-table, but thought that the woman had probably moved them since her return.

Just then she thought she heard some one moving about in Mrs. Montague's chamber adjoining, but the door was closed, and thinking it might be Mary, she continued her search, but still without success.

She was just on the point of going into the other room to ask Mary if she had seen them, when a slight sound attracted her attention, and looking up, she caught the gleam of a pair of vindictive eyes peering in at her from the hall, and the next moment the door was violently shut and the key turned in the lock.

CHAPTER XVII.

THE WOMAN IN BLACK.

For a moment Mona was too much astonished to even try to account for such a strange proceeding.

Then it occurred to her that Mrs. Montague must have returned before she was expected, let herself into the house with her latch-key, and coming quietly up stairs, had been taken by surprise to find her in her room, when she had supposed her to be safely out of her way in Havana, and so had made a prisoner of her by locking her in the boudoir.

At first Mona was somewhat appalled by her situation; then a calm smile of scorn for her enemy wreathed her lips, for she was sure that Ray would soon return. She had only to watch for him at the window, inform him of what had occurred the moment he drove to the door, and he would have her immediately released.

With this thought in her mind, she approached the window to see if he had not already arrived.

The curtain was down, and she attempted to raise it, when, the spring having been wound too tightly, it flew up with such a force as to throw the fixture from its socket, and the whole thing came crashing down upon her.

She sprang aside to avoid receiving it in her face, and in doing so nearly upset a small table that was standing before the window.

It was the table having in it the secret treasures which we have already seen. She managed to catch it, however, and saved the heavy marble top from falling to the floor by receiving it in her lap, and sinking down with it.

But while doing this, the broken lid to the secret compartment flew off, and some of its contents were scattered over her.

Mona was so startled by what she had done, that she was almost faint from fright, but she soon assured herself that no real damage had occurred—the most she had been guilty of was the discovery of some secret treasure which Mrs. Montague possessed.

She began to gather them up with the intention of replacing them in their hiding-place—the beautiful point-lace fan, which we have seen before, a box containing some lovely jewels of pearls and diamonds, and a package of letters.

"Ha!" Mona exclaimed, with a quick, in-drawn breath, as she picked these up, and read the superscription on the uppermost envelope, " 'Miss Mona Forester!' Can it be that these things belonged to my mother? And this picture! Oh, yes, it must be the very one that Louis Hamblin told me about—a picture of my father painted on ivory and set in a costly frame embellished with rubies!"

She bent over the portrait, gazing long and earnestly upon it, studying every feature of the handsome face, as if to impress them indelibly upon her mind.

"So this represents my father as he looked when he married my mother," she said, with a sigh. "He was very handsome, but, oh, what a sad, sad story it all was!"

She laid it down with an expression of keen pain on her young face and began to look over the costly jewels, handling them with a tender and reverent touch, while she saw that every one was marked with the name of "Mona" on the setting.

"These also are mine, and I shall certainly claim them. How strange that I should have found them thus!" she said, as she laid them carefully back in the box. Then she arose and righting the table, replaced the various things in the compartment.

In so doing she stepped upon a small box, which, until then, she had not seen.

The cover was held in place by a narrow rubber band.

She removed it, lifted the lid, and instantly a startled cry burst from her lips.

"Oh, what can it mean? what can it mean?" she exclaimed, losing all her color, and trembling with excitement.

At that moment the hall-bell rang again, and Mona turned once more to the window, now fully expecting to find that Ray had come.

No, another carriage stood before the door, but she could not see who had rung the bell.

She wondered why Ray did not come; it was more than an hour since he went away, and she began to fear that her captor was planning some fresh wrong to her, and he might be detained until it would be too late to help her.

She was growing both anxious and nervous, and thought she would just slip into Mrs. Montague's bedroom and see if she could not get out in that way.

Suiting the action to the resolve, she hastened into the chamber, and tried the door.

No, that was locked on the outside, and she knew that the woman must have some evil purpose in thus making a prisoner of her.

She turned again to retrace her steps, that she might keep watch for Ray at the window, when her eyes encountered an object lying upon the bed which drove the color from her face, and held her rooted to the spot where she stood!

*   *   *   *   *   *

About nine o'clock of that same morning, a woman might have been seen walking swiftly down Murray street, in the direction of the Hudson River, to the wharf occupied by the Fall River steamers.

She was tall and quite stout, but had a finely proportioned figure, and she walked with a brisk, elastic tread, which betrayed great energy and resolution.

She was dressed in deep mourning, her clothing being made of the finest material, and fitting her perfectly.

A heavy crape vail covered her head and partially enveloped her figure, effectually concealing her features, and yet a close observer would have said that she had a lovely profile, and would have noticed, also, that her hair was a decided red.

She appeared to be in a hurry, looking neither to the right nor left, nor abating her pace in the least until she reached the dock where the Fall River boat, Puritan, had but a little while previous poured forth her freight of humanity and merchandise.

As she came opposite the gang-plank a low whistle caused her to look up.

A man stationed on the saloon deck, and evidently watching for some one, made a signal, and with a nod of recognition, the woman passed on board and up the stairs to the grand saloon, where a man met her and slipped a key into her hand, then turned and walked away without uttering a word.

"Two hundred and one," she muttered, and walked deliberately down the saloon glancing at the figures on the doors of the various staterooms until she came to No. 201, when she unlocked it and went in.

Ten minutes later the man who had stood on deck as she came aboard, followed her, entered the stateroom, and locked the door after him.

The two were closeted there for nearly an hour, when the woman in black came out.

"I shall look for you at three precisely; do not fail me," said a low voice from behind the door.

"I will not fail you; but keep yourself close," was the equally guarded response, and then the heavily draped figure glided quickly down stairs and off the boat.

She crossed West street, passed on to Chambers, and turned to walk toward Broadway, passing, as she did so, a group of three or four men who were standing at the corner.

One of them gave a slight start as her garments brushed by him, took a step forward for a second look at her, then he quietly broke away from the others, and followed her, about a dozen yards behind, up Chambers street.

The woman did not appear to notice that she was being followed, for she did not accelerate her speed in the least, nor seem to pay any heed to what was going on about her. She kept straight on, as if her mind was intent only upon her own business.

But all at once, as she reached the corner of Broadway, she slipped into a carriage that stood waiting there, and was driven rapidly up town.

An angry exclamation burst from the man following her, who was none other than Rider, the detective, and he hastened forward to catch another glimpse of the carriage, if possible, before it should get out of sight.

He saw it in the distance, and hailing another, he gave chase as fast as the crowded condition of the street would permit.

Some twenty minutes later he came upon the same carriage standing on another corner, the driver as quiet and unconcerned as if he had not been dodging vehicles at the risk of a smash-up, or urging his horses to a lawless pace in that busy thoroughfare.

But the coach was empty.

Mr. Rider alighted and accosted the man.

"Where is the passenger that you had a few minutes ago?" he inquired.

The man pointed with his whip to a store near by, then relapsed into his indolent and indifferent attitude.

Mr. Rider shook his head emphatically, to indicate his disbelief of this pantomimic information, and muttered a few words not intended for polite ears as he turned on his heel and moved away.

"Fooled again," he added, "and I thought I had her sure this time. Of course she didn't go into that store any more than that other party went from St. Louis to Chicago. But it's worth something to know that she is in New York. I'll try to keep my eyes open this time."

In spite of his skepticism, however, he entered the store and sauntered slowly through it, but without encountering any woman in black, having red hair.

"She came off the Puritan," he mused, as he issued into the street again, and turned his face up town. "I imagine that she either came on from Fall River last night, or she is going back this afternoon. I'll hang round there about the time the Puritan leaves. Meantime I'll take a stroll in some of the upper tendom regions, for I'll bet she is a high-liver."

He boarded a car and was soon rolling up toward the more aristocratic portion of the city, and thus we must leave him for a while.

When Ray returned to Mrs. Montague's residence for Mona, he found another carriage waiting at the door, and it was just at this moment that Mona made her strange discovery in the woman's bedroom.

"Mr. Corbin's carriage," Ray murmured to himself as he alighted and went up the steps. "I wonder if Mr. Graves is with him, and if Mrs. Montague has returned. I hope she has not made matters unpleasant for Mona."

He rang the bell and was admitted by Mary, who wondered how many more times she would be obliged to run to the door that morning.

"Is Miss—Miss Richards through with her packing?" the young man inquired, but having almost betrayed Mona's identity, which, in accordance with the advice of the lawyers, they were not quite ready to do yet.

"She's still up stairs, sir," the girl replied. "I'll step up and tell her that you have come. Perhaps you'll wait in the reception-room, sir, as Mrs. Montague has just come in and has callers in the drawing-room."

"Certainly," Ray answered, and was about to follow her thither, when he heard his name spoken, and turning, saw Mr. Graves beckoning to him from the doorway of the drawing-room.

"Come in here," he said; "we shall need you in this business," and Ray knew that Mrs. Montague was about to be interviewed upon various matters of importance.

"Very well," he replied, then turning to Mary, he added: "You may tell Miss Richards that she need not hurry. I will call you again when I am ready to go."

He then followed the lawyer into the drawing-room and the door was shut.

"There is something queer going on in there," she muttered. "Mrs. Montague seemed all worked up over something, and those two men looked as glum as parsons at a funeral. There is cook's bell again, and Miss Ruth must wait," she concluded, impatiently, as a ring came up from the lower regions, and then she went slowly and reluctantly down stairs again.

CHAPTER XVIII.

SOME INTERESTING DISCOVERIES.

Upon entering Mrs. Montague's beautiful drawing-room, Ray found, as he had expected, that Mr. Corbin was there also, and he at once surmised the nature of the lawyer's business.

Mrs. Montague gave a start of surprise as she saw him, and lost some of her color; then recovering herself, she arose with a charming smile, and went forward to greet him.

Ray thought she looked much older than when he had seen her before, for there were dark circles under her eyes, with crows' feet at their corners, and wrinkles on her forehead and about her mouth, which he had never noticed until then, and which, somehow, seemed to change the expression of her whole face.

"This is an unexpected pleasure," she remarked, with great cordiality, "but you perceive," with a glance at the lawyers, "that I am overrun with business. May I ask you to step into the library for a few moments until I am at liberty?"

"No, if you please, madame, it is at my request that Mr. Palmer is here," quietly but decidedly interposed Mr. Graves.

Mrs. Montague flushed hotly at this interference, then seeing that she could not change the condition of affairs, and that Ray evidently understood matters, as he only bowed in the most frigid manner in response to her effusive greeting, she resigned herself to the inevitable and returned to her chair with an air of haughty defiance.

It was Mrs. Montague whom Mona had heard moving about in the chamber adjoining the boudoir.

The woman had come in just after Mary admitted that first caller below, and speeding swiftly and noiselessly up stairs, was making some changes in her toilet when the bell rang again. Mr. Corbin and Mr. Graves were at the door. She heard it, and gliding softly into the hall, leaned over the balustrade to ascertain who had called.

The moment she heard Mr. Corbin inquire for her, she grew white with passion, and her eyes flashed angrily, for she imagined that he had come to question her again regarding Mona Forester. She did not see his companion, however.

"I will give him a dose to remember this time," she muttered. Then she heard Mary inform the gentlemen that she was not at home.

"Yes, I am, Mary," she said, in a low tone, for she felt in a defiant mood, and not suspecting the fatal nature of the lawyer's visit, and feeling very secure in her own position, she rather courted an opportunity to defy him. "Invite the gentleman in, and I will be down presently."

She turned to go back to her chamber to complete her toilet, when she heard some one moving about in her boudoir.

She glided to the door, softly opened it, and looked in. Instantly her face lighted with a smile of evil triumph, though she gave a great start of surprise as she saw Mona there, and evidently searching for something.

She had already learned that the girl had managed to escape from the power of Louis and returned to New York. Therefore she now imagined that she had but just arrived and had come directly there to secure her other trunk, when doubtless she would immediately seek Ray Palmer's protection, and denounce both herself and her nephew for their plot against her.

Such a proceeding she knew would ruin all her prospects of becoming Mr. Palmer's wife, and, actuated by a sudden impulse, she hastily drew the door to again and locked it. Then she sped back to her chamber door and turned the key in that also, to prevent escape that way, and entirely forgetting in her excitement that she had intended to make still further changes in her toilet before going below.

This done, she sped swiftly down stairs, and encountered Mary in the hall.

"Lor', marm! I didn't know you had come in till you spoke," the girl remarked, with a curious stare at her.

"I have a latch-key, you know," Mrs. Montague returned, as she swept on toward the drawing-room, and the girl wondered why she "looked so strange and seemed so flustered."

Mrs. Montague entered the room with haughty mien, intending to dispose of Mr. Corbin with short ceremony, but she was somewhat taken aback when she found that he was accompanied by another legal-looking gentleman.

She had but just exchanged formal greetings with them when Ray made his appearance; but she did not suspect that he was aware of Mona's presence in the house. Mr. Graves' remark had led her to suppose that he was there by his appointment.

Mr. Corbin bowed to the young man, and remarked:

"I was about to explain to Mrs. Montague that some proofs regarding the identity of Miss Montague have recently come into my possession."

"Do you mean to assert that you have proofs that will establish the theory which you advanced to me during your last call here?" Mrs. Montague demanded, with a derisive smile.

"That is exactly what I mean, madame," Mr. Corbin replied.

Mrs. Montague tossed her head scornfully.

She was sure that the only proof in existence of Mona Forester's legal marriage was at that moment safely lying in the secret compartment of that little table up stairs. She had not seen it since her return, for she had been too busy to look over those things again and destroy such as would be dangerous, if they should fall into other hands; but she had seen them so recently she felt very secure, and did not dream that she had been guilty of any carelessness regarding them.

She knew, also, that up to the evening of Louis'
last declaration to her, Mona had no proof to produce, and, supposing that she had but just returned
from Havana, she did not imagine that either of the
lawyers or Ray had seen her to learn anything new
from her, even if she had discovered anything.

"Well, I should like to see them," she responded,
contemptuously, but with a confident air that would
have been very irritating to one less assured than Mr.
Corbin.

He quietly drew a folded paper from his breast-
pocket, opened and smoothed it out, and going to the
woman's side, held it before her for examination.

She was wholly unprepared for the appalling revelation that met her eyes, and the instant that she realized
that the paper was the identical certificate, which she
believed to be in her own possession, she lost every
atom of her color. A cry of anger and dismay broke
from her, and snatching the parchment from the lawyer's hand, she sprang to her feet, crying, hoarsely:

"Where did you get it? how did it come into your
possession?"

"Pray, madame, do not be so excited," Mr. Corbin
calmly returned, "and be careful of that document, if
you please, for it is worth a great deal to my young
client. Mr. Raymond Palmer supplied me with this
very necessary link in the evidence required to prove
Miss Montague's identity."

"And how came Raymond Palmer to have a paper
that belonged to me?" demanded Mrs. Montague, turning to him with an angry gleam in her eyes. "I have
supposed him to be a gentleman—he must be a thief,
else he never could have had it."

"You are mistaken in both assertions, Mrs. Mon-

tague," Ray responded, with cold dignity.   "In the
first place, the paper does not belong to you; it rightly
belongs to your husband's daughter.   In the second
place, it came into my possession in a perfectly legitimate manner.   On the day of your high-tea I came here
a little late, if you remember.   Your private parlor
above was used as the gentleman's dressing-room, and
I found that document lying underneath the draperies
of the bay-window.   I accidentally stepped upon it.
It crackled beneath my feet, and it was but natural
that I should wish to ascertain what was there.   When
I discovered the nature of the paper I felt perfectly
justified in taking charge of it, in the interests of my
promised wife, and so gave it into Mr. Corbin's
hands."

Mrs. Montague sat like one half stunned during
this explanation, for she readily comprehended how
this terrible calamity had happened to overtake her.
She realized that the certificate must have slipped from
her lap to the floor while she was examining the other
contents of that secret compartment; and, when she
had been so startled by Mona's rap and upset the table,
it had been pushed underneath the draperies, while,
during her hurry in replacing the various articles, she
had not noticed that it was missing.

"Yes, I understand," she said, in a low, constrained,
despairing tone.   "You have balked me at last, but,"
throwing back her head like some animal suddenly
brought to bay, "what are you going to do about it?"

"Only what is right and just, Mrs. Montague,"
courteously responded Mr. Corbin.

"Right and just!" she repeated, with bitter emphasis.
"That means, I suppose, that you are going to compel
me to give up my fortune."

"The law decrees that children shall have their father's property, excepting, of course, a certain portion," said the lawyer.

"A paltry one-third," retorted Mrs. Montague, angrily.

"Yes, unless the heirs choose to allow something more to the widow. Perhaps my client——"

Mrs. Montague sprang to her feet, her face flaming with sudden passion.

"Do you suppose I would ever humiliate myself enough to accept any favor from Mona Forester's child?" she cried, as she paced the floor excitedly back and forth. "Never! I will never be triumphed over. I will defy you all! Oh, to be beaten thus!—it is more than I can bear."

Mrs. Montague's fury was something startling in its bitterness and intensity, and the three gentlemen, witnessing it, could not help feeling something of pity for the proud woman in her humiliation, even though they were disgusted with her vindictiveness and selfishness.

"Defiance will avail you nothing, Mrs. Montague; an amicable spirit would conduce far more to your advantage," Mr. Corbin remarked. "And now I advise you," he added, "to quietly relinquish all right and title to this fortune excepting, of course, your third, and trust to your husband's daughter and her counsel to make you such allowance as they may consider right. If you refuse to do this we shall be obliged to resort to the courts to settle the question of inheritance."

"Take the matter into the courts, then," was the passionate retort. "I will defy you all to the bitter end. And you," turning with blazing eyes and crimson cheeks to Ray, "I suppose you imagined that you were to win a princely inheritance with your promised wife; that when you found this piece of parchment you would thus enable Mona Forester's child to triumph over the woman who hated her with a deadly hatred. Not so, I assure you, for my vengeance is even more complete than I ever dared to hope, and your 'promised wife,' my fine young man, will never flaunt her colors in triumph over me here in New York, for her reputation has been irretrievably ruined, and the city shall ring with the vile story ere another twenty-four hours shall pass."

"Don't be too sure, madame; don't be too sure that you're going to down that clever little lady just yet," were the words which suddenly startled every one in the room, and the next instant the door swung wide open to admit a new actor in the drama.

A brisk, energetic little man entered the room, and going directly to Mrs. Montague's side, he laid his hand upon her shoulder.

"Madame, you are my prisoner," he added, in a more quiet but intensely satisfied tone.

"What do you mean, sir?" haughtily demanded the woman, as she shook herself free from his touch. "Who are you, and how came you here?"

"Well, we'll take one question at a time, if you please, madame," the new-comer returned. "First, what do I mean? Just what I say—you are my prisoner. I arrest you for obtaining money under false pretenses—for theft, for abduction. The proof of the first charge is right here in my hand. Look!"

He opened his palm and disclosed to the horrified woman's gaze and to the amazement of the other occupants of the room two beautiful crescents of blazing diamonds.

"Heavens! where did you get them? Oh, I know—I know!" shrieked the unhappy creature, cowering and shrinking from the sight as if blinded by it, and sinking upon the nearest chair.

"Yes, I reckon you do," grimly remarked Detective Rider, for it was he, "and this clears up the Bently affair of Chicago, for here, on the back of the settings, is the very mark which Mr. Arnold of that city put upon them more than three years ago. Well, so much for that charge. Now, if Mr. Palmer will just step this way, maybe he'll recognize some of his property, and we'll explain the second and third charges."

Ray looked astonished as he went forward, but he was even more so when Mr. Rider held up before him an elegant diamond cross, which he instantly identified as one of the ornaments which the beautiful Mrs. Vanderbeck had selected on that never-to-be-forgotten day when he was decoyed into Doctor Wesselhoff's establishment and left there a prisoner, while the woman made off with her booty.

"Where did you get it?" he exclaimed, while Mrs. Montague fell back among the cushions of her chair and covered her face with her trembling hands, utterly unnerved.

"That remains to be explained, together with some other things which are no less interesting and startling," the detective returned, with an air of triumph. "And now," raising his voice a trifle, "if a certain little lady will show herself, I imagine we can entertain you with another act in this strange comedy."

As he spoke the drawing-room door, which the man had left slightly ajar when he entered, was pushed open, and Mona made her appearance with her arms full of clothing.

She glided straight to the detective's side, and handed him something which, with a dextrous movement, he clapped upon Mrs. Montague's bowed head.

It was a wig of rich, dark-red hair, which fell in lovely rings about the woman's fair forehead and white neck.

She lifted her face with a cry of terror at Mr. Rider's act, and behold! the beautiful Mrs. Vanderbeck was before them!

Ray knew at once why Mrs. Montague had looked so strangely to him as she arose to greet him when he entered.

Her face had been artistically made up, with certain applications of pencil and paint, to give her the appearance of being considerably older than she was. But he wondered how she happened to be so made up that morning.

"That is not all," Mr. Rider resumed, as he took a costly tailor-made dress from Mona's arm and held it up before his speechless auditors. "Here is the robe which was so badly rent at the time that Mrs. Vanderbeck escorted Mr. Raymond Palmer to the great Doctor Wesselhoff for treatment, while the fragment that was torn from it will fit into the hole. And here," taking another garment from Mona, "is a widow's costume in which the fascinating Mrs. Bently figured in Chicago, when she so skillfully duped a certain Mr. Cutler, swindling him out of a handsome sum of money, and giving him paste ornaments in exchange. No one would ever imagine the elegant Mrs. Richmond Montague and the lovely widow to be one and the same person, for they were entirely different in figure as well as face, the former being very slight, while the latter was inclined to be decidedly portly, as was also Mrs. Vanderbeck.

"But, gentlemen, that is also easily explained, as you will see if you examine these costumes, for there must be five pounds, more or less, of cotton wadding used about each to pad it out to the required dimensions. Clever, very clever!" interposed Mr. Rider, bestowing a glance of admiration upon the bowed and shivering figure before him. "I think, during all my experience, I have never had so complicated and interesting a case. I do not wonder that you look dazed, gentlemen," he went on, with a satisfied glance at his wide-eyed and wondering listeners, "and I imagine I could have surprised you still more if I had had time to examine a certain trunk which stands open up stairs in the lady's chamber. I think I could find among its contents a gray wig and other garments belonging to a certain Mrs. Walton, so called, and perhaps a miner's suit that would fit Mr. Louis Hamblin, alias Jake Walton, who in St. Louis recently tried to dispose of costly diamonds which he had brought all the way from Australia, for his rustic sweetheart—eh? Ha, ha, ha!" and the jubilant man burst into a laugh of infinite amusement.

"Truly, Mr. Rider, your discoveries are somewhat remarkable; but will you allow me to examine that cross?" a new voice here remarked, and Mr. Amos Palmer arose from a mammoth chair at the other end of the drawing-room, where he had been an unseen witness of and listener to all that had occurred during the last half hour.

It was he who had rung the bell just as Mona was about to enter Mrs. Montague's boudoir in search of her scissors, and who, upon being told that the lady was out, had said he would wait for her. He had called to ask his *fiancée* to go with him to select the hangings for the private parlor which he was fitting up for her in his own house.

His face, at this moment, was as colorless as marble; his eyes gleamed with a relentless purpose, and his manner was frigid from the strong curb that he had put upon himself.

At the sound of his voice Mrs. Montague lifted a face upon which utter despair, mingled with abject terror, was written. She bent one brief, searching glance upon the man, and then shrank back again into the depths of her chair, shivering as with a chill.

CHAPTER XIX.

HOW IT HAPPENED.

Mr. Rider passed Mr. Palmer the diamond cross, which he took without a word, and carefully examined, turning it over and over and scrutinizing both the stones and the setting with the closest attention, though Ray could see that his hands were trembling with excitement, and knew that his heart was undergoing the severest torture.

"Yes," he said, after an oppressive silence, during which every eye, except Mrs. Montague's, was fixed upon him, "the cross is ours—my own private mark is on the back of the setting. And so," turning sternly to the wretched woman near him, "you were the thief; you were the unprincipled character who decoyed my son to that retreat for maniacs, and nearly made one of me! Then, oh! what treachery! what duplicity! When you feared that the net was closing about you and you would be brought to justice, you sought to make a double dupe of me by a marriage with me, imagining, I suppose, that I would suffer in silence, if the theft was ever discovered, rather than have my name tarnished by a public scandal. So you have sailed under many characters!" he went on, in a tone of biting scorn. "You are the Mrs. Bently, of Chicago! the Mrs. Bent, of Boston; Mrs. Vanderbeck and Mrs. Walton, of New York; and the woman in St. Louis, who gave bail for the rascally miner, who tried to dispose of the unset solitaires. Fortunately those have been proven to be mine and returned to me; but where are the rest of the stones? I will have them, every one," he concluded, in a tone so stern and menacing that the woman shivered afresh.

"They were all together—they were all yours except two; but the cross, we—we——"

Mrs. Montague proceeded thus far in a muffled, trembling tone, and then her voice utterly failed her.

"You did not dare to try to sell too many at one time, and so you reserved the cross for future use," Mr. Palmer supplemented. "Perhaps you even intended to wear it under my very eyes, among your wedding finery. I verily believe you are audacious enough to do so; but, madame, it will be safe to say that there will be no wedding now, at least between you and me."

The man turned abruptly, as he ceased speaking, and left the room, looking fully a dozen years older than when, an hour previous, he had come there, with hope in his heart, to plan with his bride-elect how they could make their future home most attractive for her reception.

Ray felt a profound pity for his father, in this mortifying trial and disappointment, and he longed to follow him and express his sympathy; but his judgment told him that it would be better to leave him alone for a time; that his wounded pride could ill-brook any reference to his blighted hopes just then.

It may as well be related just here how Detective Rider happencd to appear so opportunely, and how Mona found the robes in which Mrs. Montague had so successfully masqueraded to carry out her various swindling operations.

It will be remembered that Mona, after she had gathered up the keepsakes belonging to her mother and returned them to the table, had found another box upon the floor of Mrs. Montague's boudoir.

When she had removed the rubber band that held the cover in its place, her astonished eyes fell upon a pair of exquisite diamond crescents for the ears, and a cross, which, from the description which Ray had given her, she knew must have been among the articles stolen from Mr. Palmer.

Instantly it flashed across her what this discovery meant.

She felt very sure that Mrs. Montague must have been concerned in the swindling of Mr. Cutler, more than three years previous, and also of Mrs. Vanderbeck in Boston, besides in the more recent so-called Palmer robbery.

Still, there were circumstances connected with these operations that puzzled her.

Mrs. Bently, the crafty widow of Chicago, had been

described to her as a stout woman with red hair. Mrs.
Vanderbeck had also been somewhat portly, likewise
Mrs. Walton, whom she had seen in St. Louis, and
these latter were somewhat advanced in years also.

Mrs. Montague, on the contrary, was slight and
sylph-like in figure; a blonde of the purest type, with
light golden hair, a lovely complexion, with hardly
the sign of a wrinkle on her handsome face.

But she did not speculate long upon these matters,
for, having made this discovery, she was more anxious
than before to be released from her place of confinement. So she had gone into the adjoining room, and
tried the door leading into the hall.

That, too, as we know, she had found locked, and
then, as she turned to retrace her steps, she was
stricken spellbound by something which she saw upon
the bed.

It was nothing less than a widow's costume, com-
prising a dress, bonnet, and vail, together with a wig
of short, curling red hair!

Yes, Mrs. Montague was the "widow!" or woman
in black whom Detective Rider had observed and
followed only a little while previous. When she
found that the man was on her track she had slipped
into the carriage and ordered the driver to take her
with all possible speed to a certain store on Broadway. Arriving there, she had simply passed in at
one door and out of one opposite leading upon a side
street, where she hailed a car, and, thoroughly
alarmed, went directly home instead of going to the
room where she usually made these changes in her
costume.

Upon reaching her own door, she quietly let herself in with her latch-key, and going directly to her

chamber, tore off her widow's weeds, and wig, and
threw them hastily upon the bed. She hurriedly
donned another dress, and was about to remove the
cleverly simulated signs of age from her face, when
she heard the bell ring, and went into the hall to
ascertain who had called. We know the rest, how she
recognized the lawyer, and imagined he had come
again to annoy her further upon the subject of Mona
Forester's child; how, almost at the same moment,
she discovered Mona's presence in the house, and instantly resolved to lock her up until she could decide
what further to do with her. And thus, laboring
under so much excitement, she entirely forgot about
the wrinkles and crow's-feet upon her face, and which
so changed its expression.

The moment Mona saw the costume upon the bed
everything was made plain to her mind. Mrs. Bently,
of the Chicago and Boston crescent swindle, was no
other than Mrs. Montague in a most ingenious disguise.

Glancing about the room for further evidences of
the woman's cunning, she espied a trunk standing
open at the foot of the bed, as if some one had been
hastily examining the contents and forgotten to shut
it afterward.

She approached it, and on top of the tray there lay
the very dress of gray ladies' cloth which she had seen
hanging in the closet of a certain room in the Southern Hotel in St. Louis. Then she knew, beyond a
doubt, that Mrs. Montague had also figured as Mrs.
Walton, the mother of the miner, in that city.

But who was the miner?

Louis Hamblin, in all probability, although she had
not dreamed of such a thing until that moment.

"It is very strange that I should not have recognized Mrs. Montague, in spite of the white hair and the spotted lace vail," she murmured, thoughtfully. But after reflecting and recalling the fact that even the woman's eyebrows had been whitened and the whole expression of the face changed by pencil lines, to simulate wrinkles and furrows, and then covered with a thickly spotted vail, she did not wonder so much.

She was amazed and appalled by these discoveries, and trembling with excitement, she resolved to learn more, if possible.

She lifted the lid of the hat-box, at one end of the tray, and there lay the very bonnet and vail that the woman had worn in St. Louis, and also the wig of white hair.

"What a wretched creature!" she exclaimed, in a horrified tone. Then wondering if Ray might not have come, while she had been there, she flew back to the window in the other room to look for him.

Yes, his carriage was standing before the door, and he would soon find means to release her, she thought.

But moment after moment went by, and no one came, while the continuous murmur of voices in the room below made her wonder what was going on there.

Presently, however, her attention was attracted to a man who was sauntering slowly along the opposite sidewalk, and she was sure she had seen him somewhere before, although, just at first, she could not place him.

"Why!" she exclaimed, after studying his face and figure a moment, "it is Mr. Rider. Can it be possible that he suspects anything of the mystery concealed in this house? At any rate, he is just the man that is needed here at this time."

She tapped lightly on the pane to attract his attention.

He stopped, glanced up, and instantly recognized Mona, nodding and lifting his hat to indicate that he did so.

She beckoned him to cross the street, and then cautiously raised the window. He was beneath it in a moment.

"Come in, Mr. Rider, and come directly up stairs to me," she said, in a low tone. "I have been locked in this room, and I have made an important discovery which you ought to know immediately."

He nodded again, his keen eyes full of fire, turned, ascended the steps, and pulled the bell.

Mary sighed heavily as she bent her weary steps, for the fifth time, up the basement stairs to answer his imperative summons.

"Is your mistress at home?" Mr. Rider inquired, in a quick, business-like tone.

"Yes, sir; but she is engaged with callers," the girl replied.

"So much the better," returned the detective; then, bending a stern look on her, he continued: "I am an officer; I have business in this house; you are to let me in and say nothing to any one. Do you understand?"

Mary grew pale at this, and fell back a step or two from the door, frightened at the term "officer."

Mr. Rider took instant advantage of the situation and stepped within the hall.

"Don't dare to mention that I am here until I give

you leave," he commanded, authoritatively, and then ran nimbly and quietly up stairs.

It was the work of but a moment to find the room where Mona was confined, turn the key, and enter.

"What does this mean, Miss Richards?" he asked, regarding her curiously. "How do you happen to be locked up like a naughty child?"

"I will explain that to you by and by; but first let me show you these."

She uncovered the box which contained the crescents and cross, and held the gleaming diamonds before his astonished eyes.

The man was so utterly confounded by the unexpected sight that for a moment he gazed at them with a look of wonder on his face.

"Zounds! where did you get them?" he cried, breathlessly.

Mona briefly explained regarding the accident to the table, which had resulted in her discovering the secret compartment with its treasures.

"Clever! clever!" the man muttered, as his eyes fastened upon the table and he comprehended the truth. "Well, well, young lady, you've done a fine stroke of business this day, and no mistake! These are the real articles, no paste or sham to fool me this time," he added, as he lifted the crescents from the box. "But—when—Mrs. Richmond Montague!— who'd have thought it?"

"This isn't all, Mr. Rider," Mona continued, in a whisper, for she feared Mrs. Montague might catch the sound of their voices.

"What! more discoveries!" the man exclaimed, all alert again, as he shut the box and slipped it into his pocket.

"Yes, step this way, if you please," and leading him to the door of Mrs. Montague's chamber, she pointed at the costume lying upon the bed.

The quick eyes took it all in at a glance, and his face lighted with a swift flash of triumph.

"The Bently affair—the Vanderbeck swindle—the Palmer robbery! Clever! clever!" he muttered, as he seized the costume, shook out its folds, discovered the thick layers of padding about the waist and hips, and eyed it with intense satisfaction. Then he revealed two rows of firm, white teeth in a broad smile, as he snatched up and twirled that dainty red wig upon his hand, examining it with a critical and admiring eye.

"And this, also," continued Mona, going to the trunk and lifting from it the tailor-made costume of gray ladies' cloth.

"Aha! ha!" chuckled Mr. Rider. "Really, Miss Richards, if you were only a man we might make a right smart detective of you. This is the very dress we have been wanting, and here is the rent. Have you still the fragment that you showed me in St. Louis?"

"Yes, it is here in my purse," Mona answered, drawing it from her pocket, and, taking the piece of cloth from it, she handed it to him.

"Here, too, is the gray wig worn by Mrs. Walton," she went on, as she lifted the lid of the hat-box and revealed its contents.

"Yes; true enough! and I'll wager that this trunk contains some other disguises which we should recognize," he responded. "But," he added, "we have enough for our purpose just now, and we will defer further examination until later. Now, Miss Richards, I am going down stairs to confront that woman with this stolen property. You follow me, but remain in the hall until I give you a signal, then come forward with these disguises. Have you any idea who is below calling on her ladyship?" he asked, in conclusion.

"No; but I am very sure that Mr. Raymond Palmer is somewhere in the house, for he was to call for me, and his carriage is at the door.

"I am glad to know that," the man cried, "and now I will make quick work of this business."

He turned and left the room with a quick step, and going directly below entered the drawing-room, just as Mrs. Montague was rudely taunting Ray about Mona.

The young girl gathered up the various articles of clothing and followed him, and we know what occurred after that.

CHAPTER XX.

MRS. MONTAGUE EXPLAINS.

It would be difficult to describe the abject distress of the wretched woman, whose career of duplicity and crime had been so unexpectedly revealed and cut short.

She was the picture of despair, as she sat crouching in the depths of her luxurious chair, her figure bowed and trembling, her face hidden in her hands.

There was a silence for a moment after Mr. Amos Palmer left the room; then Mr. Rider, who had been curiously studying his prisoner while the gentleman was speaking, remarked:

"It is the greatest mystery to me, madame, how, with the large fortune which you have had at your disposal, you could have wished to carry on such a dangerous business. What could have been your object? Surely not the need of money, nor yet the desire for jewels, since you have means enough to purchase all you might wish, and you tried to sell those you stole. One would almost suppose that it was a sort of monomania with you."

"No, it was not monomania," Mrs. Montague cried, as she started up with sudden anger and defiance; "it was absolute need."

"Really, now," Mr. Rider remarked, regarding her with a peculiar smile, "I should just like to know, as a matter of curiosity, how much it takes to relieve you from absolute need. I have supposed that you were one of the richest women in New York."

Mrs. Montague flushed a sudden crimson, and darted a quick, half-guilty look at Mr. Corbin. Then she turned again to the detective.

"Did you?—and so did others, I suppose!" she cried, with a short, scornful laugh. "Well, then, let me tell you that until I set my wits at work my income was only about twenty-five hundred dollars a year; and what was that paltry sum to a woman with my tastes?

"I do not care who knows now," she went on, with increasing excitement; "I have been humiliated to the lowest degree, and I shall glory in telling you how a woman has managed to outwit keen business men, sharp detectives, and clever police. In the first place, those crescents were presented to me at the time of my marriage. They are, as you have doubtless observed, wonderful jewels—as nearly flawless as it is possible to find diamonds. When I went to Chicago I was poor, for I had been extravagant that year and over-drawn my income. Money I must have—money I would have; and then it was that I attempted, for the first time, to carry out a scheme which I had planned while I was abroad the previous year. I had ordered a widow's outfit to be made, and padded in a way to entirely change my figure. I also purchased that red wig. While in Paris I learned the art of changing the expression of my face, by the skillful use of pencils and paint, and thus, dressed in my mourning costume with my eyebrows and lashes tinged to match my false hair, no one would ever have recognized me as Mrs. Montague.

"I had also provided myself, while in Paris, with several pairs of crescents, the exact counterparts, in everything save value, of the costly ones in my possession. I need not repeat the story of my success in getting money from Justin Cutler—you already know it; but I was so elated over the fact that I immediately went on to Boston, where I won even a larger sum from Mrs. Vanderheck."

"Yes; but how did you manage to change the jewels in that case, since you were with Mrs. Vanderheck from the time you left the expert until she paid you the money for them?" inquired Mr. Rider, who was deeply interested in this cunningly devised scheme.

"That was easily done," Mrs. Montague returned. "I had the case in my lap, and the duplicate crescents in my pocket. It required very little ingenuity on my part to so engage Mrs. Vanderheck's attention that I could abstract the real stones from the case and replace them with the others. Regarding the Palmer affair," she continued, with a glance of defiance at

Ray, "it only required a few lines and touches to my face to apparently add several years to my age and change its expression; and, with my red hair and the change in my figure, my disguise was complete.

"And the name," interposed Ray, regarding her sternly; "you had a purpose in using that."

"Certainly, and the invalid husband also," she retorted, with a short, reckless laugh. "I had a purpose, too, in calling the elder Mr. Palmer's attention to the profusion of diamonds worn by Mrs. Vanderheck upon the evening of Mrs. Merrill's reception. You can understand why, perhaps," she added, sarcastically, and turning to the detective.

He merely nodded in reply, but muttered under his breath, with a kind of admiration for her daring:

"Clever—clever, from the word 'go.'"

"With a wig of white hair, a few additional wrinkles, and the sedate dress of a woman of sixty, I passed as Mrs. Walton, the mother of a lunatic son. It was not such a very difficult matter after all," she added, glancing vindictively at Ray; "the chief requirement was plenty of assurance, or cheek, as you men would express it. My only fear was that the diamonds would be missed before we were admitted to the doctor's house."

"When did you take that package from my pocket?" Ray demanded, with some curiosity. "Was it when I leaned forward to assist you about your dress?"

The woman's lips curled.

"And run the risk of being detected before leaving the carriage after all my trouble? No, indeed," she scornfully returned. "My *coup de grace* was just after ringing Doctor Wesselhoff's bell, while we stood together on the steps; the package was not large, though valuable, and it was but the work of a moment to transfer it from your pocket to mine, while you stood there with your arms full.

Ray regarded her wonderingly. She must have been very dextrous, he thought, and yet he remembered now that she had turned suddenly and brushed rather rudely against him.

"And in St. Louis——" Mr. Rider began.

Mrs. Montague flushed, and a wary gleam came into her eye.

"Yes, of course," she interrupted, hastily; "I was also the Mrs. Walton, of St. Louis. It was very easy to hire an extra room under that name."

"And your agent was—who?" continued Mr. Rider.

"That does not matter," she retorted, sharply. "You have found me out. I have recklessly explained my own agency in these affairs, but you will not succeed in making me implicate any one else."

"Very well; we will question you no further upon that point now," said the detective; "but it does not take a very wise head to suspect who was your accomplice, and I imagine it will not take a great deal of hunting, either, to find him," and Mr. Rider resolved to make a bee line for the Fall River boat the moment he could get through with his business there. "And now, gentlemen," he resumed, turning to the lawyers and Ray, "I think we'll close this examination here, and I'll take my prisoner into camp."

A cry of horror burst from Mrs. Montague's blanched lips at this remark.

"You cannot mean it—you will not dare to take me to a vile jail," she exclaimed, in tones of mingled fear and anger.

"Jails were made for thieves, swindlers, and abductors," was the laconic response.

The woman sprang to her feet again, and shot a withering glance at him.

"I go to a common prison? never!" she said, fiercely, and with all the haughtiness of which she was capable.

"The fact of your having figured as a leader in high life, madame, does not exempt you from the penalty of the law, since you have already declared yourself guilty of the crimes I have named," coolly rejoined the detective.

"Oh, I cannot—I cannot," moaned the wretched woman, wringing her hands in abject distress. Then her glance fell upon Mona, who had quietly seated herself a little in the background, after the detective had relieved her of the clothing which she had brought into the room.

"You will not let them send me to prison—you will not let them bring me to trial and sentence me to such degradation," she moaned, imploringly.

Mr. Rider regarded her with amazement and supreme contempt at this servile appeal, for so it seemed to him.

"How can you expect that Miss Richards will succor you after your heartless and wicked treatment of her?" he demanded more sharply than he had yet spoken to her.

"Because, Mr. Rider," Mona gently interposed, "she bears a name she knows I am anxious to save from all taint or reproach; because she was the wife, and I the only child, of Walter Richmond Montague Dinsmore."

The detective gave vent to a long, low whistle of surprise.

"Zounds! can that be possible?" he cried, as he turned his wondering glance upon the lawyers.

"Yes," said Mr. Corbin, "it is the truth, and, of course, it is time that it should be revealed. I have known that Mrs. Richmond Montague and Mrs. Walter Dinsmore were one and the same person ever since the death of Mr. Dinsmore. The lady came to me immediately after that event and requested me to ascertain if he had made a will. I instituted inquiries and learned that he had tried to do so, but failed to sign it. She then revealed to me that she was the wife of Mr. Dinsmore, but that they had separated only a year after their marriage, although he had allowed her an annual income of twenty-five hundred dollars for separate maintenance. She produced her certificate and other proofs that she was his lawful wife, and authorized me to claim his fortune for her, but stipulated that she was not to appear personally in the matter, as she did not wish to be identified as Mrs. Dinsmore, after having appeared in New York society as Mrs. Montague. She absolutely refused to make her husband's niece—or supposed niece—any allowance, although I felt that it was cruel to deprive the young lady of everything when she had been reared in luxury and expected to be the sole heir, and I tried to persuade her to settle upon her the same amount that she herself had hitherto received from Mr. Dinsmore. All my arguments were without avail, however, and I was obliged to act as she required. You all know the result; Miss Mona was deprived of both fortune and home, and Mrs. Montague, as she still wished to be known, suddenly became, in truth, the rich woman she was supposed to be previously."

"Did you know of this?" Mr. Rider asked, turning to Mr. Graves.

"I knew that a woman claiming to be a Mrs. Dinsmore had secured the fortune which should have been settled upon this young lady; but I did not know that Mrs. Montague was that woman until Miss Dinsmore, as I suppose we must now call her"—with a smile at Mona—"returned from the South. Until then I also believed that she was only the niece of my friend. If I had ever suspected the truth you may be very sure that I should have fought hard to establish the fact."

"I suspected the fact when Miss Mona came to me, bringing her mother's picture, and told me her story," Mr. Corbin here remarked. "I was convinced of it after I had paid a visit to and made some inquiries of Mrs. Montague——"

"Ha!" that woman interposed as she turned angrily upon Mona, "then you did make use of that torn picture after all!"

"I took it to an artist, had it copied, then gave the pieces to Mary to be burned, as you had commanded," Mona quietly replied.

"Oh! how you have fooled me!" Mrs. Montague exclaimed, flushing hotly. "If I had only acted upon my first impressions, I should have sent you adrift at once—I should not have tolerated your presence a single hour; but you were so demure and innocent that you deceived me completely, and I never found you out until the morning after my high-tea. Then I understood your game, and resolved to so effectually clip your wings that you could never do me any mischief."

Mona started at this last revelation, and light be-gan to break upon her mind.

"How did you find me out?" she inquired, in a low tone.

"I had a letter telling me that my seamstress, who called herself Ruth Richards, was no other than Mona Montague—the last person in all the world whom I would have wished to receive into my family—and that she was having secret meetings with Raymond Palmer."

"Who wrote that letter?" Mona demanded, with heightened color.

"I do not know—it was anonymous; but I was con-vinced at once that you were Mona Montague, from the fact that you were having secret interviews with Ray Palmer, for his father had told me of his interest in her. Of course I instantly came to the conclusion that you were plotting against me, and, though I did not believe that you could prove your identity, or your mother's legal marriage, I feared that something might occur to trouble me in the possession of my fortune; so I resolved to marry you to Louis and settle the matter for all time."

"Then that was why you started so suddenly for the South?" Mona said, with flashing eyes.

"That was not my only reason for going," re-turned Mrs. Montague, flushing. "I—I had a tele-gram calling me to St. Louis, and so thought the op-portunity a fine one to carry out my scheme regard-ing you."

"And did you suppose, for one moment, that you could drive me into a marriage with a man for whom I had not the slightest affection or even respect?"

Mona demanded, bending an indignant look upon the unprincipled schemer.

"I at least resolved that I would so compromise you that no one else would ever marry you," was the malicious retort, as the woman turned her vindictive glance from her to Ray.

"Nothing could really compromise me but voluntary wrongdoing," Mona answered, with quiet dignity, "and your vile scheme was but a miserable failure."

"I do not need to be twitted of the fact," Mrs. Montague impatiently returned. "My whole life has been a failure," she went on, her face almost convulsed with pain and passion. "Oh! if I had only destroyed that marriage certificate you would never have triumphed over me like this; you would never have learned the truth about yourself."

"Oh, yes, I should," Mona composedly returned, "and even my trip to New Orleans resulted advantageously to me."

"How so?" questioned her enemy, with a start, and regarding her with a frown.

"An accident revealed to me, on the last night of our stay there, the whole truth about myself. Up to that time I was entirely ignorant of the fact that my supposed uncle was my father, for I knew nothing about the discovery of the certificate until my return from Havana."

"What do you mean?—what accident do you refer to?" Mrs. Montague asked.

"The day I was eighteen years old I asked my father some very close questions regarding my parentage, of which I had been kept very ignorant all my life. Some of them he answered, some of them he evaded, and, on the whole, my conversation with him was very unsatisfactory; for I really did not know much more about myself and my father and mother at its close than at its beginning.

"On the same day he gave me a small mirror that had once belonged to Marie Antoinette, and which, he said, had been handed down as an heirloom in my mother's family for several generations. This mirror he cautioned me never to part with; and so, when I went South with you, I packed it with my other things in my trunk. That last evening in New Orleans, while removing and repacking some clothing I dropped the book containing my mirror. When I picked it up I discovered that it contained a secret drawer in its frame. In the drawer there were some letters, a box containing two rings belonging to my mother and a full confession, written by my father upon the very day that he had presented me with the royal keepsake.

"So," Mona concluded, "you perceive that even had you destroyed the certificate proving their marriage, I should have other and sufficient proof that I was the child of Mr. and Mrs. Walter Dinsmore."

"Oh! if I had only forced the sale of all his property and gone back at once to California, I should have escaped all this and kept my fortune," groaned the unhappy woman, in deep distress.

"Really, Mrs. Dinsmore, you are showing anything but a right spirit——" Mr. Corbin began, in a tone of reproof, when she interrupted him with passionate vehemence.

"Never address me by that name," she cried. "Do you suppose I wish to be known as the widow of the man who repudiated me? Never! That was why I adopted the name of Montague, and I still wish to be known as such. Ah!—but if I have to go to—— Oh, pray plead for me!" she cried, turning again to Mona; "do not let them send me to prison."

Just at that moment Mr. Palmer's wan face appeared again at the rear door of the drawing-room.

He beckoned to Ray, who immediately left the room, and Mona, who had grown very thoughtful after Mrs. Montague's last appeal, left her seat and approached the lawyers.

"Mr. Graves—Mr. Corbin," she said, in a low tone, which only they could hear, "cannot something be done to keep this matter from becoming public? I cannot bear the thought of having my dear father's name become the subject of any scandal in connection with this woman. It would wound me very sorely to have it known that Mrs. Richmond Montague, who has figured so conspicuously in New York society, was his discarded wife; that she robbed me of my fortune, and why; that she—the woman bearing his name— was the unprincipled schemer who defrauded Mr. Justin Cutler and Mrs. Vanderheck, and robbed Mr. Palmer of valuable diamonds. I could not endure," she went on, flushing crimson, "that my name should be brought before the public in connection with Louis Hamblin and that wretched voyage from New Orleans to Havana."

"But, my dear Miss Dinsmore——" began Mr. Corbin.

"Please let me continue," Mona interposed, smiling faintly, yet betraying considerable feeling. "I think I know what you wished to remark—that she has had the benefit of all this money which she has obtained under false pretenses, and that she ought to

suffer the extreme penalty of the law for her mis-
deeds. She cannot fail to suffer all, and more than
any one could desire, in the failure of her schemes,
in the discovery of her wickedness, and in the loss
of the fortune of which she felt so secure. But even
if she were indifferent to all this I should still beg
you to consider the bitter humiliation which a public
trial would entail upon me, and the reproach upon my
father's hitherto unsullied name.   If—if I will cause
Mr. Cutler and Mrs. Vanderheck to be reimbursed for
the loss which they sustained through Mrs. Montague's dishonesty, cannot you arrange some way by
which a committal and a trial can be avoided?"

"I am afraid it would be defeating all law and justice," Mr. Corbin began again, and just at that moment Ray returned to the room, looking very grave
and thoughtful.

Mona's face lighted as she saw him.

"Ray, come here, please, and plead for me," she
said, turning her earnest face toward him; and he
saw at once that her heart was very much set upon
her object, whatever it might be.

CHAPTER XXI.

MRS. MONTAGUE TELLS HER STORY.

"What is it, Mona?" Ray inquired, as he went to
her side.   "You may be very sure that I will second
your wishes if they are wise and do not interfere in
any way with your interests."

Mona briefly repeated what she had already proposed to the lawyers, and Ray immediately responded
that it was also his wish and his father's that as far
as they were concerned all public proceedings against
Mrs. Montague should be suspended.

"Come with me to another room where we can con-
verse more freely," he added, " for I have a proposition to make to you in my father's name. Mr. Rider,"
raising his voice and addressing the detective, "will
you allow Mrs. Montague to remain alone with Miss
Dinsmore for a little while, as I wish to confer with
you upon a matter of importance?"

The detective took a swift survey of the room before answering. It was evident that he had no intention of allowing his captive to escape him now after
all his previous efforts to secure her.

"Yes," he replied, "I will go with you into the hall,
if that will do."

He knew that in the hall he should be able to keep
his eyes upon both doors of the drawing-room, and
no one could pass in and out without his knowing it,
while there was no other way of egress.

The four gentlemen accordingly withdrew, thus
leaving Mona and Mrs. Montague by themselves.

Mona seated herself by a window, and as far as
possible from the woman, for she shrank with the
greatest aversion from her, while she felt that her
own presence must be oppressive and full of reproach
to her.

But the woman's curiosity was for the moment
greater than her anxiety or remorse, and after a brief
silence, she abruptly inquired:

"How did that detective find that box of diamonds?"

"He did not find them. I accidentally discovered them," Mona replied.

"You? What were you prowling about in my room for?" crossly demanded Mrs. Montague.

"I was simply looking for a pair of scissors which I had left there the day before we went South. But why did you lock me in the room, for I suppose it was you?"

"Because I was desperate," was the defiant response. "I had just learned how you had escaped from Louis, but I had not a thought of finding you here. When I saw you in my room, however, a great fear came over me that you would yet prove my ruin. I imagined that you had just arrived in New York, and had come here to take away your things, and were perhaps searching my room for proofs of your identity. So on the impulse of the moment I locked you in, intending to make my own terms with you before I let you go."

"Did you suppose, after my experience in New Orleans, that I would trust myself with you without letting some one know where I could be found?" Mona quietly asked.

"If I had stopped to think I might have known that you would not," the woman said, sullenly. "But how did you get out of that hotel in Havana?"

"Mr. Justin Cutler assisted me."

Mrs. Montague flushed hotly at the mention of that name.

"Yes, I know, but how?" she said.

Mona briefly explained the manner of her escape, then inquired, in a voice of grave reproach:

"How could you conspire against me in such a way? How could you aid your nephew in so foul a wrong?"

"I have already told you—to make our fortunes secure," was the cool retort.

Mona shuddered. It seemed such a heartless thing to do, to plan the ruin of a homeless, unprotected girl for the sake of money.

Mrs. Montague noticed it, and smiled bitterly.

"You surely did not suppose I bore you any love, did you?" she sneered. "I have told you how I hated your mother, and it is but natural that the feeling should manifest itself against her child, especially as you both had usurped the affections of my husband."

"Such a spirit is utterly beyond my comprehension," gravely said the girl, "when your only possible reason for such hatred of a beautiful girl was that my father loved and married her."

"Well, and wasn't that enough?" hotly exclaimed Mrs. Montague. "For years Walter Dinsmore's aunt had intended that he should marry me—that was the condition upon which he was to have her fortune— and I had been reared with that expectation. Therefore, it was no light grief when I learned by accident, three weeks after he sailed for Europe, that he had married a girl who had come to New York to earn her living as a milliner. They went abroad together and registered as Mr. and Mrs. Richmond Montague. I was wild, frantic, desperate, when I discovered it; but I kept the matter to myself. I did not wish Miss Dinsmore to learn the fact, for I had a plan in my mind which I hoped might yet serve to give me the position I so coveted. I persuaded Miss Dinsmore that it would be wise to let me follow Walter to Europe, and I promised her that if such a thing were possible, I would return as his wife. Six weeks after he sailed with his bride, I also left for Europe with some friends. I kept track of the unsuspicious couple for four months, but it was not until they settled in Paris for the winter that I had an opportunity to put any of my plans into action."

"If you please, Mrs. Montague, I would rather you would not tell me any more," Mona here interrupted, with a shiver of repulsion. "My father wrote out the whole story, and so I know all about it. You accomplished your purpose and wrecked the life of a pure and beautiful woman—a loved and loving wife; but truly I believe if my mother could speak to-day she would say that she would far rather have suffered the wrong and wretchedness to which she was subjected than to have exchanged places with you."

"Do you dare to twit me of my present extremity and misery?" cried Mrs. Montague, angrily.

"Not at all; I was not thinking of these later wrongs of which you have been guilty," Mona gently returned, "but only of the ruin which you wrought in the lives of my father and mother. I cannot think that you were happy even after you had succeeded in your wretched plots."

"Happy!" repeated the woman, with great bitterness. "For two years I was the most miserable creature on earth. I will tell it, and you shall listen; you shall hear my side of the story," she went on, fiercely, as she noticed that Mona was restless under the recital. "As I said before, when they settled in Paris for the winter I began to develop my plans. I went to a skillful costumer, and provided myself with a complete disguise, then hired a room in the same house, although I took care to keep out of the sight of Walter Dinsmore and his wife. One day he went out of the city on a hunting excursion, and met with an ac-

cident—he fell and sprained his ankle, and lay in the
forest for hours in great pain. He was finally found
by some peasants who bore him to their cottage, and
kindly cared for him. His first thought was, of course,
for his wife, and he sent a messenger with a letter
to her telling of his injury. I saw the man when he
rode to the door. I instinctively knew there was ill
news. I said I knew Mrs. Montague, and I would
deliver the letter. I opened and read it, and saw that
my opportunity had come. Walter Dinsmore, with
many sickening protestations of love, wrote of his
accident, and said it would be some time before he
should be able to return to Paris, but he wished that
she would take a comfortable carriage the next day,
and come to him if she felt able to do so. Of course
I never delivered the letter, but the next day I went
to Mona Forester, and told her that her lover had deserted her; that she was no wife, for their marriage
had been but a farce; that he had not even given her
his real name; that he was already weary of her, and
she would never see him again, for he was pledged
to marry me as soon as he should return to America.

"At first she would not believe one word of it—she
had the utmost confidence in the man she idolized;
but as the days went by and he did not return she began to fear there was some foundation for my statements. Then a few cunning suggestions to the landlord and his wife poisoned their minds against her.
They accused her of having been living in their house
in an unlawful manner, and drove her out of it with
anger and scorn.

"She left on the fifth day after Walter's accident,
and I hired the butler of the house to go with her and
make it appear as if she had eloped with him. He car-

ried out my instructions so faithfully that their sudden
flitting had every appearance of the flight of a pair
of lovers. When Walter received no answer from his
wife, and she did not go to him, as he requested, he
became very anxious, and insisted upon returning to
Paris, in spite of his injury. Immediately upon his
arrival he was told that his lady had eloped with the
butler of the house, and the angry landlord compelled
him to quit the place also.

"I did not set eyes on him again for more than two
years, when he returned at Miss Dinsmore's earnest
request, for she had not long to live. He did not seem
like the same man, and apparently had no interest in
life. When Miss Dinsmore on her death-bed begged
him to let her see the consummation of her one desire
he listlessly consented, and we were married in her
presence, and she died in less than a month. Then
he confessed his former marriage to me, and told me
that he had a child; that her home must be with us,
and to escape all scandal and remark we would go to
the far West. I was furious over this revelation, but
I concealed the fact from him, for I loved him with all
my soul, and I would have adopted a dozen children
if by so doing I could have won his heart. I consented to have you in the family, provided that you
should be reared as his niece, and never be told of
your parentage. He replied, with exceeding bitterness,
that he was not anxious that his child should grow
up to hate her father for his lack of faith in her
mother, and his deep injustice to her.

"We went to San Francisco to live, but I hated you
even more bitterly than I had hated your mother, and
every caress which I saw my husband lavish upon you
was like a poisoned dagger in my heart. But he never

knew it—he never knew that I had had anything to do with the tragedy of his life, until more than a year after our marriage.

"My own child—a little girl—was born about ten months after that event; but she did not live, and this only served to make me more bitter against you; for, although my husband professed to feel great sorrow that she could not have lived to be a comfort to us and a companion to you, I knew that he would never have loved her with the peculiar tenderness which he always manifested toward you.

"When your mother fled from him and Paris she left everything that he had lavished upon her save what clothing she needed and money to defray necessary expenses during the next few months; and so after my marriage I found pocketed away among some old clothing belonging to my husband the keepsakes that he had given to her and also their marriage certificate. I took possession of them, for I resolved that if you should outlive your father you should never have anything to prove that you were his child; if I could not have my husband's heart I would at least have his money.

"One day a little over a year after our marriage, on my return from a drive, I was told that a man was waiting in the library to see me. Without a suspicion of coming evil, I went at once to ascertain his errand, and was horrified to find there the butler—the man whom I had hired to act as your mother's escort to London. He had been hunting for me for three years to extort more money from me, and had finally traced me from New York to San Francisco.

"He demanded another large sum from me. It was in vain that I told him I had paid him generously for the service he had rendered me. He insisted that I must come to his terms or he would reveal everything to my husband. Of course I yielded to that threat, and paid him the sum he demanded, but I might have saved the money, for Walter Dinsmore, who had that morning started for Oakland for the day, but changed his mind and returned while I was out, was sitting in a small alcove leading out of the library, and had heard the whole conversation.

"Of course there was a terrible scene, and he obliged me to confess everything, although he had heard enough to enable him to comprehend the whole, and then he sternly repudiated me; but, scorning the scandal which would attend proceedings for a divorce, he gave me a meager stipend for separate maintenance, and told me he never wished to look upon my face again. He settled his business, sold his property, and returned to New York with you and your nurse, leaving me to my fate. He forbade me to live under the name of Dinsmore, but I would not resume my maiden name, and so adopted that of Mrs. Richmond Montague. But I still treasured that certificate and my own also, for I meant, if I should outlive him, to claim his fortune, and also kept myself pretty well posted regarding his movements.

"Shortly after our separation my only sister died, and her son, Louis, was thus left destitute, and an orphan. I believed that I could make him useful to me, so I adopted him. We have roved a great deal, for we have had to eke out my limited income by the use of our wits. My best game, though, was with the crescents which Miss Dinsmore gave me as a wedding present, and which I had duplicated several times. Early last fall we came to New York, for in spite of all the past I still loved Walter Dinsmore, and longed to be near him.

"I felt as if the fates had favored me when I heard that he had died without making his will, and I knew from the fact that you were known only as his niece, Miss Mona Montague, that you must still be in ignorance of your real relationship toward him. So it was comparatively easy for me to establish my claim to his property. I did not appear personally in the matter, for I was leading quite a brilliant career here as Mrs. Richmond Montague, and I did not wish to figure as the discarded wife of Walter Dinsmore, so no one save Mr. Corbin even suspected my identity. If Walter Dinsmore had never written that miserable confession, or if I had at once turned all his property into money and gone abroad, or to California, I need never have been brought to this. As matters stand now, however, I suppose you will claim everything," she concluded, with a sullen frown.

Mona thought that if the law had its course with her she would need but very little of the ill-gotten wealth upon which she had been flourishing so extravagantly of late. But she simply replied, in a cold, resolute tone:

"I certainly feel that I am entitled to the property which my father wished me to have."

"Indeed! then you have changed your mind since the night when you so indignantly affirmed to Louis that you did not wish to profit by so much as a dollar from the man who had so wronged your mother," sneered her companion, bitterly.

"Certainly," calmly returned Mona, "now that I know the truth. My father did my mother no willful wrong, although in his morbid grief and sensitiveness

he imputed such wrong to himself, and never ceased
to reproach himself for it. You alone," Mona con
tinued, with stern denunciation, "are guilty of the
ruin of their happiness and lives; you alone will have
to answer for it. You have been a very wicked
woman, Mrs. Montague, not only in connection with
your schemes regarding them, but in your corruption
of the morals of your nephew. I should suppose your
conscience would never cease to reproach you for
having reared him to such a life of crime. You will
have to answer for that also."

Mrs. Montague shivered visibly at these words, thus
betraying that she was not altogether indifferent to
her accountability.

But she quickly threw off the feeling, or the outward
appearance of it, and tossing her head defiantly, she
remarked:

"I do not know who has made you my mentor, Miss
Dinsmore; but there is one thing more that I wish you
to explain to me—how came that detective to be in
my house?"

"He was passing in the street, and I asked him to
come in," Mona replied.

"Indeed! and where, pray, did you make the acquaintance of the high-toned Mr. Rider?" sarcastically
inquired Mrs. Montague.

"In St. Louis."

"In St. Louis!" the woman repeated, astonished.

"Yes. You doubtless remember the day that I rode
with you and your nephew in the street-car, when you
were both disguised."

"Yes, but did you know us at that time?"

"No, I only recognized the dress you had on."

"Ah! What a fool I was ever to wear it the second time," sighed the wretched woman, regretfully.

"I knew it was very like in both color and texture the piece of goods that Mr. Palmer had once shown me. I was almost sure when I saw that it had been mended that it was the same dress that Mrs. Vanderbeck had worn when she stole the Palmer diamonds, and immediately telegraphed to have the fragment sent to me."

"And Ray Palmer had it and had kept it all that time!" interposed Mrs. Montague, with a frown. "I hunted everywhere for it."

"He sent it to me by the next mail, and I began my hunt for the dress, although at that time I did not suspect that it belonged to you," Mona continued. Then she explained how, while assisting the chambermaid about her work, she had found the garment hanging in a wardrobe, and proved by fitting the fragment to the rent that her suspicions were correct.

"You will also remember," she added, "how you chided me a little later for going out without consulting you. I had been out to seek a detective to tell him what I had discovered."

"Ha! that was how you made Mr. Rider's acquaintance?" interrupted Mrs. Montague, with a start.

"Yes. He told me he was in St. Louis on business connected with that very case. He was very much elated after hearing my story, but when he went to make his arrest he found that Mrs. Walton and her so-called son had both disappeared. I was, of course, very much disappointed, but I never dreamed——"

"That I and my hopeful nephew were the accomplished sharpers," supplemented Mrs. Montague, with a bitter laugh. "Well, Mona Dinsmore, you have

been very keen. I will give you credit for that—you
have beaten me; I confess that you have utterly de-
feated me, and your mother is amply avenged
through you. No doubt, you are very triumphant
over my downfall," she concluded, acrimoniously.

"Indeed, I am not," Mona returned, with a sigh.
"I do not think I could triumph in the downfall of
any one, and though I am filled with horror over
what you have told me, I am very sorry for you."

"Sorry for me!" repeated the woman, with skeptical
contempt.

"Yes, I am truly sorry for you, and for any one
who has fallen so low, for I am sure you must have
seasons of suffering and remorse that are very hard
to bear, while as for avenging my mother, I never
had such a thought; I do not believe she would wish
me to entertain any such spirit. I intend to assert my
rights, as my father's daughter, but not with any desire for revenge."

Mona's remarks were here suddenly cut short by
the return of the four gentlemen, and Mrs. Montague
eagerly and searchingly scanned their faces as they
gravely resumed their seats.

CHAPTER XXII.

MRS. MONTAGUE'S ANNUITY.

Mona, too, regarded the lawyers with some anxiety,
for she felt extremely sensitive about having her
father's troubles and past life become the subject of a
public scandal.

Ray noticed it, and telegraphed her a gleam of hope from his tender eyes.

The proposition which he had made to the lawyers upon leaving the room was in accordance with his father's request.

Mr. Palmer had begged that all proceedings in the case of the robbery might be quashed.

"I would rather lose three times the amount that woman stole from us than to have all New York know the wretched truth," he said to Ray, after calling him from the drawing-room. "To have it known that she robbed us and then tried to fortify herself by a marriage with me! I could not bear it. I have made a fool of myself, Ray," he went on, with pitiable humility, "but I don't want everybody discussing the mortifying details of the affair. If you can prevail upon the lawyers to settle everything quietly, do so, and, of course, Rider being a private detective, and in our pay, will do as we say, and, my boy, you and I will ignore the subject, after this, for all time."

Ray grasped his father's hand in heartfelt sympathy as he replied:

"We will manage to hush the matter, never fear. I am very sure that Mona will also desire to do so, and though I should be glad to have that woman reap the full reward of her wickedness I can forego that satisfaction for the sake of saving her feelings and yours."

Then, as we know, he returned to the drawing-room where Mona called to him to come and plead for the same thing.

The lawyers were both willing, for Mona's sake, to refrain from active proceedings against Mrs. Montague if she would resign all Mr. Dinsmore's property; but Mr. Rider objected very emphatically to this plan.

"It has been a tough case," he said, somewhat obstinately, "and it is no more than fair that a man should have the glory of working it up. Money isn't everything to a person in such business—reputation is worth considerable."

They had quite a spirited argument with him; but he yielded the point at last, provided Mr. Cutler would consent, although not with a very good grace, and then they all went back to Mona and her unhappy companion.

But Mrs. Montague put a grave front upon her critical situation.

"Well, and have you decided the fate of your prisoner?" she inquired of Mr. Rider, with haughty audacity, although her face was as white as her handkerchief as she put the question.

"Well, madame," he retorted, with scant ceremony, "if it had been left with me to settle there would have been no discussion with you—you would be in the Tombs."

"Well?" she asked, impatiently, seeing there was more to be said about the matter, and turning to Mr. Corbin.

"We have decided, Mrs. Montague, that in the first place, you are to relinquish everything which you inherited from Mr. Dinsmore at the time of his death."

"Everything?" she began, interrupting him.

"Please listen to what I have to tell you, and defer your objections until later," remarked the lawyer, coldly.

"Yes, everything. You are also to give up all jewels of every description that you have in your possession to make good as far as may be the losses of those who have suffered through your dishonesty. You are then to pledge yourself to leave New York and never show yourself here again upon pain of immediate arrest, nor cause any of the revelations of this morning to be made public. Upon these conditions we have decided, for the sake of the feelings of others, to let you go free and not subject you to a trial for your crime—provided Mr. Cutler agrees to this decision."

"But—but I must have something to live on," the miserable woman said, with white lips. "I can't give up everything; the law would give me my third, and I ought to inherit much more through my child."

"The law would give you—a criminal—nothing," Mr. Graves here sternly remarked. "Let me but reveal the fact that Mr. Dinsmore wished to secure everything to his daughter, and how you defrauded her, and you would find that the law would not deal very generously with you."

"But I must have money. I could not bear poverty," reiterated the woman, tremulously.

"Mr. Graves—Mr. Corbin!" Mona here interposed, turning to them, "it surely becomes the daughter's duty to be as generous as the father, and——"

"Generous!" bitterly exclaimed Mrs. Montague.

"Yes, he was generous," Mona asserted, with cold positiveness, "for, after all the wrong of which you had been guilty, he certainly would have been justified if he had utterly renounced you and refused to make any provision for you. But since he did not, I will do what I think he would have wished, and, with the consent of these gentlemen," with a glance at Ray and the lawyers, "I will continue the same annuity that he granted to you."

"That is an exceedingly noble and liberal proposition, Miss Dinsmore," Mr. Corbin remarked, bestowing a glance of admiration upon her, "and with all my heart I honor you for it."

Mrs. Montague did not make any acknowledgment or reply. She had dropped her head upon her hands and seemed to be lost in her own unhappy reflections.

Mr. Graves and Mr. Corbin conferred together for a few moments, and then the former remarked:

"Mrs. Montague will, of course, wish to give these subjects some consideration, and meanwhile I will go to consult with Mr. Cutler regarding his interest in the matter."

He left immediately, and Mr. Corbin and Mr. Rider fell into general conversation, while Ray and Mona withdrew to the lower end of the drawing-room, where they could talk over matters unheard.

Mr. Graves was gone about an hour, and then returned accompanied by Mr. Justin Cutler himself.

After discussing at some length the question of Mrs. Montague being brought to trial he finally agreed to concur in the decision of the others.

"For Miss Dinsmore's sake I will waive all proceedings," he remarked, "but were it not for the feelings of that young lady," he added, sternly, "I would press the matter to the extent of the law."

Mrs. Montague shuddered at his relentless tone, but Mona thanked him with a smile for the concession.

Mrs. Montague then consented to abide by the conditions made by the lawyers, and, at their command, brought forth her valuable store of jewels to have them appraised and used to indemnify those who had suffered loss through her crimes.

Ray laid out what he thought would serve to make Mr. Cutler's loss good, selected what stones he thought belonged to his own firm, and then it was decided that the real crescents should be given to Mrs. Vanderheck if she wished them, or they should be sold and the money given to her.

Mrs. Montague was then informed that she must at once surrender all deeds, bonds, bank stock, etc., which she had received from the Dinsmore estate, and would be expected to leave the city before noon of the next day.

She curtly replied that she would require only three hours, and that she would leave the house before sunset. The house, having been purchased with Mr. Dinsmore's money, would henceforth belong to Mona, therefore she and Ray decided to remain where they were until her departure and see that everything was properly secured afterward.

Having decided that these matters should not be made public, nothing could be done with Louis Hamblin, and Mr. Rider, much against his inclination, was obliged to forego making the arrest on the Fall River boat.

Mrs. Montague hastened her preparations and left her elegant home on West Forty-ninth street in season to meet her nephew a little after the hour appointed in the morning. Mr. Corbin previous to this handed her the first payment of her annuity, and obtained an address to which it was to be sent in the future, and thus the two accomplished sharpers disappeared from New York society, which knew them no more.

The next evening Ray and Mona were talking over their plans for the future, in the cozy library in Mr. Graves' house, when the young girl remarked:

"Ray, would you not like to read the story that my father concealed in the royal mirror?"

"Yes, dear, if you wish me," her lover replied.

Mona excused herself and went to get it. When she returned she brought the ancient keepsake with her.

She explained how the secret drawer operated, showed him the two rings and the letters, then putting Mr. Dinsmore's confession into his hands, bade him read it; and this is what his eager eyes perused:

"My Dear Mona:—You who have been the darling of my heart, the pride of my life; you have just left me, to go to your caller, after having probed my heart to its very core. I can never make you know the bitterness of spirit that I experience, as I write these lines, for the questions you have just asked me have completely unmanned me—have made a veritable coward of me when I should have boldly told you the truth, let the consequence be what it would; whether it would have touched your heart with pity and fresh love for a sorrowing and repentant man, or driven you away from me in hate and scorn such as I experience for myself. You have just told me that I have made your life a very happy one; that you love me dearly. Oh, my darling, you will never know, until I am gone, how I hug these sweet words to my soul, and exult over them with secret joy, and you will never know, either, until then, how I long and hunger to hear you call me just once by the sacred name 'father.'

"Yes, Mona, I am your father; you are my child,

and yet I had not the courage to tell you so, with all the rest of the sad story, this morning, for fear I should see all the love die out of your face, and you would turn coldly from me as you learned the great wrong I once did your mother.

"I told you that your father is dead. So he is, to you, and has been for many long years; for when I brought you from England, when you were only two years old, I vowed that you should never know that I was the man who, by my cowardice and neglect, ruined your mother's life; so I adopted you as my niece, and you have always believed yourself to be the child of my only and idolized sister. But, to begin at the beginning, I first met Mona Forester one day while attending my aunt to a millinery store, where she had her bonnets and caps made. She waited upon her, and I sat and watched the beautiful girl, entranced by her loveliness and winning manner. She was a cultured lady, in spite of the fact that she was obliged to earn her living in so humble a way.

"Her parents had both died two years previously, leaving her homeless and destitute, after having been reared in the lap of luxury. I saw her often after that, we soon learned to love each other, and it was not long before she was my promised wife.

"But my first sin was in not giving her my full name. I was afraid she might be shy of me, if she knew that I was the heir of the wealthy Miss Dinsmore, and so I told her my name was Richmond Montague. About that time, my studies being completed, my aunt wanted me to go abroad for a couple of years.

"She also wished me to marry the child of an intimate friend, and take her with me. She had been planning this marriage for years and had threatened, if I disappointed her, to leave all her money to some one else.

"Now comes my second sin against your mother. If I had been loyal and true, I should have frankly told my aunt of my love for Mona Forester, and that I could never marry another woman, fortune or no fortune. But I shirked the duty—I thought something might happen before my return to give me the fortune, and then I should be free to choose for myself; so I led Miss Dinsmore to believe that on my return I would marry Miss Barton. I wanted the fortune—I loved money and the pleasure it brought, but I did not want Miss Barton for a wife. She was proud and haughty —a girl bound up in the world and fashion, and I did love sweet and amiable Mona Forester.

"Now my third sin: I was selfish. I could not bear the thought of leaving my love behind, and so I persuaded her to a secret marriage, and to go to Europe with me. I never should have done this; a man is a coward and knave who will not boldly acknowledge his wife before the world. I hated myself for my weakness, yet had not strength of purpose to do what was right. We sailed under the name of Mr. and Mrs. Richmond Montague, and Mona did not know that I had any other; but I took care that the marriage certificate was made out with my full name, so that the ceremony should be perfectly legal.

"We were very happy, for I idolized my young wife, and our life for six months was one of earth's sweetest poems. We traveled a great deal during the summer, and then settled in Paris for the winter. We had rooms in a pleasant house in a first-class locality; our meals were served in our own dining-room, and everything seemed almost as homelike as if we had been in America.

"One day I took a sudden freak that I wanted to go hunting. Mona begged me not to go; she was afraid of fire-arms, and feared some accident. But I laughed at her fears, told her that I was an expert with a gun, and went away in spite of her pleadings, little thinking I should never see my darling again. I did meet with an accident—I fell and sprained my ankle very badly, and lay for several hours in a dense forest unable to move.

"Finally some peasants found me, and took me to their cottage, but it was too late to send news of my injury to Paris that night. But the next morning early I sent the man of the house—who was going through the city on his way to visit some friends for a week, with a letter to Mona, telling her to take a carriage and come to me. She did not come, and I heard nothing from her. I could not send to her again, for there was no one in the cottage to go, and no neighbor within a mile. I was terribly anxious, and imagined a hundred things, and at the end of a week, unable to endure the suspense any longer, I insisted upon being taken back to Paris in spite of the serious condition of my foot and ankle.

"But, oh, my child, the tidings that met me there were such as to drive the strongest mind distracted. The landlord told me that my wife had fled with the butler of the house. At first I laughed in his face at anything so absurd, but when he flew into a towering passion and accused me of having brought disgrace upon his house by living there unlawfully with a woman who was not my wife, I began to think there must be some truth in his statements. In vain I denied the charge; he would not listen to me, and drove me also from his dwelling.

"I was too lame and helpless to attempt to follow Mona, but I set a detective at work to find my wife, for I still had faith in her, and thought she might be the victim of the landlord's suspicions. The detective traced her to London, and brought me word that a couple answering the description of my wife and the butler had crossed the channel on a certain date, and had since been living under the same roof in London.

"Then I cursed my wife, and said I would never trust a human being again. I was a long time getting over my lameness, but I still kept my detective on the watch, and one day he came to me with the intelligence that the butler had deserted his victim, and the lady was ill, and almost destitute.

"That Mona should want or suffer, under any circumstances, was the last thing I could wish, even though I then firmly believed that she had deserted me; while the thought that my child might even lack the necessities of life, was sufficient incentive to make me hasten at once to her relief. But I have told you, Mona, that she was dead, and I found only a weak and helpless baby to need my care. The nurse told me that the lady had wanted to go to America several weeks previously, but her physician had forbidden her to attempt to cross the ocean. She told me that a gentleman had taken the room for her and had been very kind to her, but the lady had been very unhappy and ill most of the time, since coming to the house. I questioned her closely, but evidently Mona had made a confidante of no one, and she had lived very quietly, seldom going out, and seeing no one. I could not

reconcile this with the fact of her having eloped with
the butler, and I realized all too late that I should have
come to her the moment I learned where she was, demanded an explanation, and at least given her a chance
to defend herself. My darling might have lived, if I
had done so, and my child would not have been mother-
less.

"I was frantic with grief, and tried to drown my
sorrow by constant change of scene. I traveled for
two years, and then was summoned home to my aunt,
who was dying. She insisted that my marriage with
Miss Barton should be immediately consummated, and
I, too wretched to contest the point, let them have
their way. Miss Dinsmore died soon afterward, but
without suspecting my previous marriage. Then I
confessed the truth to my wife, and told her of the existence of my child. I saw at once that she was deeply
wounded upon learning of this secret of my life, but
I never suspected how exceedingly jealous and bitter
she was, or that she had any previous knowledge of the
fact, until a little more than a year after our marriage,
when I accidentally overheard a conversation between
her and the man who had been her accomplice in ruining your mother's happiness and mine. That elopement, so called, had always seemed utterly inexplicable
to me until then.

"I learned that day that Margaret Barton had
known of my marriage with Mona Forester almost
from the first, that she had followed us abroad, and
came disguised into the very house where we were
living; that she had intercepted my letter, telling Mona
of my accident, and made the poor child believe that
I had deserted her, and that I had not really married
her, but simply brought her abroad with me to be the

plaything of my season of travel, after which I was
pledged to marry her, Margaret Barton. She repeated
this cunning tale to the landlord, and then, when he
drove my darling forth into the street, she hired the
butler to follow her, and thus give her departure the
appearance of an elopement. It was a plot fit to eman-
ate only from the heart and brain of a fiend, and I
wormed it out of her little by little, after the departure of her tool, who had traced her to this country,
hoping to get more money for keeping her secret.

"I cannot, neither do I wish to describe the scene
that followed this discovery. I was like a madman for
a season, when I learned how I had been duped, how
my darling had been wronged and betrayed, and driven
to her untimely death, and I closed my heart and my
doors forever against Margaret Barton. I settled an
annuity of twenty-five hundred dollars upon her, then
taking you, I left San Francisco. I came to settle in
New York.

"You know all the rest, my Mona, but you cannot
know how I have longed to own you, my child, and
dared not, fearing to alienate your love by confessing the truth. I am going to conceal this avowal in
the secret drawer of the mirror, that I have given you
to-day, and some time you will read this story and
perhaps pity and forgive your father for the culpable
cowardice and wrong-doing of his early life. That
woman stole the certificate of my first marriage and
all the trinkets I had given your mother; but I swear
to you that Mona Forester was my lawful wife—that
you are our child, and in a few days I shall make my
will, so stating, and bequeath to you the bulk of my
fortune. I will also in that document explain the secret of this mirror so that you will have no difficulty

in finding this confession, your mother's rings, and some letters which may be a comfort to you.

"Now, my darling, this is all; but I hope you will not love me less when you learn your mother's sad story and my weakness and sin in not boldly acknowledging her as my wife before the world. Oh, if I could hear but once, your dear lips call me 'father' I could ask no greater comfort in life—it would be the sweetest music I have ever heard since I lost my other Mona; yet it cannot be. But that God may bless you, and give you a happy life, is the earnest prayer of your loving father,

"WALTER RICHMOND MONTAGUE DINSMORE."

Ray was deeply moved as he finished reading this sad tale.

"It is the saddest story I ever heard," he said, as he folded the closely written sheets and returned them to Mona, "and Mr. Dinsmore must have suffered very keenly since the discovery of the great wrong done his wife, for his whole confession betrays how sensitive and remorseful he was."

"My poor father! if he had only told me! I could not have loved him less, and it would have been such a comfort to have known of this relationship, and to have talked with him about my mother," said Mona, with tears in her beautiful eyes.

"Well, dear, we will begin our life with no concealments," said Ray, with a tender smile. "And now, when may I tell Mr. Graves that you will come to me?"

"When you will, Ray," Mona answered, flushing, but with a look of love and trust that made his heart leap with gladness.

"Then one month from to-day, dear," he said, as he bent his lips to hers.

And so, when the roses began to bloom and all the world was in its brightest dress, there was a quiet wedding one morning in Mr. Graves' spacious drawing-room and Mona Dinsmore gave herself to the man she loved.

There were only a few tried and true friends present to witness the ceremony, but everybody was happy, and all agreed that the bride was very lovely in her simple but elegant traveling dress.

"I cannot have a large wedding or any parade with gay people about me, for my heart is still too sore over the loss of my dear father," Mona had said, with quivering lips, when they had asked her wishes regarding the wedding, and so everything had been done very simply.

It is doubtful if so young a bride was ever made the recipient of so many diamonds as fell to Mona's lot that day.

Mr. Palmer, true to his promise, had all the recovered stones reset for her, and made her a handsome gift besides. Mr. and Miss Cutler presented to her a pair of beautiful stars for the hair, and Ray put a blazing solitaire above her wedding-ring, for a guard.

After a sumptuous wedding-breakfast, the happy couple started for a trip to the Golden Gate city, while during their absence, Mr. Palmer, senior, had his residence partially remodeled and refurnished for the fair daughter to whom already his heart had gone out in tender affection.

A notice of the marriage appeared in the papers, together with a statement that "the handsome fortune left by the late Walter Dinsmore had been restored to the young lady formerly known as Miss Mona Montague, now Mrs. Raymond Palmer, who had been fraudulently deprived of it, through the craftiness of a woman calling herself Mrs. Dinsmore."

Mona did not wish anything of her father's sad story to be made public, and so, it was arranged that this was all that should be given to the reporters, to show that she was Mr. Dinsmore's heiress, and would resume her former position in the world upon her return from her bridal trip.

THE END.

Good Fiction Worth Reading.

the young lady formerly known as Miss Maud Mor-
rison, now Mrs. Raymond Palmer, he had been
fraudulently deprived of; and mentioned the railway of a
woman calling herself Mrs. Dinsmore.

Maud did not wish anything of her father, but
sought to be made public, and see it was arranged that
should be all that should be seen by the reporters, to
show that she was Mr. Dinsmore's heiress, and would
resume her former position in the world upon her return from her bridal trip.

THE END.

Good Fiction Worth Reading.

A series of romances containing several of the old favorites in the field of historical fiction, replete with powerful romances of love and diplomacy that excel in thrilling and absorbing interest.

A COLONIAL FREE-LANCE. A story of American Colonial Times. By Chauncey C. Hotchkiss. Cloth, 12mo. with four illustrations by J. Watson Davis. Price, $1.00.

A book that appeals to Americans as a vivid picture of Revolutionary scenes. The story is a strong one, a thrilling one. It causes the true American to flush with excitement, to devour chapter after chapter, until the eyes smart, and it fairly smokes with patriotism. The love story is a singularly charming idyl.

THE TOWER OF LONDON. A Historical Romance of the Times of Lady Jane Grey and Mary Tudor. By Wm. Harrison Ainsworth. Cloth, 12mo. with four illustrations by George Cruikshank. Price, $1.00.

This romance of the "Tower of London" depicts the Tower as palace, prison and fortress, with many historical associations. The era is the middle of the sixteenth century.
The story is divided into two parts, one dealing with Lady Jane Grey, and the other with Mary Tudor as Queen, introducing other notable characters of the era. Throughout the story holds the interest of the reader in the midst of intrigue and conspiracy, extending considerably over a half a century.

IN DEFIANCE OF THE KING. A Romance of the American Revolution. By Chauncey C. Hotchkiss. Cloth, 12mo. with four illustrations by J. Watson Davis. Price, $1.00.

Mr. Hotchkiss has etched in burning words a story of Yankee bravery, and true love that thrills from beginning to end, with the spirit of the Revolution. The heart beats quickly, and we feel ourselves taking a part in the exciting scenes described. His whole story is so absorbing that you will sit up far into the night to finish it. As a love romance it is charming.

GARTHOWEN. A story of a Welsh Homestead. By Allen Raine. Cloth, 12mo. with four illustrations by J. Watson Davis. Price, $1.00.

"This is a little idyl of humble life and enduring love, laid bare before us, very real and pure, which in its telling shows us some strong points of Welsh character—the pride, the hasty temper, the quick dying out of wrath. . . . We call this a well-written story, interesting alike through its romance and its glimpses into another life than ours. A delightful and clever picture of Welsh village life. The result is excellent."—Detroit Free Press.

MIFANWY. The story of a Welsh Singer. By Allan Raine. Cloth, 12mo. with four illustrations by J. Watson Davis. Price, $1.00.

"This is a love story, simple, tender and pretty as one would care to read. The action throughout is brisk and pleasing; the characters, it is apparent at once, are as true to life as though the author had known them all personally. Simple in all its situations, the story is worked up in that touching and quaint strain which never grows wearisome, no matter how often the lights and shadows of love are introduced. It rings true, and does not tax the imagination."—Boston Herald.

Good Fiction Worth Reading.

A series of romances containing several of the old favorites in the field of historical fiction, replete with powerful romances of love and diplomacy that excel in thrilling and absorbing interest.

DARNLEY. A Romance of the times of Henry VIII. and Cardinal Wolsey. By G. P. R. James. Cloth, 12mo. with four illustrations by J. Watson Davis. Price, $1.00.

In point of publication, "Darnley" is that work by Mr. James which follows "Richelieu," and, if rumor can be credited, it was owing to the advice and insistence of our own Washington Irving that we are indebted primarily for the story, the young author questioning whether he could properly paint the difference in the characters of the two great cardinals. And it is not surprising that James should have hesitated; he had been eminently successful in giving to the world the portrait of Richelieu as a man, and by attempting a similar task with Wolsey as the theme, was much like tempting fortune. Irving insisted that "Darnley" came naturally in sequence, and this opinion being supported by Sir Walter Scott, the author set about the work.

As a historical romance "Darnley" is a book that can be taken up pleasurably again and again, for there is about it that subtle charm which those who are strangers to the works of G. P. R. James have claimed was only to be imparted by Dumas.

If there was nothing more about the work to attract especial attention, the account of the meeting of the kings on the historic "field of the cloth of gold" would entitle the story to the most favorable consideration of every reader.

There is really but little pure romance in this story, for the author has taken care to imagine love passages only between those whom history has credited with having entertained the tender passion one for another, and he succeeds in making such lovers as all the world must love.

CAPTAIN BRAND, OF THE SCHOONER CENTIPEDE. By Lieut. Henry A. Wise, U. S. N. (Harry Gringo). Cloth, 12mo. with four illustrations by J. Watson Davis. Price, $1.00.

The re-publication of this story will please those lovers of sea yarns who delight in so much of the salty flavor of the ocean as can come through the medium of a printed page, for never has a story of the sea and those "who go down in ships" been written by one more familiar with the scenes depicted.

The one book of this gifted author which is best remembered, and which will be read with pleasure for many years to come, is "Captain Brand," who, as the author states on his title page, was a "pirate of eminence in the West Indies." As a sea story pure and simple, "Captain Brand" has never been excelled, and as a story of piratical life, told without the usual embellishments of blood and thunder, it has no equal.

NICK OF THE WOODS. A story of the Early Setlers of Kentucky. By Robert Montgomery Bird. Cloth, 12mo. with four illustrations by J. Watson Davis. Price, $1.00.

This most popular novel and thrilling story of early frontier life in Kentucky was originally published in the year 1837. The novel, long out of print, had in its day a phenomenal sale, for its realistic presentation of Indian and frontier life in the early days of settlement in the South, narrated in the tale with all the art of a practiced writer. A very charming love romance runs through the story. This new and tasteful edition of "Nick of the Woods" will be certain to make many new admirers for this enchanting story from Dr. Bird's clever and versatile pen.

For sale by all booksellers, or sent postpaid on receipt of price by the publishers, A. L. BURT COMPANY, 114-120 East 23d Street, New York

Good Fiction Worth Reading

A series of romances containing several of the old favorites in the field of historical fiction, replete with powerful romances of love and diplomacy that excel in thrilling and absorbing interest.

GUY FAWKES. A Romance of the Gunpowder Treason. By Wm. Harrison Ainsworth. Cloth, 12mo. with four illustrations by George Cruikshank. Price, $1.00.

The "Gunpowder Plot" was a modest attempt to blow up Parliament, the King and his Counsellors. James of Scotland, then King of England, was weak-minded and extravagant. He hit upon the efficient scheme of extorting money from the people by imposing taxes on the Catholics. In their natural resentment to this extortion, a handful of bold spirits concluded to overthrow the government. Finally the plotters were arrested, and the King put to torture Guy Fawkes and the other prisoners with fivral vinne. A viva intanss luvi stary runs through the entire romance.

THE SPIRIT OF THE BORDER. A Romance of the Early Settlers in the Ohio Valley. By Zane Grey. Cloth, 12mo. with four illustrations by J. Watson Davis. Price, $1.00.

A book rather out of the ordinary is this "Spirit of the Border." The main thread of the story has to do with the work of the Moravian missionaries in the Ohio Valley. Incidentally the reader is given details of the frontier life of those hardy pioneers who broke the wilderness for the planting of this great nation. Chief among these, as a matter of course, is Lewis Wetzel, one of the most peculiar, and at the same time the most admirable of all the brave men who spent their lives battling with the savage foe, that others might dwell in comparative security.

Details of the establishment and destruction of the Moravian "Village of Peace" are given at some length, and with minute description. The efforts to Christianize the Indians are described as they never have been before, and the author has depicted the characters of the leaders of the several Indian tribes with great care, which of itself will be of interest to the student.

By no means least among the charms of the story are the vivid word-pictures of the thrilling adventures, and the intense paintings of the beauties of nature, as seen in the almost unbroken forests.

It is the spirit of the frontier which is described, and one can by it, perhaps, the better understand why men, and women, too, willingly braved every privation and danger that the westward progress of the star of empire might be the more certain and rapid. A love story, simple and tender, runs through the book.

RICHELIEU. A tale of France in the reign of King Louis XIII. By G. P. R. James. Cloth, 12mo. with four illustrations by J. Watson Davis. Price, $1.00.

In 1829 Mr. James published his first romance, "Richelieu," and was recognized at once as one of the masters of the craft.

In this book he laid the story during those later days of the great cardinal's life, when his power was beginning to wane, but while it was yet sufficiently strong to permit now and then of volcanic outbursts which overwhelmed foes and carried friends to the topmost wave of prosperity. One of the most striking portions of the story is that of Cinq Mar's conspiracy; the method of conducting criminal cases, and the political trickery resorted to by royal favorites, affording a better insight into the statecraft of that day than can be had even by an exhaustive study of history. It is a powerful romance of love and diplomacy, and in point of thrilling and absorbing interest has never been excelled.

Good Fiction Worth Reading.

A series of romances containing several of the old favorites in the field of historical fiction, replete with powerful romances of love and diplomacy that excel in thrilling and absorbing interest.

WINDSOR CASTLE. A Historical Romance of the Reign of Henry VIII., Catharine of Aragon and Anne Boleyn. By Wm. Harrison Ainsworth. Cloth, 12mo. with four illustrations by George Cruikshank. Price, $1.00.

"Windsor Castle" is the story of Henry VIII., Catharine, and Anne Boleyn. "Bluff King Hal," although a well-loved monarch, was none too good a one in many ways. Of all his selfishness and unwarrantable acts, none was more discreditable than his divorce from Catharine, and his marriage to the beautiful Anne Boleyn. The King's love was as brief as it was vehement. Jane Seymour, waiting maid on the Queen, attracted him, and Anne Boleyn was forced to the block to make room for her successor. This romance is one of extreme interest to all readers.

HORSESHOE ROBINSON. A tale of the Tory Ascendency in South Carolina in 1780. By John P. Kennedy. Cloth, 12mo. with four illustrations by J. Watson Davis. Price, $1.00.

Among the old favorites in the field of what is known as historical fiction, there are none which appeal to a larger number of Americans than Horseshoe Robinson, and this because it is the only story which depicts with fidelity to the facts the heroic efforts of the colonists in South Carolina to defend their homes against the brutal oppression of the British under such leaders as Cornwallis and Tarleton.

The reader is charmed with the story of love which forms the thread of the tale, and then impressed with the wealth of detail concerning those times. The picture of the manifold sufferings of the people, is never overdrawn, but painted faithfully and honestly by one who spared neither time nor labor in his efforts to present in this charming love story all that price in blood and tears which the Carolinians paid as their share in the winning of the republic.

Take it all in all, "Horseshoe Robinson" is a work which should be found on every book-shelf, not only because it is a most entertaining story, but because of the wealth of valuable information concerning the colonists which it contains. That it has been brought out once more, well illustrated, is something which will give pleasure to thousands who have long desired an opportunity to read the story again, and to the many who have tried vainly in these latter days to procure a copy that they might read it for the first time.

THE PEARL OF ORR'S ISLAND. A story of the Coast of Maine. By Harriet Beecher Stowe. Cloth, 12mo. Illustrated. Price, $1.00.

Written prior to 1862, the "Pearl of Orr's Island" is ever new; a book filled with delicate fancies, such as seemingly array themselves anew each time one reads them. One sees the "sea like an unbroken mirror all around the pine-girt, lonely shores of Orr's Island," and straightway comes "the heavy, hollow moan of the surf on the beach, like the wild angry howl of some savage animal."

Who can read of the beginning of that sweet life, named Mara, which came into this world under the very shadow of the Death angel's wings, without having an intense desire to know how the premature bud blossomed? Again and again one lingers over the descriptions of the character of that baby boy Moses, who came through the tempest, amid th' angry billows, pillowed on his dead mother's breast.

There is no more faithful portrayal of New England life than that which Mrs. Stowe gives in "The Pearl of Orr's Island."

GOOD FICTION WORTH READING

A series of romances containing several of the old favorites in the field of historical fiction, replete with powerful romances of love and diplomacy that excel in thrilling and absorbing interest.

THE LAST TRAIL. A story of early days in the Ohio Valley. By Zane Grey. Cloth, 12mo. Four page illustrations by J. Watson Davis. Price, $1.00.

"The Last Trail" is a story of the border. The scene is laid at Fort Henry, where Col. Ebenezer Zane with his family have built up a village despite the attacks of savages and renegades. The Colonel's brother and Wetzel, known as Deathwind by the Indians, are the bordermen who devote their lives to the welfare of the white people. A splendid love story runs through the book.

That Helen Sheppard, the heroine, should fall in love with such a brave, skilful scout as Jonathan Zane seems only reasonable after his years of association and defense of the people of the settlement from savages and renegades.

If one has a liking for stories of the trail, where the white man matches brains against savage cunning, for tales of ambush and constant striving for the mastery, "The Last Trail" will be greatly to his liking.

THE KNIGHTS OF THE HORSESHOE. A traditionary tale of the Cocked Hat Gentry in the Old Dominion. By Dr. Wm. A. Caruthers. Cloth, 12mo. Four page illustrations by J. Watson Davis. Price, $1.00.

Many will hail with delight the re-publication of this rare and justly famous story of early American colonial life and old-time Virginian hospitality.

Much that is charmingly interesting will be found in this tale that so faithfully depicts early American colonial life, and also here is found all the details of the founding of the Tramontane Order, around which has ever been such a delicious flavor of romance.

Early customs, much love making, plantation life, politics, intrigues, and finally that wonderful march across the mountains which resulted in the discovery and conquest of the fair Valley of Virginia. A rare book filled with a delicious flavor of romance.

BY BERWEN BANKS. A Romance of Welsh Life. By Allen Raine. Cloth, 12mo. Four page illustrations by J. Watson Davis. Price $1.00.

It is a tender and beautiful romance of the idyllic. A charming picture of life in a Welsh seaside village. It is something of a prose-poem, true, tender and graceful.

For sale by all booksellers, or sent postpaid on receipt of price by the publishers, A. L. BURT COMPANY, 52-58 Duane St., New York.

GOOD FICTION WORTH READING

A series of romances containing several of the old favorites in the field of historical fiction, replete with powerful romances of love and diplomacy that excel in thrilling and absorbing interest.

ROB OF THE BOWL. A Story of the Early Days of Maryland. By John P. Kennedy. Cloth, 12mo. Four page illustrations by J. Watson Davis. Price, $1.00.

This story is an authentic exposition of the manners and customs during Lord Baltimore's rule. The greater portion of the action takes place in St. Mary's—the original capital of the State.

The quaint character of Rob, the loss of whose legs was supplied by a wooden bowl strapped to his thighs, his misfortunes and mother wit, far outshine those fair to look upon. Pirates and smugglers did Rob consort with for gain, and it was to him that Blanche Werden owed her life and her happiness, as the author has told us in such an enchanting manner.

As a series of pictures of early colonial life in Maryland, "Rob of the Bowl" has no equal. The story is full of splendid action, with a charming love story, and a plot that never loosens the grip of its interest to its last page.

TICONDEROGA. A Story of Early Frontier Life in the Mohawk Valley. By G. P. R. James. Cloth, 12mo. Four page illustrations by J. Watson Davis. Price, $1.00.

The setting of the story is decidedly more picturesque than any ever evolved by Cooper. The story is located on the frontier of New York State. The principal characters in the story include an English gentleman, his beautiful daughter, Lord Howe, and certain Indian sachems belonging to the Five Nations, and the story ends with the Battle of Ticonderoga.

The character of Captain Brooks, who voluntarily decides to sacrifice his own life in order to save the son of the Englishman, is not among the least of the attractions of this story, which holds the attention of the reader even to the last page.

Interwoven with the plot is the Indian "blood" law, which demands a life for a life, whether it be that of the murderer or one of his race. A more charming story of mingled love and adventure has never been written than "Ticonderoga."

MARY DERWENT. A tale of the Wyoming Valley in 1778. By Mrs. Ann S. Stephens. Coth, 12mo. Four illustrations by J. Watson Davis. Price, $1.00.

The scene of this fascinating story of early frontier life is laid in the Valley of Wyoming. Aside from Mary Derwent, who is of course the heroine, the story deals with Queen Esther's son, Giengwatah, the Butlers of notorious memory, and the adventures of the Colonists with the Indians.

Though much is made of the Massacre of Wyoming, a great portion of the tale describes the love making between Mary Derwent's sister, Walter Butler, and one of the defenders of Forty Fort.

This historical novel stands out bright and pleasing, because of the mystery and notoriety of several of the actors, the tender love scenes, descriptions of the different localities, and the struggles of the settlers. It holds the attention of the reader even to the last page.